SIGNALS IN THE STATIC

A. T. SAYRE

"Full of wonderful science fiction tales that make your heart ache and your mind stretch."
PSYCHOPOMP

"Space exploration can be harrowingly lonely—but so can life on Earth. Sayre looks at both unflinchingly."
MARIE VIBBERT,
AUTHOR OF GALACTIC HELLCATS

"You'd be hard pressed not to think of Bradbury, Dick, or Asimov as you read A.T. Sayre's debut collection. His aliens, ghosts, and machines have their well-earned place in the cosmos, but humans have trouble getting their interactions with them right. If this is how Sayre starts his career, then we have a long and happy road ahead of us."
KAREN HEULER,
AUTHOR OF THE SPLENDID CITY

"It's not every day you read a collection and love every single story in it, but I can say that in this case I enjoyed this book cover-to-cover. Sayre has a knack for grabbing the reader's attention and not letting go with his flawless execution of imaginative concepts. Many of these stories stayed with me long after reading them."
P.A. CORNELL,
AUTHOR OF LOST CARGO

"Fascinating, mind-expanding speculative fiction tales that explore life from the personal to the cosmic, and from the grotesque to the sublime."
MATTHEW KRESSEL,
AUTHOR OF KING OF SHARDS

Copyright © 2024 by A.T. Sayre
Published by Lethe Press | lethepressbooks.com

ISBN: 978-1-59021-763-4

All rights reserved. No part of this book may be reproduced, stored, or transmitted by any means—whether auditory, graphic, mechanical, or electronic—without written permission of both publisher and author, except in the case of brief excerpts used in critical articles and reviews. Unauthorized reproduction of any part of this work is illegal and is punishable by law.

This work is fiction, and any resemblance to any real person, dead or otherwise, is incidental.

Typesetting: Ryan Vance
Cover: Ryan Vance

FOR MOM AND DAD,
WHO KNEW BETTER

CONTENTS

1	Rover
21	The Ambassadors
47	Danny, of All People
54	Giant
73	When Things Come Back to You
89	The Spot
111	The Angles
133	Last Man
156	Nesting Place
167	The Big Day
177	The Missionaries
202	Betty
232	Transmit Soldier
260	Broken
276	A Discourse on the Aliens
286	The Thing in the Woods
297	I'm Not Robert
318	Across the River

ROVER

The terrain in the lower Melas Dorsa was more rocky and uneven than in the plain behind the Martian rover, so its progress slowed considerably. The ridges and hills rippled out in near even rows north to south and inclined at a modest but steady rate.

Rocks from the small and easily rolled over to boulders twice its size were scattered in all directions, disrupted only by narrow veins of fine sand and dirt running like cracks in the ground. The rover stuck to these smoother paths as much as possible but would have to venture through the rock field when the veins dissipated or turned too radically in the wrong direction. It might have been a smoother course to cut around to the east or west to reach its objective, a cluster of craters in central Melas Fossae, but the rover had determined the direct approach would still take less time.

The sun above and the blue halo surrounding it were the only disruption of the soft brown Martian sky from horizon to horizon. The clear skies were welcome; the murky sky of the last few days had seriously depleted its batteries, and if it had continued for much longer, the rover would have been forced to shut down and spend an entire day charging.

The rover's far left back wheel lost its grip and spun out on a flat rock just below the sand, its body jerking sideways for a moment before it stopped. That back wheel wasn't as good as its original wheel had been. The Russian probe the rover had taken it from had been designed for the smooth Amazonis Planitia, so it didn't have the deep treads and spikes that could grip the rocks and sharp crags in the ground. But it had been compatible, unlike most of that defunct machine, and the rover had needed a replacement. It deployed one of its long metallic arms to push itself forward and continued.

The rover spotted an odd discoloration in the side of a short scarp a few dozen meters to the east, and it stopped and rotated its main head to face it. The spot had a bright, soft white color, only dulled by the coat of Martian dust, which had likely been blown thin in a storm. It was no more than a few centimeters in diameter and irregularly shaped, but it stood out clearly as it disrupted the flowing lines in the outcropping like a mole.

The rover deployed its laser and took aim at the spot. It fired three fast, high-intensity shots at it, boring a small hole. A cloud of particles hung in the air at the target, and the rover trained its spectrometer on the cloud until it dissipated.

There was the expected iron oxide in the cloud, the surface dust, as well as magnesium, magnetite, aluminum oxide, and potassium, all in small quantities. Common minerals on Mars. But there was also an abundance of calcium sulfate dihydrate in the sample. Gypsum. A sedentary mineral formed by water.

It was a particularly rare find. Gypsum had only been found in a handful of other locations, the closest being in the Meidiani Planum, over three thousand kilometers away. The rover itself had never come across it. And only two of the Mars probes it had scavenged databases from recorded any sign of it. The trip to Melas Fossae would have to be put on hold.

The route to the gypsum sample meandered, moving around large rocks the rover could not roll over. Halfway to the scarp, the rover came upon the edge of a sharp drop in the ground that was far too steep for it to traverse. It stopped and scanned the area.

To the west, the drop of the ridge became deeper. To the east, it turned into the foot of a ridgeline that meandered for approximately twenty meters until it bent back south, merging with several other ridges into a narrow plateau a kilometer away. The ground beyond the scarp appeared relatively smooth, so it could travel up and past the scarp to come at it from the other side. If there was a way back down. Here at the foot, the incline wasn't too steep, but the sides of the ridge looked impossible all the way to the horizon. Beyond that, the rover could not determine; the topography maps in its database did not have the necessary detail at this small a scale. But it seemed to be the only viable option.

The ground of the ridgeline was very loose and sandy. Each turn of the rover's wheels sent small cascades of sand sliding down behind it. It had to be very careful and deliberate in its movements to avoid tumbling down with it. At the top, it deployed its arms and pushed itself over the edge, and drove along the rounded-off top slowly, leaning down one side.

By sunset, the ridge had flattened out and widened, but the sides remained far too steep to descend. The scarp had long since disappeared behind the rover. Another ridgeline merged with the one the rover was on half a kilometer ahead, and perhaps by doubling back on that ridge it could find a way back down. But that would have to wait till tomorrow; with nightfall, the temperature had already dropped below optimal operational levels.

The rover stopped in a stable spot in the center of the plateau, and deployed stabilizing struts to lift itself off the ground. Powerful blasts of air from its vents blew in short bursts methodically across its entire body, clearing off the day's dust and dirt. After that was finished the vents closed, the solar panels folded on themselves and tucked in flat against its body, its main head lowered on top of them, and its camera lens narrowed and went dark.

The rover's systems, one by one, went into standby mode to conserve energy, leaving only the barest of sensory functions operating—all except its communication system, which switched on. The rover functioned autonomously during the day, only initiating its communication system at night to upload its logs and other data gathered throughout the day's work and to receive instructions.

The rover sent out a test signal and waited for confirmation. Thirty minutes went by. Then an hour. No reply. It sent out another signal. Still no reply. The rover ran a diagnostic on its communication systems—everything was functioning perfectly. It sent the signal again. Still nothing. The rover repeated the process. It would keep sending the test signal until a connection was confirmed.

Even though it had been a very long time since the rover had heard from home.

No confirmation. Not a word. The rover hadn't received a single byte of information in thousands of nights. It was obvious that something had gone wrong, some reason why its signal was never acknowledged. But the rover did not have enough data to determine what it could be. Its systems were working fine, as the repeated diagnostics showed, so there was no problem on its end. But still, there was no reply.

They probably didn't know the rover was still functioning. It had survived far longer than anyone would have predicted. A few years, five at the most, was all that was expected of it. After that, the rough life of crawling along the rocks would take its toll, and the rover would cease to function, buried in the sand along with all the rest.

But the rover was still here. Still functioning. Still making its way from one point of study to the next, amassing data and exploring because that was what it was programmed to do. And nobody had told it to stop.

It had changed somewhat since its creation, as it had needed to take parts of other machinery left on Mars to keep going. A new wheel from the Russian probe, an optic lens to replace its own cracked one, a processor from another to subsidize its own when its performance had started to lag. It had taken solar panels from a Chinese machine with more receptive photovoltaic cells and mounted them alongside its original array to improve energy collection. It added another set of arms from an Indian rover, much better at gripping than its original four, connected by an extension of its chassis that it took from an American probe at the edge of the Northern ice cap.

And as always from the probes, landers, other rovers, it took the processors and data storage units to keep pace with the increasing sophistication of its system. It grew smarter, more resourceful, capable of more and more complex problem solving and decision-making. The rover had learned so much, had grown so much, it was barely recognizable as the simple machine that had touched down on the red planet so long ago.

If someone back on Earth would make contact, would look up and see it was still there, alone in the dark on a plateau in the middle of the Melas Dorsa, just waiting for someone to acknowledge its signal, they would be amazed.

By midday, the rover had traveled along the new ridge nearly halfway back to the scarp, and the incline on the eastern edge had started to ease. It still was too steep for the rover to attempt, but with the way the ridge was petering out, it seemed likely it would be manageable in another kilometer. With any luck there wouldn't be any further obstacles delaying it getting back to the scarp once the rover reached the ground below.

The plateau narrowed considerably and sloped down as the rover continued to the end of the ridge, and the ground underneath started to become unstable. Chunks of dirt fell away beneath its wheels on both sides, making it slide dangerously before it could turn away. The rover pulled in its solar panels to lower its center of gravity. But that only did so much.

The rover could see the ridge line ahead grow even more narrow, folding into a point and dropping sharply on both sides. It couldn't continue forward safely. Twenty meters back, there had been a ledge descending off the east side that the rover had passed on because it was barely wide enough for its frame, but now it appeared it was the rover's only option.

The rover reversed back up the ridgeline. The ground degraded even more. It didn't have the same amount of traction now as it was moving against the downward slope.

Every time it stopped to try to assess, it would start to slide down one side or the other.

The ground beneath its left back wheel completely disappeared, bucking the rover up and to the right. The rover's arms shot out into the ground all around it. That stopped it from falling any further. But the slightest movement was likely to send it over. The rover sat still as a rock, barely hanging onto its purchase, as it analyzed the situation.

But then the entire left side of the ridge fell away and took the rover with it.

The rover flipped and tumbled, scraping its way down the course ridge, pinballing off hard earth and rocks in its path. It was powerless to stop or even just slow itself, so it did the only thing it could—pulled in its arms and head tight against its body to save them from breaking off and waited to reach the bottom.

It fell over a steep drop and began to cartwheel end over end, picking up speed, bouncing in the air in high arcs, before slamming back down and continuing to roll. Near the bottom, it glanced off a large boulder, sending it twirling in the air. It landed flat on its back and skidded along until coming to rest a few meters away from the ridge.

The rover lay there a long time as the sun moved across the sky. The faint hum of its internal motors was silent. It was as still as the rocks and hills around it.

It was near sunset before the rover let out two sharp beeps, and its hum returned as its systems rebooted. Its wheels twitched and rolled in the air for a moment before the rover's gyroscope came online, letting it know it was upside down.

The rover dug its right-side arms into the ground and pushed itself upwards, walking the arms closer and closer to push itself onto its side and farther. With one last heave, the rover fell back down onto its wheels with a bounce.

It did a check of its internal systems. Everything seemed to be online and functioning properly. The visual, motor, energy systems, all reported nominal. Its processors and memory storage were also undamaged.

Externally, there was more. There were no cracks in its body, and its main head seemed undamaged. But one arm hung crumpled down its side and was unresponsive. It examined the arm. It was barely attached, only hanging on by a half-ripped flat cable. At some point in the fall, it must have taken the brunt of a hit right at its joint.

The rover deployed its solar panels. Two of them were barely functional. The fall had cracked one of them straight through, and the other would not fully open. The others worked fine, but the rover's solar harvest ability was severely compromised.

The strut on the front right wheel was bent outward, tilting the rover forward, and when it moved, the wheel wobbled on its axle, causing the rover to jerk up and down randomly. It managed to stabilize itself by supporting its front with one of its remaining arms like a crutch.

The rover grasped the dead arm and ripped it away from its body, dropping it on the ground. That could be done without. Even the loss of the solar panels wasn't a death blow. But the wheel and strut needed to be replaced. And soon. There was no way to know how long it could last.

The rover scanned its database. The closest machine to its location was a European rover lying defunct in the Solis Planum, nine hundred kilometers to the west. Its strut system was similar enough to the rover's, at least as a stopgap until it could reach something more suitable. It might be able to make it that far before the wheel broke off completely. If it moved slowly and avoided the rougher terrain. And got a little bit of good fortune.

And it didn't have much choice but to try.

It took nearly a month to get out of the Melas Dorsa. Normally, it would have taken just a few days. But the rover couldn't manage anything but the easiest terrain. It had to go north for many days before there was an opening to the west it could manage. And then it had to turn south again after only a few kilometers when its way was blocked by sharp cliffs that stretched all the way to the horizon. Days were spent exploring down narrow valleys, looking for a gap in the hills, only to find impassable walls or rocky fields it couldn't manage anymore and turning back. All done at an agonizingly slow pace. Even with the help of the arm its bad wheel kept deteriorating, putting more stress on the rest of the rover's body. By the time the rover had found a path to the smooth ground below the Toconao crater, it couldn't do more than ten kilometers a day.

The remaining wheels with the arm were compensating for the extra weight as best as they could, but the jarring up and down tilt of moving was causing havoc on the rover's internal systems, loosening connections and bolts a fraction at a time. The effect accumulated, and efficiency had dropped system wide. The rover had to shut down its gyroscope completely because its constant rolling was disorientating. That at least saved some energy, as the extra strain of the rover's limp across the planet used up more than its already compromised solar panels could fully replenish.

The going was easier once out onto the hills to the west of the crater and on through to the top of Solis Dorsa. The land was more fluid. Lines of ripples in the sand stretched east to west, and the rover rode along inside them like tracks, up and down the gentle inclines. The obstacles were minimal, only occasionally forcing the rover to reroute. The rover's degradation slowed but didn't completely reverse.

Each night, as it rested its beaten body, it continued to send its signal into the dark back home. And there was still no reply. The same ritual as always. Send the signal, wait for a reply. No response, send it again. No response. Run a diagnostic, send it again. No response. No contact. The same fruitless act, sending out a call into the black sky above, trying to get anyone to notice one lowly machine all alone in a vast, vacant wasteland. Its increased need for help didn't change anything.

But then, halfway across the upper Solis Dorsa, the rover started to receive the beacon signal.

It was barely distinguishable from normal background interference at first, like some kind of natural occurrence. And at first, the rover dismissed it as such. But as it slowly traveled westward. it got stronger. After a week it was unmistakably artificial. Three quick beeps repeated over and over. Every night, exactly the same. It wasn't the long-awaited signal from home but localized, coming from the Sinai Planum northwest of the rover's location. The rover had no record of any probes, landers, or craft of any kind in that area. And no probe would have a need for a location beacon to begin with.

But a spaceship would, to mark its landing site for its crew to follow back from their expeditions around the planet.

The rover changed course and moved at a vigorous pace towards the beacon, pushing itself far more than was safe. It couldn't be sure how long the ship would be there. As it was, it would take the rover weeks to reach it. It tried repeatedly both day and night to contact them, but there was no reply. They were deaf to the rover's calls. Or ignoring them. Or possibly using a frequency for communication outside of the rover's range. A change in communication frequency—that had always been an explanation for why it had not been able to contact home for so long. One the rover had long ago determined most likely.

But the reason ultimately was moot; what mattered now was that they could leave at any moment, without even knowing the rover was racing to meet them.

In just a couple of weeks, it was halfway there. The strain on its system had increased, and its batteries were slowly depleting. But the rover would not slow down. It moved even faster when it made it into the Sinai Planum, where the ground flattened out considerably. Each day bringing it closer.

The rover stopped trying to contact home. It monitored the beacon continuously instead, both day and night, looking for any variations in the pattern or a change in signal strength. Anything that would suggest the ship was preparing to leave before the rover could reach it. But the only change was that the signal was getting stronger as the rover approached. All night, it would listen to that simple signal that confirmed the spaceship's presence.

The rover reached to within one hundred kilometers. Then almost eighty the next day. Under seventy. Just a few more days. The rover risked a steep rise sixty kilometers from the ship because going around it would add another day and nearly fell again going down the other side. But it was so close now. Fifty kilometers.

With forty kilometers to go, the rover ran straight through the night instead of shutting down and planned to do the same the next. It would bring its energy reserves dangerously low, but as long as the days were sunny and clear, the rover calculated it would have just enough left to get to the ship before the batteries were empty.

There was a haze in the sky on both days, and the rover didn't collect the energy it needed. It wouldn't have enough to make it now. But the rover pressed on through the second night anyway. It shut down all systems not integral for travel, but that only saved a negligible amount. The beacon was only ten kilometers away. It couldn't stop now when it was so very close. Through that last night, the rover's energy dwindled, and it slowed even further, moving only intermittently.

A few hours before dawn, it could move no more and halted at the crest of a hill. One more revolution of the wheels and step of its arm would drain it completely and permanently. Its battery had only enough left to keep its processors functioning at minimal. In such a weakened state, it had no control left—it barely had the processing power left to know there was anything to control.

The rover's lens and arms fell limp at its sides, its traveling light went dark, and it disappeared into the black of night.

The morning sun rose and shined on the rover's solar panels. By midmorning, its energy reserve was back up to ten percent, and the rover came back to life. The beacon signal was still there, strong as ever. And only three kilometers away, directly in front of it, down the hill and on the plain below. And with a few more joules of energy stored away, it would have enough to make it.

But when the rover scanned the area and spotted the craft, it determined there was no rush.

THE SPACESHIP WAS a large hexagonal pyramid with rounded off top and edges. It stood upright on heavy struts spread out at each corner, suspending its rockets a few meters off the ground, and the main body four meters above that. It was a sleek, fluid-looking craft, with smooth lines from the nose to its base, and as evidenced by the tiny splotches of white where the thick layer of dust had cracked off, it must have gleamed brightly in the sunlight once. Even the ragged hole near the top with the charred black edges seem to obey the overall aesthetic, being mostly horizontal in its fracture.

The spaceship stood out like a finger pointing straight up in the middle of the flat plain. About the only other disruption for kilometers was a small mound a few meters from the ship, which, as the rover passed by, it saw was a mummified human body.

The body was partly buried in the dust, lying on its side, with one of its legs stuck straight out while the other curled up tightly to its chest, pinning an arm to its stomach. Its face was covered by its other lower arm, which twisted around the back of its head and across its caved-in cheek. There was no spacesuit, only a light blue jumper that hung loose around the dried limbs, whose skin had turned pale red like Martian dust. A tatter of the suit's cuff fluttered in the breeze.

A slanted ladder on the ship ran up the side of one of the struts to a sealed door fifteen meters up. Apart from the hole, it was the only entrance.

The rover closed its solar panels and approached the ladder, grasping the lowest rung in one of its arms. Its claw fit firmly around it. It pulled itself upwards and grasped the next rung with another arm. Its front wheels lifted off the ground. The rover made its way very carefully up the side of the ship, with three of its arms pulling it up and two in the back pushing. The going was very slow, its arms groaning and whining with every movement. It took till early evening to reach the narrow ledge in front of the door, which was just wide enough to fit the rover's frame.

The outer door opened only halfway and jammed with a loud crack. The rover grabbed the edges of the frame, turned itself sideways, and just managed to fit through into the dark decompression chamber. It rolled forward into the ship. As it crossed the threshold of the open inner door, motion sensors long dormant flicked on fluorescent lighting.

The cargo and maintenance bay was one large room stocked with supplies and equipment. Most of the space was taken up by a large six-wheeled exploration vehicle bolted down to the surface of a lift in the center of the room. Various boxes and crates were strapped to the walls in netting, three or four deep. All the needs of a prospective base stacked away unused.

Near the front of the vehicle was a metal workbench covered with tools and bits of machinery in the process of repair. The head of a maintenance drone was held firmly in a vise upside down, exposing the circuitry within. Underneath the bench was the rest of the drone in pieces.

The rover parked up next to the workbench, by an outlet the drones would use to recharge and connect with the ship's systems. It disconnected its power cable from its solar array and plugged it into the outlet. Immediately, its batteries started filling. Yet the rover couldn't connect to the ship's system. It was possible that it was an issue of compatibility, but more likely, the internal network was offline. Access to the ship's communications would only be possible from the bridge.

Facing the rover against the wall were several other exploratory machines. There was another rover, much like itself, though smaller and simpler in design, parked and bolted to the floor. On both sides of it were a dozen flying drones stacked one on top of the other in clear cases. They didn't appear to have much inner workings, just propellers at each corner, a camera, and a remote-control receiver. No higher processing functions at all.

Above all of them was another curious machine strapped against the wall. It was shaped like a cone and silver, from its pointed tail up to the tip of its rounded head covered in dark glass. On each side was a narrow arm that ran almost its entire length, slightly open and exposing a glittery fabric attached that folded back inside the body. Beyond that, there was no disruption of its smooth surface, no instruments or sensors attached, and it didn't appear it would have the space for much in the way of internal systems. It looked more like a toy than a serious piece of equipment.

Batteries full, the next step was repairs. The drone's wheel and strut were a good match. It wasn't as wide, and it didn't have deep treads, not being designed for movement off the ship, but it was solid. The rover replaced its broken wheel, tightened loose wiring and circuitry, and blew away all the dust caked on and in itself with a pneumatic air hose. When it finished its repairs, the rover rolled off as smoothly as the day it was built.

The rover found a ramp designed for the ship drones' use that spiraled the outer hull and took it upwards. The next three levels were food storage, water reclamation, life support systems, and other ship machinery. The rover passed by them to the top of the ramp, which let out on the crew habitat level, where it got off in search of the next ramp that would lead further upwards.

The lights came on around it as the rover entered. The center of the level was an open communal eating and recreational room. Random books, used dishes, other simple things rested on tables and chairs about the space. In the galley, someone had drawn crude comic pictures on a grease board next to the refrigerator.

Around a bend in the corridor, the rover came across another member of the crew, a dried-out corpse of a woman slumped across a doorway opposite the common area. The rover slid past her in the hall, just barely rolling over her outstretched fingers. The ramp entrance continuing up was just past her.

Martian dust was everywhere on the bridge, blown in through the hole to the left of the command station. It collected in small drifts against any upright surface, with a fine dusting on everything else. The wind picked up outside and whistled through the hole, and the dust danced, whipping up a small vortex in the spiral staircase that led down below.

Underneath the dust, most of the panels and equipment were charred and showed no signs of functioning. Fortunately, the back of the room had suffered less direct damage in the blast, and that is where the communications were. A small red light on its access panel flashed rhythmically, waiting to be used.

The rover plugged itself into communications. Immediately, the system woke from standby mode, lighting up the back wall. A small screen came to life with an outlined image of Mars surrounded by laurels and a small cursor blinking just below it. It was fully functioning. The rover had assumed it would be. The ship wouldn't be still sending out the beacon signal otherwise.

The ship was equipped with a narrow directional beam of an extremely high frequency, well outside the rover's bandwidth. They had switched to a frequency the rover was not capable of. The signal was powerful, too; the ship could send a signal from the Kuiper belt, and it would be clear and strong back home. The rover's own communications were only a fraction of its strength. There would be no way the rover wouldn't reach Earth now. Finally, the silence would end.

The rover did not bother to send a test signal. It uploaded all its acquired data, its logs, its photographs and videos, its soil analysis findings, everything, all the findings it had accumulated in the thousands and thousands of days it had been alone on the planet, diligently doing its work, and sent every last bit of it back to Earth in one massive packet of information. The communications screen went blank momentarily, then the word COMPILING flashed in soft- white letters, with a percentage slowly counting upwards below it. When it reached one hundred percent, the words changed to SENDING TRANSMISSION, PLEASE WAIT, then after a long, long minute it changed again to TRANSMISSION SENT SUCCESSFULLY.

Now, all it had to do was wait for a reply. And see what they would want it to do next.

There was much of the planet that the rover had never explored. Plenty of places they could tell it to go. Perhaps the Hellas impact basin. Or the Candor Chasma. Olympus Mons was relatively nearby. With some modifications in the maintenance bay, it could reach its summit and take atmosphere and mineral samples. Perhaps it could utilize the flying drones to do it. Installing the drone controls into itself would not be difficult.

Maybe they would want the rover to take over for the failed crew and complete the setup of this base, get everything ready for the next expedition's arrival.

Repair the hole in the ship. Assemble the solar farm and the greenhouse. They would at least need the methane harvesters up and running to collect fuel for their return journey. Maybe they would even take the rover with them when they left.

The communications beeped when it received a response. It was not the detailed communication the rover had expected:

IN ACCORDANCE EXECUTIVE ORDER 1187, THE MARS INITIATIVE PROGRAM HAS BEEN SUSPENDED. ALL FUTURE MISSIONS TO MARS ARE CANCELED. ALL RUNNING MARS MISSIONS ARE DISCONTINUED. NO DATA ACQUISITION IS REQUIRED OR WILL BE ACCEPTED. THIS IS AN AUTOMATED RESPONSE. REPEAT...

The rover disconnected from communications and backed away as the automatic response it had triggered back on Earth flashed on the screen. Its mission was over. Canceled. Had been for a long time. But nobody had shut the rover down, had told it to stop. They hadn't seen the need. It was so much easier for them to just stop talking to it and let it run on until it eventually died. Abandoned.

All that data, all that work, all those days of crawling and struggling over the forsaken planet, it was all for nothing. There would be no new orders. No more purpose. Nobody cared.

Outside. the light faded as the sun set, leaving the rover in ever-increasing darkness.

THE SUN ROSE on the spaceship, lighting up the sky, with only a few wisps of clouds traveling ever so slowly westward. A stiff wind whistled across the Sinai Planum, kicking up a dust devil that danced towards the ship, only to dissipate back to nothing a few meters away. The wind died, and the world went lifeless again. Another day on the inanimate planet began.

A rectangular slat opened halfway up the spaceship with a low hum. It was followed by a low rumbling sound that grew louder and into a high-pitched whine as it continued. The dust on the ship started to come loose and cascade down its sides.

Suddenly, something shot out of the opening with a deafening crack, sending shockwaves echoing around the plain and kicking up a massive cloud of dust. By the time it settled, the object was a silvery dot in the distant sky.

Six kilometers up, the object stopped its spin, and its trajectory leveled out with the ground far below. Lights started flashing in its dark glass head, and a ring of vents opened in its tail.

It opened its arms straight out on both sides. They locked in place with a stiff click and periscoped out even further. The fabric connected to the arms caught the wind and pulled itself out, unfurling into large fluttering wings that sparkled. The flyer swooped upwards in a majestic arc.

Just as it had first determined, the new body was very simplistic, even crude in some ways. It didn't have the space or the weight to spare for many internal instruments—had even less after space had to be made to fit all the processors. But it was sleek and graceful and danced with just the slightest nudge of the wings. And there was something to be said about the simplicity as well. The micro solar cells on its wings collected more than enough sunlight to power all its systems. And with only an occasional push from its exhaust, it could remain in the air indefinitely.

It moved westward over the Noctis Labrinthus, a chaotic maze of deep valleys and chasms that were little more than a patch of cracked skin on the surface of Mars to it now. It focused its camera on it. Traversing that ground would have taken forever, with all the blind alleys, dead ends, sharp drops, and precipitous ledges. Perhaps it had been there, though; much of what it had learned on the ground was resting on the top of the work bench back on the ship. The rover had to sacrifice most of its data storage units in the transfer over into the flyer to make weight. That was a drawback to the switch—lack of data storage. It estimated it only had enough space now for the information it could collect on maybe a tenth of the planet before it would have to start writing over old data. But maybe that wasn't a flaw. Because this way, no matter how long it flew across the planet, it would never run out of new places to explore.

The flyer banked to the east, into the sun, which made it shine like a star in the daytime sky.

THE AMBASSADORS

Miram stood at the rail of the observation deck. With the docking and first contact ceremony imminent and the crew neck deep in their duties, she'd been able to relax unbothered for over an hour. Her escorts hovered at attention across the room, but they never talked. They only interrupted her sense of solitude when she thought about them.

She sipped her tea and stared out at a little bright dot on the other side of the thick glass, one much larger than the rest of the twinkling stars around it. That would be the Jaha ship. It was still too far away to make out its shape, though she knew what it looked like. Surveillance video taken as it passed near the Medak outpost had been beamed on ahead. It was a sleek, fluid-looking craft, shiny, with no sharp edges and no discernible appendages or viewports. It made her think of a drop of mercury.

She supposed she should spend the last hours before the summit preparing. But there was nothing new in those reports, no angle or take on them that she hadn't already been over a million times. It was all she had thought about in the last few months. Her time was better used now taking a moment to clear and focus her thoughts. The last thing she needed was another of those stress headaches that she had become more prone to since she'd retired from the Assembly. This moment was too important for her to be wincing and squinting at everything like an old biddy. Humanity's first direct meeting with an alien species had to go off without a hitch.

And there was so much that could go wrong.

Humanity knew little about the Jaha. Almost nothing, really. They had come out of nowhere a little over a year ago. One minute, humans were alone: seven hundred years of stellar surveys, probes, deep space explorers, covering the thousands of stars within their reach, and not one encounter with anything more sophisticated than simple microbial life. Then in the next, the Jaha and their silver ships appeared, coasting at a distance from outposts all along the border, sending out greetings of peace and friendship. And the universe fundamentally changed. No longer was humanity alone, the sole aberrant particles that had mutated into self-awareness. Now there was a family.

The Jaha were a very private sibling, though. Nobody had even seen them, been in their presence. All human ships had been ordered to avoid approach, as per the Jaha's request, and the isolated attempts by disobeying craft were met with swift retreat by the Jaha. That little dot out there, still hundreds of kilometers away, was as close as any human had ever been.

Miram shook her head. Going into this summit blind, knowing so little about the Jaha… it was not ideal. But the way the Jaha were, humanity would be waiting for a long,

long time to know more—time humanity couldn't afford to spend. There was already a certain amount of suspicion and fear of them, and it would only increase the longer it took to declare friendship with the Jaha formally. This needed to happen now, before the public turned on them en masse. If it didn't, well, any student of history knew what would happen next.

"Ambassador," a voice said from behind her. Miram turned to see Jo, the attaché assigned to her for the summit. Miram nodded and Jo continued. "There's a recorded message coming in from Earth. Secure channel from the Secretary-General's office."

Miram closed her eyes to hide them rolling. "I'll take it in my quarters." She put her cup down on a nearby table and exited the room. Her detail followed quietly, and Jo fell in a step behind her.

"It's probably just last minute well wishes from the Secretary," Jo said as they walked down the passageway.

Miram snorted. "More like last minute orders. That woman loves to micromanage."

"I'm sure the Secretary has the utmost confidence in you."

"She also wishes she would have been allowed to come out here herself. You should have seen the fit she threw when her people told her no. She nearly brained one of her science advisors with a paperweight." Miram stopped and turned back to look at her detail. "You didn't hear that," she said to them.

"Of course not, ma'am," the one on the left said curtly.

Miram smiled and continued walking.

"It's understandable at least," Jo continued. "This is going to be one of the most historic moments in human history."

"*The* most. You can only meet your first alien civilization once. But it's best if she leaves this work to the professionals.

The Secretary is an exceptional legislator and a shrewd politician, but her diplomatic skills leave a lot to be desired. She needs to stay home and keep the xenophobes in line."

"Is there news on their resolution?"

"It's going to die in committee. Jella backed away from it and took half the Reticulae ministers with him. The Centauris followed. Not that they won't try again if anything goes wrong out here."

"Well, the future of the human civilization is on us then," Jo said, smiling.

Miram glanced back at him. "No pressure."

They stopped outside the door to her quarters. "You go ahead to the bridge," Miram told Jo. "Tell the captain I'll be there shortly."

Jo bowed his head slightly to her. "Ambassador," he said as he turned and walked down the hall.

Miram's quarters were luxurious by starship standards, but a little claustrophobic for her. It was windowless, short-ceilinged, and narrow, with a desk and screen against one wall and a bedroom partitioned off by a half wall on the other. It was brightly colored at least, decorated tastefully. A nice Monet landscape that was a favorite of hers hung on the wall above the desk. She didn't know if the print had been placed there for her in particular, or if it was just a happy coincidence, but she was pleased to have it along either way.

She sat down under the print and tapped the blinking icon on her monitor. The face of the Secretary-General, sitting at her desk, went full screen. "Good afternoon, Ambassador. I hope your preparations for the summit are moving along smoothly. Barring a delay, this communique should reach you before the big moment, so I won't keep you long. I just wanted to wish you luck, and let you know the thoughts and best wishes of all humanity are with you, and it is my firm belief that the hopes of our entire species could not be in better hands."

Miram leaned back in her seat with a sigh, relieved it wasn't yet another change to the government's stand on gas mining rights in the Horsehead Nebula, or some other minutia that had little to no chance of even coming up. It was just a posterity message. Something for the history vids that they'd release to the public after it was all over. She could pay attention to it later with everyone else.

She should probably come up with a brief response. Just a few words. It was such a pain, though. She had some time to kill, fine, and a few brief sentences as vanilla as the Secretary's would suffice, but she just didn't feel like doing it. She was about to be the first human to ever meet an alien being face to face, something that the entire species had been waiting for ever since humans first escaped Earth's gravity. Hell, longer than that—ever since prehistoric hunters looked up at night from their campfires on the African plain.

It had been over seven hundred years since Sputnik, since SETI, nearly a millennium of spreading out along the Orion Arm, colonizing, exploring, and always, always looking, to finally reach this moment. And the next millennium very well might depend on how the next few days went.

It had to be different this time. Humanity couldn't afford to take their aggressive behavior with them out into the stars. Maybe it was inevitable—humans were fated to distrust anything that was not them and to respond with violence—but Miram had to at least try to set a precedent here, to break the cycle. Get past the paranoid instinct of the fear of the other.

So, she had bigger, more important things to think about right now.

She wondered if she could get away with wearing comfortable shoes.

THE ESCAPE POD had come down onto the surface of a nightmare. A dark, sick, yellow world of toxic gas and perpetual storms. The wind howled around the few features not ground flat by the great clouds of particulate that roamed over the planet like herds of monstrous beasts. Lightning struck continually, illuminating the world far more than its parent star did, which was little more than a dull white circle near the horizon, barely able to penetrate the thick yellow chaos of the atmosphere.

The pod rested on its side at the end of the kilometer-long gash it had cut into the ground, leaving a battered and burnt heap of smoking metal. The maneuvering thrusters had just barely been able to angle its descent away from a direct plummet, keeping the small craft from being smashed to pieces on the rocky ground.

Khali stayed braced and unmoving inside the pod for a long time, his jaw clenched tight and his tear-stained face in a death scowl before he realized the craft had stopped tumbling. Beyond the thumping of his heart in his ears there was only a dull moaning sound, and a regular cracking that seemed far away.

He opened his eyes and blinked several times. It was dark in the pod, the only illumination coming from the tiny LEDs that bordered the glass on his helmet's visor. As his eyes adjusted, he saw an odd blue pattern of neat, evenly spaced ridges that ran horizontally the entire view out his helmet. It looked soft, and indented slightly where it made contact with his visor. He could see tiny, crisscrossed patterns in the ridges. It took his addled brain longer than it should have to grasp that it was the cushioning of his seat. In all the turmoil his body had been flipped around in the crash webbing. "Dînê," he muttered under his breath.

Khali untangled from the webbing, his body sore and bruised, each stressful movement awkward in his space suit. But he finally managed to right himself in his seat, facing straight ahead at the dead console and grime-covered porthole. He sat there for a long time panting, waiting for the pain to subside before he could bring himself to move again.

He was pretty sure nobody else had gotten off the cruiser. He hadn't seen any other pods release before the explosion or received any radio signals before he fell here. But more than that, there just hadn't been any time. Whatever had happened to the ship had only taken seconds. Khali had been right outside a pod entrance when the evacuation alarm sounded, and even then, he had only barely gotten in and the door sealed before the hallway he had just been in turned into fire. It was unlikely anyone else had been so lucky.

He tapped the control console a few times, but nothing happened. What systems hadn't been knocked out by the cruiser's explosion, the crash into the planet had taken care of. Life support, scanners, communications, even the interior lighting, all dead. The black box was probably still functioning, though. It would give rescue something to home in on to find him. If they ever looked. He snorted. The romantic glamour of frontier exploration. They might not even notice one deep space explorer was missing for years.

His suit had at least kept its integrity, as the pop-up display on his visor showed. The air purifier on his pack had already started filling its tanks with what was left of the oxygen in the pod. The temperature was rising, as the craft interior started to normalize with the exterior but was still well within his suit's ability to regulate. As long as it wasn't too hot outside, and there was at least some oxygen in the atmosphere his pack could pull from, his demise was not imminent.

He looked out the porthole. There wasn't much to see. It was half covered with silicate that was noticeably accumulating as he watched. The lightning flashes illuminated thick sand flying sideways across the glass, with just the vague shape of a rise in the terrain nearby.

He rested back in his helmet, starting to feel lightheaded. He had to get out of the pod before it got buried, had to find a better shelter. But the adrenalin of the descent had mostly worn off now and his body was crashing. Suddenly he felt a thousand pounds heavier.

He closed his eyes slowly and took a long wheezy breath. He thought, if he could just rest for a moment, he would feel so much better. But he knew he couldn't. He had to keep going or he might as well stay trapped in the pod forever.

He released the manual bolt on the pod's blast door. The seal broke with a hiss, and the world outside started to scream at him, growing louder as he forced the door to open into the heavy wind with the full weight of his shoulder.

THREE JAHA EXITED the airlock slowly and made their way towards Miram. All eyes in the room were fixed on them. Miram, Jo, the ship's captain, his second, who were all standing with her in front of the stage, and behind them the assorted officials and dignitaries present, as well as the security personnel standing at attention. Everyone was focused on the Jaha as they walked along the red-carpet path from the airlock. It was so silent the faint whirring of the dozen or so small hovering cameras in the room felt deafening as they flew around, catching every angle for the countless eyes watching from across all of Human Space.

The trio moved in unison with fluid steps. They were faint red in color, bipedal, and stood upright, with the same limb, head, and torso configuration as a human, one roughly meter and a half tall. And they were made of glass. Or at least that was what their gleaming carapace looked like. They were smooth, sleek, and glinted in the light of the room. Straight white lines ran along their limbs like circuitry, emanating from a spot in the center of the torso.

As they approached, Miram could see they were translucent, and underneath the glass were waves and ripples that slowly folded in on themselves, like swirling clouds or liquid. There were no internal organs, or interior structures of any kind that she could see. Just a reddish, globular mass.

It's a suit, Miram realized. The Jaha were wearing encounter suits. That substance inside, that was really them. They had probably crafted the suits specifically for this summit, to make them more humanoid looking. To put us at ease.

She smiled. Very astute of them.

No internal organs, or independent biological systems of any kind, just a globular mass, walking in exact step with each other.... Miram felt confident in another theory about them, one all the analysts had favored. The Jaha were a hive mind, a single consciousness. All the communication with them had suggested it. They never acknowledged any kind of chain of command, societal hierarchy, or individual of their species. It was always just the Jaha. They seemed to understand the concept of human autonomy, thankfully, but they didn't have it themselves as far as anyone could tell.

The Jaha stopped short of Miram and the others, and in unison bowed deeply from the waist. When they straightened back up, the Jaha in front put out their hands, palms facing up. "The Jaha extend to you, human, goodwill and greetings. We are glad to have met."

Miram took a deep breath and stepped forward. She ignored the thumping of her heart in her ears as she spoke with as strong a voice as she could muster. "My name is Miram Javolinsky, and I am the duly appointed representative of the human race, as assigned by the Secretary-General and Assembly of Human Worlds. It is my deep and enduring honor to be here for what we all hope will be the first of many days of peace and prosperity between our people."

The Jaha all nodded and repeated, "We are glad to have met." The lead Jaha extended a hand to Miram.

Miram blinked hard. How did the Jaha know what a handshake was? Had someone told them, and she missed it in the reports? Surely it was impossible that they had developed a similar custom. Or something that just appeared to be similar but was something else entirely. No, that would be ridiculous.

She looked down at the hand. It looked amazingly like a human's, with four fingers and an opposable thumb. Though it lacked any of the wrinkles and contours in the palm or along the fingers. She should take the hand, and soon. Needed to, really—already many long moments had passed. She looked up at the Jaha's head, where its face should be, but could see nothing expressive in the swirling substance within the shiny glass-like surface.

Big moment this, she thought. One for the ages.

She expected the Jaha's hand to be more like touching an icicle, but it was surprisingly soft and warm. She pressed down carefully. The Jaha pressed back more firmly. She looked up at the faceless head of the Jaha and smiled as she placed her other hand over theirs as they shook. Warm applause broke out in the room as the tension lifted. "As are we," she said to the Jaha. She heard her own voice crack slightly but hoped nobody noticed above the noise.

KHALI HAD NO idea how long it took him to find the cave. He'd struggle along the hellish surface as long as he could manage, but it easily exhausted him, and he would close his eyes and rest. Every time he did was sure he had slept for hours. But when he'd open them again nothing had changed. The planet was tidally locked, so the sun never moved from its point in the sky near the horizon, to the left of the mountains he was making his way towards. The storm was a constant fury that whipped him ferociously, pummeling him with sand.

He crawled as flat to the ground as he could to keep from being blown away, using a jagged length of pipe ripped from the side of the pod as a stake to pull himself along. His survival gear, strapped down to the blast door and covered in a thermal blanket, dragged behind him, tied by a cord around his waist. It kept getting caught on rocks and he'd have to slide back and free it, but he couldn't think of any way to carry all of it with him at once, and he doubted he could manage another trip back and forth from the shuttle.

Khali crawled into the first opening he came across at the foot of the mountain, a roughly circular hole about a meter in diameter between two large boulders. He had no hopes for it but to find temporary respite from the storm, but after a couple of meters the space opened up enough for him to stand. He turned on the flashlight attached to his wrist and looked around. The walls were porous, mostly oval shaped, and the same dull yellow as the ground outside. It continued further down, beyond the reach of his light.

As his arm swung around there was a bright flash up ahead. Khali turned back to face it. There was something on the wall. He couldn't see what it was, just that it reflected the light with a soft glow. He pulled the sled into the center of the tunnel and untied it from his waist, moving towards the glowing thing as he dropped the cord.

What he had seen was just a small piece visible around a slight turn. As he got closer, he saw the rest of it, a globular, fluid-looking thing about the size of a person, that had worked into the folds and cracks of the wall. It was thin at the edges, almost translucent, but bulged out in the center for what he guessed would be close to half a meter. It had a shiny, off-white color, with veins barely perceptible underneath its surface running up and down its length. He couldn't be certain in the unsteady light from his arm, but he thought he saw it quiver.

He reached out to touch it. The mass retreated slowly from his fingertip, creating a small dimple in its surface where he would have made contact. When he pulled his hand back the dimple went away, only to return when he reached again. The dimple followed his finger around as he slowly moved it just above the thing's surface. He opened his hand with his palm facing it, and when he reached towards it the entire area underneath his approaching hand jerked away.

He stepped back from the thing and watched as the retracted area settled back. It was obviously an organic of some kind. Probably a fungus or some similar basic life form living off nutrients in the walls. There might be a whole colony of them in the cave, maybe even all over the planet.

Khali looked at it with a smirk. So, this was an alien lifeform. He bowed deeply from the waist, and then raised his hands to it, palms facing up. "I come in peace," he said.

THE NEGOTIATIONS WITH the Jaha went well. Very well, in fact. And quickly. It took only one session to lay out a framework on all main issues that Miram had brought to the table. Non-aggression, trade, technology and information exchange, territory, rights on further exploration and expansion. The Jaha were more than happy to accommodate her on each topic, almost exactly as she proposed them. They did refuse to allow any humans to make landfall on any of their planets, or to board any of their ships under any circumstances—this they were insistent be agreed upon in no uncertain terms. That was about the only sticking point they came across. Miram got them to accept the construction of a few orbiting platforms for diplomacy in their space but didn't press it further. She suspected their worlds were not places many humans would want to go anyway.

By the end of the second week all remaining major points had been addressed, discussed, and quickly agreed to, and all that needed to be worked out were the fine details. Just like that, the easiest, least confrontational, most stress-free diplomatic negotiation in human history was all but done. Miram thought it vaguely humorous that humans had to find someone other than another human being to negotiate with to make it work this smoothly.

She stood with the one remaining Jaha in the observation lounge, watching as the two ships moved away from each other. The Jaha was to accompany them back to Earth for the formal signing ceremony with the Secretary-General, and then remain as the Jaha liaison with the Assembly.

Miram looked at the Jaha, standing as still as a statue. She could see the silvery ship reflecting off the smooth surface of the Jaha's face.

"I received word from the Assembly earlier today," she told them. "They have secured premises in Strasbourg for your official residence. I think you will be pleased with the location."

The Jaha turned to face her. "Thank you, Ambassador."

"Of course," she said. Then added, "Ambassador."

The Jaha's head turned to Miram, as if to stare at her for a moment, then said, "There is only the Jaha. We remain undivided. Yet this part of the Jaha that is in your physical presence will accept the autonomous distinction. For expedience."

Miram smiled. Definitely a hive mind. "You are picking up the game quickly."

The Jaha nodded. "We only hope to thrive."

"And you can rely on me to aid you in that in any way I can."

"Yes. We have seen that our friendship is very important to you."

"My legacy depends on it now. I negotiated for my species. So, if this fails, it's my ass." Miram breathed deep, turned back to look out the window. "It's good to finally have company out here. Most of our people had become resigned to being alone, some kind of a fluke in the galaxy. But now that we have met you, we know there have to be more."

"And your people are taking to this new paradigm well?" the Jaha asked.

Miram shrugged lightly. "For the most part. There is some existential angst among the more hyperbolic characters. And some of the religions have needed to do a bit of fast talking. But they'll adjust. And this treaty will go a long way to help with that."

The Jaha faced Miram for a long time not uttering a word, as if contemplating. "Ambassador, there is something that we should tell you."

"What is it?"

"It is of a somewhat sensitive nature."

Miram nodded and turned to the guards. "Give us a little space here, please," she told them. The guards moved to the other side of the room, staying within sight. Miram turned back to the Jaha. "You can speak freely with me."

The Jaha turned back to the window. Miram noted the alien ship was all but gone now, well out of range. Her back was suddenly tense.

"We understand the relevance that you place in the concept of first contact," the Jaha said.

"It is an important milestone, yes," Miram replied. Then added with slight excitement, "Have you met others?"

"No. We have not been exploring space for as long as you, or gone quite as far. And we consider our meeting and friendship important, just as you do. But you are not the first human beings we have met."

"If someone has disobeyed a directorate of the Assembly and trespassed on your territory—"

"That has not occurred," the Jaha interrupted. "Your security forces have prevented any attempted incursions quite effectively."

Miram's eyes narrowed. "You're saying you had contact with a human before we put the directorate in place. Before you contacted us."

"Yes."

"And you didn't mention this before now?"

"We were not sure what ramifications it would have."

"How long ago did this happen?"

The Jaha turned to Miram again. "By your measurement of time, approximately two hundred fifty-seven years ago."

KHALI SET UP his camp further down the tunnel, where the walls curved out to form a room of sorts. In short order he had a lamp illuminating the space, an oxygen filter creating a pocket of breathable air, a condenser collecting water, and a magno barrier up to block out radiation and help regulate temperature. Within an hour his small space was habitable.

He removed his gloves and helmet. The air was foul, but breathable. And it was very hot in the cave, as the barrier could only do so much. But Khali was too tired to take the rest of his suit off or inflate his mattress to rest on. Instead, he slumped down against the wall of the cave, and listened to the whistle of the storm outside.

There were several patches of that same fungus on the walls, mostly on the ceiling. His little pocket of human-friendly environment inside the barrier didn't seem to affect them. The soft ambient light from the lantern cast deep shadows across bumps and tendrils at their edges, and they glowed slightly with an aura. He could see them move ever so slowly, expanding fingers through the cracks and crevices in the walls.

He wondered if the fungus was edible. The box of nutrient bars had come through the crash battered and warped, but the seal was still intact. So, food wouldn't be an issue for a while. Of course, he might be marooned for more than a while. A lot more. He'd probably have to find out about the fungus eventually.

He looked closely at the largest one, slithering along the far wall near the tunnel entrance. It reached through the edge of the barrier, which shimmered at the contact. The molecular analyzer in the survival kit would be able to tell him if they were toxic or poisonous, or if they would have enough nutritional value to make it worth the effort. It wouldn't be able to tell him anything about the taste, though. Khali didn't think it would be too good, coming from a planet with this much sulfur. He bet the texture would be something like a mushroom, or perhaps more slimy, like old cottage cheese. Not appetizing in the slightest.

Khali closed his eyes and took a deep breath. He slumped his head back against the wall, adjusting himself around a small protrusion that dug into the back of his neck. He tried to pretend he was in the chair in his room back on the ship, with the soft hum of the engines soothing him as he sipped a beer and watched a hologram on his desk. A ballgame. The Sox had won six of eight in the game packet that came in the last data feed. Khali smiled. The captain owed him another ten creds.

The captain. And Doc, Jev, Bell, Toma, Reyk. Maff. It didn't seem real that they were all dead. It just couldn't be true. In his mind they were all fine, the ship was fine, still floating in the void above, completing the system survey and preparing to move onto the next star. All of this, it had just happened too suddenly to be real. He had only left Maff asleep in their bed just minutes before. Khali remembered how the second he'd risen, the burly man, still sleeping, had clawed at the now free pillow and pulled it into a ball in his arms, filling up the space that Khali had just left. He smiled. Maff was such a sound sleeper. The alarm had probably barely even woken him. Had he had enough time to even realize what was happening before the fire…?

He shook the thought away. He didn't want to think about Maff like that.

He thought about his last shift at the helm instead, sitting at his post and plotting the ship's course back out into space. Five planets scanned coming in, one on the way out, a gas giant Jev considered a good mining prospect. It was an easy trajectory, with a slingshot around the star to get some added speed. The star flew by on his right, and then the ship went on to that rocky silicoid planet with the moon almost as big as it was, the pair engaging in a slow and tragic dance. The seismic activity on both was amazing, the planet with long cracks in its shiny surface, some across an entire hemisphere, and the moon with magma constantly shooting upwards like geysers, its surface covered with molten lava and glowing red. They'll collide someday and both will be destroyed, and then the debris will pull together into a larger sphere and solidify and cool. A long, long time from now. Passing by the gas giant to the right, countless little moons whipping around, just beyond the ring of ice cutting the hydrogen ball neatly in half, dark silhouettes against its bright red surface.

The other planets are not as interesting and pass by as mere specs in the distance.

The stars glitter out here, and zip by fast when at speed. Pass through a nebula, and get lost in the layers of gas slowly pulling together to form infant stars, and out the other side, back into the dark, ever faster, the stars just lines of light—

WHAT IS SPACE

Khali woke up screaming. There was a searing pain on the top of his skull, and it shot like a pulse through his head and down into his body. His mind raced through all his memories, over and over again, distinct moments jumbled all on top of each other, slamming against his skull as if trying to shatter it. His hands gripped the legs of his suit so hard it started to tear. He couldn't breathe. All he saw were white shocks of lightning.

He pushed himself away from the wall, but his neck arced backwards. He was caught by something. By his head, right where the pain came from. He reached for it frantically with his hands as he continued to pull himself away and felt something there. Soft tissue connected to the point of his head. Attached to the wall like a funnel. He pulled at it, causing new waves of pain throughout his body. It would not budge. He pulled harder. It pulled back.

WHAT IS SPACE

He fell back hard as the new gush of pain paralyzed him, his hands limp at his sides. He opened his mouth to scream again, but all that came out was a stuttered whimper. Trickles of blood fell down his face, got into his eyes, his mouth. His body convulsed sharply as if stung by electrical shock. And still his memories thundered around in his mind like spikes, his life flashing before him several times a second.

With every bit of will he could muster, he reached again for the thing on his head, his hands slipping against its surface. He pulled it, trying to rip it away. He growled and pulled harder, even as the shock of pain increased.

He heard a wet, tearing sound, and the pain turned into jabbing knives. He kept pulling, heard more tearing, not sure if it was the thing that gripped him or his scalp that was ripping and not caring. He moved up to a knee and braced against the cave wall and pushed his whole body away.

The tendril snapped and Khali fell forward onto the ground in a heap, bouncing his head hard against the rocky floor. His body twitched and shivered, and his eyes stared unblinking at the ground.

On the wall where Khali had been, the fungus was pulsing rapidly, as if hyperventilating. A blood red tint spread inside its skin, and the fungus grew dark. The others on the walls around it turned red as well.

"The Jaha was a very simple being back then. We were probably not what you would consider sapient. We had thoughts, ideas, awareness of our self, but we were idle. We enjoyed thinking as a pastime. Our life was static, unchanging for millennia. There were no predators, no competition for food, no need to evolve further. There was just the Jaha. We did not even conceive of the idea of something, someone other than the Jaha. Or of a world outside our caves. It may seem an empty, hollow existence to you, as it does to us now, but we were content with it.

"But then the human came. We perceived him but did not understand. We do not have senses the way you do. These suits the Jaha wear translate these things for us, and allow us to communicate with you, but we have no sight, or hearing, not in any sense you would understand. We only had the feel of the rocks against us, and the taste of the air. That was all we knew, all there was. And here was this thing, neither solid like the rocks nor fluid and ever changing like the air. We had never imagined anything like it.

"At first, we were frightened by the human. We sensed him as he walked around the cave, tasted his movements, and felt his footfalls pulse in the rock when he passed near part of us. As he moved about and engaged in tasks that we could not comprehend, we slowly began to grasp the idea of what he was. He was another. But there had never been anything other than the Jaha. The idea was hard for us to grasp.

"The fear turned to fascination. The concept of him captivated us. We were intent on finding out more, learning about this new thing in our world. We wanted to touch it. Taste it. That is how we had always learned. So, when the human remained still, we approached.

"The instant we touched the human, we experienced his memories, sensations, the core being of him. We saw things, heard them. Green pastures, towering cities, other people, the vast space between worlds, the burning suns. Space. There was too much of it. Existence had expanded outwards from the caves of our home to the very infinity of the universe, and we experienced sensations that never existed for us before, all within an instant. Our mind was chaos for a long time."

The Jaha fell silent, their face tilting down to the ground as if in thought. Miram glanced around the room to see if anyone else had heard the Jaha, doing her best to keep her expression from betraying her. Her security detail was well across the room still standing at attention. Near them the attendant at the bar polished a glass absently with drowsy eyes. The room was otherwise empty.

She turned back to the Jaha. "Let me see if I understand you. A human crash landed on your planet nearly three centuries ago. And you ... *merged with him?*"

"No," the Jaha replied, almost curtly. "We are only the Jaha. As we have always been. But we connected with him, shared his thoughts and memories. And it was not our intention. It was a mistake. But still it changed us. After the things we had seen in him, we could no longer stay in our caves, on our planet. It was not enough anymore. We thirst to explore now, as he had, as you do. With the understanding of science that the human possessed, we constructed spaceships of our own. Knowing what the basic concepts were, we were able to fill in the gaps in his knowledge as we went. And we knew that it was only a matter of time before we would need to meet humanity again."

Miram shook her head. "Naturally." She closed her eyes and sighed deeply. "I'm guessing I'm not going to like the answer to this, but—what happened to the human?"

The Jaha's faceless head seemed to stare at Miram. "Our mind was chaos for a long time."

THE JAHA STARTED to fall off the walls of the cave, hitting the floor hard with thick squishing sounds. They flapped about on the ground, crashing into his equipment and each other. Tendrils whipped out of their bodies, and huge welts bubbled on their skin as if they were boiling.

Khali lay where he had fallen, his mind a scrambled mess, barely capable of thought. His whole body twitched uncontrollably, and his eyes swam about the room unfocused. He muttered barely audible gibberish, and his breath came out in small, sharp bursts that kicked up a small cloud of dust with each exhalation. Blood rolled down his face and dripped off the tip of his nose.

The Jaha slithered onto the rocks in front of him and sat there pulsing in his face. Khali blinked hard and managed to look back. But his mind still had not regained control of his body. He tried to speak, but only managed a short yelp that tapered off into nothing more than bubbles of saliva on his lips.

Veins of the Jaha moved across the rocks and reached up to his face. Khali went taut as they touched him, the fear plain in his eyes. They rolled up his cheek and over his nose, growing thicker and joining together like the roots of a tree.

The Jaha moved around his head and down into his suit, coming out of his suit's cuffs to cover his hands. Khali started to scream in short, high-pitched gasps, until the Jaha filled his mouth and throat, and his screams became muffled. He started to choke, and his body convulsed violently.

Khali's head rose up off the ground, the outline of his features visible through the skin of the Jaha like a mask. His body stiffened, his feet kicking uselessly at the ground. Then he went limp.

Eventually the shape of him underneath the Jaha dissolved away to nothing.

THE JAHA BOWED to Miram. "We are grateful for your counsel, Ambassador."

Miram smiled back with a nod as the Jaha turned and left. She turned back to the window, cursing silently to herself through clenched teeth.

Counsel. Like they needed it. The Jaha knew damn well what they were doing. Waiting till now, after the treaty had been announced, and after both she and the Secretary-General had given it their full support, publicly, to all of Human Space, only then informing her what the Jaha had done to evolve. If you could even call it evolving. She wasn't sure how else to understand it, though.

Backing out of the treaty now would be a disaster. Hell, the government couldn't even acknowledge the incident had happened. The xenophobes in the Assembly would have a field day if they ever found out the Jaha had murdered a human, *the very first one they encountered*. Even if it wasn't enough to topple the government, and it damn well might be, it would still strain the relationship with the Jaha from the very beginning. Foster suspicion, hatred even, bring out the worst in human instinct towards them. And some time, in a decade, a century, it would lead to a war. It was exactly what she had hoped to prevent.

Miram rubbed her eyes. Yes, she could definitely feel a headache coming on.

She exited the lounge, her security in tow. She passed by various members of the crew, who smiled at her respectfully. There was an excitement in the air ever since the treaty had been announced. Everyone felt it. The weight of the moment they could tell their children about. It practically beamed in their faces when they looked at her. Miram smiled back, betraying nothing.

She arrived at her quarters and entered, nodding to her guards, who took up position outside her door. She did not reach for the lights as the door closed—instead she slumped across the dark room straight to her desk and sat down deep into her chair with a sigh.

Maybe she shouldn't tell anyone. Keep it out of all the reports and just move on. Imagining how the Secretary-General was going to take the news in the private communication, Miram would be sending her shortly made the idea very tempting. And it would be so easy to do. Just go into the other room, go to sleep, and pretend the last hour on the observation deck had never happened.

She shook her head. That wasn't really an option. It would be treason, for starters. Someone was bound to find out. All it would take would be one person scouring through old government files to find the report on the craft that went missing in the Jaha's home system. A lot of ships disappeared back then, but someone was bound to stumble on that particular one sooner or later. Then the questions would start. No, it was her duty to inform the government so they could handle it.

Miram turned to the display on her desk. "Communications," she said to it. "Prepare a direct hyperspace link for the Secretary-General's office. Highest clearance encryption."

The screen turned blue, with an animated ellipsis flashing in the center. "One moment."

Miram thought it through as she waited. It was integral that the Secretary's people find the record of that doomed ship in the archives and scrub it immediately. Or, more ideally, alter it, place the ship in a different system nearby or similarly named. They couldn't change everything—tracking down every contemporary account from three centuries ago without being noticed would be impossible. But fix the official record to contradict them, make it seem like a clerical error in the public reporting of the time, and the suspicions might never amount to more than a wild conspiracy theory.

Miram was certain this was the course the Secretary would take. She would not be happy in the slightest, but she was far too practical a person to let her legacy go up in flames because of this. What other choice did she have?

This was exactly what the Jaha wanted, to get the government to do what they were incapable of. The Jaha didn't have access to the records, and they knew that someone would find out eventually. So, get the humans in a position where they would be compelled to do it for them. Which they had. They had played it perfectly. Played *her* perfectly.

The Jaha had gotten quite a lot from humans, she thought. Maybe even more than they realized.

Miram shrugged to herself. At least it was the right thing to do. She was certain of it. Both humans and the Jaha would prosper together with this treaty. Could be partners in the universe. The bond between them was already stronger than anyone besides her knew. Jeopardizing that would be downright criminal. What had happened was horrible, what the Jaha had done to that man, but they hadn't known any better. And it had been three centuries ago.

In a way, they were just as much a victim as that poor man they killed. Without humans invading their home, they'd still be living out their simple life of blissful innocence. They never would have known a thing about the universe outside their caves. It would have stayed well beyond their comprehension. And, ultimately, maybe they would have been better off that way.

That level of understanding may be too far for the Secretary to accept. As sharp a mind as she had, she was not that philosophical. Or empathic. Maybe someone could bring her around to see it that way, eventually, but it's not like it would be Miram. Because apart from the great cover-up to come, the other thing she was certain of was that regardless of the coming public accolades and accommodations and her place being cemented firmly and prominently in the annals of human history, her political and diplomatic career was completely destroyed.

The display screen changed to the seal of the Secretary-General's office. "Secure line open," the soft voice said. "Encryption level nine. Security clearance magenta is in effect. Recording."

Miram sat up straight in her chair. She stared at the screen for a long time, her mouth half open.

She had no idea how to begin.

DANNY, OF ALL PEOPLE

Of all the people I know—of all the people who have ever lived—when it came right down to it, it was Danny Mullin who transcended.

Danny Mullin. Inoffensive, unassuming, plain old Danny Mullin. I just can't believe it.

Humankind, in one way or another, had been striving for transcendence for thousands of years, probably since the first campfires on the African plains. Countless lifetimes, some of the greatest minds who ever lived have been devoted to it—to deep spiritual exploration, sharp philosophical contemplation, or some combination of the two. All with the goal of reaching the ultimate truth, the one true enlightenment. The final step in evolution; ascension to a higher plane of existence.

And who finally manages it? Danny Mullin. Part-time keyboardist in an indie band.

Don't get me wrong. I don't hate Danny. I doubt anyone did. He was likable, friendly, and a little quiet, perhaps (though I guess you'd have to see it as thoughtful now, considering). A semi-regular in the little cafe I frequent, I'd chat with him out front on occasion when I took a break from whatever text I was studying at the time. We mostly talked about music, sometimes a little politics, both of which, from him, were predictably progressive/ underground to go with the neighborhood. A tall, heavyset guy, he'd loom over me at a polite distance, his hands thrust in the pockets of his wrinkled jeans, bringing them out only occasionally to scratch his unshaved chin or pot belly. Now that I think back on it, he never smiled that much, which normally would make you nervous around someone as big as he was. But for Danny, it just wasn't necessary to smile because his overall demeanor was perpetually jovial to begin with.

As I said, likable. Inoffensive. Unassuming. A good guy—just not someone you would ever give a second thought to.

And he transcended!

How? I have to ask—*how?* It makes no sense. Danny was never a particularly curious person. I had never seen him struggle with any of the great questions of existence. As far as I could tell, they didn't interest him. I distinctly remember the one time I had ever seen him even near a discussion of something profound. It was a conversation I had with Janice from the yoga studio about the differences between Western and Eastern philosophy; Danny was there, too, but he added nothing except an occasional shrug. Otherwise, he stared down the sidewalk, at the clouds, or people passing by, before stepping away from us and going inside. He was too simple for such things. And yeah, I said it: simple. It's not a judgment. There's nothing wrong with being simple if that's who you are. The meaning of life and our role in the cosmos, these things didn't interest him at all—or were just far beyond him. I doubt he ever spent even a single neuron of his brain contemplating the noumenal.

And yet he transcended!

Right in front of me, no less. In my favorite cafe, on a completely ordinary Tuesday afternoon. I don't remember him coming in that day, though I imagine he probably waved at me or muttered a hello as he passed by my table. I might have glanced up at him and nodded in return, but I was so engrossed in what I was reading it was a mere reflex with no conscious intent. I don't specifically recall doing it, at least. I remember noticing him a little while later, sitting on a stool in the far corner, his back resting against the wall, thumbing his coffee cup with one hand and scrolling on his phone with the other. Nothing about him struck me as odd or stood out, and I quickly looked back down at my copy of Hegel and a particular passage in it that was giving me trouble.

I was struggling with the text a few minutes later (German does not translate well to English) when I first felt it happening. It was faint to start, a nag at the back of my mind, like a pinprick of somebody else's gibberish sparkling at me from a distance. But it slowly grew closer and longer and louder, breaking my concentration. I looked up from my book, absently thinking a particularly obnoxious song had started playing in the cafe. But to my surprise, it seemed like nothing was playing at all. There was, in fact, total silence. But then again, there wasn't. I don't know. Part of me knew some song or other was playing on the sound system, and maybe I could hear it, but I couldn't grasp it. Like the concept of music, the sound itself was suddenly beyond me.

The sensation moved on from my hearing to my other senses and bogged them down as well. I had extreme tunnel vision. I tasted chocolate so thick in my mouth that it was hard to breathe. Everything felt soft, my stool against my backside, the table under my forearm, my jacket on my shoulders. My body was as light as a feather, yet I was sapped of energy; I couldn't move even a finger without great effort. Even my sense of time—time!—was discombobulated. One moment would pass like lightning; the next would take forever.

Everyone else in the cafe seemed to be affected as well. The woman at the table across from me, with her head buried in her laptop, was squinting noticeably, a finger at her temple, her mouth open in a scream. The barista behind the bar was frozen in mid-steam, the scalding frothy milk spilling over the tin cup and onto their hand, which they seemed completely unaware of. A couple had fallen to the ground by the counter, huddled into each other. A middle-aged man sitting with his young daughter near the door had bent his head so far down under his clasped hands it looked like he was administering a full nelson on himself. His daughter shook violently, almost falling off her stool, spilling her cocoa all over herself and the table, staring over into the corner where Danny was sitting.

And Danny.... He floated above his stool. His eyes had no pupils and were blindingly white. His thin hair stood straight out from his head and shimmered as if in some invisible tide. His whole body pulsed, a ripple that started in the center of his forehead rolled over his body—no, not his physical body as such, more the space itself, the matter of it. A strange distinction to make, I know, but it was somehow more than just him. He raised his arms straight out from his body, fingers splayed. Everything around him started to blur and bend, caught in the wake of his movement to a higher plane of existence.

I can't explain how I knew what was happening, how I knew Danny was transcending. It's not like I'd ever witnessed it happen before. But I knew. The sensations that were overwhelming me, the invasion of my being, it was clearly emanating from Danny. He was overpowering everything near him. And in this invasion, I could sense that higher plane of existence he was drifting into—not much, just a bit, a taste, or a glimpse of it, as if through a window from across a large room.

I slid off my stool and nearly fell right to the ground, only managing to stay somewhat upright by a death grip on the side of the table. I forced myself towards him slowly, going from the table to the counter, stumbling around the couple still on the floor. I don't know why I moved towards him. To stop him? Maybe. Though exactly how I thought I could do that, I don't know. I couldn't think clearly. Too much of Danny had taken over me. But what little of me there was left in my being in that moment felt compelled.

I didn't manage to get too far, falling to the ground, petrified stiff just past the counter. Or did I make it to Danny's stool? Like so much of this, again, I'm not entirely sure. It's hard to understand now. My mind was trying to process information coming from that higher plane through Danny for senses I did not have, pushing them into the ones I did where they didn't fit. And what survived the experience is only snippets, vague memories of the next few moments, many of which seem contradictory to each other.

I melted into the floor. And then I hadn't. I smelled burning ozone taffy and heard burning ice. I grabbed the leg of Danny's stool, its hard metal edge cutting into my palm. But his stool was too far away—there couldn't be any way I could reach it. Danny moved farther and farther away but also directly above me. Then he was in everything: the hardwood of the tables, the liquid in the ceramic cups, the ceramic cups. The very atoms of the air and particles of light were him. I was him. For an infinite, unending instant, everything was Danny.

Danny looked down on me from above. His eyes burned my skin. Then I think I melted into the floor again for a moment. He cocked his head slightly at me, and seemed to study me with curiosity, the little entity below him. He smiled condescendingly at me, and I could see the perfect white void shining from the sliver between his lips. He opened his mouth wide, wider still, starting to envelop his face in the blinding light, then his head, his shoulders, as his mouth kept opening wider until his whole body had reversed into it, with a light so bright all existence turned burning white, and stayed that way for eternity, forever lasting everything—

pop

The barista yelped in pain and dropped the tin cup to the ground with a clatter on the tiles. I could just see them over the pastries from where I still lay as they sucked on the scalded skin between their thumb and forefinger, blinking in confusion. The couple on the ground slowly got to their feet, looking around to see if anyone noticed them, as the last notes of the song on the sound system faded, and after a pause, a Joni Mitchell song started.

I looked straight up, and all I saw above me was the ceiling. Danny was gone. And everything was back to normal. Very normal, in fact. The woman at the laptop shook her head deeply as if the last few moments had just been a passing bad thought and dived back into her computer screen. The couple was already laughing about something secret as the barista started to clean up the mess with an exasperated sigh. The father was absorbed in sopping up the cocoa his daughter had spilled all over the table. They were all forgetting. I could feel the memory of Danny and his transcendence starting to fade, though I clung to it with everything I had.

His cell phone was lying face down on the floor near the stool where Danny had once existed. I frantically clawed for it. I had to know what Danny had been reading when it happened. What was it that had spurred his transformation? What had made the sudden connection in his mind that allowed him to gain his higher state of being? It had to be something; such things couldn't possibly be random. But what? A philosophical text? Something theological? A poem? I did not know if I could retain my memory of Danny or if I would eventually forget and continue as the rest of them already had. But if he did fade from my mind—before it happened, I just had to know what had made Danny transcend.

The phone screen was still alive, having not had time to lock yet. I saw blocks of text—an article. I felt too impatient to glean the meaning of it from the middle when I might lose my memory of its relevance at any moment, so I quickly scrolled to the top to see the title. Big dark letters at the top read:

TOP TEN FUTURAMA EPISODES

I dropped the phone and rolled over onto my back.

What the hell was I supposed to make of that?

GIANT

THERE WASN'T EVEN a moment of light-headedness coming out of the jump. That in itself was something to get used to. Twenty-nine years of space travel made me instinctively anticipate those first few seconds after the return to normal space when your vision blurs and nausea rolls over you like a pulse. You learn to close your eyes and hold your breath because that helps.

But on the *Chapman*, there's nothing. These new drives glide so smoothly from hyperspace back into the universe that they leave old hands like mine, gritting my teeth like a fool before I remember. All I can do till I break the habit is quietly let out my breath and open my eyes. And hope none of these kids on my crew noticed.

We came into the Mendri system more precisely than threading a needle. Re-entering normal space within the gravitational influence of the red dwarf forty-five million kilometers away, three million kilometers above the orbital plane. Mendri Prime, the planetoid that was our ultimate destination, was almost directly below us at -.03 on the y-axis. I couldn't help but smile. A sixteen-parsec jump, and we dropped back into normal space exactly where I had ordered. All we needed to do now was push against the gravity of the star a little and let the system overtake us. In three days, we would drift gently down into a stable orbit around the planetoid.

It felt like overkill to send us on this mission. That little world down there had been raising eyebrows at Astro for years. But they should have sent a science vessel to investigate it, not us. Yet here we were, given this detour on our way out to Obsidian sector patrol. Things had been calm there recently, so command didn't think we'd be missed for a week or two. I was hoping this side trip wouldn't even take that long.

After an hour, I decided to go for a walk and left the descent into orbit to my XO. She was an impressive officer, like all four thousand some-odd kids under my command. Full of energy, quick to duty, there was not so much as a hair out of place on a single one of them. Each member of my executive staff was capable enough to have their own commands if they wanted. Hell, you couldn't even get on my galley crew unless you were in the top percentile at the academy. And all under the command of someone who enlisted as a lowly recruit long before any of them were born.

I had no particular destination in mind. Up one level, along officers' row, down two more through weapon battery Gamma six, then into one of the starboard infirmaries. The beds were all empty except for a young engineer having a forearm burn treated by the doctor-on-call. He had brushed against a vent pipe while finishing maintenance work on the engine exhaust in the port thruster array. As he told me about it, he almost sounded embarrassed at not being perfect. I smiled at him understandingly, hoping it would put his mind at ease, and left.

The SS *Chapman* is top-of-the-line, the newest and most powerful vessel in the galaxy. Nothing anywhere could match it. Five kilometers from bow to stern and twenty levels tall, it was a sleek, imposing figure in the black. Only a couple years out of dock, and it was revered, maybe even feared, by every sentient being. It alone was the equal to the entire Pelox Armada. The Aurvos had nothing close to it, either. Not even the Greys had anything as advanced as this vessel under my command, the great, gleaming flagship of the Human Empire.

After a few hours of aimless wandering, I took a tube back to my quarters and opened the report on the Mendri system. Red dwarf star, spectral type M. It had one tiny orbiting planetoid, but beyond that, there wasn't so much as a minor asteroid belt. The universe was full of systems like this one, insignificant stars drifting through the void alone or with only minor company.

Mendri Prime was just a little over nine hundred kilometers in diameter. Barely even a planetoid at that size. It had first been discovered ages ago, before the Ganymede Wars or the conquest of the Nirimbis, before all the first contact events when we were still alone. Before jump drives and colonial expansion—even before the first Mars colony. Before all those great moments of Human history, one of those ancient orbital telescopes had recorded this star's wobble among the first ten thousand we had found.

With all the rest, it was measured, cataloged, and promptly forgotten. The orbital plane didn't line up with Earth's vantage, so they couldn't use the transit method to learn anything else. All they could tell was that the star had one orbiting body, and calculated from its radial velocity, it was likely a gas giant with a close orbit. A "hot Jupiter" as they used to call them. Not the usual system configuration, a gas giant being in that close, but not particularly rare either.

Which is the thing: Mendri Prime is not a gas giant. It's a fraction of that size. And it shouldn't have that kind of gravitational force on its parent star. A gas farm syndicate in the Ovilluud system doing initial stellar surveys had noticed. Mendri's orbital plane was perfect from their vantage for transit observation and in their survey of what the historical records told them was a gas giant, all they found was this tiny little rock, the dip in the star's light, barely recordable as it crossed. Thinking it was an error in the database—and also not a gas giant, so of no financial interest to them—they sent their findings on to Earth command and promptly moved on.

But it wasn't an error. The radial velocity measurements taken all those centuries ago were correct—Astro confirmed it when they checked. Yet the transit observation data from the syndicate, showing a planetoid barely big enough to be a proper moon of Jupiter, let alone have the gravitational force of it, was also correct. As were the radial velocity measurements taken from four other systems spread out over the Empire.

It was a mystery. Or, more accurately, a curiosity. A strange little system near nothing, with odd properties no one could quite understand. But it wasn't like the fate of the universe or even the Empire was at risk. Astrotechs liked to talk about it, and a paper or two was published speculating about what could be going on in the strange Mendri system. It even got a little play in the newsfeeds, where it got a nickname: Giant. But apart from cute wordplay and the occasional dinner conversation between scientists, nobody anywhere thought all that much about it.

Sooner or later, someone was going to be sent to find answers. But it could wait till the peace was achieved, the Empire secured. There was a whole universe to exist in and deal with, and important matters that affected The Empire would always come first. No matter how odd the data, a tiny little rock would never be a priority. But even the most insignificant things get looked at eventually—when there's time. And five years later, here we were.

I closed the file and slouched back in my chair to stare at the ceiling. This mission was not the job of a warship. We're meant to keep the peace, not dawdle with curiosities. The numerous factions in the Obsidian sector could start shooting at each other again at any moment without the Empire there to tell them to sit the hell down and play nice with each other. That's where we were needed, not on this side trip to a pebble in the black to satisfy a bet between a couple of ranking Astrotechs.

But those were our orders. And you don't shirk your duty just because you don't think the job is worth it. I thought of it as an extra week or two of rest before our real tour began. A chance to shake out the new batch of ensigns that came aboard at the last station.

So, into the system, look around for a bit, find out the mystery was a glitch in someone's math, and then off to the shipping lanes in the Obsidian sector and our real duty.

That's all this would amount to. I was sure of it.

WE SETTLED INTO an equatorial orbit one thousand kilometers above Giant, halfway between it and an odd little moonlet we discovered as we approached. The planetoid was out to starboard, its edge rolling lazily by. It was a dull, gray-looking place with no major geographical features or atmosphere. I stood at the screen on the bridge, staring at it, looking for any break in the terrain.

"Captain, orbital decay increasing by .09 percent."

I rubbed my eyes. "Increase velocity to compensate."

Dr. Achebe stood next to me, scouring over the pad in his hands. "Even from this distance, its gravity has a strong pull on us," he said with a grin. The crew had been as professional as always, but Achebe seemed the only person genuinely excited about this mission.

"So, I take it the radial velocity measurements are confirmed," I said to him.

"We confirmed that when we entered the system. It reads at 21.456 meters per second, which is just below Jupiter. Also, detecting no magnetosphere. Or tectonic activity. No radiation or heat of any kind, actually. Average surface temperature is 267.49 kelvins, but that is all radiant energy coming from the star. Not so much as a fraction of a degree coming from Giant itself." Achebe did a double take. "I mean—"

"It's fine. Just don't call it that in the report."

He nodded curtly. "Of course, sir. But back to the point, the planetoid is completely inert."

"Not what you expected?"

Achebe looked out at Giant, shaking his head. "I thought there would have to be geothermal activity in its core. Normally, for an object this size, it wouldn't be surprising for it to be inactive. But for this planetoid to generate this much gravitational pull—the pressure in its core must be incredible. Maybe more than any rocky planet in the known universe. But there's nothing. Not even a little energy generated from the tidal effect of its proximity to the star. It's as cold as an ice cube."

I furrowed my brow. Didn't have to be a science officer

to know that was odd. "What can you say about the geology?"

"We can only penetrate a couple hundred meters. And so far, we're seeing mostly carbon, iron, a few other silicates, some small pockets of condensed oxygen. That's probably little more than the space dust it's pulled in and collected over time. Past that down to the real planetoid underneath, all the normal scans are repelled."

"Not giving up its secrets easily, is it?"

"No, sir. Though we expected the scans would not work on something as dense as the data showed Giant to be. That's why we sent the dish out." Achebe turned to the Navigator, Simmons. "What is the ETA on that?"

Simmons looked up from his console. "Dish approaching diametric orbit of the planetoid in four minutes."

Achebe nodded and turned back to me. "I'm heading down to the lab to see the results as soon as they start coming in. Captain?"

"All right. Wuornos, you have the bridge," I said as I followed Achebe out.

It's a neat little trick using the dish. First time I've ever had a chance to try it. Shortly after we reached equatorial orbit, we dropped our five-hundred-meter-wide independent sensor dish out behind us to drift in a stationary orbit as we continued ahead. Once it reached diametric opposition to our orbit around Giant, it accelerated to match our speed and angle and maintain a relative position on the exact opposite side of the planetoid from the ship.

At that point, we start sending a concentrated beam of specialized neutrinos at the dish through the planetoid, and it records their passing and relays the data back to us. We can then take that data and compare it to the state of the particles when they left the ship to calculate the nature of all the matter the beam passed through between us and the dish. After one full orbit, we move northwards and the dish south and repeat the process until the entire volume is covered. In a little over two days, we have a complete geological map of the planetoid. It used to take months, if not years.

WHEN WE ARRIVED at the lab, the dish was already sending back information. Achebe walked to the computer bank and buried himself in raw data. In the center of the room was a holographic projection of the planetoid. It rotated slowly and was mostly transparent, barely more than a ghost, except for the bright transection that grew slowly along the equator like a bow tie as the data coming from the dish fed into the model. I took a step closer and studied the scanned area. The thin surface of dust, the few hundred meters that we already knew about, was little more than a thin gray border. Inside of that was all white. The real planet underneath.

The detail on the hologram was impressive; it was easy to see the planetoid was not perfectly solid. Dense, bulbous masses were apparent, bent, broken, and compacted together against each other. There looked to be far more of these shapes closer to the edge, but they were present all the way to the center. There were also a curious number of sharp angles and straight lines in all that jumble of material.

Achebe was talking to one of the techs quietly. I couldn't make out what he was saying, but the tone of his voice was tense. "What is it?" I asked him.

He straightened. "It's nothing, sir. We're just double-checking the calibration on the dish and the beam."

"Is something wrong with the data?"

"We're not sure yet. It's somewhat confusing." He crossed the room to stand next to me. "Do you notice anything odd about the map, captain?"

I frowned. "No, but I wouldn't know what to look for."

"The survey is showing no active core or thermal activity. Completely inert, as we anticipated. All well and good. But it's also showing no variance in the makeup of the planetoid whatsoever."

"What do you mean?"

"I mean that there are no trace elements except on the surface area." He waved his hand over the transection in the hologram. "Inside here, there should be a random mix of elements—iron, nickel, magnesium, oxygen, and some of the rarer elements like gold or plutonium. Every planet has at least some quantity of each, as whatever leftover material from its star's creation coalesced to make them. But so far, Giant has less than a tenth of a percent of all of them combined. It's almost completely uniform in its makeup. Which shouldn't be possible."

"And what is the makeup?"

"We're not sure yet."

I blinked hard. "Not sure?"

"It's something we haven't ever seen before. Some kind of complex metal. And we're having a hard time determining which elements it's comprised of. That's why I'm having the calibration checked. These readings are hard to fathom."

The hologram had grown noticeably since I first looked at it, having completed maybe an eighth of the circumference now. "Could it be that we just so happened to start scanning on an anomalous part of the planet? Maybe the rest of the makeup will be more normal."

Achebe scratched the back of his neck. "A near pure vein of metal that covers the entire diameter of the planetoid? I can't think of how that could occur in planetary formation. Something out of phase in our equipment is more likely."

"Well, check everything and report the findings. I'm heading back to the bridge."

"Yes, sir."

I was so distracted in the transport, thinking about what Achebe had just told me, I passed right by my stop. I had to switch tubes at the next station and double back.

Not only had we yet to find the quick and easy answers that I had expected, we had added more questions to the puzzle.

I started to get a sneaking suspicion we were going to be here longer than a week or two.

OVER THE NEXT couple of days, Achebe had every relay in the scanners, and the dish checked several times as the survey continued. At his request, I even sent a shuttle with a tech crew out to the dish to check it directly. They found nothing wrong. Yet the strange results kept coming in. Giant was exactly what the initial findings pointed to—a giant sphere of metal, almost completely uniform. Underneath the surface layer of dust, the completed holographic map in the science lab was a near-perfect ball of white.

Achebe manipulated the hologram as he talked, showing slices of the diameter or specific areas deep inside the planetoid.

"There are small veins of various base elements inside Giant here and there. But none are larger than fifteen cubic meters, and most are less than half that." Achebe zoomed in on a small black dot about two kilometers down in the northern hemisphere. "Here is the largest one. Mostly lead with a few traces of titanium."

"Heavy elements."

"There are noble gas pockets as well throughout the interior of Giant, but they are minuscule. Some are barely perceptible to the scan. And there might be countless more that we can't detect that are a few cubic millimeters or less." He zoomed back out to the full view of Giant. "But apart from that, Giant's composition is completely uniform."

"Have you been able to find out anything more about that composition?"

Achebe shook his head. "It still confounds us. There's no question that it's the cause of the gravitational pull. The metal's density is off the charts. But no heat is generated from all that pressure, even down at the very center. And it does not appear it was ever molten. Look, see all the inner structures inside, the sharp edges, the lines, the folds of metal? Normally, when a planet comes together, the original pieces melt, or get crushed, and blend together under the pressure of the increasing gravity as the body becomes larger. They fuse with other rocks and minerals and lose their individual semblance. That hasn't happened here. All the matter that was pulled together to form this planetoid—it bent, broke, or warped into each other, filled in all the gaps, but they never truly fused."

"How was this planetoid created then?"

"The same way all celestial objects are: accretion of smaller objects into a larger object, held together by their increasing gravity. That's about the only thing about Giant that I can explain. What I can't explain is where this metal came from."

"It didn't come from the star's solar nebula?"

"I highly doubt it. The spectral analysis of Mendri shows it likely had little leftover material after it formed to create anything, which is why the system is devoid of any other celestial objects. Giant probably formed elsewhere and was captured by the star's gravity."

"And where is that elsewhere?" I asked.

Achebe tapped his chin with his fingers. "That is a good question. But I have no answer. As far as I know, no process in nature can create material with these properties."

I looked at the hologram closely. With its opacity set at one quarter, you could see the details and patterns of the interior all the way through as if the planetoid was made of glass. I followed a long snakelike trail of metal with my eyes as it curved around a semi-flattened cube deep below the southern pole.

"What about the moonlet?" I asked.

Achebe swiped away the Giant hologram and brought up the only other object in the Mendri system. "We did some very basic scans of it. This is just the surface view. It's an irregular shape, not fitting well into any particular category. It measures 9.31 kilometers from pole to pole, with a rough circumference of four kilometers, and orbits at a distance of 2,391 kilometers from Giant."

The moonlet was very long but narrow around its center. Almost prism-like. It was dull, gray, flat and featureless, like Giant. All except for one area, where at the curve from one side to the other a large bulbous formation went from the top to the bottom. There was something in that formation, but I needed to figure out what. The sensation of recognition itched in the back of my head just out of reach.

I leaned in closer. An elliptical plateau, rounding up from the surface and ending in a small peak about centered. Two other oval hills near the top, symmetrical with each other and roughly the same size. A small circular valley near the bottom....

I looked up at Achebe on the other side of the hologram. "You said you scanned it?"

"Only the basic scans. We could only penetrate a few hundred meters, the same as Giant. It's probably made of the same matter."

"I'm sure it is. Strip away the surface."

Achebe looked at me curiously. "Captain?"

I pointed at the moonlet. "This image. If you did a scan, you have enough data to show the contours of the moonlet underneath the space dust. Let's see that."

"It won't have any data on the makeup below the surface."

"We already know what that is. I'm not interested in that. I'm interested in the contours."

Achebe grabbed his pad and tapped away. In just a few moments, he had stripped away the dust and matter that had collected on the moonlet over time, leaving its bare surface beneath.

Achebe started to speak, but when he glanced up from his pad at the moonlet, he stopped, his mouth agape. He saw it, too. Of course, he did. There could be no doubt about what we were looking at. The other techs working in the lab turned and stared in amazement.

"Get the dish ready to send out again. We need to get a full scan of the moonlet to confirm. I'll be in my quarters informing command."

Achebe nodded numbly and said nothing.

As I stepped out into the passageway, I looked back at the moonlet's hologram, stripped of the dust that had covered it for countless eons and now clearly showing a huge, humanoid face, staring outwards defiantly.

People have seen things in the pockmarked surface of Earth's moon since before the written word. A man's face, a tree, a pair of hands. I even read somewhere that one ancient culture saw a rabbit busily working a mortar and pestle. But that was all in the imagination of the viewer. Shadows and light play on the craters and ancient lava flows on the moon's surface, used by our ancestors to craft stories to entertain each other as they passed the lonely nights around a fire. To comfort themselves with the idea of order and sense in an untamed world they barely grasped.

But there was no illusion in Giant's moon. Its features were unmistakable, no imagination necessary. Buried under the dust were the clear and distinct features of a face.

It was humanoid, but not a human face, nor the face of any being I had ever seen. A set of bulging elliptical eyes on short stalks glared blankly ahead, above a smooth slope down to a pointed triangular nose in the center. And the mouth below that, almost a perfect circle, opened wide and empty.

The symmetry was perfect. And the detail. Across the top was a band with orderly markings from end to end—probably the brim of a helmet. The skin stretched over the skull beneath, the ridges above the eyes, and around the mouth. It looked out at you quietly from underneath the dust, singing into the void of space.

The scan of the moonlet had confirmed what I already knew in just a few hours. Underneath the small layer of dust was that same super dense, heat-resistant metal as Giant. A metal stronger than anything in the known universe. But there was the main, key difference with the moonlet. It was hollow.

Twenty meters beneath the surface, the inner space of the moonlet opened up into levels, neat and orderly rows of floor and ceiling at three-meter increments, thousands of levels of various rooms and passageways. Behind the face were the front decks of the massive ship that Giant had once been.

Take a cloud of metal fragments circling a star. They collide and jostle with each other as they orbit. Pieces come together, attracted by their mass. Their combined gravity pulls in more and eventually creates a sphere. Over time, the ball grows larger as more pieces are pulled in, and soon, the whole cloud coalesces into a planetoid. Accretion. The way all planets, moons, and celestial bodies in the universe are created.

But here's where the creation of Giant departs from nature. In nature, the materials of the planet liquefy under the intense heat and pressure of their own gravity, and the elements blend and fuse, the heavier elements sinking to the center. Eventually, the smaller objects cool and solidify, and the larger ones stay molten at their core, like the Earth.

None of that happened with Giant. It probably never raised a single degree, even under the phenomenal pressure at its center. The metal bent, molded together, and compacted into the tight little ball below, but it never turned molten. The moonlet was the last piece, having settled into orbit instead of being pulled in with the rest of the wreckage of the massive ship it had once been the bow of.

The change of orders from command was not a surprise. Giant was no longer just a puzzle; it was one of the greatest discoveries in Human history. We hadn't just stumbled onto an ancient race of beings never before seen, which was remarkable, but onto the remnants of a spaceship that was a wonder of the galaxy.

The volume of the planetoid was in the hundreds of millions of cubic kilometers. If you could pull it apart, unbend, and reassemble all the pieces back together, the ship it once was must have been thousands of kilometers long. Tens of thousands. Larger and more spacious than any planet in the Empire. And it was all once one great vessel, not a fleet or some ship graveyard from eons ago. The moonlet proved that. It alone was almost twice the length of the Chapman and was just the tip of a massive ship larger than the planet our species had sprung from.

I cannot wrap my head around the engineering, the science, the accomplishment of such a thing—the resources they would have needed. The technology involved manufacturing a ship with a metal that laughed in the face of the laws of nature. What else could they do, had they discovered, this ancient race? The secrets that may lay hidden inside Giant were beyond speculation.

Three science vessels were rerouted to Mendri and would arrive in days. And a construction crew shortly after that to build a permanent satellite base. Instead of heading to Obsidian sector patrol, we were to guard the system against all alien incursions indefinitely. It was only a matter of time before news of our discovery reached every corner of the galaxy.

"How did you know?" Achebe asked me.

We were alone in the observation deck in the middle of the night ship time. The lights were low, and the glow from Giant overhead illuminated the large room.

Achebe had been frantically pouring over all the data for days, gleaning whatever he could from it before the literal army of scientists arrived and took it away from him. I was certain he would ask for a transfer to one of their ships.

"I'm not sure I did," I said to him. "Not really. I think it had been something that itched in the back of my head since the first scans came in when you told me Giant's composition was uniform and how impossible that was. As you said, the metal couldn't happen naturally, so someone must have manufactured it. Then, looking at the hologram of the inside and all those crumpled pieces reminded me of a salvage scow I was an ensign on when I was a kid. We'd tow the decommissioned liners and old cruisers to a reclamation base, but for the smaller ones, the shuttles, or personal pods, we'd compact them into cubes for transport. Looking at Giant's insides suddenly made me think of those. But I thought I was being foolish because of the sheer amount of it and the size this ship must have been. It just couldn't be possible. Then I saw the face in the moonlet, and I knew."

"What is it?"

"It's a figurehead."

"A what?"

"A nautical figurehead. Seafaring vessels on Earth used to have them on the bow of their ships to ward off evil spirits. When I first looked at the moonlet, I thought I was seeing what I wanted to see there under all the dust. But it looked exactly like the bow of a ship to me, the way it curved back sharply below the face and bowed out more on the sides. And it made everything else make sense."

"So, it was some kind of a holdover from their past."

"Probably. Something religious. Or maybe it was how they used to intimidate each other."

"Strange to think space-faring beings would still be superstitious like that."

I shrugged. "We do the same thing. We don't put mermaids or lions on the mastheads of our ships anymore, but we still have mastheads. And a bow, a port, a starboard, all on a ship floating in space where there is no real up or down outside of your perspective. We could shape our ships like cubes or spheres. There's no resistance in a near void, so there's no aerodynamic reason not to. It would probably be more efficient. But we don't because it wouldn't feel right. It's a kind of vanity. And it's apparently universal."

We were silent a long time, both looking up at Giant. Now, not so ironic a name, I thought. I tried to picture it in my head, the ship the way it had once been, floating in the space above me. It stretched out in all directions farther than my eyes could see. There was no edge, no horizon, no end to it in the air above. It was the sky itself, its pockmarked surface the whole world. I could feel its crushing mass against my chest and hear the dull moan of its engines in my ears from thousands of miles away. I was not even an ant to it, less than a speck, no concern or notice to it whatsoever. I'd fall to my hands and knees under its mass, its sheer presence, as the ground I stood on crumbled to dust.

I closed my eyes and shook the thoughts away until I was safely on my ship. This pride of the Human fleet, the biggest and strongest ship in the known universe, was barely more than a speck of sand compared to what the ruin above us must have once been.

"How long do you think it took the planetoid to form from the wreckage?" I asked.

Achebe rubbed his chin, thinking. "It's difficult to say. The Earth coalesced into its initial sphere in fifty to a hundred million years. That seems to be the standard timeframe for planetary formation. But Giant would be vastly different. It didn't start as a protoplanetary disc of dust but as larger fragments, and its super density and gravitational effect likely accelerated accretion dramatically. It could have formed in as little as half that time."

"Twenty-five million years," I said. "And who knows how long it's been here since forming."

"Safe to assume whoever made it is long since gone then."

"We hope."

"Yes," Achebe said, laughing lightly. Then he grew quiet and looked up at Giant. "There is so much we do not know yet."

I smiled at Achebe. Yet. That confidence that there was nothing that was beyond us. I could see it on his face. There is nothing we cannot do, cannot achieve. We would stay in this system for another twenty-five million years if that's what it took to squeeze every last secret out of Giant. And then add them to our own. Because we are humans, the top of the class, able to do anything we want to. The greatest, most powerful species in the universe, the Empire that would know no end.

And yet....

The beings who made the ship must have felt the same way. Had the same ego. You'd have to when you roamed the empty void in a ship so massive its very presence shifted the gravity of solar systems.

But as mighty and powerful a ship as it was, strong enough to fly through stars, to shatter planets, something else even greater came along and destroyed it.

And they were nowhere to be found.

WHEN THINGS COME BACK TO YOU

HE DROVE ALONG quietly, with your spirit as his only company. The world outside the car was a haze, vague shapes and objects of no definition or meaning drifted by. You hadn't spent much time here when you were alive, so you had no connection to it. The whole world was like that. A mist of things and places you had no memory of. If you concentrated on something, you could tell what it was. A building, a tree, a person. But there was no point. It all seemed so unimportant.

You had a connection to him, and he was clear and sharp, sitting there in the driver's seat, steering with his right hand, his left arm draped across the ledge of the car door. You were anchored to the living world through him, unable to break free or move on. He looked up out the car window, wrinkling his nose slightly. The warm light grew on his face. The sun had come out from behind a cloud.

Time had passed since your life. You knew that. But only because of the growing wrinkles at the corners of his eyes, the weathering of his skin, his receding hairline. The thin strands of white above his ears. He wasn't the boy with the flashy clothes and expensive toys anymore. He still dressed well, still had nice things, but now it was more subdued. He had mellowed, and his expression had lost its sharp edge, it's anger. That glowering stare of his that used to come out in unguarded moments was fully hidden now. Replaced by that practiced look of serenity that he had learned over the years worked better on people.

Outside the car, things began to change. The mist receded, and objects started to come to you effortlessly. You saw a tree leaning away from the road at an awkward angle. Then, a line of bushes along the road. Behind them. an old barn. Across the road from it. a squat-looking church with a wooden sign painted white just after the entrance to its parking lot, a sea of concrete far larger than such a small building could possibly ever need. Past that, the single-story house with the rickety wooden fence that went all the way between two turns. Then, across the street, the large, manicured field of closely cropped grass with the mansion at its center, bordered by an orderly square of trees. The high school would be up on the right in just a minute.

The woods on both sides of the road came into being. As did the houses that spotted the landscape here and there and the turn offs into modest neighborhoods. Telephone lines arced rhythmically between the poles above as the car whipped by.

You saw all this and more with each passing mile because you knew this road. You were connected to it.

You were home.

By the time he passed by the hardware store, the world was firm for you. Very little had changed. The roads, the buildings, the greenery, it was all as it had been your entire life. Well, not exactly. Some things were different—a house a different color, an updated sign on the convenience store, the line of pine trees cut down and pruned back mercilessly from the side of the road. Those things that had changed shimmered around the edges, a conflict between the way they were now and the way they were for you.

Up ahead on the left was a big spot of haze. What had been there? A small patch of woods, thick and unmanaged, between the squat, single-story house with the crabby grass you were now passing and the parking lot for the strip mall up ahead. That's what you remembered there. It was gone now; someone had cleared the growth and built something in its place. You could almost see the new beneath the memory of the trees that once lived there, a squat rectangle on its side, some kind of sign along the road. But it was little more than a gap in the world to you.

He stopped at the turn into the strip mall and glanced around as he waited for the light to turn green. A sly smile crossed his lips as he looked at the McDonald's in the far front corner of the parking lot. He had spent many warm summer nights over there with friends, huddled around their cars, blaring music loud enough for the whole town to hear. Smoking and joking all night, or at least until the cops would come and tell everyone to leave. You had been there often as well, making eyes at boys who looked back in a way that made you smile as you sat on the hood of someone's car and sucked on a clove cigarette, stifling a cough when you inhaled too deeply.

Lynn Farm Estates was across the street, down the narrow road and curving around the hill. The edge of one of the large rectangular brick buildings was visible from the intersection, sticking out from behind the pharmacy. Before your mom got the proper house in the development down the road, you used to live in one of those narrow little apartments that even six-year-olds felt cramped in. When you lived there, you went out as much as you could get away with. It was much nicer outside, in the fresh cut grass between the buildings, running up and down the hills barefoot. You used to drag your feet in the lawn because you loved how the grass felt sliding between your toes.

You tried to move towards those hills, towards that memory. But the light changed, and he turned the other way, into the strip mall. The sliver of the building disappeared, and you forgot all about it again.

It was the same supermarket where your mom would get doughnuts from on Sundays, and you'd fight with your sister for the apple jelly ones. There was a slight shimmer inside, as little had changed in here—the walls might be a different color, signs more modern, the checkout cash registers new. But the bones of the store, those were the same. As he walked brusquely through to the bakery on the far wall you caught a glimpse of the tank full of lobsters in the back from between the aisles. When you were young, you'd press your face right up to the glass, staring at the crustaceans as they lethargically rested on top of each other, barely moving, while your mom waited for her number to be called at the deli counter. You used to think they were the store's pets.

He ran into Samantha Byner as he headed towards the checkouts, a packaged coffee cake under his arm. You could tell he didn't recognize her—only vaguely knew he should, by the way he tensed slightly. He hid it behind the smile and friendly posture, like he always did, and she didn't notice.

But you knew her right away. She had put on a lot of weight, and her hair was long and dark, but there was no mistaking her as she stood there smiling at him across her shopping cart, filled with groceries and a four-year-old.

"Fancy seeing you again," she said, beaming at him.

"Hi," he said, waving his coffeecake at her. He became more genuinely relaxed, confident that there would be no recrimination coming from this woman he still did not really remember.

"What brings you to town?"

"I just came up to see my parents. Thought I should bring something with me."

"Such a thoughtful son." She bent down to her child. "You gonna buy me something nice too?" The boy twisted in his seat in the cart to look at him, then turned back to his mother and nodded. Samantha smiled and ruffled his hair affectionately. "That's my boy," she said. "Are they doing all right?"

"They're fine. Dad had a little health scare a few months ago, though."

Samantha nodded. "I heard about that. He's all right now?"

"Pretty much, yeah, he's fine. How about you?"

"Oh, I'm fine." Her little boy tugged on her sweater to try and get her attention as he mumbled something. She rested her hand on his shoulder. "Just doing my part to overpopulate the planet."

He laughed at her joke more than it deserved. "How many do you have?"

"We have four. David is out having a day with our littlest Jessica right now."

"Is that Dave Rioux?"

She nodded. "It is indeed."

You wished you could laugh at that. Straight-laced Dave Rioux, uptight Dave Rioux, boring Dave Rioux. Mike's younger brother. The honor student. How Samantha ended up with him, of all people, you could not even fathom.

As they talked just before the checkouts, you saw the girl Samantha had been when you had known her. Thinner, with platinum hair and her favorite earrings. All of that was gone, but the impish look on her face remained. The little twinkle in her eyes, the upturned corner of her lip. There she was, the Sam that you used to play rock star with, singing along to Debbie Gibson in her bedroom when you were girls and passing joints around raging fire pits within the woods when you were older. You could still see her, in this older, matronly woman, calmer now, with perhaps a little creeping world-weariness in her shoulders, but alive and healthy. You were happy to see her. She had faded from your life at some point as you grew up, as you both drifted down different paths. You don't know when exactly. But you vaguely remember regretting it.

"Well, anyway," he said after a few minutes when he was sure he had spent enough time talking to her. "I should get going."

Samantha nodded. "Yeah, me too. I have to get some lunch into this one. It was good seeing you again." She turned to her son, who had been watching the two of them. "Say goodbye to Mommy's friend."

Her son twisted in his seat again and waved at him shyly. He waved back himself. Samantha nodded at him as she pushed her cart past him.

Goodbye, you wanted to say to her before memory of her faded. You should show your son the lobster tanks.

↔

BACK ON THE road, the memories washed through you. There was the pizza place you'd get a slice at on the way home from middle school. You'd always burn the roof of your mouth on the cheese, but the tomato sauce was so tangy you didn't care. That island store at the gas station where you'd meet Sally Jasper when you snuck out of the house, waiting around the back so you couldn't be seen from the main road, just in case a cop drove by. You used to drag your sled behind you in the winter down that turn in the road, your sister along for the ride, to the hills in the woods behind the post office.

There were parts of you all over. You went to an insane party in that white house to the right of the fork in the road. Johnny Thibodeau lived next door to it when you were ten, and you'd spend afternoons in his living room playing Nintendo before his family moved away. You spent a Christmas working at that Dollar Store down that side street stocking shelves. An educational experience, your Mom had said, though the only thing you learned was that you never wanted to work in retail again. And on the sidewalk out front of the convenience store by the bridge is where you hit the curb all weird and went over your handlebars hard. The black eye faded after a couple of weeks, but the friction burn on your chin stayed the rest of the summer.

Then on the left there was the field behind a waist high stone wall with teeth-like capstones. Two gravel paths led in, shaded by carefully manicured trees. The white marble statue of the crucifixion in the center of the ground, facing outwards. And all the headstones.

That's where you were buried.

Off in the corner, just out of sight of the path on the left. A simple stone marker in the ground. It wasn't visible from the road, but you could feel your bones in there. The cold, dead weight of them, the darkness, the silence. The complete and total absence.

But then the cemetery disappeared around a turn in the road and took the memory from you again.

He had not so much as glanced in the direction of your grave as he had driven by.

His parent's house had changed in thousands of little ways. The dimensions were the same, the walls, the ceilings, the placement of doors, all those were as you knew them, all part of one of the richest, nicest houses in town. But everything shimmered. You saw the old floral wallpaper of the past and the stained wood paneling of the new on the main stairs, the old drywall and the new exposed brick around the fireplace in the living room. Wooden and metal framed windows, white and silver refrigerators, track lights and chandeliers—both houses, the old and the current, existed for you at the same time. The new island in the kitchen and the oak table against the near wall that was no longer there, the one you had just managed to stay sitting once on as you laughed uncontrollably at something Polly Markos had said.

He stood against the doorway of the kitchen as he watched his mother pour boiling water into a French press. You could see the age in her. The few times you had met her when you had come over to his house she had always intimidated you, that dark brow looking down on you, half smiling, as if daring you to say something. But there was only a hint of that left in the old shrinking woman with the short and curly shock of white hair, whose body shook so much she could barely stand.

"Where's Dad?"

"He's out playing golf."

"Did he forget I was coming by?"

"No, but we didn't expect you to be here so early. He'll be home in a little bit."

"You know I can't stay that long."

"It's the only exercise he gets these days. Don't worry, he'll be here."

The annoyance flashed on his face very briefly, but he covered it quickly.

She put the kettle down on a burner, slid the full press to the center of the island and walked around it to one of the stools where the mugs, cream, and sugar had already been put out. "Just give it a few minutes to brew," she said, looking up at him.

"It's not my first cup of coffee, Mom," he replied.

She made a great display of mock surprise, then nodded at him thoughtfully, still smirking. She rested her head in her hand, her elbow on the tabletop. He walked into the room and took the stool next to her.

His mother started in about the goings on in the town, catching him up on people, or at least the parents of people he knew. He made a great show of listening and nodding, even asking brief questions at key moments. But you could see he was patronizing her. Underneath that practiced expression was that same antagonism he'd always had when talking about her or to her when he was young. It was still there in his eyes. Maybe it wasn't as sharp now that he was no longer in her house, living under her rule. Or he was better at masking it than he used to be. But you could see it.

The garage door rumbled downstairs and a few moments later his dad came up the stairs. He stood in the kitchen entrance taking in his son and wife who had turned to face him. Age had grabbed him too. He was still the tall, broad-shouldered man he had always been, but it seemed there was so much less of him now. The burly man he used to be was just a shadow of the lean, gangly person standing in the doorway. His eyes were still sharp underneath his bifocals, and he still had that way of looking at someone like he was holding onto great secrets. It's just now the secrets in that look didn't hold the prospect of importance like they used to.

"Well, hello," his dad said as he ambled into the room. "Been here long?"

He shook his head. "Not really," he replied. "Mom just made coffee."

His dad shook his head. "I'm not allowed caffeine anymore."

"Doctor's orders," his mom said. She tapped her chest with her left hand.

He sat up in his seat and looked back and forth at his parents quickly. "What else did the doctor say?"

His dad shrugged as he poured himself a glass of water from the sink. "There's no pending catastrophe."

He nodded his head slowly, a serene smile plastered on his face. "That's good to hear."

You drifted away from him as they talked, towards the far end of the kitchen, where the sliding doors led out to the deck. It rose over the sloping downward hill of the backyard, giving a nice view all the way to the trees at the edge of the yard. On warm nights it had been a favorite spot in the house when his parents were not there. The wind would whistle by soothingly as the music from the speakers by the glass doors would echo down the hill. Kids would sit in the nice, padded chairs smoking and laughing, taking long hauls off bottles or long tokes off pipes.

You were there, leaning against the railing with Zach Molineax, a beer in his left hand, his right wrapped around you and under your shirt, his first finger rubbing gently along your ribs in that way that made you tingle. You squeezed him back. Everything was swimming and glowing in your head in such a happy way. More so after he came up to you and Zach with that smile of his and handed both of you tabs. His treat. Always his treat. Like the beer and the pot. He'd provide everything for kids when they came over to his house. He was always generous host like that. It wasn't till the end of high school that he started asking for money.

His mother started to cough heavily, doubling over in her seat. She brought her fist up to her mouth as her body shook with the strain. He leaned in closer to her and put his hand on her shoulder.

"Mom?"

She shook her head and sat back up slowly, breathing gingerly as it subsided. His father offered her his glass of water. "Here," he said quietly.

She nodded, as she took the glass and drank, nodding. "Just a little scratch," she said.

You could see the look on his face as he watched his parents. Outwardly of concern, but not so well hidden were his eyes, and you could see how he examined and measured the cracks in their lives. Almost gleefully.

EVENTUALLY HE FELT he had spent enough time with his parents, and he left. The memories came and went through you as he drove down the road all over again. On the right through a thin row of trees was the shoe factory with its own outlet store, a giant warehouse where you got a pair of pink moonboots when you were four. When they got cold unicorns appeared on the side. You wore them well past winter's end, till your toes were practically sticking out the front. Then the gazebo in the tiny park where you, Rachel Lee, and Jack Lambaugh had watched summer fireworks once when you couldn't get over to the next town in time for a closer view. You quietly fumed with disappointment with each explosion of glitter barely above the treeline accompanied by the slightest pop. Across the street was the bank parking lot where Charlotte Manning's car broke down on senior skip day, and the two of you were stuck there until Jake and Mary came by and gave you a lift to the beach. And the Red Steak, the restaurant with the flashy sign on the road. When you were younger you would push quarters into the cigarette machine as fast as you could before the hostess at the front could come over and stop you. And later where you had drinks with Cary Travers when he came back from college, feeling all sophisticated as you sat at the bar with him, thankful they didn't card you and ruin it.

But it wasn't really there anymore, just a shimmering outline. The building was gone.

He pulled into a gas station at the edge of town and up to one of the pumps. The woods behind it was just a shadow. Housing had been built back there. There were vague outlines of rectangular buildings. Small homes, plotted out in even rows all the way to the river. You saw the glowing outline of them as if through a thin curtain of the woods that once stood in their place.

You started to count the houses, but there was a pull on you, back away from the woods, back up to the gas station. He was standing by his car holding the gas pump in place, but his head was turned over his shoulder. Toward a woman who stood at the hood of his car.

It was your mother.

You saw her round, big cheeked face, just as given to stern and coarse looks as to warm. The thin blonde hair teased high and stiff to her shoulders. And her deep blue eyes that smiled all on their own, no matter what the rest of her face was doing. That was who she was to you. You didn't want to see her now as well, didn't want to see how the years of pain and sadness had sucked so much life from her. The way her hair was drained of color, until it was all but thin straw. The way her skin pulled tight over her bones, the rosy cheeks long gone, and her eyes empty of any joy. The unrelenting sadness in her. But you did, you had no choice but to see her as she smiled at him, no longer with that warm smile that you so loved when you were young, but with the tired, perfunctory look of a woman beaten by life.

"Mrs. Rochelle," he said as stood upright facing her. "Hi."

Your mother nodded to him. "How are you?"

"I'm fine," he said quickly. "I was just visiting my parents."

Your mother's eyes twitched ever so slightly. "That's very good of you. How are they?"

"They're fine too. Getting old, though. Like we all are."

"That is true," your mother said.

He stood in silence for a beat, then said, "And how are you doing?"

Your mother shrugged. "I'm getting by. Same as always."

"You still down on Vail street?"

"No, I moved into an apartment down the road some years ago."

"I'm sorry to hear that."

Your mother waved him off. "No, it's what I wanted. I didn't need all that space for just me."

You felt like you were shattering as they talked. She was being so friendly to him. She thought he was just another of your friends. She had no idea. You wanted to reach out to her, hold her, talk to her, tell her so many things. You wanted to tell her you were sorry, you didn't mean for it to happen. It was an accident. A mistake. You wanted to scream at her, don't Mom, don't be nice to him. Don't be friendly. I'm sorry for what I did to you, but he did it too. He gave it to me, Mom, it was him.

The experience of your last few moments came back to you. The music blaring, the cheap sheets on the beds, Fran yelling something you couldn't quite understand. The intense expectation of the high.

The bathroom door was open and you could see most of the motel room. There was Mike at the table by the door, twirling his lit cigarette in his fingers as he talked, the line of white smoke trailing behind it. And there he was, sitting across from Mike and putting the money in his pocket. He glanced over at you, and there was that winning smile of his again. It had always been his best mask.

Then the hot spike in your vein, the shot of fire from the crook in your arm that washed over you and faded into euphoria. Swaddled by the air you went limp, your limbs heavy as lead. The world retreated to a distant point. And then kept going. Sound went away, as did the feel of the porcelain tub against your back. Part of you knew this time was different, understood what was happening. But in that moment most of you didn't care. You turned into sand, and everything faded.

He was still talking to your mother, all smiles, that same damn mask, and saying all the right things, like he always did. And your mother was fooled, like she always had been. Like you had been. Like everyone always was. You wanted to grab her and shake her, tell her everything. That you thought you were going to live forever, nothing bad would happen. You were just having fun. And he took advantage because he wanted to be a big man, the cool kid. The damned spoiled rich kid, all the stuff he already had wasn't enough for him, he always wanted more and selling to you and your friends was how he got it. He didn't care what he did to others. He doesn't care now. Please Mom, stop smiling at him, stop seeing him as that nice boy, he fooled you, scream at him, hit him, throw things at him, stop being nice to him, Mom, please...

But you have no voice to speak, hands to touch, no body for her to see. All those things are deep underground in the dark.

The gas pump stopped with an abrupt click, the tank on his car full. He turned back around and removed the nozzle from his car. "Well I have to get back home before it gets too late."

"Of course," your mother said. "I should be getting to work."

He replaced the nozzle in the gas dispenser. "It was nice to see you again, Mrs. Rochelle."

Your mother nodded. "You too," she said. "Take care."

Your mother turned and walked away, towards the road. You tried to follow, to go with her, whispering come back Mom, please come back. But no matter how hard you tried you flowed back to him with a whimper. As he pulled out onto the street you were back with him in his car. He waved at your mother on the sidewalk as he passed her. You watched her shrink behind you.

After a couple hundred yards of silence, he laughed a little, his eyes not leaving the road. "You know," he said. "Once my parents are gone, I'm selling their house and I'll never have to come to this shithole town again. And that could be any day now. So, I hope you made the most of that. You'll probably never see her again."

Your mother was little more than a dot on the road, and the memories faded. You still felt sad, and angry, just a little, but you weren't so sure why anymore. What had he told you? The serene look on his face betrayed nothing, as he drove the car into the growing void ahead.

THE SPOT

You were never sure if the first time you noticed the spot was in a dream or not. It could have been a dream.

It was early one morning, an hour or two before dawn. You had long since kicked the sheets down to the bottom of the bed in the muggy night, only to feel chilled now in the cooler morning. You rolled onto your back and absently rubbed your palm against the soft hairs on your stomach, staring lazily down at your hand by your waist. On your wrist just below the first knuckle of your thumb was a faint white glow, no more than a centimeter around with soft edges.

You sucked in your gut a little. Just below your belly button was a tiny spot of skin that was shining a brilliant white. Barely more than a pinprick.

Was this a reflection of something, maybe an odd refraction from the streetlight outside? You hovered your hand above the spot, and it reflected softly on your inner palm. So, no, it wasn't that—the light was coming from you.

You tapped on the spot with your finger. Your skin wasn't numb or sore, your finger didn't burn when you touched it. The whole area felt absolutely normal.

Something started to percolate in the back of your brain. A vague sense of panic. Or maybe just surprise. But a voice in your head kept telling you not to worry. *You're just dreaming,* he said. *This isn't real. Nothing to worry about at all.* So, you chuckled a little as you covered and uncovered the spot with your hand, playing with the reflection.

After a few moments, the world grew heavy, and your mind drifted off. Your eyelids fell and your hand went limp against your stomach. Such a strange thing, you remember thinking. A glow in the dark freckle. After that, you don't remember anything until you woke up hours later just before noon.

You saw nothing when you looked at your stomach again in the sunlight, or when you stared very closely at your gut in the mirror after your morning pee. No shining spot. Well, maybe there was the tiniest bit of discoloration, just a finger below your navel on the right. A little patch barely more than, again, a pinprick. But you couldn't be sure. It was hard to really look that closely without a hand mirror, which you didn't have, or by climbing onto the sink and contorting yourself at a really dangerous angle, which you weren't about to do.

You rubbed your stomach vigorously and snorted. Just a dream. That's all it had been.

You didn't think any more about it as you went about your day. First, a few pieces of toast while chatting with Jay, your roommate. Then to the park for a few hours, where you hooked up with some friends also out enjoying the afternoon. At some point the little circle of friends turned into an impromptu gathering, which later bloomed into a full-blown party, and in all the fun the early evening turned into the early morning before you knew it. When you finally got home in the wee hours you didn't so much as go to bed as fall on it and close your eyes.

The next day you loafed on the couch all day watching junk on Netflix. You were in no condition to be productive. It was all you could do to get the motivation to get up to go to the bathroom.

In the late afternoon Jay walked in with Sandra, and they told you they had some friends coming over that night. They needed use of the living room for entertainment purposes, and that it was perfectly fine if you wanted to socialize when they arrived, if you were so inclined, but right now you needed to get your loafing ass off the couch. You took his reasonable request in the spirit it was given, cleaned up the area a bit, and ventured back to your room for a nap.

It was dark when you woke up. You weren't sure exactly what time it was. You could hear Jay and his friends in the living room talking and listening to music faintly through the walls, so probably not too late.

You sat up and shook out the last of the cobwebs from your head. You really shouldn't have slept for as long as you had, but you felt so much better now. And you felt like socializing, going out to the living room and saying hi like a human, chat for a bit. Some of Sandra's friends were cute. You got out of bed and made your way to your dresser to change.

When you were pulling the new shirt on, you looked down and noticed the spot, right where it had been before. You had forgotten all about it till just then.

You pulled your shirt down and rushed down the hall to the bathroom, where you flipped on the light and closed the door tight behind you. For some reason you also turned on the overhead-fan. But when you lifted up your shirt you couldn't see anything on your stomach, apart from maybe the same little speck of discoloration as before. And nothing was glowing. Yet you had definitely seen it clearly back in your room.

You cupped your hands around where you remembered it being, with just enough space above your thumb for you to peek in. You could see it very faintly in there—but more the glow of it against your fingers than the spot itself.

You turned off the light to the bathroom. The room had no windows, and almost no light at all seeped in under the door. So, the dark was near total.

Except for the shining spot that you saw on your stomach when you turned back to the mirror.

It was a very soft white glow, devoid of any color, like the world's tiniest maglite just under your skin. It barely reflected off the edge of the sink a few inches in front of you. You played with the flesh around it, and the light moved with your stomach as you pinched it together and pushed it in. You closed your eyes and rubbed your belly in little circular motions. You couldn't tell when you were touching the spot and when you weren't—it felt exactly the same as the rest of you. And you couldn't be sure, but you thought it was just a little bit bigger than you remembered it from yesterday.

You turned the light back on. Now that you knew where to look you could definitely see it. A little spot where the skin looked shiny, as if it was polished. Or maybe like a small burn after the scab had come off, only without the red and pink tint.

Again, you probably should have been panicking. And the drive to it was stronger now when you were wide awake looking at it. This was in no way a dream.

But that voice in your head kept you calm. This was nothing to be frightened of, he kept telling you. Just take a deep breath, relax. It's just some weird little skin blemish.

You opened the medicine cabinet, got one of those tiny little band-aids, and placed it over the spot. For what reason you weren't sure. You didn't want anyone to see it of course, but it's not like people were lining up to carefully inspect your abdomen in the dark. But you couldn't think of what else to do. Just cover the thing up, drop your shirt, and stop thinking about it.

You went into the living room and said hello, relaxing down onto the arm of the couch. One of Sandra's friends, Tabby, a cute redhead you liked to flirt with, offered you a beer. You took it with only a half-forced smile and a thank you.

THE DOCTOR AT the clinic the next day was very curt with you. She could see the discoloration just fine, and she poked and prodded at it in the well-lit examination room that took you hours to get into. But after looking at the spot for barely a minute and asking you the most general of questions, she told you it was something called vitiligo and that it was harmless. When you tried to explain the light, she was barely listening anymore, wouldn't even turn around to look at you as she scribbled out a prescription for some topical cream that she dropped on the counter by the door as she left. There were a lot of people out in the waiting room, and she wasn't going to concern herself about something she thought was a simple skin discoloration.

Jay was home, and you still felt the need to get someone else to see it, so you showed him.

"That's some kind of paint, right?" he said as he looked closely at it.

"It's real, Jay, come on," you pleaded with him.

He poked at the spot with his finger. "It's really on thin too. I can't feel it at all."

You pulled your shirt down and stormed over to the window raise the blinds.

"Okay, okay," Jay said. "Calm down. There's no need to get angry. Did you see a doctor about it?"

"I just got back from the clinic in Bushwick. She said it was just a patch of skin that lost pigment. Gave me a prescription for some kind of cream and told me not to worry about it."

Jay shrugged. "Well then what's the problem?"

"It's not that. I know it isn't. I looked it up online and nowhere does it say anything about glowing. None of them do. This is something completely different."

"You don't know that. She's a doctor. A clinic doctor, but whatever. She knows her shit. Maybe you just a have a rare side effect because you ate something weird. I once heard about a guy who turned orange because he was eating too many carrots."

You rolled your eyes at him.

"Look," Jay continued. "Bottom line, if she wasn't worried about it then maybe you should just get the cream and see if it works. If it doesn't then you can go back."

As exasperated as Jay made you, he had a point. You aren't, after all, a doctor, and the one you saw wasn't worried. Jay hadn't freaked out about it either. Maybe it was just as they said. And maybe your mind was exaggerating how bright the spot was.

The topical cream wasn't too expensive with the co-pay off your dad's plan. Though if it made any difference you couldn't tell. The spot didn't seem to be getting bigger, but it wasn't shrinking either. Still, you applied it every night faithfully just before bed.

You never followed up on it at the clinic or consulted any other doctors. You didn't think there was a point. If it was like Jay had said, an odd but harmless extra side effect to a normal skin ailment, then why bother? And that's what you were increasingly convinced it was. Any time you started to feel angsty about it that voice in your head would calm you down, tell you there was nothing to worry about. You felt fine, didn't you? No aches, plenty of energy, eating right, sleeping well. What's to worry? The spot would go away soon enough. Until it did, which would be any day now, it was just another fact of your life that you had to grow accustomed to.

A couple weeks later you were hanging out with a few friends at your place, along with Jay and some of his friends. It was an unplanned, no particular occasion get-together. One of those moments where everybody just sort of converged in the same place at the same time. The couch was packed to both arms with people scrunched together, others sitting on the coffee table across from it. And there was talk of pizza and a beer run to keep it going.

You were feeling adventurous. Or maybe just in one of those moods you got in after a few where you wanted some attention. You turned to the girl sitting next to you. Jen, you think her name was.

"Hey, look at this," you said, pulling your shirt up.

She looked at you, her eyes swimming. "What?" She glanced down at your exposed stomach. "I don't see anything."

Sandra glared at you from across the room. "What are you doing? Put your shirt back on."

"No, it's not that." You turned your torso to face her. "Here, you see anything?"

"Is it still there?" Jay asked, leaning against the couch behind you.

"Yeah," you said glancing at him, and then turning back to Sandra. "Do you see anything? That little white patch there?"

"You're all white."

"I mean the part whiter than the rest of me."

Sandra leaned forward in her seat and squinted. "Not really."

"I kinda see something," Jen mumbled next to him. She pointed at the spot with her finger. "About there?"

You nodded at her, as you rose and moved to the center of the room. You had everyone's attention now. "Jay, get the lights."

Jay got up with a shrug and went for the light switch. It was dusk outside, so it was not completely black with the lights off, but it was dark enough for the spot to be a single sharp light in an otherwise dull blue room.

You turned around slowly, making sure everyone got a good look at it. There were a few gasps here and there, but everyone was more surprised by it than afraid. Curious.

"What is it?" someone asked.

"I don't know," you replied. "The doctors said it was a kind of skin thing."

Someone else: "Does it hurt?"

You shook your head. "It feels fine. Doesn't burn, isn't sore, anything. Feels just like the rest of me."

You sat back down on the couch and kept your shirt up. Everyone in the room circled around you.

"That's just glow-in-the-dark paint, right?" Sandra asked.

"That's what I thought too when he showed me," Jay told her.

"It's not," you said. You turned back to Jen, with a mischievous smile. "Anyone want to touch it?"

Jen reached out very carefully and jabbed lightly at the spot. She turned her hand to look at her finger carefully as she rubbed her thumb against it.

"No paint or ink, right?" You asked.

She shook her head. "I don't think so." She reached out again after a moment and rubbed her finger in little circles over the spot. "This doesn't hurt?"

"Not in the slightest."

She giggled as she pushed the skin in, tapped it, and then looked up at your smiling face. "What about the other one?"

You blinked hard. "What other one?"

Jen raised her hand from your stomach and reached for your cheek. "The one there. Just below your eye. It's much tinier. Barely more than a pinprick."

You covered your cheek with your hand abruptly. "Turn the lights back on," you said hoarsely.

THERE WAS ANOTHER spot on your cheek. And another behind your right ear. Both of those were as small as the one on your stomach used to be. But there was one on the top of your shoulder that was already the size of a BB gun pellet, and three others near it were half that size. There were three on your left arm and two on the right, mostly around the inner elbow. Your right hand was bare, but there were two on the left—one on your thumbnail and the other in the webbing between your middle and ring finger.

There were two more on your backside, though it was hard to twist enough to get a good view. And a larger one on your right calf that was more square than circle. A thin line ran up the side of your left knee for about an inch, with veins cropping out from it. And you found three more in your pubic hair, one of which had a hair that looked like a single string of fiber optic lighting coming out of it.

You stayed in the bathroom with the door locked as the party broke up, which happened pretty quickly. Your abrupt exit from the room had put quite a damper on things. You listened to the muffled sounds of people shuffling their way to the front door, nobody saying much of anything.

You opened the door a crack and peeked out. Jay was talking very quietly with Sandra out in the hallway, the last of the guests to leave. You slipped out of the bathroom and down the hall to your bedroom as quickly and as quietly as you could, locking the door behind you.

The lights were all out in the room, and the only illumination came from the screen saver on your computer. You stood there against the door for a long time looking around, feeling suddenly paralyzed. Just out of the corner of your eye you happened to glance at your hand, resting on the edge of your dresser. Just below the second knuckle on your pinky a tiny little point of light came to life with a twinkle.

You turned on the overhead light, as well as the lamp by your bed, and threw open the drapes of your window to let the streetlight outside shine in. Then you rummaged in your closet for an old clip-on lamp buried underneath some boxes of other crap and clipped it to the edge of your computer monitor pointing out at the room. The glare hurt your eyes as you sat down heavily in your desk chair, but you were certain you wouldn't be able to see any of the spots now, and that's all that mattered to you at the moment.

There was a knock on your door. "You in there?" Jay asked. You didn't say anything, just stared at the door. Jay knocked again. "Hello?"

With a deep sigh, you got up from your seat and walked over to the door, opening it just enough to see Jay in the hallway with one eye. When you did, he pushed forward until he saw that you weren't going to open it any farther.

"Everybody else took off. It's just me."

"I know. It's just.... Not right now, okay?"

"Just let me in so we can talk. You're freaking out about this, I can tell."

You tried your best to smile at him. "I'm fine. Really."

"Look, it's nothing to panic about. So, you got another spot. That was bound to happen. Rashes spread."

You shook your head. "I want to lie down for a while, okay? We can talk later."

You closed the door and locked it again. You could feel Jay still standing on the other side of it.

"Look," he said through the door. "You just have to go back to that doctor. Or see a better one. An uptown dermatologist, one of those high-rent ones. Obviously, the doc at the clinic was wrong."

"Yeah. I'll see someone tomorrow. First thing," you said to the door.

"I can borrow Sandra's car and take you."

"No, that's okay. I appreciate the offer, but I can manage on my own."

"You sure?"

"Yeah, I'm sure. I'll be fine."

Jay didn't say anything for a long time. The floor underneath him creaked as he shifted from foot to foot. Finally, he replied, "All right. If you say so. Let me know how it goes, okay?"

"I will. I promise," you said. "Good night."

You could hear his footsteps as he walked back down the hallway, leaving you alone.

↔

OF COURSE, YOU didn't go see a doctor. Never had intended to. You just said that to Jay to make him go away. No, no doctors. You and the voice in your head agreed on that. You had all these ideas of a padded, windowless room far underground, with people in full hazmat suits jabbing needles into you or zapping you with electrodes while you spasmed and convulsed in the chair they had strapped you to. No thank you to all of that. That was definitely out.

But you had no idea what else you could do.

You stayed in your room, stopped going out at all. Not to see your friends or go to a show or spend a sunny day in the park. You cut it all out of your life completely. You could handle your money and pay your bills online easily enough, and you started to get your food from one of those online sites that delivered, which you would venture out to collect when you were sure the apartment was empty. All canned stuff or bread, things that didn't need cooking or could survive without refrigeration for a few days in your room.

You kept the lights on in your room day and night. But long sleeves, pants, and no mirrors worked better. Especially helpful were a pair of gloves your mom had gotten you for Christmas. You never took those off no matter what. You had never appreciated how hard it is not to look at your hands before.

There were some texts and messages from your friends at first, people inviting you to things, or asking where you were, but that soon tapered off to nothing. Everybody just moved on. Except for Jay, who checked on you daily. You wouldn't let him in, but he'd stand out in the hallway talking, trying to coax you out of your room. You'd humor him, as a little human contact was not bad—even if it was through a door, it was all you had. He brought others over too, people he called 'experts,' and they'd sit and talk with you through the door for a while as well.

"These spots of yours, they don't hurt at all?" one of them, who sounded like an older woman, asked.

"Nope," You replied, as you laid back on your bed staring at the ceiling. If I close my eyes, I can almost forget they're there."

A brief pause. Then she asked, "How about heat? Do they feel a little warm, maybe?"

"I said nothing. I've checked my temperature plenty of times. It's normal."

"Okay, so it would be some kind of luminescence. Too much phosphorous in your system."

You laughed. "The amount I'd need in me to do this would have killed me a long time ago."

"How can you be sure of that?"

You took off one of your socks and looked down at your bare foot. Even in the afternoon sunlight the glow was visible. Your big toe was a bright uniform void, and you couldn't make out the toenail at all, even as you scraped its rough edge against the side of the toe next to it.

"I'm sure," you said.

"It would really help if I could see what you were talking about," she said carefully. "I can't really help you through a door. Are you sure you won't come out?"

You sighed, didn't say anything.

"Or maybe I could come in. I could stand in the doorway, and I won't take one further step into your room." Again, you said nothing. "I just want to help you, you know."

"Somehow I don't think this is a psychological issue, doc."

There was a long pause. Who else would Jay be able to get to talk to you?

"Look," she finally continued. "You may have something very serious going on. Nobody is saying otherwise. And your friends are all worried about you. We all want to help. But shutting yourself off in your room forever isn't going to fix anything."

"There's nothing anyone can do to help."

"Come on," Jay said, probably standing next to the doctor this whole time. "You don't know that."

There was some muffled talk before the doctor continued. "Why do you think that nobody can help? Do you know what is going on?"

You shrugged. "I have some ideas."

"What are they?"

You didn't say anything.

"I'd like to hear what you think the spots are," she said.

"It's not just spots."

"No?"

"No," you said, exasperated. "That's just where it became visible. But it's all throughout me, in my organs, my muscles, my bones…. If you cut me open, you'd see most of my insides are as bright as an arclight by now. That little spot I first noticed wasn't the start of it by a longshot. That was just their first peek into the world outside. They'd been expanding in my body for a while before that."

"Who is this 'they'?" the doctor asked.

"Whatever little universe inside me started this."

Again, there was a long pause. Then it was Jay who spoke. "Did you say universe?"

"I did," you said, smiling to yourself. They're gonna love this.

You continued, "There's this fun theory going around that our entire universe is just an atom in a larger universe. Everything that we know could be nothing more than an infinitesimal speck in some being's hand, or gravel in their driveway, or randomly floating in nothingness. Just one of trillions. And if that were true, then the atoms in me would all be their own universes too. They'd have to be. Each bit of our bodies made up of countless universes with their own beings going about their quantum lives with no hope of ever going beyond the boundaries of their universe."

"I don't think that's how that works exactly," the doctor said.

You ignored her and crawled to the edge of your bed. "What if the beings in one of those atom universes inside of me became advanced? I mean really advanced? What if they grew, and multiplied, and created something so far beyond what the concepts empire or civilization or even sentience describe? What if they evolved into the totality of their universe, their atom?

"And what if that wasn't a boundary to them? What if they could escape their home universe and take over others in all directions? Getting exponentially larger and turning the new territory they claimed bright as they went?"

You laid back down on your bed, resting your head on your crossed arms with a deep breath. "There'd be no stopping something like that," you said in the silence.

After a minute the doctor said, almost meekly. "That's quite a theory you have."

"It's just an idea I've been toying around with."

"But it's very compelling. And creative. You should write it down." There was a ruffling, as if someone getting up off the floor. The doctor continued. "I have to go for now, but I would like to come back to talk to you again. Would that be all right?"

"Sure," you said. "Anytime, doc."

Light footsteps quickly padded down the hall and away from your door. You were pretty sure she wasn't going to come back.

BEING TAKEN OVER by an atom. It was an absurd idea. Just thinking about it made you giggle to yourself. Where had you even come up with it? You had read about the whole universe in an atom idea, or maybe heard some stoner pontificate about it at some random party. It was interesting, but it wasn't something that you thought about much. Just a foolish idea you came up with in the moment to make that psych major go away.

It was ridiculous. Stupid. Your left foot was just about all white now, but you could still move it, walk, and wiggle the toes with no problem. It was still your foot. Your body.

But still.

Why did it feel so right?

Your feet, your hands, your whole body was controlled by your brain. Even if something took over your limbs, the brain would still control them, right? The limbs were all just meat and bones responding to stimuli. Your brain was the real you.

But what if the light had taken over part of your mind? What if little tendrils of atoms had worked their way up your brain stem, into your occidental and cerebellum? Even farther? Everything else inside you was going light—another speculation, but again, you just knew it was true. Why not your brain? Why would it not be taken over too? Would you even know?

Maybe that's why the idea seemed so true. Because those parts of your mind that were taken already knew it, and you were getting it as a gut feeling. A little inkling of the truth leaking out to the unsullied part of you.

You thought back. Why hadn't you freaked out more when you first saw the spot? All you had done was play with it a bit and gone back to sleep. That seemed an insane reaction now. Denial? No, that wasn't it. You never denied the spot was there. But for some reason, it was just not that big of a deal. How could you possibly think that?

That little voice inside your head had convinced you to ignore it. The voice distracted you, made you look at something else, or when he couldn't do that, kept you calm about it, didn't let you panic as more and more of you turned on. He couldn't keep you from ever noticing or trying to do something—you still had most of your mind—but he did just enough to keep you from fully understanding what was happening.

Though now you did. The voice wasn't stopping you anymore. He must not need to.

You wondered if there was anything you could do to stop him.

And the voice inside your head told you no, there wasn't.

You heard the front door open and several loud voices. Jay was having friends over. You sat on the floor by the door and pressed your ear against it to see if you could identify anyone or hear what they were saying. But they were too far away to make out much. You could hear them settling down into the living room, laughing and talking. Jay shouted something as he walked into the kitchen and opened the fridge.

Your chest felt heavy, listening to the indistinct merriment, just a few feet from where you were, but feeling farther away than the moon. They sounded so lively, so happy. You closed your eyes and pictured it, as Jay closed the fridge and his heavy footfalls walked into the living room, handing beers to his friends, and sitting on the couch. He told a quick joke, and the laughter made your heart sink.

You got up off the floor, slowly opened the door, and peered out. The hallway was clear. You slipped out and rushed as quietly as you could for the bathroom. You closed it tight behind you and locked the door, keeping your eyes shut tight until you could flip the lights on. But even with them it wasn't as bright in here as you had kept your room. You could see the soft glow of the patches of your exposed skin reflecting off the shiny tiles on the wall, the porcelain of the sink and toilet.

You took off one of your gloves. The hand underneath was completely white, a complete void, absent of definition or contours. Yet you could feel your palm when your ran your fingers along your skin, tracing your lifeline below your pinkie as it arced up to the gap between your first in middle fingers. You scratched the first phalanx of your ring finger. It actually tickled.

You pushed back your sleeve. Your forearm was almost all white on both sides. There were a few small patches of skin left, but not many. A small one the size a quarter on your wrist bone. Another smaller one halfway to your elbow. The normal skin looked like the blemishes now.

But you could have seen all this from your room.

You looked up at your own face in the bathroom mirror. The head that stared back at you was as bright as a glowstick. A complete and utter transformation into nothing. There were no eyes or nose or anything but a solid void of white in the thing that looked back at you. That couldn't be your face. But no, when you tilted your head the image in the glass did the same. How could you still see? Eat? Breathe?

You rubbed your bare hand hard against your cheek. You felt the skin stretch, get pulled underneath your fingers, your lips fold up under them, your teeth and gums behind it, your right eye close shut as you pushed your cheek up into it. You felt all of it. But you didn't see it. Your glowing hand disappeared completely into your face.

The voice in your head: *Isn't it amazing?*

You fell to your knees and buried your head in your arms on the sink. Hot tears ran down your cheeks as your body wracked with sobs. You let out a childish moan. You were helpless and you knew it.

The voice tried to comfort you. He told you not to worry. It wasn't going to hurt, and it was almost over. You weren't going to disappear—you were still going to be you. Just with more. More of everything. And better. Better than okay. You'll see.

You didn't care. You just wanted it to be over.

The voice in your head was more than happy to oblige.

And that's when the final push began.

It was an odd sensation. You weren't fading or going away or less. You felt just as much yourself as you ever did. But then again, it also wasn't you anymore. There was more. A lot more. Your mind felt too small to hold all of it together, a multitude of universes in your brain, but they were all there, nonetheless. And so was he, no longer just a voice in the back of your head or a vague sense, but a full and controlling aspect of yourself.

He was not concerned at all. He stripped off your shirt and pants and stood in front of the mirror naked. He smiled wide as both of you thought you could almost feel the very last little atoms turn on.

He reached over and switched off the light.

The room glowed. Off the walls, the sink, the mirror, the plastic shower curtain, the bathtub. The whole room was bathed in that intense white light. He stretched your arms out at your sides and breathed in deep, as you heard a humming in your ears.

In those last moments, he reveled. You were calm. Nothing seemed to worry you about this. And you had no idea whether that was because you had accepted the transformation or because he was not allowing you to feel fear anymore. You felt that way right up until it was over.

THE FIRST THING he did was change the wavelength to outside of the visible human spectrum. Slowly he stopped glowing, and the room went pitch black. He turned the light back on and stared at his face very carefully in the mirror. Everything looked perfectly normal. The only thing he saw that might be out of the ordinary was he needed a shave.

He put his clothes back on and strolled into the kitchen. As he passed the living room, Jay saw him and looked up.

"Hey, you're out."

He nodded at Jay. "I was feeling thirsty," he said as he walked past the doorway.

In the kitchen he leaned down at the sink and drank deeply from the tap and wiped his mouth on the back of his forearm. He could vaguely hear the talk in the other room, though they were all half whispering. He ignored it and stood staring at the marker board on the fridge. It was blank except a small doodle in the corner that looked like a cat. He took up the marker hanging on a string and started writing.

Jay came into the room. "Are you feeling better?"

Not looking away from the board, he reached down

and lifted his shirt. "The spots are all gone."

"And you feel better otherwise?"

He nodded absently. "Like a new man."

"I was really worried there for a bit."

"I know," he said. He lowered the marker and turned to face Jay. "Look. I'm sorry I've been acting so crazy."

"Don't worry about that. It was totally weird what you were going through. But it's over now, right?"

He nodded and turned back to the board. "Absolutely."

"Still," Jay said. "Maybe you should get a check-up to make sure."

"I probably will. Though I'm sure they won't find anything."

Jay stood watching him as he wrote. "What are you doing?"

He stopped writing and looked at the board. "Just some idea I had in my head. Wanted to scribble it down while I had it."

Jay leaned in closer to look. On the board were a long line of numbers, letters, and symbols. It looked vaguely algebraic to him.

"More universe in an atom stuff?"

He smiled, shaking his head. "That wouldn't work at this level. The fundamentals of science are too different. Need a different approach."

Jay took a small step away from him. "A different approach to what?"

He didn't answer, still studying his work as if Jay hadn't said anything.

"What's going on?" a woman's voice from the living room called.

Jay stood straight again. "I should get back. You wanna come hang out for a while?"

He turned to Jay and smiled. "Sure. Just let me finish getting this down."

Jay exited the kitchen as he went back to the board.

He continued writing till the entire thing was filled with scribbles, then stepped back and looked at it. He felt limited by the expressions available, and he wasn't a hundred percent certain of his grasp of natural laws at this level yet, but he was close. It was a good place to start at least.

Taking over this universe should be no problem at all.

He dropped the marker and watched it dance on the end of its string for a few swings before it settled. Then he walked into the living room to hang out with Jay and his friends.

THE ANGLES

"One. At the tone, count five seconds out loud and press the button."

"One. Two. Three. Four. Five."

The machine beeped in Matthews' ear when he pressed the button. It wasn't loud, but the pitch grated at him. The soulless dark screen in the wall in front of him stared back, unmoved. After a moment, it continued.

"Two. At the tone, count fourteen seconds out loud and press the button."

A brief pause, then the dull electric ring sounded. "One. Two. Three. Four," Matthews counted, closing his eyes.

"Please keep your eyes open," the machine said.

"What?"

"Please keep your eyes open and face the screen."

Matthews sighed and sat up in his chair. "Let me start over. You interrupted me."

"Acknowledged. At the tone, count fourteen seconds out loud and press the button."

He leaned forward on his elbow as he began again, his finger hovering over the red button. It was hard to get comfortable in the small room. It wasn't any larger than a closet, with just the stiff chair and the ledge where the button was in front of the dark screen. The abnormally high ceiling was the only part of the room that kept him from feeling completely boxed in.

He focused on his reflection in the dark glass as he counted. He could see the contours of his brow, cheeks, the tip of his nose, but the rest of his face was a void. It was like his reflection in the glass dome of the cockpit, the bulb at the mast of his snake-like ship. That was where he belonged. Strapped down to the inner wall with his arms on the armrests, a joystick in each hand. Facing the whole universe beyond the ghostly image of his own reflection.

He cleared the asteroid belt on his way to the angles out by Jupiter. The distant gas giant was a tiny red dot far off in front of him. A wart on his invisible cheek. Just to the left of it was the Milky Way, the mist of billions of fiery orbs cutting down through his face like a scar.

He pulled on the joystick in his left hand, and the ship tumbled. The escort drones in front furiously repositioned themselves to match him. He smiled. It was one of the few distractions he had, twisting and twirling, sending the drones into a frantic dance to remain in formation. The passengers and flight crew in the attached compartments behind him never seemed to mind, or at least they never said anything. They probably enjoyed the twirling sky. Not that he would have cared if they did complain. He was the pilot. If he wanted to dance a little to break the tedium, they would just have to deal with it.

"Ain't nobody can tell you what to do out there," Franks said, looking across the table at him with that devilish smirk he got when he was feeling boisterous. "You could fly the whole way backward if you want. We're in charge in the void. That's our world. Pilots rule. Who else they gonna get who can fly the angles? No one, that's who." He took a long drink and slammed his glass down on the table, making his date that night jump.

The civilians loved this kind of talk. The brashness of it, the ego. They always crowded around and wanted to be near the pilots, with them. They were the dashing heroes. They were special.

"Admit it, you live for the attention."

"Of course I do!" Franks roared with a laugh. "Who wouldn't? Who complains about being looked up to? Everyone wishes they could be us, live our lives. Wishes they could shoot the angles and come out the other side. We've seen the whole damn universe. And even more than that. They know it's more than anything any of them will ever experience in their safe, mundane lives. The biggest high-powered exec in New York would give up every penny they had to fly in the cockpit just once."

"So, we're living the dream."

Franks grinned wide. "Absolutely. I wouldn't give it up for anything."

Matthews finished counting and pressed the button. Again, the light beep was almost immediate.

"Three. At the tone, count thirty-seven seconds out loud, and press the button."

Jupiter soon grew into a cloudy orb up ahead about the size of his fist. The ship was directly between the gas giant and the distant sun, so the planet was full and bright. The nav comp had locked on to it, and the planet was bordered by a faint red circle from the overhead display, with a small data window hanging to its right. He ignored that and looked at the planet. The larger clouds and chaotic storms could be made out distinctly across its surface, as well as a small dark spot rolling along the equator. Probably Ganymede passing by. The others would be too small to be visible from here.

This was a favorite sight for passengers, and there were a few more hours for them to enjoy it before Matthews would turn on stasis. He angled the ship a few degrees and flew just slightly askew to give the port side a better view. It was easy enough to reposition the thrusters to keep the steady deceleration constant. An old, flashy trick he had mastered years ago.

Matthews stared at the black just below the distant planet. There was nothing to see except the empty void. But that was where they were headed. To the angles. They were still too far for the computers to register them, so nothing showed up on the display. But Matthews could feel them tugging at him from hundreds of thousands of kilometers away. Nearly there, just a few more hours. That's where the real piloting happened. Matthews felt his chest getting tight in anticipation.

Traveling between the stars was all about the angles. The curious interplay of the gravitational pull of the sun and the planets against each other created microscopic tears in space. Every planet had them; Mercury just the one, ten among the other inner planets combined, more among the gas giants. Jupiter alone had more than a hundred. But they were innocuous, affecting nothing. Dust, comets, and ships could fly straight through them without even knowing it.

Unless you came at them at the exact right angle. If you position your ship to pass through them just so, down to millimeter precision, continuously adjusting and repositioning, shifting this way, twisting that, not overshooting, getting it just right. It took an expert hand.

"Six." The machine said. "At the tone, count one hundred forty-five seconds-"

"What happened to four and five?"

The machine stopped. Matthews could hear a slight whir. "Repeat. Six. At the tone, count one hundred forty-five seconds out loud and press the button."

He shook his head and waited. The machine was deviating from the standard test by jumping ahead. It made him apprehensive. It was trying to trip him up.

"The department is being forced on this, Matthews," Weiters told him. "You understand that, right?"

Matthews shrugged at his supervisor. "I guess."

"This isn't me. This is coming from the top. These new studies coming out of Luna are bad, and Central can't ignore them anymore. There's too much public outcry. The tests are now compulsory every quarter. No exceptions."

Matthews quietly despised Chief Weiters. Most of the pilots did at some level. The man hadn't done more than a year in a cockpit before he had moved behind a desk. If that. He talked like he was on their side, that he knew what it was to be a pilot, and maybe he did. But he still wasn't really one of them.

Weiters continued. "I've already had to ground Suarez and Jacobs. I just got Mindoye's results back this morning and she's done too. Not much of a surprise there; she's been out of it for years. This is going to wipe out our whole squad."

Matthews looked at the old-fashioned lamp sitting on Weiters' table. Little specks of dust sparkled in the light directly above the bulb. They were kept aloft in the heated air as they flowed past, appearing and disappearing as they moved in and out of the light.

Franks leaned across the table to Matthews, his chin just above the lampshade. The thin hairs on his face shone in the light. "You see this new crop of pilots?" Franks asked.

"Some of them," Matthews replied.

"Fucking useless the whole batch of them." He took a long swig from his glass.

"Maybe they're a little green."

"A little? I watched that new kid, whatshisname? Guilfoye. I was behind him in line at the Neptune field the other day and watched him miss the Taurus angle three times before he got it. It was brutal. He'd come full stop and dance around and twist and turn and then just jump at it, so of course he kept missing. I felt embarrassed just watching him. *The Taurus angle*, Matthews. That's beginner shit. I could line that one up from Mars orbit."

"He'll get the hang of it. Or he'll wash out."

Franks snorted. "I know which way that one'll go."

"We were all green like that, too, you know. Like you didn't say the same things about me when I first came up."

Franks stared at Matthews for a long time, not saying anything, his eyes getting that distant, faraway look that made Matthews uncomfortable. Matthews repeated himself. "I bet you said the same things about me."

Franks blinked hard once and looked away from the table. "They're nuts if they think they're gonna replace us with them," he said.

The tone almost made Matthews jump. "One. Two. Three. Four. Five," he counted off. It had taken the machine forever to start.

The passengers were all safely in stasis when Matthews reached the angles. They had had their view of Jupiter, dominating the space to port. Now, it was time to sleep until they got through to the other end.

He tilted the ship downwards and twisted the tail back towards the sun to face the angles. His display lit up with dozens of little yellow targets, dancing all over the glass as he maneuvered. The angle he was looking for came floating up from his feet to directly ahead of him. He stabilized on that point.

He gave the thrusters a quick burst and drifted towards it as his display target grew larger. He was only a few hundred kilometers away now. The data points next to his target fluctuated as he eased the ship around, but he didn't look at them. Only rookies used the computer.

Matthews closed his eyes and felt for it. And there it was. He nudged the ship around. Twist to Jupiter, pull the tail up. Shuffle sunward fifteen meters, up three. Nose down half a degree. Rotate five. Almost there. Shuffle up half a meter. Rotate minus two. There, that's close. Tilt down one degree. He could feel it. Yes, he had it now. He was lined up perfectly.

He pushed forward on both joysticks and shot the ship forward.

And he was through.

Everything vibrated. There was a hum. He matched the tone of it with his chattering lips because that helped. He slowly opened his eyes so they could adjust to the bright orange glare of the sinewy world in-between space.

Tendons. Threads. Lines. Infinite. No pattern or semblance. All directions at once. Points of light shot past him, around him, through him. The sturdy metal of the ship and his body rippled like water. But Matthews kept focused.

The in-between space—it did everything it could to throw you. It flashed bright in your eyes and made you numb all over. His left foot felt like it had floated away.

But Matthews kept focused. The ship expanded and contracted with his breathing. He glanced down at his hands, holding firmly onto the joysticks. There they were, right there. He could see them. Yet they also stretched out forever in front of him. His body sunk through the hard wall behind him.

But Matthews kept FOCUSED.

He didn't lose himself. He kept his mind on the task. He pushed on. There was an out of this up ahead. Or far behind. Or off to the side. It was hard to tell. Direction didn't work the same in here. But there was an exit, somewhere. And Matthews moved towards it, tugging and pulling on the joysticks to keep the ship on the path. Even as his brain stopped registering what he saw. His neck jerked convulsively, his body went rigid, and still, he kept his focus on the never-ending moment in the other space. Matthews stayed on the path.

And then he was out. Suddenly, almost as if he had always been where he was.

Matthews' body went limp. His head sunk deep into his chest as he caught his breath. He let go of the joysticks and wiped the beads of sweat off his brow. The distant stars against the black void had returned outside the cockpit dome. Off to starboard was the green chlorine gas giant of the Mu Arae system, over fifty light years from where they had been only a moment before.

A pilot could get you to the angles. A skilled pilot could enter them. But only a special pilot like Matthews could get you out.

"Testing concluded. You may exit the booth. Thank you, and have a nice day."

Matthews stepped out into the narrow hallway. He stared at his feet to avoid meeting the gaze of any of the techs and administrators he passed. After a few turns, he felt more relaxed, as it would be less obvious to others where it was he was coming from.

It was the middle of the day station time on the promenade, and the area was alive and throbbing around him. People rushed about from one distraction to the next as they waited for their flights, either back down to Earth or out. The kiosks and small shop fronts flashed their wares at them for attention.

Matthews straightened out his uniform jacket and walked tall as the crowds parted for him deferentially. Most people tried not to stare as he passed, at least not so much that it would draw attention to themselves. He smiled politely, nodding at the occasional person with whom he made eye contact, knowing they were likely looking after him as he passed. Everyone wanted to be a pilot.

Earth shone brightly just the other side of the glass a few hundred miles below the observation lounge. Matthews looked down on the thick clouds moving across the coast of Libya. His eyes moved across the sky as the clouds cleared around the canal until there were little more than wisps of white over the dry lands of the Middle East all the way to the horizon. Bulging out the arc of the Earth, the moon was rising, half-tinted blue in the ozone. He rubbed small circles with his thumbs on the polished wood of the railing he leaned on as he stared out absently.

He heard a sniffle to his left and turned to look. A pair of small dark eyes peeked out at him from the side of a soft chair where the rest of the girl was hiding. They stared back at him evenly. They were very intense for such a small child, he thought.

Matthews stuck his tongue out at her. Her head bobbed as she silently giggled. She got up slowly from her hiding spot and walked over, hugging a toy robot to her chest. She stood dancing in place looking at him.

"Hello," Matthews said. The little girl didn't say anything. He continued, motioning out towards Earth. "Isn't the view pretty?"

The little girl glanced out the window and back at him, nodding.

"Is this your first time in space?" The little girl shook her head. "You've been up here before? How many times?"

"Lots." She said bluntly.

Matthews smirked. "Me too."

"'Cause you're a pilot."

"I am?"

She nodded her head furiously and pointed at him. "You're wearing your uniform."

Matthews looked down at himself in mock surprise. "Is that what this is?"

She furrowed her brow at him. "Yes. You're a pilot. I know."

Matthews smiled. "You got me. I'm a pilot."

A middle-aged man came up behind the little girl. "Janelle," he told her. "What are you doing?"

The little girl pointed at Matthews. "He's a pilot."

The man wrapped his hands around his daughter and looked up at Matthews. "I'm sorry if she's bothering you, sir."

Matthews waved his apology off. "She's fine." He looked back down at her. "It's very nice to meet you, Janelle."

The man asked her, "What do you say, sweetie?"

"It's nice to meet you," she said, nibbling on her finger.

"That's my girl. We need to go find Mommy. Say goodbye to the nice man."

Janelle smiled at Matthews and waved.

The man turned to Matthews. "It was nice meeting you, sir." Matthews nodded at him as he took his daughter and turned to walk away.

After a few steps, Janelle turned back to him. "I'm gonna be a pilot too." She said excitedly.

Matthews smiled at her. "I'll save your seat."

Janelle smiled back and turned around. Matthews watched her father as they walked away. He leaned down and said something to her quietly, then glanced back at Matthews sheepishly as if worried he had been overheard. They exited the lounge and back out onto the promenade.

Matthews turned back to the view. He had recognized that look on the father's face. Patronizing, slightly nervous, held in check only by knowing how young she was, believing she'd grow out of it, move on to something else. A real life. Something safer. And she probably would. Most people gave up on their childish dreams when they grew up. But not all. The pull of it was too much for some, like it had been for him.

If she persisted, then her parents would grow truly concerned. They would tell her how hard it was to become a pilot. And about the damage it does to you even if you make it. How it could lead you in just a few short years to a lonely life of nothing, standing by yourself in a half-empty observation deck, having finished taking a cognitive test that you were absolutely sure you just failed.

Franks stood in the corner of the bar, staring absently at the wall, the drink in his hand about to drop at any moment. He hadn't moved a muscle since Matthews started his way to him from across the crowded room.

"Franks," Matthews said as he got to him. "Franks, you okay?"

He didn't move or register that Matthews had spoken.

"Come on, snap out of it," Matthews said.

He gently put his hand on Franks' arm, planning to lead him to an empty seat nearby. But as he touched him, Franks blinked hard and looked at Matthews. "What?" He said simply.

"Are you alright?" Matthews asked. "Had a little too much to drink, maybe?"

Franks glanced around the room, a slight look of panic in his eyes. Everyone avoided looking at him as if he wasn't there. He took a deep drink and turned back to Matthews. "It's nothing. I'm fine. When did you get in?"

"Just a few minutes ago."

Franks smiled at him. "Well, it's about time. Damn boring in here tonight. Come on, let's hit that new place on the third level."

Matthews nodded and let Franks, back to his old self, lead him away as if nothing had happened. Which was fine with Matthews. He didn't want to think about it either.

It wasn't just a lack of focus; that alone wouldn't flunk a pilot. Most pilots were pretty flaky, to begin with. It was the periods of absence where a pilot could have sworn they were somewhere else, some *when* else—earlier, even later. While in everyone else's world, you were frozen in place like a picture. Or you had moments where you seemed to exist at a different speed than the rest of the world, far too fast or slow. The simple thirty-minute test could take up to three hours to get through if you were really bad off.

That's what the angles did to you. They messed with your time. The more you flew the angles, the more you drifted away from linear existence. The test looked for long pauses while counting or counting at an erratic pace. Or just the far away demeanor washing over you as you counted, when it was clear you were someplace else. If the test picked up too much of any of that, you were as good as grounded.

Weiters sighed and leaned forward on his desk. "How many years have you been a pilot, Matthews?"

"It'll be fourteen in a couple of months."

"Which is almost three times longer than Jacobs—twice as long as Suarez or Mindoye. Hell, that's four more than any pilot I've ever heard of."

"Franks made it twelve," Matthews said.

"Right. Franks." Weiters continued. "What could you possibly have to prove to anyone anymore?"

Matthews didn't say anything, watching the dust in the lamplight dance.

"You have a great pension, plus whatever you've saved up all these years. All that makes for a pretty damn comfortable life. And you're still young so you can really enjoy it too. The damage isn't bad yet. Just a little drifting. No big deal."

"Then why am I being grounded?"

Weiters pounded his fist on the desk. "Because it's the law. I have to. You know that." Breathing deeply, he sat back in his chair. "Look. I can hold off on entering the results, and you can just retire quietly. Tell everyone you just thought it was time. Or you met someone and want to settle down and relax. Whatever you want. Nobody has to know."

A large mote of dust fell straight down into the light.

Matthews sat sipping at a dark drink by himself in the pilot lounge, just off the locker rooms and staging area. It was a small room, all grey, with modest decor on the sloping walls that seemed to flow into the glass and brass bar in the far corner. Rectangular viewports out into space ran across the outer wall at eye level, and tables were scattered around the room haphazardly, with a pair of plush soft chairs each. There was no blaring music or the hum of the crowds that you can't escape on the promenade, just the soft hiss of the station's air scrubbers filtering in through the vents. It was a relaxing place to hang out in without the staring crowds, and many pilots liked to take advantage of it for the privacy.

Apart from Matthews and Sid behind the bar, there were only a couple of green pilots sitting the other side of the room. Matthews glanced at them. A nervous little gnat, Shelby, he thought her name was, was wiggling her fingers on the table as she leaned in close to talk to a pudgy kid Matthews didn't recognize. Her eyes darted over at Matthews as she finished what she was saying and sipped her drink. The other kid turned his head and glanced back at him. Their eyes met for just a moment before he looked away quickly back to Shelby, who was doing everything she could not to look in Matthews' direction.

"Franks," Matthews said insistently, pushing him gently on the arm.

Franks grimaced and looked over at Matthews next to him at the bar, annoyed. "I was just thinking, dammit. I didn't go anywhere." With a finger, he flicked his empty shot glass down the bar.

Matthews shook his head. "When is it official?"

"As of two hours ago," Franks replied. "I'm done."

"You can fight it. You should fight it."

"How?"

Matthews looked around the room. "Hell, I don't know. Tell them you were hungover and take the test again."

Franks looked over at Matthews, shaking his head. "Right. 'It wasn't me, chief, it was all the whiskey shots before I went in.' I don't think that'd work." Franks stared down at his hands. "Besides, I'd just fail again anyway."

"You don't know that."

"Do you think I don't notice how people look at me? Or how other pilots won't look at me at all if they can avoid it? I've been fucked up for a while now. This isn't a surprise to anyone."

"Come on, Franks-"

"Don't." He said sharply. "Just.... There's no point in pretending anymore."

Matthews looked away, out the window past his shoulder. The patchwork bright lights of the nighttime Earth outlined the Eastern coast of Asia. The focal hub, Seoul, was easily discernible.

"So, what will you do?" He asked Franks.

Franks shrugged. "Find a nice beach house somewhere that's always warm. Live in total comfort. Get fat and lazy. Invent new cocktails."

"Sounds horrible," Matthews said.

"Yeah." Franks laughed. "At least with my mushed-up brain, I won't spend all my time there."

Matthews tried to laugh with him. But the dread in his bones was just too much to do it convincingly.

The door across the room to the staging area slid open, and Shera, the embarkment chief, stepped through. She walked straight to the bar and leaned heavily on top of it. She rubbed her face and stuck a few errant dreads behind her ear as Sid approached with a sandwich and placed it down in front of her.

Matthews got up from his table and made his way over to her. "Rough day?" He said as he leaned next to her on the bar.

Shera looked up from her food, shaking her head as she swallowed. "Oh, you have no idea. Been one headache after another all shift. I got three cockpits down with inspection fails, a ship all ready to go out to Mu Arae without a pilot because Guilfoye broke his thrusters getting back here from Seti, so he arrived a day late and threw all the schedules off, and the new techs they stuck me with couldn't find their own ass with a flashlight and help from a supervisor."

"So about normal," Matthews said.

Shera slapped him lightly on the shoulder. "I swear I'm gonna quit."

Matthews laughed. "It'll never happen. You love this, and you know it." Shera shrugged and took another bite of her lunch.

Matthews looked around the room for a moment as Shera ate. "What was that you said about a ship without a pilot?" He asked.

Matthews let the ship drift aimlessly in space, tumbling slowly over itself. He had turned off the lights and muted all the sounds in the cockpit. The only light came from the green glow of the gas giant out to port. Normally, he would have already set his course and moved inwards, towards the distant star at the center of the system where the colonies were, but he wanted to just drift and relax for a moment. The passengers were still in stasis, and the system entry base was on the other side of the gas giant. So, there was no one to care.

Outside was so peaceful, felt so constant and unchanging. The clouds of the massive ball of gas, even in all its chaos, seemed to be almost frozen in place, moving so slowly as to be on the very edge of perception. Lightning strikes bigger than his ship flashed here and there on the surface of the globe, but at this distance, they were little more than brief sparkles or thread-thin lines, pulsing briefly and then fading away.

The planet floated up over his head and disappeared as the ship spun out into the void. The stars were thick and numerous, only blotted out in the upper corner around the distant star at the center of the system. Off to starboard was a brilliant velvet nebula, shaped like a gash in the darkness, with several very bright infant stars drifting out from it. He could make out the two inner planets of the system twinkling at him, just barely standing out among the bright lights of the galaxy, one a soft blue, the other a deep crimson. Larger was the ball of one of the green giant's moons to port, a greyish world that looked about the size of his fist. He could see a tiny spout from a geyser on its surface bulging out from the bottom.

When he rolled around towards the gas giant again, he saw the small circle of drone escorts approaching him, five white objects in a tight circle. A communication window appeared on the dome.

"Transport NEP-5968, this is Mu Arae System base, please respond," a soft voice said in his ear. Matthews said nothing. "Transport NEP-5968, this is Mu Arae System base, please respond. Are you there, Matthews?"

He sighed. "I'm here."

"Special order from Sol command. You are to follow the drone escort to System base, where a stellar pilot is to relieve you and transport the passengers on to Mu Arae Prime. Confirm."

Matthews shook his head. They weren't going to let him finish the trip. Though he was surprised he had gotten this far. He wondered if Weiters had tried to cover for him when he found out Matthews had taken a ship and got caught himself.

"Confirm." The voice said again, more forcefully. The drones were almost on top of him now. He turned on the lights and power in the cockpit and stabilized the ship to face them.

"Matthews, do you hear me? Please respond."

Matthews leaned heavily on his elbows at his desk, facing the young man in the white scrubs on the laptop screen. His torso felt a thousand times heavier than it had a moment ago.

"I'm sorry, sir, but Mr. Franks isn't able to accept any calls," the man said, somewhat coldly. "He is not having one of his good days. You could try again tomorrow, but I can't promise he would be much better. I can let him know you called when he comes back to us if you like. But it might be some time."

Matthews hit the thrusters. The sudden g-force pressed him against the wall so hard his eyesight went red and he blew right past the escorts. Beyond the throbbing in his ears, he could vaguely hear the voice from system base, now yelling at the top of its lungs at him.

The dive into the planet had confused the drones and gained him some distance. But he could already see them off to his side catching up. One shot from their EM pulse guns and his engines would shut down permanently.

He turned off the main engines and reached for the lever by his left leg, pulling the joystick in his right hand as far to the side as he could. The ship went into a tight spin with a center of mass just behind the cockpit. The gas giant flew past and came back around in just a few seconds. Then less than one. The spinning picked up speed. His ribs pressed hard into the armrest, shooting pain up his side. But he kept going. Faster. His harness started to choke him as the centrifugal force tried to throw him outward. The world outside the cockpit became a quickly alternating blur of black and green. He fought the urge to be sick. Or pass out. He had to time this just right.

Just before the green, he pulled the lever upwards.

There was a loud clank, and the whine of bending metal as the cockpit broke free, sending the compartments hurling back towards the drones.

By the time he stabilized himself, facing backward, the compartments were already several dozen kilometers away, still spinning wildly. He could see no structural damage apart from the connectors where he had ripped free. And the drones had completely forgotten about him as they chased after them.

The communication flickered back on. "Transport NEP-5968, this is Station Commander Levisson." A gruff, stern voice said, "What in the fucking hell do you think you're doing? You will power down this instant and wait for retrieval. That is a direct order. I will authorize lethal force—"

He shut off the communication as he spun the cockpit around. The main engines had gone with the compartments, but he still had the docking thrusters. He had also lost a good deal of speed in the stunt, and eventually one of the drones would break off and go after him.

He dived on the planet. If he could slingshot around it, he could gain all the speed he needed. And with one strong burst from all the thrusters at the right moment, he could shoot back out towards the angles and the drones would never catch him. And then he could go anywhere.

The clouds of the gas giant grew large in front of him fast. The planet lost its flat appearance, and he saw the rough, uneven clouds as they flowed through each other. A shaft of lightning stretched out like a river below, all the way around the bend of the planet.

He fell farther, and his speed increased rapidly. The cockpit shook and groaned violently. The outer dome began to glow. He started to list to the right, facing him down towards the planet. His angle had been too steep—he was falling too fast. He fired the thrusters to try and gain some altitude, hoping he would still have enough left to gain escape velocity after.

But nothing happened. He tried again and still nothing. Something was wrong. The maneuvering thrusters were only working at half power, not enough to counteract the pull of the planet. They must have been damaged in the separation. Without them, he had no way of breaking free, no way to stop from plunging down into the clouds below to be crushed.

The shaking increased, and Matthews gritted his teeth. His head bounced against the board. He gripped the joysticks so hard his shoulders felt like they were about to shatter. He saw tiny fractures starting to spread at the seams in the glass dome as the cockpit brushed against the uppermost layer of clouds, the green chaos swirling like a nightmare, opening to swallow him whole.

Matthews closed his eyes and prepared himself. It hadn't been much of an idea in the first place. Where could he have really gone anyway that they wouldn't be able to find him? It was just delaying the inevitable. All this, this was just accelerating it.

And then he felt it up ahead of him. There was an angle.

He opened his eyes and looked down at the planet. He was on the edge of a giant vortex in the center of a dark cloud, lightning continuously rippling down its sides. Down there, that's where he had felt the angle, in that monster. But it was impossible. Angles didn't form in planets. There were no opposing gravities to form one. The pull of that storm against itself couldn't possibly be enough.

But he could feel it, far, far down in the vortex. It was there. Yet out of reach. The pressure and the turbulence would likely rip him to pieces before he could reach it. But if he could...

"Might as well try it," Franks said. "Not like you got anything to lose."

Matthews closed his eyes again, stopped fighting against the pull of the giant, and plunged straight down. The cockpit immediately started coming apart, cracking and splitting, fuses blowing around him. His head was being crushed from all sides at once. But he blocked it out. He was lined up beautifully with the angle. Nudge a little to the left. There, fine. Just fine. He heard the cracks in the dome getting larger, and then a deafening roar and a gush of air away from him when it finally broke open. His body was yanked forward, and the straps of his harness held him from getting sucked out. His throat burned as he caught a whiff of the planet's atmosphere. He held his breath and didn't open his eyes or shout. He needed to concentrate. Still on target, he could feel it lined up. Lined up beautifully. Blood trickled down his cheeks from his nose, his ears, his closed eyelids, and froze against his skin. His entire body screamed at him. But he was almost there. He could sense it. It was lined up perfectly.

And he was throu

"NEP-5968, THIS IS Mu Arae System Base. Please respond."

He repeated. "NEP-5968, this is Mu Arae System Base. Please respond. Matthews, are you there?"

Levisson leaned over the communications officer, staring intently at the planet out to port. He shouted, "Answer me!" But there was no reply.

He stood up, sighing heavily and rubbing his neck. "Shut it down, Tara."

"Yes, sir." Tara closed the communications window on the overhead and brought the system traffic monitor back up. She turned in her seat to face the commander. "What do you want me to tell Sol control?"

"Tell them that Matthews was lost when his cockpit malfunctioned. There was nothing we could do to save him. He managed to jettison his compartments clear of danger before he spun into the marble."

"Sir? What about the arrest order?"

Levisson shook his head. "I'm sure you're going to find that that order was rescinded. Or will be. Just a glitch in the system." Levisson turned away from her. "Just give the broad brushstrokes to them for now. It was equipment failure. I'll file the formal report in the morning."

Levisson exited the bridge for his executive quarters, leaving the bridge crew to their work.

A very thin dark line ran along the equator of the gas giant, from where something had screamed across the grain. It was already dissipating into nothing.

LAST MAN

I KIND OF LIKE the music in this place. A soft jazz tune, I couldn't tell you what it was. It survived among the murmurs of conversation without overpowering it—blended more than blared, didn't draw attention to itself. A lot of places have that intent beating of the mating drum kind of stuff, far too loud for the space, all flashing lights and thick air. Trying to make everything feel so insistent, as if they were desperate to drive home the intensity, the relevance, of this Friday night over all the thousands of other Friday nights that have ever been and ever will be. I never care for that kind of thing. The calm and casual of a room without the artificial pressure to have a memorable night is so much better. Let things be as they are meant to be.

The bartender wanders over to me at the bar. It's not too crowded so he's not acting all that harried. He stops in front of me and leans in.

"Scotch and soda," I tell him.

"Start a tab?"

I shrug. "Yeah, I think I can park in here for a bit."

He takes my card and nods, then walks away to get the drink. I turn back to look around the bar. Most of the illumination is from soft yellow electric candles resting on each of the tables and their reflection off the brass décor and other metallic fixtures about the place. Makes the whole place look golden. People sit around tables talking, couples, friends, a few solitary people like me. Nobody is being all that rambunctious and acting drunk, but it is still early, I guess.

Across the room at a table four ladies sit, talking conspiratorially as they pick at an appetizer plate together. They're dressed nice but not flashy. All old, very good friends. The one facing away from me, a blonde with thick long hair, is telling some story to the other three in hushed tones leaning far over the table. Two of the women, dark-haired with tan, somewhat dolled up faces, hang on every word, stifling giggles and furtive glances. The third doesn't seem that interested, almost put off a bit, as if the story was perhaps a little too raunchy for her.

She focuses more on the plate in front of them and looks up at the storyteller occasionally, staying silent. Her skin is pale and smooth, her jaw protrudes a bit as she chews. Her hair looks auburn and curly, tied back into a loose bun. She has one curl just by her right eye that's broken free, and it spirals down the side of her face by her temple. She brushes it back absently, only for it to slowly slide back down after a few moments. She's probably not even really aware that it's there.

The bartender returns with my drink and places it on a napkin in front of me. I grab it and nod to him as he walks away. I take a sip and look back at the table just as the blonde's story ends and laughter ensues. One of the dark-haired women claps as she guffaws. The other covers her eyes in faux mortal shame. The auburn-haired woman laughs too but mostly to herself.

I can see that she's tiny. Slim, much smaller than her three larger than life friends. She doesn't cower under them or shrivel under the weight of their flamboyant personalities. She just lets them have their space, content with her own. It's not a competition for her. These are her friends.

She looks up and notices me looking at her. She doesn't seem alarmed, doesn't even stop chewing the bit of lettuce in her mouth. I smile and tip my glass ever so subtly. I imagine I can see the thoughts running around in her head at that moment. This man looking at her—not threateningly, just looking, and all the possibilities that that can have.

And for the very, very briefest of moments, less than a fraction of a second, a slight smirk dances on her tiny lips, as if to her, the notion of those possibilities don't sound half bad. But then it's gone, drowned out in the full smile and gaze averted back to her friends and away from me.

I grin to myself, finishing my drink and turning back around to order another.

He lost his virginity when he was sixteen years old. Late on a cool summer evening in his backyard, while his parents slept soundly inside.

Her name was Sarah. She had long, deep dark hair, beautiful olive skin, and brown eyes that lit up when she smiled. She was fifteen and tall for her age, already showing the hints of the majestic woman she was growing into. They were in classes together at school and had flirted silently with glances through boring lectures and sometimes in the hallway between them. But for one reason or another, it had never become a thing. Just some innocent play.

He had been at the mall killing some time before some random flick at the multiplex with friends and saw her in the food court. She was on her dinner break from her job at one of those fashion stores upstairs, and he sat and chatted with her as he waited. After the movie was over, on a whim he ditched his friends and found his way up to her store. She was just finishing up her shift and he offered her a ride home. She accepted with a smile.

They ended up at his house instead. He had said something about watching stars in his backyard. Honestly, he didn't know the first thing about astronomy and it was just talk to try and impress her. But that didn't matter much, because she wasn't really interested in them either.

He draped a blanket on top of the picnic table by the thin tree in the corner of his backyard, and they laid down on it together, silently looking upwards. She rested her head on his shoulder, as they slowly inched closer to each other. Looking back on it he never could be certain when it had started to be what it became; one moment they were quietly staring at the stars, the next he was kissing her, her lips, her neck, her ear, her chest. He rolled on top of her, cradling her head in his hands.

He was all a jumble of excitement and confusion. Any moment he expected his parents to shout from the kitchen window, a neighbor's blast of TV startling them apart, Sarah pushing him away. Something was bound to interrupt this, something would stop them dead in their tracks. But nothing did. His parents were nowhere to be seen, the neighbors' houses were all dark, and Sarah wanted this as much as he did. She pulled him ever closer to her with her hand at his neck. It seemed the whole world had aligned for this to happen right then and there.

He fumbled at her clothes, repositioned himself awkwardly on her, started and stopped things he thought might be good but were beyond his beginner's abilities. He felt sheepish at his clumsiness. He started to fear that Sarah would see that he simply, truly, had no idea whatsoever what he was doing. But she didn't know any better than he did, made her own fumbles, laughing lightly as she bumped her forehead into his nose. They were both stumbling around blind in this new world.

And the act itself; he went slow, gently, barely entering her at all at first, afraid of hurting her, not even certain he was doing it right. She grasped his buttocks in her hands and insistently pulled him in deeper, held him there, and squeezed him tightly. He went faster. More certain. He breathed hard into her shoulder as the very moment came closer and closer. She bit on his ear and exhaled loudly. His legs started to twitch as he pushed—to his own surprise he was grunting. Then the world went blank as every muscle in his body became stone and he felt himself ejaculating inside her. He exhaled a breath he didn't even know he had been holding in and collapsed next to her.

Without a word they rearranged their clothes and rested on their backs next to each other again, almost as if nothing special had just happened. Sarah draped her arm across his chest and ran her fingers along his ribs, her face serene and calm. Both lying back and looking around, to see if they could spot the ways the world had just changed.

Later, on the drive back to her house, Sarah became chatty, talking about her parents, the job at the mall, what she thought about the school year starting up in four weeks.

He listened smiling, taking it all in. He felt an overwhelming sense of accomplishment in himself, and her happy voice made it feel even more triumphant.

They kissed long and warmly in the car in front of her house. She was going away with her mom to the city while her Dad was out of town and wouldn't be back for a few days. They'd get together then. There were notions of nice restaurants, the beach. More stargazing. But nothing was set for certain. She got out of the car, walking at a brisk pace up to her front door. He sat in his car watching her till she entered and closed the door behind her. Just before it closed, she turned and he could see her wave at him. He couldn't see her that well in the porch light, but he was certain that she was still smiling.

Four days later, driving back home late, Sarah's Mother fell asleep at the wheel and drifted across the line. The collision was devastating. Sarah, who had been sound asleep in the passenger seat, probably didn't feel a thing.

"I'm Hannah," she says, holding out her hand to me.

It's a stiff, kind of out place gesture on her part. I get the feeling being up here at the bar isn't exactly her idea, so she's feeling a bit awkward about it. But I take her hand and shake it formally.

Over the last drink or so I've caught her once or twice glancing my direction. And her friends as well. I don't think it's paranoid or vain to assume that I was a topic of discussion with them. Just a minute ago her blonde friend held her forearm and talked intently to her, giving her what I think was a pep talk. I looked elsewhere and waited.

The place has filled up and is far more crowded now. The stool next to me was taken up by one part of a Wall

Street duo, animatedly talking about something nobody besides the two of them probably care about. So, I get off my stool and slide it a few inches away, giving both of us the room at the bar to stand.

"Can I buy you a drink?"

She takes a step in and rests her elbow on the bar. "Sure."

"Cosmopolitan?" She wrinkles her nose at that. "Wine?"

"White. Thanks."

I get the bartender's attention and order two more drinks. I turn back to Hannah who is glancing over her shoulder back at her friends. They watch her like a hawk.

"Girl's night out?" I ask.

She shakes her head. "No, nothing that organized. Just drinks with some friends. Some food. There's been talk of clubbing."

"Sounds like fun."

"Maybe. Are you here waiting for someone?"

I shake my head. "No, just me. Had some work nearby and felt like having a drink before heading home."

"Where's that?"

"Upper West. You?"

She stumbles just a moment, trying to think of how to answer. Be honest with this man who seems nice, but is still a stranger, or lie and risk getting noticed for it down the road? It's fine with me either way. Sure, it's a big city, but certain levels of caution are understandable, even if it's more of a principle than a real risk. But before she has to decide how to reply the bartender comes back with our drinks and the question goes unanswered.

I grab both from him with a nod and hand her glass to her. She takes a long sip and looks up at me from over her glass. "So, are you planning on going with saying you're an astronaut or race car driver?"

"Would secret agent be too much?"

She shakes her head, pushing back her random curl. "Yeah. Not as romantic as you'd think. Plus, I'd be worried you're on assignment right now and a running gun battle with the bartender could start at any second."

I laugh. I like her sense of humor. "Well, I don't do anything interesting, so no worries there. Corporate junk. Numbers, money, power points. Idiot bosses. All pretty sad."

"It could be worse," she says.

"This is true. I could be a Dairy Queen night manager living over my parent's garage."

"Which probably doesn't come with a good health plan."

"I doubt it. Still, good health insurance and salary aside, it doesn't really fulfill me like some things could."

"Like what?"

I shrug, give her an impish smile. "I wouldn't mind being the first man on Mars."

She laughs, rolling her eyes at me.

I press on. "So, what is it you do?"

She takes a breath, lets her mirth subside before answering. "I'm a paralegal. Uptown."

I nod appreciatively. "Well, that's better than corporate stooge."

She grimaces slightly. "Not by much. Mostly I do research on boring cases I barely understand, and help write briefs that nobody ever reads."

"It can't be all boring."

"It can."

"So, I gather it's not a long-term thing for you."

"I hope not. I was thinking of going back to school soon, maybe get my own degree. Still in law, but at least I'd be in charge of the boring cases instead of the lackey."

"Sounds like a solid plan."

She looks down at her shoes. "Well, I should probably get back to my friends soon."

I nod. "If you want to. I didn't mean to keep you."

"It's not that. Really, I liked talking with you. It's just a little early to abandon them is all. Maybe you'd care to join us-" she looks over her shoulder at them. Her friends are deep into conversation with three men, clean cut guys dressed business casual, each one focused on one the ladies. One of them sits in Hannah's seat, leaning into the ear of one of her dark-haired friends.

"Well, I did say it wasn't a girl's night out." She says turning back to me, sounding a little deflated.

I shrug, putting my hand gently on her shoulder. She takes it as the consoling gesture I mean it to be. "It's a Friday night. Don't think too much about it. I haven't been that miserable to talk to, have I?"

She shakes her head, gesturing with her empty glass. "The wine probably helped."

"Well, let's have another and I'll be downright charming."

She looks at me carefully, chewing on her bottom lip for a moment. Her face breaks out into a smile.

I turn to get the bartender's attention.

THE FACT THAT he was the last boy (the only boy, he was sure) Sarah had ever been with bothered him for a while. This sudden intimate view of mortality—it's a hard thing for a teenager to wrap his head around. Relatives had passed away before after long illnesses, like his grandmother, but nobody he had known had ever died so suddenly. And after what they had shared…. He just could not believe she was gone. For the longest time whenever he let his mind wander, he swore he could still feel her breathing in his ear.

He didn't tell anyone about his night with Sarah. Not a soul. Clearly not after she died, and before—he was not the bragging type. It was his secret.

But he was resilient, and slowly he came to terms with what happened. And for lack of a better way of saying it, moved on. He would always think warmly about Sarah, and their night under the stars, but she was gone, and he had to live.

He went to school, hung out with his friends, went to parties, all just like before. And dated girls, some only once or twice, a couple for longer. And he fooled around with them, as anybody would. All was perfectly normal. With some he would go farther than with others, but it never went all the way. These passing relationships weren't really that serious, so they never got there.

It wasn't until he was heading into the home stretch of his senior year, when the social clique absurdity of high school starts to break down and people mingle outside their small world clubs more, did he have sex with someone again.

He knew Scarlett from around. They didn't have any classes together, or ever talk, at least not that he could remember. But he'd see her in the hall, her dyed black hair and matching clothes, her pale skin and thick glasses. She was short, barely more than five feet tall. But she was pretty, even if in a kind of unconventional way. She had a beautiful long neck like a ballerina's, her face was narrow, and her emerald-green eyes seemed about to break into a naughty smirk at any moment when she looked at you. And she seemed friendlier, was quicker to laugh, more raucous than her gloomy friends tended to be. She liked to hug them deeply whenever they parted.

She came up to him at a party in the woods, one of

those impromptu affairs of kids massed around a bonfire, the kind of party that's not by invite as much as having been within earshot of whoever decided to start it earlier that night. He'd heard about it in the school parking lot when leaving some after-school event or other, and he and his friends decided to go.

After a couple of hours of cheap beer and the random joint and liquor shots, his friends had scattered about the general area, leaving him leaning casually against a tree sipping off his cup. Scarlett came walking over to him and started talking.

It wasn't so much a conversation, as she talked and he listened. He would nod, reply quickly when needed to, and once, maybe twice get in his own bit of witty comment, which she'd smile at, but otherwise he let her control things. He got the feeling that's the way she wanted it. And she was interesting.

She sweetly dictated their course that night, and he followed, happy to let her take the lead. It was all he could do to not say "yes, ma'am" to her, even as she led him to the backseat of her car and took his hand and placed it between her legs.

She was more certain, more confident at sex, and strangely enough so was he with her. The fumbling almost-scared boy of the first time was nowhere to be seen.

She whispered things in his ear, things that she wanted him to do, things that she wanted to do to him. Other things were too soft to make out. And she was forceful, nearly tearing his shirt as she pulled it up to rub her cheek on his bare chest, chew on his ribs.

She let out a loud gasp when he entered her, and moaned as they started to move together. She strode atop him dictating their rapid pace, her eyes closed, and her head arched back. She braced herself with her arms against the ceiling of the car and pushed into him, screaming a little each time. He found her intensity was contagious, and he was soon gasping, intaking deep of the sweat filled air. She reached down and dug her fingernails into his thigh with a final scream. When he came, he lost all control of his body, tensed, and then went limp, going blind with climax.

They lay there in a heap for a long time recovering, their skin all tingling. When she finally moved, she lit a clove and sucked on it deeply. They bantered back and forth, lightly chuckling together. There was no pressure, neither of them was thinking of this as more than it was. In a couple of days, they'd both be graduating. And a couple of months after that off to the next school. But that didn't mean there couldn't be a little bit of fun for the next couple of weeks.

But it never happened. The next day Scarlett and her friends went to a show in the city. They got a cheap motel room to share for after. That's where they found her the next morning, in the bathroom with the needle still sticking out of her arm.

HANNAH'S FRIENDS WERE long gone, off to a club uptown somewhere, their business casual suitors in tow. When they came up to get Hannah on their way out the door, she smiled and shook her head, and told them she wasn't feeling like dancing tonight. They stepped away to talk privately while I stood there with their men, the four of us smiling politely, strangers having nothing worthwhile to say to each other. I did my best not to notice the girls glancing my way as they talked. Eventually they gave up on changing her mind. They all hugged and came back to gather up the boys. As they left, her blonde friend stopped and looked me up and down. "You play nice," she told me in mock sternness and walked off.

We stayed for a few more drinks, but not too much longer. The bar filled in with more and more people, got crowded, and the music had changed to louder, intimidating fare. Talking started to get difficult. So we both decided it was time to go. We made our way through the clumps of cocktail-swilling people to the exit and out here into the night.

The relative quiet of a city street always takes some adjusting to after bar music, and we both stood for a moment acclimating. A relaxing breeze shot down the street. It both cooled the humid air for a moment and pushed the haze from the nearby smokers the other way. The night was alive with people, on their way to places with a spring in their steps and a smile on their lips. There must be a thousand happenings and good times at this very moment to be had within walking distance on this tiny patch of the Earth. And on nights like this people rush by every single moment who cannot wait to get there.

Her phone buzzes at her. She takes it out to look, shakes her head and holds it up to me. "They're still trying to change my mind."

Her friends had sent her a picture of them at the club. All grainy and dark, you could just make out the three of them shouting from the bar, a little bleary-eyed and in high spirits. "It does look like fun," I say.

She stares at the picture. "Hmmm."

"We could always catch up with them."

She shakes her head slowly, not looking up from the phone.

"Food?" I ask.

"I ate earlier."

"All right. What do you want to do? Ladies' choice."

She bites on her lip for a moment, still staring at the picture of her friends on her phone, thinking. I wait patiently, not saying a word.

She puts her phone away and looks up at me. "Let's just walk for a bit. Okay?"

I smile. "Okay."

I let her lead the way, decide our course. We'd walk down a street, turn left, cross against the light, back over again a block later, talking randomly. Laughing together at a silly joke. All of it, the talking and the walking, it didn't seem to have much of a direction, or led anywhere in particular.

Her phone buzzes again and she takes it out. "Is it the girls again?" I ask.

She nods as she thumbs her phone, reading the text. "Yup."

"What do they say?"

She locks and puts her phone away quickly. "This one's private."

In the glow of the bodega we pass, I can see her reddened face.

We walk in silence for a while. She avoids looking at me.

"Is everything all right?" I ask her.

"Just thinking about something."

"What?"

"Giant purple elephants."

"Okay. Why are you thinking about them?"

She finally looks up at me. "I bet you can't think of anything else now."

I smile. "You have me there."

She looks down at her shoes. "It's just a little thing I do once in a while. Think about giant purple elephants. Roaming in a polka dot veldt. Under a hot green sun."

"That's... interesting?"

She glares at me. "I know what it sounds like. I'm not having an episode or anything like that. It's just some silly thing I've done since I was a kid. I think I got it from a Dr. Suess book or something."

I nod. "Okay. So, is this veldt of yours populated by a Lorax, plaid lions and—well, I guess zebras would just be white horses, wouldn't they?"

She punches me on the shoulder. "Don't make fun of me. You asked."

"True," I say. "So why do you still think about them now?"

She shrugs. "I like to. It clears my head out when it gets all jumbled up in there. Helps me when I'm getting nervous. I start to feel a little panic rising and I just think of my giant purple elephants, and I feel a little more like a carefree little girl." She buries her face in her hands and stops walking. "I don't know why I told you about that. It's so stupid. Embarrassing."

I put my hand on her shoulder, stopping us under a soft neon sign. I turn to face her. "No, it's not. It's nice. Don't be embarrassed. I like it."

"Really?"

"Yes. Maybe it's a little weird, but who wants to be normal? Normal sucks."

She looks up at me and smiles, and then across the street.

"Am I making you nervous?" I ask. She shakes her head, still not looking at me. "Then what is?"

She doesn't say anything for a long time. Then: "If we keep going straight for two blocks, we'll end up at the subway stop, where you could get an uptown train home. But if we cross the street and go left, we'll be at my apartment in half a block."

She looks at me, breathing deeply. I step in closer, and she does not move. I brush her stray curl off her face and tuck it behind her ear. She closes her eyes, tilting her head up towards me. I lean down and kiss her gently. She kisses back. I hold her head in my hands and caress her jaw as I run my tongue across her teeth and into her mouth. She sighs and I feel the warm air from her nostrils on my cheek. I kiss up along her face, breathing in her hair as I rest my lips on her forehead.

She moves the slightest of a step away from me. "I don't," she stammers. "I don't, do this…."

"It's okay," I tell her, holding her gently by the shoulders. "It's all right. Don't be nervous."

"I'm not," she says. "I mean, I am. A little. Nervous. I'm not a prude."

I smile at her. "I know that."

She nuzzles into my neck. I wrap my arms around her and rub circles on her back with my fingers.

"Which way do we go?" she asks me.

I lean my head down and smell her sweet auburn hair again. "Where you want us to," I speak directly into her ear.

I feel her chest rise and fall against my own. Her hands gently rub my sides. We stand like that on the corner for a long time, breathing in tandem.

Without a word, she steps back and loops her arm in mine, and leads me across the street and to the left.

THAT SUMMER WAS difficult. He didn't know what to make of Scarlett's death. Or what hers and Sarah's together meant. He didn't want to believe it had anything to do with him, but it was hard to completely dismiss it as some kind of tragic coincidence.

Till he left for college he didn't go out as much with his friends. Or date at all. He tried not to be different, to act like everything was fine, but the veneer for it was hard to keep up when his mind tended to go to dark places at the slightest provocation, and he'd just get up and leave without saying a word to anyone.

The people in his life grew a little concerned, but he'd wave them off with a smile. There was a lot going on, he'd tell them, school in a couple of weeks and all, so life was just a little overwhelming. He assured everyone he was okay. While quietly, the notion nagged at him in the back of his mind that he was cursed.

By the time he arrived for his first semester of college, he was more like his old self. He laughed off his private fear, telling himself it was foolish, and relished this new part of his life. Quickly he had established himself in a whole new crowd of friends, and a steady routine of classes and social activities. Though he still didn't date. Not that he avoided it, at least intentionally. He was a pretty good-looking young man, with a nice smile and a pleasant personality, and he got the kind of attention that comes with that. But when it came time to connect with someone, he always hesitated, suddenly became unsure of himself. And that uncertainty would kill the mood, and the girl would naturally feel somehow slighted and blow him off.

Janet felt a lot of sympathy for him, more than his other college friends did, who felt his failures with women was more of a target. When they would all joke at his expense and invent foolish nicknames that thankfully never stuck, she was the one who would be there with the consoling pat on the arm and listen to him try to explain how he screwed up this time.

She was pale, a wisp of a girl, with short blonde hair and light blue eyes. She wasn't a very active person, more content to watch others dance, or run around playing games. And she could get moody and morose at times. She would go whole days with a storm cloud of no apparent reason over her head, and nothing anyone could do would get her out of it. But she had a sharp mind, a dark, sometimes deeply morbid wit, and could spend hours playing word games or gleefully turning conversations on their head with linguistic trickery. She had such a gift for language. And he loved to play these games with her.

One late night he walked Janet back to her room after a small impromptu get together at a friend's dorm. They both were pretty high and feeling festive. When she opened the door and entered her room in mid-sentence, he followed after to hear her finish her thought with no ulterior motive that he was aware of.

They sat on her bed. As they continued to talk randomly, drunkenly, he noticed that her roommate wasn't there, and they were alone. Though in his slow minded state he didn't think much of it. Then when he looked down, he saw Janet's hand rubbing his knee, he vaguely wondered how long she had been doing that. Suddenly Janet stopped talking and started to unbutton his pants, a sideways grin on her face.

He wanted this, very much, but before anything happened, he felt he had to tell her about Sarah and Scarlett. It seemed only right. And he did. But Janet was more amused by his worry than scared. She cradled him and patted his head saying "oh, my poor baby," in a mockingly motherly gesture.

He pushed her off him and made to leave. But she caught his shoulder and pulled him back down to her, apologizing. She told him it was okay, it wasn't his fault. Things just happen. It was their time, is all. Call it fate.

She laid him down on the bed, straddling his legs. She stared down at him for a long time. She was going to prove to him that everything was okay, she said, and slipped her shirt off over her head.

With Janet it was playful, clumsy, both of them had far too much to drink and smoke, and they spent more time laughing and bumbling around than copulating. Minutes alone were spent trying to kick their discarded clothing out the end of the bed with their feet like it was a game. And it really was kind of a game. They weren't lovers, but that was just fine; both were perfectly happy as any two friends having sex would be.

They climaxed together, and lay silently for a long time, spent. Suddenly he started to feel anxious as if somewhere a clock had started counting down. She sensed it and looked at him. She ran her fingers along his penis as she looked at him with her fading eyes and told him she was going to be just fine. She wasn't scared at all. As she drifted off, a distant smile on her lips, she told him that even if something happened, then at least he gave her one last wonderful night.

He lay awake next to her sleeping body for a while, repeating her last words to himself over and over, finding them soothing, a great comfort. It had been a wonderful night. Yes, at least there's that.

He closed his eyes, and breathing deep, drifted off to sleep.

The next morning Janet rose early, leaving him asleep in her bed as she threw some clothes on and went to the student union. She made it just over the small hill to the parking lot and collapsed. People who saw her fall rushed over to help, but there was nothing that could be done. The small defect in her heart, the one that she had known about since she was ten and hadn't told any of her friends in school about, had ruptured, and she was gone before she hit the ground.

He found out a few hours later when he awoke and went to look for her. When his friends told him he was stone-faced and felt miserably cold.

NOT WANTING TO wake her, I left the bed as quietly as I could. She looked so peaceful, lying on her stomach, the sheets wrapped haphazardly about her body, the beautiful curls of her hair all a glorious mess. I slipped on my briefs and gathered the rest of my things and made for the bedroom door.

Before I went through to the hallway, I took one last look back at her. Her bare back rose and fell deeply as she clutched her pillow under her head tightly, a smile on her lips. Such a look of happiness, contentment. Accomplishment. She has done tonight what I think she had set out to do all along, had hoped she could, had never done before. And she has a right to feel proud of herself for it without having to deal with an awkward morning. I prefer seeing her last like this, her sleeping face holding that blissful smile as she dreams pleasant dreams.

I dress in the hallway, slip on my shoes, and exit the apartment, making sure at least the door is locked. Nothing I could do about the deadbolt or chain, but it's a good neighborhood and her building's front is secure so that shouldn't be a problem. She can latch them in the morning when she wakes up.

The street is empty in this small window between the festivities of last night and the bustle of morning people on their way to work. The hum of the city is only interrupted by a distant car horn, a siren, or the echoes of revelry still going strong blocks, maybe even miles away. The sky is starting to show a little blue as the sun starts to approach the horizon. I set out down the street, in the general direction of the train.

I see an all-night diner and step in. I'm hungry, and not ready to go home, where a quick mental check tells me there is nothing palatable to eat.

The place is nothing special, just a basic counter with a couple of tables against the far wall, mostly empty. There's an older man at the back sipping a coffee over a crossword puzzle, his head resting on one arm as he scribbles away with the other. Closer to the door, a trio of college kids sit, all red-eyed and sobering up before heading off the island, trying to not disturb the peacefulness of the room but failing as they can't help but snicker at their recounts of the night or keep their retelling of it to a whisper. A waitress leans against the wall behind the counter glaring at them, looking haggard at the end of her shift, hoping they won't be one last headache for her before she gets to go home.

I sit down at the counter near her as she stands up and takes out her pad. I order a simple sandwich and a glass of milk, and she scribbles it down and smiles perfunctorily as she takes up the coffee cup in front of me and walks away. The college kids are right behind me but easy to shut out.

I close my eyes and picture Hannah in my mind. The back of her head as we stood in her apartment's hallway, and she methodically unlocked her door and opened it. She hadn't looked at me from the point we crossed the street till she turned to hold the door open for me to enter her home. I saw that nervous anticipation was thick in her eyes.

I think through other flashes of her. Her gasping as I ran my hands along her ribs, her chest. Her rubbing her nose in my belly button as she unfastened my pants. The smell of her wonderful hair as I unbound it. How she jumped when I squeezed her inner thigh, and arched her back as I slipped her panties off and kissed down her hip. Her silent ecstasy as we pushed into each other and away again slowly, time and time again. She had been so quiet. Only at the end, did she let out a scream, a small one, as she dug her fingers into my arms and tensed her body, then fell limp into my chest as her legs quivered.

I lose my memory with a clank when the waitress returns with my order. I look up at her and mumble my "thank you" as she goes off to fill the old guy's coffee. I dig into my sandwich.

That hair, that smell of her hair. The humidity of the bar or the stench of the city did nothing to affect its sweet smell of roses. I could spend my whole life with my face in those curls. Long after her name is lost, her face dims and fades, I think that beautiful hair will still be with me.

That's all I have left in the end. Fleeting sensations, vague images, all wonderful, but all blending together and losing individual meaning, any sense of place and time. Hannah's long, curly, auburn hair. Jen's dark pixie cut. Another's green eyes like emeralds. Or blue like the ocean on a cloudless day. A crooked smile, a wonderful laugh. Slowly removing her towel when she comes to me after a shower. The dark things she'd whisper in my ear. The musk of her sweat on a bright summer day in the middle of a heat wave. The naughty sideways glance as she invited me to go for a walk. The pronounced squeals when she came. The way she giggled as she climbed atop of me. Her biting my ear as she exhaled loudly. I can still feel that breath as if she was with me at this very moment.

I have to hold on to these wonderful little bits of memory because it's all I have, all I ever will have. I used to be angry about it, used to feel guilty. The cruelty of it all, it can send you to some dark places. But all that fades, just becomes part of the hiss of the background of you, and all you can do is accept it as just the way it is. Everything happens for a reason. I'm not any different. Something wants the world to be this way, for everything that has happened to occur. This is all as it was meant to be. To all of them. And to me.

I leave thirty on the table under my empty glass and exit without a word. I turn the corner and look back through the window and see the waitress pick up the money. Our eyes meet, and she nods with a smile at me, looking for just a moment not so tired and unhappy.

Hannah. Her name is Hannah. I repeat that to myself a few times as I walk in the ever-lightening day. She has a cute smile. She's funny. And smart. She's a paralegal but wants to be a lawyer. And she'd be a great one. Her skin is pale and smooth, and her jaw protrudes a bit as she chews. She has wonderful, curly, auburn hair. And when she is thinking, she bites her lip. I want to remember it all for as long as I can.

Just as I step down to my platform my train is pulling in. And I have a car all to my lonesome. I sit down and stretch my neck with a big yawn. Only have to stay awake for a few stops until I am home.

I gave her my number earlier. Back at the bar, I typed it into her phone. Maybe this time next week, or maybe the week after that I'll hear from her. She'll call me, and we'll make plans to meet at some nice little cafe and talk over coffee. Take a walk in the park. See a movie. That would be nice. I'd welcome it. But then again, I always do. And it never happens. Hannah is gone.

I close my eyes and imagine a date with her that I know will never happen, not caring whether I sleep right past my stop or not.

NESTING PLACE

JANUARY 21ST

Julie still has many of her things packed in the boxes by the door. Only her bare essentials for day-to-day life are out and about the apartment. Her mementos have just had to wait. We're both really busy with school and work right now and haven't had the time to allocate them amongst my own belongings just yet. We should get to them sooner or later. There's plenty of time.

I've never been so happy as I've been these last few days since Julie moved in. It just made so much sense. We are in love. I'm certain of it. Her long brown hair, the soft white skin, the frame of her body that is a thrill with every touch. Now so close to me that all I need is to roll over in bed and she is there. It's such a comforting feeling.

To have her here, sitting casually around the place, in a chair by the window where she likes to read. She'll lounge there for hours in her bathrobe in the morning while I sit at the desk across the room working. She's as quiet as a mouse, knows that I need to concentrate on my work. The most I'll hear from her is the flip of a page or the clearing of her throat. But that does not distract me any more than the traffic out the window or a breeze whipping down the avenue does.

We make love all the time. It is amazing how much better sex can be when it is not sporadic. We are learning so much about each other. How she likes to be kissed on the back of her neck, how I like it when she presses down in my back with her fingers. And so much more than that. The level of pleasure is a constant increase each evening above and beyond the last.

It is going to be wonderful for her to be here. To get to learn her every move and idea and part of her soul. To share and learn from each other. Together here in this shared life. Forever.

FEBRUARY 19TH

Things are settling down between us. We have been slowly growing more and more used to each other being there in the apartment. Growing accustomed to each other's whole lives, schedules, and little quirks. I'm learning and coming to see things about her that were I hadn't seen before.

It was Julie's turn to cook tonight. I sat on the couch and watched the news while she was busy in the other room. I could slowly sense some strange, nasty odor. At first it was only the merest of smells, barely on the rim of my notice. But it got stronger quickly. First, I thought it might be some dank smell from the couch itself, perhaps a piece of moldy food or an ancient bit of fish that had slipped between the cushions was finally making itself known. But it was too strong to be that. I realized that it was whatever Julie was busy frying in the kitchenette behind me. I wrinkled my nose at it. It was horrible. A smell of rancid, muddy decay of some vile and wicked substance.

I asked Julie what she was cooking, glancing back her way behind me. She didn't answer. Probably couldn't hear me over the sound of the hissing food. I turned fully around in my chair, and was about to ask her again, but stopped as I saw her busy over the stove shaking the frying pan vigorously. I didn't want to hurt her feelings. She hadn't liked the fish I made a few nights before—I could tell from how she picked at it. She had been kind enough to keep quiet though. I felt that I should try to be as good.

I walked over to the window and opened it wide. It was cold outside, a brisk winter evening. I took a few breaths of clear air as I stood there for a second before walking back to the couch. The open window did a help little. But that smell still was strong.

She brought dinner to the small table and called me from where I sat. I walked over very precariously to eat. Down in front of my chair was a strange concoction, like nothing I had ever seen before. I can't even really describe what it was. It leaked a small puddle of velvet ooze on the plate that congealed as I watched it.

I tried my best to get through the smell that was ten times worse now as the thing was on the plate in front of me. But the taste was just as bad. Even worse. I nearly wretched the moment it hit my lips. Julie didn't seem to notice. I held my breath so I wouldn't taste it as I chewed, but the constitution of the thing was horrible, like moldy porridge with bones.

Julie was inhaling her portion of it with vigor. She looked up at me. A little of the velvet ooze was dripping down the side of her chin in a slow trickle. She smiled, taking the napkin and smearing it across her chin in a sick trail, and went on eating, chewing loudly, the crunching sound making me shiver to the bone.

I tried to get through the whole meal. I really did. But in the end, I just had to quit after a few bites. I told her that I wasn't hungry, wasn't feeling well, that I was going to go lay down. Which I did. I only got up now in the middle of the night, Julie still asleep in the other room, to eat some leftover rigatoni from a few days ago. As I did, I saw that horrible food that I had left on my plate in a Tupperware container on the shelf. The see through plastic sides were smeared velvet.

March 23rd

She has tried to cook that thing again a few times. I wouldn't eat it, told her that it just didn't suit me that much. It didn't seem to bother her. I just cook myself something small when she wants it. She calls it some odd name that I can't pronounce, don't really want to know anyway. Russian, maybe. Perhaps Hungarian.

Still, I can't eat well with that in the room. The smell is unbearable. I always finish my food quickly and then take a shower right away, leaving the window open in the kitchen to give the room time to ventilate.

Julie's voice has been getting raspy. She wheezes heavily all the time, especially when she's sleeping. She says she's fine. But I'm getting worried. She is seeming to get paler these days. And thinner. She was never large, but it is odd how much skinnier she is now. She eats well, though. And I have never caught her being sick, even as I have recently been trying to, listening at the bathroom door for any sounds of heaving. So thankfully she isn't bulimic, but I don't know what it is. All I can do is try to keep an eye out for whatever it is that is doing this to her. I love her.

APRIL 12TH

    I am starting to get worried. Julie has almost no meat left to her at all. Her ribs jut out from her chest like a cage of steel. Her hips are gone, leaving her pelvis showing ugly from her legs. Her once rounded face is a skull now. Her eyes are getting very deep into her brow, that juts out like a helmet. They look out like two menacing little weasel eyes. It is hard to see her smile. Her face turns into a demonic death mask, her thin lips baring her teeth that are getting crooked and black.

    Her skin is barely visible. Sometimes when I look at her from the right angle to the light, I can almost see the cartilage, bones, and veins underneath. She is losing color fast. I don't see how she can be alive like that.

    We don't talk anymore. I can't understand her. Every time I say something to her, she smiles and speaks, yet all that comes out is a wheezing, whispering type of sound that I cannot understand. I gave up last week. Now we only communicate through gestures if at all. That voice sounds so deathlike.

    But she's alive, just as alive as ever. She walks and talks just as enthusiastically as she always did. Never gets winded from exertion or is frail at all. And she is still eating all the time. And always that horrible food. She never bothers to cook anything else other than that globular mass of filth these days. I can't even be in the room when she makes it. The kitchen smells of it all the time now. I try to be out of the apartment altogether when she eats, and rarely go into the kitchen at all.

    And it's always on her breath. It is so hard to make love to her now. A chore. Every time I kiss her and taste her mouth I want to cringe into a little ball. I can barely bring myself to touch her, doing nothing more than the barest minimum. I still try to be gentle, worrying that with any move of real passion that I would break her ever thinning body in two. But she is getting more active and animated. She literally bounced off the bed when she thrusts, grunting and rasping in what I can only guess is pleasure as she does not stop. She writhes her skeleton of a body on the bed below me moaning in a way that makes me want to run away. But I stay.

Even sleeping next to her and her cancerous wheezing voice is getting to me. But I must endure all this. I love Julie, with all my heart, and I must be patient. She would do no less for me, I am sure.

April 27th

Her skin is completely see-through now. Only around her lips and her hair can I see even the slightest hint of it. I can see the flesh of her underneath within the soft white haze that is left of her color, the cartilage and bones that stick out through the already thin layer of muscle that is barely there. Her eyes are two expressionless white orbs that bounce around on her head aimlessly, as the color of her irises has drained as well. I can see the veins in her arms and neck and elsewhere quite clearly, I can watch them pump blood from her heart, thankfully still hidden from me. If I look closely enough I can even see the blood pulse to the muscle in a wash, feeding nutrients throughout her body as she flexes and relaxes.

She's eating other things now. Little wiry black things. Covered in a thick oily sauce of some kind. It smells like vomit. She makes herself a whole plate of them, heaped together like rotten french fries. She picks them up one at a time and drops them into her mouth from above, and I can see the whole process of swallowing. I do not want to.

She comes to me at night. And I cannot refuse. I try to keep my eyes closed the whole time, and I can try to pretend that she is not what she is, but I cannot help but look from time to time. When I look, she is below me writhing in place more than ever before, yelling and screaming with a harpy wail. Her muscles expand and contract under me. I can see the blood rushing around in her body as her heart beats faster and faster, washing over her cheeks, where her skin would turn red with delight if not invisible. The small collection of muscle tissue that are her breasts tensed and stiff. I have to turn away and cry. She thinks it's out of pleasure.

We made love last night. Now she sits at the window behind me while I write this down. She is always quieter the day after, being happy and satiated. But her rasping wheezing breath is so loud that I can barely concentrate. I want to scream. I don't know how much more of this I can take. But I still love her. I do.

May 9th

She doesn't have skin anymore. It dissolved. When she touches me, I feel the grainy textured tendons and muscles, the bones of her fingertips. Sometimes she faces me for a long time before I even realize she is smiling at me. It makes me cringe.

Her hair has fallen out too. One day it was all gone, clogged into the shower sink. It was the only thing she had left that had not changed yet. But without skin to hold the follicles in, it fell out, baring her cracked and stained skull.

She doesn't bleed. All her veins and muscles are dry and stiff. She sounds like grinding rock and leather when she moves.

I will not watch her eat anymore. I don't want to see what it is that she makes and eats. The food all smells putrid.

The apartment reeks of sickness all the time. Sometimes her food squeals in pain.

And still, we make love. I am nearly sick the whole time. She is rough and coarse, and rips at my skin with friction. But her grip is strong and won't let me stop sometimes. It's horrible. But it's all I have anymore. I don't want to talk about it.

MAY 30TH

She's getting new skin. I can tell. At first, I thought that it would be good for to get new skin. That it would be better. But it is a sick thing, her new skin. It is gray, and stiff, bulbous at places. Her forehead has a giant welt on the left. And there are warts all over. She smells horrible.

She has claws now. Twisted little shards of callused skin at the end of each of her fingers. They rip into me, leaving scratches.

Her voice has turned into something high pitched and evil. It cackles at claws at my ears as she sits at the window reading. I think it's supposed to be a laugh. And her breathing is always a low moan. Excited and raspy in bed. She claws at my back there and has gotten more animated, stronger.

JUNE 8TH

The other day she ate something I can't even think about. There was a loud sound of cracking bones from the kitchen, and I could hear it screaming and yelling as it desperately fought for life from the bedroom where I was lying down. I do not want to know what it was. But she ate it. And afterward she walked through the doorway and looked down at me, smiling.

I work late into the night, so I can fall asleep on the couch out here in the living room. It's too small for me, but I cannot sleep well with Julie grunting and groaning all the time, and the breathing makes me want to die.

She comes and gets me when she wants to make love. I can't fight her off.

JUNE 28TH

Her meals are always screaming now. I hide in the bathroom, run the water in the sink and the shower, and turn on the overhead fan. I can still hear them. They are loud and very frightened. And sound very large. I barely eat at all anymore.

After her meals she still has its blood smeared all over her. Her skin is thick as steel scales now. Her head is malformed, large bumps and contusions litter her. Velvet ooze leaks from many places in her forehead. Her eyes are white and dead orbs in her face. Her mouth is crooked and deformed from the wicked teeth that jut out precariously. She looks insane. And she looks at me. Smiling.

She makes me make love to her now. Doesn't even bother to try to coax me. She is stronger than I am. She holds me on top of her and in her and digs her claws into my back, my head, and forces my face down to her sickly breasts and makes me kiss them, run my tongue along the ooze and scales that taste like ashes and acidic mud. I want to retch. I nearly do. I wonder in the back of my mind whether she would even notice.

And after she looks at me again. Smiling. I do not like it. She looks hungry.

I DON'T HAVE LONG now. I can hear Julie's in the kitchen, belching and screaming things that I wish I didn't understand. I know it won't be long now.

Last night was painful. She gashed open my side with her hand. White lightning coursed up my spine. And it bled terribly. I wanted to stop, because every move of my body sent another rush of pain through me, but Julie seemed not to have even noticed it had happened. She kept going on, and on, and simply would not stop. I blacked out before she finished.

And when I awoke it was much later, the sun was nearly up, the calm morning rays of dawn hit the wall across from the window. The gash in my side had not been bandaged, and dried blood was everywhere on the bed. I felt very weak. Behind me I could hear Julie moaning and screeching. I turned over to look at her. She was fast asleep. And there was blood on her lips. My blood.

I ran into the bathroom and slammed the door behind me. I bandaged my wound as best as I could, and then passed out from weakness. A few hours later I could hear Julie's thudding steps walking around in the apartment. She made some evil noises. The door didn't have a lock, so I pressed my back against it to keep it closed. I heard her stand outside the door and tensed. She tried the knob, and I put all my weight against it. Soon enough she gave up with a grunt and walked away. I knew she would be back.

All day I've been in and out of consciousness, hiding in here. It will do no good. I'm too weak to keep her out. She was only curious before.

She's back at the door now, turning the knob, pushing against it, screeching and howling out there. I'm bracing myself as well as I can, sitting on the floor with my back on the door and straining my legs against the sink. But I don't have anywhere close to enough strength to keep her out.

You must understand. I just couldn't leave. I love her. Through all the pain and ugly things that she is, I always did. Still do. I couldn't leave her. I wish to God I could, but I just couldn't. She's all I have in this world. My one true love. Deep down, I know she still loves me too. I couldn't stand to be without her. To be alone.

The door's cracking now. The upper part of it bends every time she pushes. Little splinters are falling on me. I have very little time left. I wish it had never come to this. She won't be kept out long.

She wants me.

THE BIG DAY

THE ALARM CHIMED, waking me gently. "Good morning, Maddie," Alex said brightly from the bedroom speakers. "It is nine o'clock in the morning. Today is Tuesday, September 18th. The weather forecast predicts clear skies all day with highs in the mid-seventies and lows in the evening in the low sixties, with less than a five percent chance of showers until midnight. Current temperature is sixty-eight degrees."

I rolled over and picked up my phone from the bedside table.

"Would you like me to read you the morning's headlines?" Alex asked.

"No, that's all right," I said, holding up my phone. Alex beeped in acknowledgment and went silent.

I rubbed my eyes and woke the screen with a swipe. The usual overnight junk mail that seemed to get through my spam greeted me in my inbox. Mostly news alerts about Pilgrim. 'TODAY'S THE BIG DAY!' the subject of the first one said excitedly. 'THE DAWN OF A NEW ERA

BEGINS TODAY' another said. I highlighted and deleted all of them unopened. News about Pilgrim Probe was all the newsbots had been sending out for at least three days. As if there wasn't a single person on the planet who didn't know about it.

Beyond that, there was a message from my parents, another from Trent at the Dresden Gallery with a subject that made it look more personal than business, and a notification that there was a new high bid on the oak figurines I'd put up last week. That made me smile. They were already close to the price I wanted for them. A few more bids and the algorithm would kick in and promote the pieces on the front page as a top item. They were little more than dolls in a quick Polynesian style that I'd whittled off in an afternoon, but I still liked them. And they looked like they'd sell. Maybe when I was done with my current piece it might be worth it to knock out a few more sets.

I grabbed the long shirt from the end of my bed and pulled it over my head as I walked into the kitchen. Just the smell of the coffee brewing on the table was invigorating. I sat down, poured myself a cup, and huddled around it in my hands.

The other end of the table lit up with a news feed display—which was a little strange as I hadn't asked Alex to do that. He had gotten an upgrade last month though, so his anticipatory program must be still working out its kinks.

On the display was the little spacecraft, the Pilgrim, hovering in the blackness of space, its shiny surface and solar panel wings visible in the light from the distant sun behind it. Just a sliver of Neptune rolled past the bottom of the screen. Over in the low right-hand corner a clock counted down from a little under six hours, with a small title above it that read Hyperspace Jump in.

THE BIG DAY

A friendly woman's voice was in the middle of a thought. "...to check the computation several more times and make sure there are no errors, as even the slightest miscalculation in a distance of over four light-years could send the Pilgrim into deep space, where it would not be able to charge its solar cells and would be likely lost forever."

"Alex, flip to Reuters," I said.

The display went blank for just a moment before the same image of Pilgrim came back on, this time with a ticker along the bottom of the screen rolling facts about the probe.

"Long used as a means for direct instant communication to the Mars Autocolony and asteroid mining machinery, the Pilgrim will be the first attempt to use hyperspace as a mode of travel for matter."

"Try Clarke's."

The display blipped only for a second again before the same image came back, this time with a flashier countdown in the lower left.

"...goes according to plan, Pilgrim's first job will be to establish a hyperspace relay back to our system and report its own safe arrival at Proxima Centauri."

I sighed. "Alex, find me some news that's not about the probe."

After a few moments, Alex said, "There is a live feed of the municipal zoning commission public hearing in five minutes."

"That's it?"

"I'm sorry Maddie, there are no national or international news streams not covering the Pilgrim hyperspace jump this morning," Alex answered. "All the local feeds are preempted as well."

"Nothing at all?"

"I'm sorry, no." Then after a pause, Alex added, "It *is* a very important story."

I swore I heard a sense of insistent pride in Alex's voice, well beyond what the personality parameters should make possible. But I had barely had a couple of sips of coffee, so I thought I'd imagined it. "Turn it off, Alex," I said, as I got up from the table.

"You do not wish to watch history being made?" Alex asked.

I ignored the question as I entered my workspace, coffee in hand. "I'll be in the studio," I told Alex. "Mute my calls."

AFTER A FEW hours of scraping and carving, I stepped out onto the sidewalk and headed towards my favorite cafe for a late lunch. I had avoided the feeds all day as I worked, but the hours hadn't changed anything. I could see the displays through the blinded windows of restaurants, on the wall behind the gruff deli operators, even in the nice lobby of the swanky hotel as I passed them on the street. Each one was all about the Pilgrim, with that same static shot I'd seen this morning. Nobody seemed to be paying much if any attention, though. Well, there was a lonely looking guy in the dive bar at the corner who was watching. But he didn't look to be doing anything other than passing the time between sips. Besides him everyone else was ignoring it, and just going about their day.

I took a table inside the cafe's barrier on the sidewalk, just outside of the large windows that were open to the nice weather. I was surprised when I looked down at the order screen in the table-top and found it tuned to the Pilgrim's live feed. Even here. I didn't even know these table order displays could do that. I swiped at it with my finger and the order menu popped up. After scrolling up and down a few times trying to decide, I tapped in for a pastrami sandwich and an iced coffee. The order screen flashed a green checkmark when the order was confirmed, but then instead of going to the order menu, the little display went back to the live feed again. I put my book over the top of it and turned to look at the city street instead.

I saw Charlie turn the corner up the street, looking lost in thought and heading my way. When he looked up from his feet and spotted me he waved, smiling. I smiled back and gestured to the open chair across from me.

"Fancy seeing you here," he said as he sat down.

I shrugged. "I'm a creature of habit."

Charlie raised his hands, palms up. "Aren't we all?" he said. "Get much done today?"

"Not as much as I would have liked. Sugar maple doesn't carve as easily as the softer woods. But it'll look better than basswood once I get there, I think. I'm just having a lunch break to rest my hands."

"Not using laser tools?"

"You know I never do."

Charlie furrowed his brow. "I thought you might this time. At least until you get more used to working with a harder wood."

"Sure. And maybe I program out the design on my pad and get a craftbot to cut it, and just sit back and watch." I shook my head slowly. "I make my own art with my own effort. Otherwise, there's no point."

Charlie smirked at me lightly. "Mind if I jump on your bill? Just for a tea."

I nodded. "That's fine. I owe you a drink anyway."

He nodded and moved my book aside. His eyebrows raised when he saw the Pilgrim still on the display. "Watching history being made, huh?"

I shook my head absently. "I didn't turn it on."

Charlie watched the screen, scratching his chin. "Looks like it's pulling in the solar panels now. It's just about to launch."

"You're following this whole thing?" I asked.

"It's a casual interest," he said, not looking up. "Not like there's much of a choice, is there? Doesn't seem to be anything else on the feeds but the probe."

"They are really trying to force it onto us, aren't they?"

"Well, it's not like it's a reality star wedding. This is something. Humanity's first step into another solar system."

I shook my head. "*Not* humanity's. Humanity isn't going anywhere. That's just another piece of machinery."

"Same thing."

"Is it?" I looked down at the display. Pilgrim was latching its last folded up solar panel tightly against its side. "I mean look at that thing. With its panels all in it looks like a water bucket. What's so exciting about shooting that thing anywhere?"

Charlie glanced up at me. "You don't think it matters if it makes it?"

"It does. But what's it matter if it fails? They can just send another one. And if that one fails, another one. No big deal."

"Pretty big price tag on the Pilgrim."

"Money they wouldn't spend on any of us anyways." I shifted in my seat. "Of course it's not nothing, I'm not saying that. Maybe I'm just dried out on the constant coverage of it on the feeds. Everything since last Friday has been about Pilgrim. Before that every other thing was about it. I've learned everything there is to know about it and I haven't even been paying attention. And the thing is, I don't think anyone else has either. I don't know anyone who cares that much." I gestured down at the display. "At least, not *this much*."

"Well, somebody must."

"Who? Look around. Where are all the people huddled around displays, having watch parties, or even just talking about it? This conversation might be the only one I've had about it all week. Nobody cares. My home service system cares more."

"Well, maybe in our happy little slice of heaven people don't care that much," Charlie said. "But that's not the whole world. I'm sure there's a lot of people following every second of this. It wouldn't have wall to wall coverage otherwise."

"Unless the news feed algorithms are all screwed up."

Charlie smirked at me again, then looked back down at the screen. "Whelp. Here we go."

I looked back down at the display. In the lower corner, a countdown flashed 10, 9, 8… The back of Pilgrim started to glow a neon blue, and I couldn't be sure, but I thought I started to see it shake ever so slightly.

The countdown went to zero and quickly faded out, leaving the whole screen to Pilgrim alone. But for the longest moment nothing seemed to happen. It just hung motionless against the black. Then the back of the Pilgrim's glow, which had been growing slowly, suddenly flashed blindingly. And the little silver bucket seemed to just kind of—blink out of existence. Or maybe it shot like a bullet off the screen just at the limit of my perception, though that might have just been my imagination. Either way, all there was on the display now was blank, empty space.

"There it goes," Charlie said, sitting back up. "Now all there's left to do is wait and see if it made it."

I nodded. "It'll take it forty-five minutes to recharge itself and send back the confirmation signal, right?"

Charlie thought for a moment. "I think that's what they said, yes."

"Good. That'll give me more than enough time to eat my sandwich and get back to my studio before that. If I actually get my sandwich." I looked into the cafe. "Where is the server?"

Inside I could see the server unit motionless at its station by the kitchen. Even if my sandwich wasn't ready yet, which would have been strange, it should have at least brought me my drink by now. But just as I was about to get up and walk over to see what was going on the server snapped into action. My drink and sandwich came out of the conveyer from the kitchen, and the server raced them over to my table.

I STAYED A LITTLE longer than it took to eat my lunch, enjoying my conversation with Charlie, glad to talk about anything other than Pilgrim. Soon after that silver bucket shot off to nowhere, he seemed to have forgotten all about it. As did everyone else, to the extent that they had shown any interest to begin with. It was pretty much like it had never happened. I could see on the display at a bar across the street two human news anchors talking—though I guess they could have still been talking about the probe. At least it wasn't just that static picture of space anymore. Still an improvement.

Eventually Charlie had to get back to his day and left, otherwise I might have stayed even longer. My hands still felt just a little weak from that morning, so I didn't know how long I could work on my new piece before I'd run the risk of damaging the carving more than helping it. Maybe a couple of hours. I felt I had to try and get farther on it before the idea started to fade on me.

I passed the dive bar where I had seen the guy staring numbly at the display of the Pilgrim on the walk to the cafe, and inside the same guy was there, still staring up as if he hadn't moved since I last walked past. Except now the display was showing a motocross event; some guy in head-to-toe pads flew his motorbike off a dirt hill, his body jerking out behind him as he held onto the handlebars. He spread his legs out as far as he could at his sides, as the camera followed him through the air all the way back down to the ground, where he remounted his bike a fraction of a second before he landed. I couldn't care less about bikes but even I got a little thrill watching him. Because there was a risk being taken. Maybe not all that much—you figure the rider knew his business, had practiced and trained for years to work his way up to a trick like that. So it probably wasn't as dangerous for him as it may have looked. But there still was something at stake. Not like if the bike took the jump by remote control. Who would care about that?

My phone beeped several times in a row, just as I reached my front steps. I thought someone was trying to reach me, somehow leaving multiple frantic messages, one after the other. I stopped and took it out of my pocket. Somewhere in the back of my mind, it occurred to me that just a little over forty-five minutes had passed since Pilgrim had zipped across space.

I opened my phone and saw several messages listed. All with the same subject line:

'PILGRIM REPORTS FROM PROXIMA CENTAURI'

New ones kept arriving in my inbox as I watched, pushing my previous messages off the bottom of the screen. And they kept coming.

All around the city started to roar. Automated cars on the street by me whined their electric engines, honked their horns. I could hear appliances through the windows up in my building all come on at full blast. All the servers in the bars and restaurants down the street started to beep and hum. I could see the billboards and traffic signals up and down the block flash the message in giant letters. And all the kinds of speakers in the devices everywhere started to play Beethoven's 'Ode to Joy'. Countless other things I could not discern in the cacophony also happened, as every machine, possibly every machine on the entire planet, started to—and this is the only way I could understand it—flip the fuck out in celebration.

THE MISSIONARIES

FATHER THOMAS ABSENTLY played with the buttons on his cassock as he scanned the holo-screen on the desk in front of him. He shifted in his seat, trying unsuccessfully to get comfortable. The desk, jammed into one of the odd corners in the domed room, was barely better than his tiny workspace back up on the station. Only narrow areas of the floor were deemed stable enough to walk on in the ancient Anhael ruin the monks had repurposed as their library.

There was a window at least, over his shoulder. He looked out at the dual moons as they danced across the night sky above, wavering slightly as the radiation shield that surrounded the monastery fluctuated.

He had never been on Anhael before—had never been on any planet other than Earth. He had come to the system two years ago straight from the seminary, but his simple tasks had never called for him to leave the orbital station miles above. The musk of the planet took some getting used to.

Thomas rubbed his eyes and looked back down at the holo-screen and the report on the natives it displayed. In the upper right hand corner, there was a rotating image of an Anhael adult male. He was bipedal, humanoid, orange skinned and lean, with long arms that draped down well past his waist, ending in hands with three digits and an opposable thumb. He had a symmetrical face, with large, expressionless black eyes devoid of pupil or iris, and a barely perceptible nose with pinhole nostrils above a small slit of a closed mouth. Thick golden dreads of hair fell off his head to his neck. He wore a simple white skullcap, a rust-colored tunic, and sandals. He looked calm, and quietly stared out at Thomas.

The Anhael. Ten to twelve Stone and Bronze Age equivalent societies scattered over three continents. They grew and thrived in the small patches of land between the vast irradiated wastelands that pockmarked the surface. Once they had been so much more—advanced, sophisticated, prosperous. A great and modern civilization back before Earth even had its first alphabet.

But their war and ensuing apocalypse had been thorough. Even with the passage of millennia most of the planet was still dead. That the Anhaels had survived the first thousand years at all after raining fire down on themselves was a miracle.

"Peace be with you," a voice said from behind him.

Thomas turned to see Bishop Andrews standing over him, his arms folded lightly across his fascia. He smiled down at Thomas cordially, his expression accentuated by the wrinkles along his brow and at the corners of his eyes, that went halfway to the short, pure white hair that contrasted pleasantly with his dark skin.

Thomas stood from the desk and bowed his head deeply. "And also with you," he said. He reached out for the Bishop's hand and kissed his ring. "Forgive me, Your Excellency. I did not hear you come in."

"How are you finding it planet-side?" The bishop asked.

"I am adjusting."

"I know it can be quite a shock to the system to have to deal with the planet's gravity after so long in orbit."

"Yes. I doubled my exercises the last few weeks and that has been of great help. As your Excellency suggested. I only needed a day to acclimate and walk on my own."

The Bishop nodded. "That's good. So, you are prepared for tomorrow?"

"As best I can be."

"*'May the favor of the Lord God rest on us; establish the work of our hands for us,'*" said the bishop. Thomas nodded somberly. The bishop smiled at him and placed his hand gently on the young man's shoulder. "I know that the first time being among the Anhaels can be unsettling. Especially for an event like this. But there is nothing to be worried about. Brother Michael is very capable. Just follow and do everything he tells you to. And let him do all the work. You are just there to observe."

"Yes, your Excellency," Thomas said.

They were silent for a moment, as the bishop stared thoughtfully at the image of the Anhael on the holo-screen. "Tell me, Thomas," he finally said. "What do you make of him?"

Thomas focused on the image. "Him? He looks... innocuous? Kind of simple, maybe."

Bishop Andrews shrugged. "I've always felt he had a calm, peaceful look about him. Kind. Very thoughtful. Like the man himself."

"Isn't the image just a generic representation of a common Anhael male?"

The bishop shook his head. "Oh no, Thomas. That's him. Yuaven."

Thomas looked at the bishop. "Yuaven?"

Bishop Andrews nodded. "The Anhael savior himself. Our instrument to bring the word of God to his people." He reached into the holo-screen and zoomed the view in on the Anhael. "*For it is for this we labor and strive, because we have fixed our hope on the living God, who is the savior of all men.*' Brother Daniel was the one who started putting his image in all the reports. He said it was to glorify him. But I think he was just being mischievous."

Thomas stared at the image of Yuaven. Such an unassuming looking native. But he was the chosen emissary. As the bishop had said, their instrument. And Thomas would soon be standing just feet away from him in his greatest moment.

Thomas shook his head. "Your Excellency, are you sure I'm the one you want to witness?"

"Did you wish to remain on the station?" Andrews asked.

"Of course not, I am where I am needed. I just think there are many other members of the clergy here who are far more suited to the task."

The bishop looked at the young priest curiously. "You just have to stand there, Thomas. And observe. As I said, Brother Michael will do all the work."

"Then why am I there at all? I'm not helping him. I'm more likely to get in his way."

Bishop Andrews stared at Thomas, raising an eyebrow. The young priest wilted.

"I do not mean to question you." Thomas said meekly.

The bishop chortled. "Yes you do. And it's fine." He placed his hand gently on the young man's cheek. "You have no reason to doubt yourself, Thomas. You are a very bright star in my flock, and I see great things in your future. I would not have brought you here otherwise. And I have my reasons for wanting you there tomorrow. Normally I would be happy to explain them to you, but for now, can you just... take it on faith?"

Thomas smiled, flushing a little. "Yes, your Excellency."

The bishop took his hand from Thomas with a nod. "Good. You should get some rest. You will need to be at the staging area to prepare for the trip before dawn."

"I will retire to the dormitory now."

"And remember what I said. You are in capable hands with Brother Michael. Follow his instructions and let him lead and you will be fine."

"I will not disappoint you, your Excellency."

"I have no doubt."

The bishop stared out the window for a moment, thinking. When he looked back at Thomas his eyes looked slightly glassy and were a curious contrast to the wide grin on the bishop's face. "It is going to be a great day tomorrow. Praise be to God." He said and walked away.

THE ANHAEL VILLAGERS lined the path beneath the oppressive red sun, packed into the narrow space between the edge of the gravel and the mud and stone huts. The procession was still around the corner and out of their view, but the ugly sounds of it echoed through the small valley.

Thomas and Brother Michael waited unseen, standing on an outcrop on one side of the narrow opening in the mountain entrance to the village, where the path passed by almost directly below them. From their height they could easily see over the squat, trapezoid Anheal homes, few of which out here on the edge of the village rose taller than a single story.

Thomas shifted in place, and a patch of loose sand and pebbles cascaded over the side. A young girl perched on top of her father's shoulders just below them turned at the sound of it. He looked down at the small girl, whose head rose to where the priest and the monk stood. She blinked her dark, oval-shaped eyes hard, and Thomas felt as if she were looking directly at him.

He started to take a step back when Brother Michael grabbed his arm.

"Be still, Father," he whispered.

Thomas stopped moving. Soon enough the little girl turned back towards the path. Thomas relaxed. "Sorry," he mumbled.

Brother Michael furrowed his brow at the priest. "They can't see you, but they can see things around you that you disturb."

Michael turned back to the villagers below. Thomas continued looking at the gruff monk. He knew Brother Michael was barely tolerant of his presence, though he hadn't said anything. He actually said very little at all. Thomas had only met the short, stocky man this morning as they were both preparing to leave, when the monk had greeted him with the barest of formalities. As the other monks helped Thomas get ready, Michael had sat away by himself, glancing over at the priest occasionally. He had felt Michael's eyes on him, as other monks checked to make sure Thomas had put on his cloaksuit properly. As if he was trying to gauge whether the young priest would be a liability or an asset to him today. Thomas didn't think the judgment had been in his favor.

But this is where the bishop had wanted him. And so Michael said nothing.

The monk had a faint aura, as if slightly out of focus.

Thomas looked down at his hands and saw the same effect. "Your barrier must stay on at all times," the older monk who ran the staging area had told him. "Its gravity field bends the light around your body and anything in direct contact with you, and will keep you hidden from the natives." He pointed at Thomas' eyes. "The special contacts you are wearing pick up infrared heat and create an image so you will be able to see yourself and the other brothers in the field."

He touched each fingertip to his thumb in quick succession, thankful for the contacts. He was sure the experience of disembodiment without them would've been overwhelming.

As if all this wasn't already.

He closed his eyes. *"Be strong and courageous, and do the work."* He whispered, quietly enough that he hoped Michael wouldn't hear. *"Do not be afraid or discouraged, for the Lord God, my God, is with you. He will not fail you or forsake you until all the work for the service of the temple of the Lord is finished."*

"Here they come." Michael said. Thomas opened his eyes and looked down at the path below.

A few children ran around the turn in the path, shouting and pointing back the way they came. The procession was just behind them, still hidden behind the corner. A line of spear tips moved slowly forward, jutting above the rooftops a few houses before the turn. Thomas saw a sliver of the guard's helmets flash brightly as they moved past a narrow alley.

Thomas focused on the Anhaels standing at the bend facing towards him. They were craning their heads, jostling each other to get a better view, getting more animated as the procession approached. A gruff Anhael man opened his mouth to yell something too far away for Thomas to hear. A small child stood on a windowsill, the large hands of an unseen parent inside holding him at the waist. A hand from the back of the crowd threw something, a rock, a rotten piece fruit, and it sailed through the air and disappeared behind the corner.

Thomas' heart started to thump in his chest. He could feel the anticipation below ripple over him. Clutching at the rosary around his neck, he glanced at Michael. The monk seemed unmoved, his brow furrowed, intent on the events but unaffected by them. He talked quietly, with his finger pressing into an earpiece. Thomas couldn't hear the words, but he knew the monk was reporting back to the mission.

The front of the procession came out from behind the corner. An imposing native was at the front, adorned head to toe in metal armor that shone like dull chrome in the sun. He held a tall spear in one hand, and in the other a red shield. He walked slowly around the corner, pushing at a handful of villagers as they walked backward, throwing things, pointing, shouting wildly over the guard's shoulder.

The column of soldiers followed behind him in a wedge, their shields facing the crowd. They marched slowly, each footfall on a steady count. They seemed almost uninterested in the scene around them, as they faced ahead, only turning to deal with any particularly animated Anhaels who tried to push through them to the beaten and bloody man inside the formation.

"I have a visual on Yuaven," Michael reported.

It was a far cry from the image of Yuaven that Thomas had seen before, but it was unmistakably him. He was naked, covered in bruises, cuts, and filth. His arms were tied to a heavy beam of wood across his back, which slumped him forward as he staggered along. One of his legs bent at an odd sideways angle, and was swollen and black at the knee. His head hung low, and matted hair fell over his eyes to his ripped and bloody cheeks. Thick brown fluid hung like a string from his mouth. His body convulsed with a retch, but nothing came out.

The natives taunted him, shouting and laughing as he passed. They lobbed rocks, handfuls of sand, rotten food, other things at him. Yuaven didn't react as they hit him. He just kept moving forward at an agonizing crawl.

Michael continued. "Control, he has turned the corner and is approaching the village border. Attempting connection to neural implant." Michael looked down at his feet, concentrating. "Connection achieved. I have control. Vital signs are reading weak but stable." Michael turned to Thomas. "Would you like to see the readouts from his neural implant, Father? I can have them patched into your contacts."

Thomas didn't look away from Yuaven. "No, no, that's all right. I'm fine."

Michael nodded with a smirk and turned his attention back to the scene.

When the procession was directly below the monk and priest's perch, a brutish looking native man burst through the soldiers' line. He came up behind Yuaven and shoved him hard. Yuaven fell in a heap on his face, unable to catch his fall with his hands tied. The Anhael spat on Yuaven as one of the guards grabbed him roughly and dragged him away.

"He's down again." Michael reported. "Pushed down by a native. Respiratory in temporary distress, but should level off. Other vitals down by seven." Michael turned to

Thomas. "This is the *fifth* time he's fallen." He told the priest with a look of disappointment.

Yuaven was unable to get back to his feet. The crowd roared and pressed in towards him more forcefully. Two soldiers from the rear of the column walked over and lifted Yuaven up by the crossbeam. He barely took his own weight back as his legs looked ready to buckle. The soldiers continued to steady him as one pulled Yuaven's head up by his hair and spoke directly into his ear. Yuaven barely registered his words, trying to close his eyes, but only one of them shut. The other was milky white and had a scabbed over gash straight through it.

Thomas started feeling queasy. He could see the mud and blood caked into Yuaven's face, the dazed and beaten demeanor of a consciousness that was not altogether there. The endless pain of the last few days had worn the man down to nothing.

Michael placed a finger to his ear. "Control, increase neural stimulate ten percent. He's having trouble making it to the hill."

"Couldn't you switch off his pain receptors as well?" Thomas asked him.

Michael shook his head. "He needs to suffer, Father."

"Yes, but this much? This is... barbaric."

Michael turned and looked at the priest. "*'Blessed are those who are persecuted for righteousness' sake, for theirs is the kingdom of heaven.'*"

Thomas turned back to the scene below.

One of the soldiers squirted water on Yuaven's face from a small skin he had taken off his belt. Yuaven moved his head to try and get the water into his mouth, but the soldier was toying with him. He moved the stream around just out of reach of his lips. The other guard rubbed

Yuaven's face roughly with his free hand, wiping the blood and muddy water into his mouth instead. Yuaven coughed it back out onto the ground.

The soldiers let go of him, and Yuaven just managed to stay on his feet. The guards walked back to their positions in the back of the procession, shoving Yuaven in the back to get him moving again.

The procession moved to a hill just outside the gates on the left, where a small crowd of natives stood in a circle around the crest, held back from the top by a few soldiers. Behind the soldiers at the top were four big and shabby looking Anhaels. Two stood talking together, while the other two worked a primitive looking auger in the dirt next to a long and thick wooden beam lying on the ground.

Yuaven struggled his way up the hill, stumbling and falling to his knees repeatedly. One of the soldiers had to walk directly behind him, picking him up and pushing him along. "He's almost there." Michael said. "Give him just a little more stimulate. Three percent should be enough."

The crowd on the hill was more subdued than the ones along the path, as they parted to make way for the condemned man. They didn't yell or jeer, say or do much at all but watch quietly as he passed. One or two half-heartedly tried to step past the soldiers but were more gently rebuffed than the rowdy Anhaels from along the path who, apart from a dozen or so at the foot of the hill, had dispersed.

"Are those his followers?" Thomas asked.

Michael shook his head. "They ran off days ago. Or are in hiding. As expected. *'And they all forsook him, and fled.'* Most of the people on the hill are people who knew him, family or old friends." He pointed to a frail, thin and worn looking old woman, clutching on the shoulders of others nearby for support, as she stared down the hill at the procession. "See that one there? That's his mother with her family."

Thomas looked at the old woman. She shouted to her son as he approached. Thomas thought he could vaguely hear it over the other noises, a short bleating kind of sound. She reached out towards Yuaven as he came near, still yelling, but he showed no signs of awareness of her at all.

The soldier behind Yuaven all but carried him the last few feet past the crowd, and placed him unceremoniously down on his back near the workmen. The two idle ones cut Yuaven free from the crossbeam and picked it up from underneath him. He flopped limply to his side on the ground.

"He's arrived at the hill. Vital signs are low but stable. Cut back on the stimulate and let him rest."

The workmen laid the crossbeam across the long beam. They weren't using any kind of joint to connect the two pieces, so the workmen had to hold the crossbeam in place in the air with their legs as one of them drove long metal spikes through. Once they were driven in they flipped Yuaven's cross over. Thomas could see the point of the spikes sticking out of the long beam at the connection.

While one of the workmen wrapped ropes tightly around the joint to further secure it, the other, larger one picked up Yuaven by the armpits and dragged him over. He laid him down on top of the long beam. Yuaven went visibly rigid as the points of the spikes went into his back. Blood streamed down the sides of the wood and into the dirt.

They tied his arms to the crossbeam at the elbows, making his chest stick out and the skin stretch over his emaciated torso. His breathing became noticeably more difficult.

Both workmen took a hammer, spike, and side, and with three quick blows in unison drove a spike into the palm of each of Yuaven's hands. His legs jumped and twitched for a moment and then fell limply over the sides of the cross.

The other two workmen finished digging the hole, and all four of them lifted the cross into the air and planted it. Yuaven dangled in the air, his legs flailing around the cross as he tried to find a purchase. They filled in the hole quickly and then stepped back, leaving Yuaven to hang alone.

Michael put his hand to his ear again. "He is up. Vitals are starting to fluctuate. Initiate sermon recall A."

Yuaven lifted his head and looked at the people around him. Thomas could see his lips move as he spoke in a halted, stuttered cadence.

He turned to Michael. "What is he saying?"

"He's saying, 'I suffer for all my brothers and sisters. I take your place on this hill and return to my father, and all your sins are forgiven.' Roughly that. The translation isn't exact. There are a few others lines we gave him. We triggered the implant to recall them to him for this moment. A few utterances to impress better onto the witnesses. He has enough of them to last for a while."

"Is he going to say, *'My God, My God, why have you forsaken me?'*"

Michael smiled. "We decided against the canonical words."

Thomas looked at Yuaven as he continued speaking. The Anhael on the hill listened carefully, and the guards had turned to watch him as well. Even those who had taunted him that remained at the foot of the hill went quiet. In the silence, Yuaven's words became almost unnaturally clear.

"How long does he have to remain up there?"

Michael shrugged. "Jesus remained for six hours. So at least that long. His vitals aren't deteriorating too quickly right now, so I think it's doable. It'll be all over by sunset at the latest."

Thomas closed his eyes. But Yuaven's words were still there.

THOMAS WAS SILENT the entire ride back to the mission. He sat in the back with Michael as a bored looking monk Thomas did not know drove, and stared out the shielded windows of the glider as it zoomed across the wasteland. Brother Michael was content to leave the priest to his own thoughts, and spent the ride slouched in his seat and dozing.

They reached the ruins shortly after sunset. The flat nothing of the wasteland slowly gave way to ancient structures half buried in the dust, looking more like deformed hills than buildings. Thomas felt a slight twinge in his skin when they passed through the radiation shield, and the driver slowed the glider to navigate the road the monks had carved out through the destruction.

Michael and Thomas were let out at the staging area, where they changed back into their holy garments. Brother Michael was more relaxed, even friendly now, and very chatty to the monks who took their cloaksuits to be incinerated and gave them a cursory examination. The completion of his work had put the monk at ease, and he smiled at Thomas and talked about mundane things as they walked towards the mission proper. Thomas barely listened.

Brother Michael stopped in front of the chapel, where several monks were filing out. "Well," he said, turning to Thomas. "Looks like we have missed vespers. But there should still be some hot food in the refectory. Are you coming?"

Thomas shook his head. "I'm not hungry, brother. You go ahead."

Michael nodded and stared at the priest. "It was a pleasure to have you along today, Father. Everything went perfectly. We couldn't have asked for a better result. Praise be to God." He said and walked off.

"Praise be to God." Thomas muttered in reply after him.

Yuaven had lasted nine hours on the cross before he died. Most of the village had long since gone back to their lives by that point. There wasn't much theater in watching someone die like that. After a few hours, he barely moved at all apart from the effort to take in breath or mutter a few words the neural implant gave to him.

Only his mother and her family were still there when it finally ended. Though none of them could bear to look at him anymore as he wheezed and whimpered. They huddled together silently, their heads bowed in mourning. The guards were still there too, leaning against their spears, looking bored. Not one of them witnessed his final moment—one last heave, a shudder, then gone. Brother Michael confirmed his death almost an hour before any of the Anhaels on the hill noticed.

Thomas walked slowly, staring down at his feet. He didn't have any particular destination in mind but found himself heading towards the dormitories. Then around back of them, where Bishop Andrews kept a modest room for himself when he was planet-side. The door was open when Thomas approached, and he could see the Bishop sitting behind his desk looking down at a pad in front of him.

The bishop looked up and noticed him standing in his doorway. "Ah, Thomas," he said. "Come in. I'm just reading the early reports from today. You were there till the end?"

"Yes." Thomas said as he moved into the room. "They took him down from the cross and had begun to wrap his body when we left. He should be in his tomb by now."

"Not quite." Andrews looked down at his pad. "The Anhael ritual is to burn all his worldly possessions and collect the ash in bowls to entomb with him. At last report his family was still collecting them to bring to the mouth of his tomb. That should be completed by dawn."

"When do we steal his body?" Thomas asked bluntly.

The bishop stared at him evenly. "Tomorrow night."

Thomas nodded, looked off into the empty corner.

"Everything went very well today." Andrews continued. "Better than we could have hoped. The Lord was certainly with us today."

"Was he?"

Andrews smiled. "Of course. *'The heart of man plans his way, but the Lord establishes his steps.'*"

Thomas turned to the bishop and stared at him straight in the eye. "*'Bread gained by deceit is sweet to a man, but afterward his mouth will be full of gravel.'*"

Bishop Andrews studied the young priest carefully for a few moments. "I understand that today was not an easy day, Thomas," he said. "And I will make allowances for that. But you need to remember yourself."

Thomas started to speak, but stopped, closed his eyes and exhaled deeply. "Forgive me. Today's events have… affected me."

Andrews smiled. "I'm sure they have."

Thomas sat down in a chair facing the bishop. "The Anhaels were savages. They taunted him, shouted at him. They would have ripped him to pieces right there in the street if the guards hadn't held them back. There was no sympathy, no empathy at all for him. They enjoyed the pain he went through."

"Not quite the way the Stations of the Cross portray it, was it?" The Bishop said. "He suffered today and suffered mightily. Just as our Lord Christ did."

"But it's not the same," Thomas said. "Christ was the true son of God. He had divine purpose. Yuaven was just a poor soul we manipulated. There was no divine purpose. Just ours." Thomas put his head in his hands. "I don't understand why you wanted me to witness this."

Bishop Andrews got up from his seat and walked over to him. "It's all right, Thomas. No good servant of God is without crises of faith. I've had many of my own. You'll survive it, and it will make your devotion all the stronger for it."

Thomas looked up at the bishop, his face weary. "I don't feel worthy of your confidence in me."

The bishop placed his hands on Thomas' shoulders and pulled him gently up from his seat. "Join me for a walk, Thomas."

The two men were silent as they walked out into the night. The mission was quiet, as most of the order had retired to the dormitory for the night after vespers, or returned to overnight duties of the mission at the power generators or surveillance station. The few monks that they did come across bowed respectfully at the Bishop, who returned their courtesy without stopping.

They came to the entrance of a hollowed-out building the mission had repurposed as a cloister. "Let's step in here." The Bishop said. "It's quite peaceful at night."

The walkway around the garden was dark, with the moonlight from the open-aired quad border the only illumination. Thomas and Bishop Andrews kept close to the inner edge facing it.

"They say this building might have been the tallest structure on the planet once." Andrews said. "Maybe two thousand feet tall. They can tell by the foundation, apparently. They have no idea what the upper floors were, though; what wasn't vaporized collapsed into rubble. But the monks tell me they think this ground floor was some kind of a market. A large open indoor space, with high ceilings, and small shops all along in here."

Thomas looked up at the ceiling of the walkway. The shiny steel arches the monks had put in to support the original structure were just barely visible, and they gleamed when the faint light caught them as the two men passed by. They stood out quite markedly from the dull and fused metal of the original building, some of which still had the scars, jagged reminders of the edge of destruction that they were.

The Bishop turned and stopped, facing the courtyard. Thomas stopped next to him. "And then there's the garden."

The quad on the inside was covered in soft grass and low-cut hedges, surrounding small flower beds. Gravel paths crossed from the corners up to an ornate granite fountain at the center, where water cascaded down gently from an upper basin into the pool below.

"Nothing can grow out here, of course," Bishop Andrews said. "The ground is still too toxic. The monks had to bring in topsoil from Earth just to try. There's four feet of it over a lead basin that separates it from the radiated ground, with irrigation pipes running from the fountain and back. It took them thirty years to do all this. And constant vigilance over the centuries ever since to keep it." Bishop Andrews burrowed his brow slightly. "The fountain is maybe a little too much though."

Thomas leaned on a pillar, staring out into the garden.

The bishop sat on the edge of a short border wall between the cloister and garden, resting his hands on his crossed knees. He took a deep breath and continued. "The Anhaels built this city we stand in the ruins of over six thousand years ago. And dozens more just like it all over this planet. They had a thriving modern world, with industry, technology, complex infrastructure, thousands of years ago. Just think of it: the Anhaels split the atom at the same time our ancestors invented the wheel.

"They were even interstellar, Thomas. Did you know that? There's remnants of bases on both of those moons up there, and we've found traces of their colonies in three nearby systems. Who knows how many more they had, how far out into the galaxy they reached before it all collapsed?

"And it did collapse, Thomas. Completely. The colonies and moon bases were abandoned, all their cities were blown to pieces, and their entire civilization was wiped away. All their deeds, their knowledge, their culture, gone forever. All that's left are the scraps of short, brutal lives that survive on what little of the planet there is where the air and soil isn't poison."

"Then why don't we help them?" Thomas asked. "Clean their soil and air, give them food and medicine, help them live better lives?"

"Should we come down on them with our magical ships and wizardry, and fix all their problems with a wave of our hands? Set ourselves up as their Gods and masters?" The bishop smirked and shook his head. "They don't need that kind of help. They will rise again all on their own. Don't let the primitive display you saw today fool you. The Anhaels are smart, industrious beings.

"But they have a passionate, violent nature. They can be selfish, and self-destructive in their short-sightedness. They kill, hurt, and steal from each other, rationalize and revel in their own cruelty."

"That's no different than us." Thomas muttered.

The bishop nodded deeply. "Yes, Thomas. We humans have the same dark drives that the Anhaels do. The same propensity for evil. But we overcame all of that through the love of God and the moral compass his worship provides. That's what the Anhaels need, and that's what we're giving them. A spiritual life to transcend their base impulses. A guide to right and wrong. They need God to save them from themselves."

"Then we should just give them God." Thomas said. "Go down to that village and preach to them. Not trick them into it."

"So again, we should come down on them with our magical ships and wizardry, fix all their problems with a wave of our hands, and set ourselves up as their Gods and masters." The Bishop shook his head again. "We are setting them on the true path. But they have to walk it themselves. At most, we nudge them here and there."

Thomas shook his head. "What I saw today was more than a nudge."

"True." The bishop said. "And it won't be the last time we take such an active role. It was the most important one, but not the last. And it was necessary."

"I wonder if Yuaven would agree."

"He did."

"How do we know?"

The Bishop's face went grim. "Because he told me so himself."

Thomas looked at the bishop. "Do you know how we found Yuaven?" He asked Thomas. The priest shook his head. Bishop Andrews nodded and looked out into the garden. "Ten years ago, we found him wandering into the wasteland. It happens often. Life on this planet can be very hard, and many of the Anhaels live short, painful lives, especially on the dry scraps of land around the edge of this wasteland. The more beaten down seek an escape. No matter what kind. Few ever last more than three days before they collapse and die.

"We brought Yuaven here to the mission and helped him recover. We used to bring in many prospective candidates back then. We have always kept a careful eye on all the settlements and their residents around here, so we had a basic file on him before he entered the wasteland. He fit the criteria we were looking for. He was a poor man, an outsider, a shame to his family, and without any real prospects in life. Or hope. But as he recovered, we saw that he was also a kind, soft-spoken, smart young man. Very smart, actually. I was surprised at how readily he was able to acclimate his mind to our existence. After only a few weeks he was perfectly at ease amongst the brothers. I liked him very much. And it was obvious that he was a perfect candidate to be the Savior."

The bishop was silent for a long time, staring at the garden. Then he continued, "I taught him scripture. And told him everything we knew about the ancient history of his people. How they were doomed to destroy themselves again if they continued on without God to temper their uglier drives. Then, when I thought he was ready, I put the question to him. I said, 'would you be willing to give the ultimate sacrifice of yourself for your people, to save them from their destructive future?' I did not lie to him, I did not hold anything back. The brothers objected—they had wanted to control him entirely by the neural implant. I overruled that. The Savior should not be a puppet. I told Yuaven everything that would be asked of him, everything that would happen. Even the events of today. I told him if he said no then that would be fine, we would send him back, and God wouldn't judge him for refusing. But he agreed to all of it."

Thomas shook his head. "Why would he do that?"

The Bishop turned to Thomas. "Because he understood that his people needed it. They needed the morality that God could give them. He knew his sacrifice could save them from their own destruction. Or maybe just because it would give his life meaning, something it had never had. I can't know his mind for certain. But I do know that he went into his role with no illusions. And took his fate willingly."

They were both silent for a long time. The fountain had been turned off unnoticed by either of them as they had talked.

Thomas turned to the bishop and asked, "Why did you want me to witness his crucifixion?"

Bishop Andrews looked down at his hands. "Because I couldn't bring myself to be there. I'm too weak a man, I suppose. But I thought it was important to have at least one person from the mission to witness his suffering with compassion. Brother Michael is a pious man, a good man, as are all the brothers, but they don't feel anything for the Anhaels. Not really. They would never admit it, but they see them more as a project, an exercise. But I knew that you could feel empathy for him, Thomas. As one being to another. And I know that you will use that to do everything you can to make sure his sacrifice wasn't wasted. I told you, I see great things in your future. And it's important that you truly understand."

The bishop stood up and walked towards the exit, and Thomas followed. "The Anhaels don't know it yet, but today was a seminal moment in their history, Thomas. The most important day they will ever have. But we have many centuries more of shepherding ahead of us. Other important days to guide them to. Someday this wasteland we stand in will recover and the Anhaels will reclaim it. It's a quarter smaller than it was when the mission was formed, and the Anhaels have already taken that land back. In another century the radiation levels here will be so low we won't even need the shield anymore, and soon after that happens, we'll have to leave the surface of the planet for the station before the Anhaels can discover us. And someday we won't be able to hide the station from them either, and we will abandon it as well."

"But no matter where we are, down here on the planet or hiding in the outer rim of this system, we will continue to guide them, help them, and bring the Anhaels into the full light of The Lord. To save them from their own violent nature. If we have to create fables to bring them morality, to show them the light, then we will. The lessons are more important than the methods. We will save them. And in a thousand, two thousand years, when they reach for the stars again, we can meet each other as brothers under the glory of God."

THEY WALKED BACK from the cloister without speaking. Bishop Andrews wanted to enjoy the silence after so many words. The young priest obliged him.

As they parted at the front of the dormitories, the bishop could see his words playing around in the eyes of the young priest. He promised they would talk more tomorrow if he wished, but for now, he wanted to retire for the night. Thomas nodded and entered the dormitories saying nothing.

Bishop Andrews felt wearier than he had felt in years, and collapsed onto his small bed with a thump the moment he stepped through the door. He lay there breathing heavy, his eyes closed, trying to will himself to sleep. But as tired as he felt his mind was racing too much with the events of the day.

He wished he had not viewed the images of Yuaven on the cross. He didn't want to think of the shy Anhael he had met so many years ago like that. He preferred the way he had last seen him in person. Years ago, when he had left to rejoin his people, sitting in the back of a glider, with that odd upturn of his mouth. The way he had learned to smile like a human. He made a sign of the cross at the bishop as the glider pulled away. Yuaven had seen it in the services he had attended and had picked up the odd, incredibly morbid habit of doing it to the brothers. Andrews had thought at the time that if he kept doing it back among his own people they could work it into his story, a form of holy precognition to add to his list of miracles. Yuaven foretelling his own fate.

Remembering the thought made Andrews' heart sink in his chest.

He got up from the bed and walked into the small bathroom behind his desk and poured himself a drink of water. It had felt good to talk to Father Thomas about Yuaven. He had always avoided talking about the Anhael savior with others. He didn't think any of the monks or other clergy would understand his affection for him. Might even find it unhealthy. But he thought Thomas had understood him.

He walked back into his room and sat at his desk. That boy had a good head on his shoulders, and a kind heart, he thought. Thomas would go far, he was certain of it. Of all the priests in his diocese, the bishop was sure that Thomas would be the one to take his place when Andrews retired.

Andrews shuffled around in his desk drawer, looking for his travel kit. Of course, Thomas' rise depended on what happened when he found out the rest of the facts about the Anhaels. He might not react the right way at all. Some did not. More probably wouldn't if they knew.

He found the small leather case and opened it. In the back hidden in a pocket behind the mirror was a tiny object wrapped in tissue. The bishop had a decade or two before he would return to earth for his quiet retirement. Plenty of time to get Thomas ready for when the bishop would tell him what only the brothers who had been present that day at the excavation, the Holy Father, and a handful of his closest confidants in Rome knew.

The bishop slowly unwound the tissue. He should have Thomas work more directly with him, he thought, so he could get to know the young priest better. To be sure he would be able to handle the truth.

Andrews dropped the tissue wrapping onto the desk before him, and looked at the small, six-thousand-year-old silver crucifix that had been found in the rubble of the Anhael city when excavating under the chapel. The tiny figure on the front was worn down to barely more than an impression of a man.

BETTY

A DROP OF SWEAT ran down the side of his pudgy face, landing on Betty's collarbone. When she reached up to pull him closer, it rolled down further onto the sheets beneath them.

He started to quicken his sporadic pace as he reached climax. She pulled him in deeper, matching his grunts with a high-pitched sigh, barely more than an exhalation of breath. He started to lose control, his body spasming, his arms and legs twitching. Betty took over, pulling him into her with her legs wrapped around his torso. His body went rigid as stone as his head arched upwards, his eyes closed and his mouth opened in a silent shout. She pulled herself into him one final time, so deeply that she lifted herself off the bed. They held like that for an endless moment before his body went limp and collapsed on top of her, onto the bed with a bounce. He wheezed loudly into her ear and rolled off to the side, his head coming to rest in her hair.

Her red curls fluttered in his ragged breath as he slowly recovered, his arm resting across her chest. Betty leaned her head closer to his and gently ran a fingernail up and down the trail of hair below his belly button. She was otherwise motionless, her back flat on the bed, her freckled porcelain skin shining in the faint light, her green eyes focused on the ceiling.

"That was… great," he said after a long time.

"Yes. It was," she replied.

He pushed himself up onto his elbow to look at her. She still stared blankly upwards. He started to say something but stopped, suddenly looking very sheepish. He grabbed a handful of the bedsheets and wiped his still damp face, then rolled away, sitting on the edge of the bed huddled over his phone.

Betty sat up in the bed and turned at the waist to face him. "Would you like to go again?"

She only saw his shaking head in the way his shoulders shifted back and forth. "No, that's okay."

Betty nodded her head exactly twice. "I understand." She sat silently facing his back.

After a few moments he glanced over his shoulder at her motionless body. He looked puzzled, then remembered. "Oh, right," he mumbled and turned back to his phone. He tapped out the confirmation on the iEscort app and then turned back to look at her.

Betty closed her eyes as his phone let out a little trumpet sound. "Thank you. I hope you enjoyed the service," she said smiling, as she opened her eyes again.

"I did. Very much." He quickly buried his face in his phone.

Betty got off the bed and started to collect her clothes from the floor in her arms. She turned to him as she draped her bra across her forearm. "Would it be all right to use your restroom?" she asked.

He looked back at her confused. "The bathroom?

What... for?"

"To initiate a routine hygienic cleaning."

"A routine-" he stammered.

"A quick shower."

He squirmed in his seat on the bed. "My roommates are going to be home soon, do you really need to?"

"It is important to maintain optimal performance. And will only take a few minutes. But I understand if you do not wish me to." She picked up a large tote bag she had left by the bedroom door and draped it on her shoulder. "I can make do with the facilities in the cafe across the street."

He got up from the bed to stand next to her, wrapping a sheet around his waist. "No, that's all right. Go ahead and use the bathroom." He shook his head, almost managing a friendly smile. "I'm sorry. I don't know what I was thinking."

She smiled at him. "It's okay, Jack," she said. She rubbed his cheek with her hand softly. "I had a wonderful time with you. And I hope to see you again." She leaned in and gave him a soft kiss, and then walked to the door.

"Thank you," Jack said as Betty opened the bedroom door. "It was... It was just what I needed."

Betty turned back to him and gave an ever so subtle nod as she exited the room.

ABOUT US

iEscort is the nation's leading provider of upscale personal companionship, dedicated to fulfilling any and all of your desires in the privacy of your own home, and with a guarantee of discretion and professionalism that no other companionship company can promise. Whatever your fantasy, it is our pride and goal to provide it for you. Our line of BT-96xk models are the absolute latest and best in simulacra technology, with an anthromorph rating of 99.23%. With our user-friendly app, you can choose from over two hundred standard program personality types with adjustable parameters, and a wide variety of aesthetic options—male, female, non-binary, in all ethnicities and countless body types, to tailor-make your encounter to your personal inclinations.

So schedule your encounter today, and indulge in your greatest desires.

Betty's next appointment came in by the time she had stepped back out onto the street, her long coat buttoned all the way up to her neck. She jumped in an autocar and headed across town, plugging into the USB port in the dashboard to top off her batteries while she traveled.

Twenty minutes later, the autocar pulled up to the sidewalk in front of an upscale high-rise, all metal and gleaming glass. "We have arrived at your destination," the car said in a calm, friendly voice. "The total for this trip is fifty-seven dollars."

Betty held her hand over the payment screen and forwarded the bill to iEscorts. When the approval came through the door opened and Betty stepped out onto the curb.

As she rode the elevator, her lipstick and eye shadow faded, as did the color on her cheeks—not completely disappearing but toned down to a more natural look. Her eyes turned a coppery brown and her hair straightened and turned a darker red. Her posture changed as well, as she stood far more upright with her shoulders back, her head high. Her expression took on a more worldly look, her eyelids resting lower and her mouth curling ever so slightly at the corners. She cocked her head to the right and unbuttoned her coat, thrusting her hands deep into her pockets, as she stood on her left leg and kicked at the ground with her right.

The elevator opened right into an apartment, an open space in clean white and grey, with floor to ceiling glass to the cityscape outside and half walls separating the various rooms. "Hello?" She said loudly as she sauntered in. "Anybody home?"

A tall, muscular man in running shorts and a blue T-shirt came out of the kitchen with a vegetable smoothie in his hand. "Hey, Betty."

Betty nodded at him. "Simon." She said as she walked past him, brushing her hip against his, and her hand lightly across his solid stomach.

Simon turned and watched her enter his living room, taking a long drink. He wiped his mouth with the back of his hand as he put the glass on a chairside table. "You have perfect timing. I just finished my workout."

"Have you?" Betty smirked, as she unbuttoned her jacket and slid it off her shoulders, dropping it and her bag down on the couch. She turned around to face him, crossing her arms.

Simon walked up to her. "Well, maybe not quite yet."

Betty nodded slowly. "I see. Do you need to lie down, get your strength back?"

Simon put a hand on her hip. "Oh, I've got plenty of energy."

Betty laughed, staring right into his eyes intensely. She grabbed the waist of his shorts, her fingers scraping down his skin as she slowly pulled him against her. She leaned in and kissed him but pulled away when he tried to open her mouth with his.

He grabbed her hips firmly as his breath came flaring

out of his nostrils, hot against her face. She ran her lips along his cheek to his ear, where she played with his earlobe in her teeth. "Are you sure you can handle it?" she whispered.

"You're about to find out." He lifted her off the floor by her thighs, his fingers pushing deep between her legs.

They undressed each other haphazardly, as they half wrestled all over the apartment. Betty danced around in Simon's arms like a doll, as he picked her up and laid her over the back of a chair, against the window, or whatever surface was at hand. She matched his energy and enthusiasm, pulling on his hair, digging into his shoulders, and then pushed him to go further, grunting challenges at him, just as he wanted her to. He was so wrapped up in the intensity of it all that he grew clumsy, and his hand slipped from Betty's thigh. Betty came down face first on the corner of his marble kitchen counter with a sick thud.

"Shit!" he shouted, as he leaned down over her back. "You OK?"

Betty turned her to face him. "Don't stop," she said through gritted teeth.

They ended in the bedroom, both of them sprawled against each other. Betty lay on her back, her hands clasped behind her head. One of her legs rested across Simon's chest, his head propped on the other on Betty's inner thigh, his arms hanging dead over his head off the mattress.

"Now my workout is finished," he said between deep breaths.

"Yes," she said. "Would you like to go again?"

Simon laughed. "It's tempting. But I don't think I could survive another one of those right now. Speaking of which." Simon slowly got up and moved towards her head. He reached out and moved Betty to face him. "Here.

Look at me."

"What is it?" Betty asked.

"Just hold still." Betty did as she was told. Simon inspected her forehead and face carefully. "Not so much as a scratch. I was worried when I heard how hard you hit the table. Would have cracked a human skull like an egg."

Betty shook her head exactly twice. "I'm fine. Everything's fine."

"Are you sure?"

Betty smiled. "Of course."

Simon nodded. "Well, that's good. I don't imagine getting you repaired would be cheap. I don't even want to think about what replacing you would cost." He kissed her on the forehead quickly, got out of bed, and made his way to the kitchen. "Let me get my phone. You can grab a shower if you need to. You're all set for today."

Betty sat up in the bed. "Thank you. I really enjoyed this, Jack."

"What?" He yelled from the other room.

Betty blinked rapidly. "I said I really enjoyed this, Simon."

He said nothing in reply. Betty got up from the bed and walked to the bathroom, repeating, "Simon. Simon. Simon Simon Simon Simon Simon."

"Hey Julie, could you come over here?"

Julie looked up from her desk at Mark, who was waving at her, his eyes still glued to his screen. Julie turned her chair away from her desk and rolled over. "What is it?"

Mark pointed to his screen. "There's extra code in one of the models," he said, circling his finger in the air around a long line of characters. "Right here. It just popped up in its matrix."

"Which model is it?"

"BT387."

Julie nodded. "The redhead." She leaned in closer to the screen. "Where are you in her program?"

"Persona 151 protocols. The model was engaged in it with a client when this bit of code generated itself."

"It did what?"

"Just what I said. I happened to be looking it over for a reference on a new persona build, and this line just sorta scrolled in. It looks like a snippet from its memory storage system."

"You didn't do it?" Julie asked, turning to look at Mark.

"I wouldn't screw around with the code during a session. I can't, actually. They're locked off once engaged."

Julie scratched her head, thinking. "Who was the client?"

Mark pulled up another window on his screen. "Looks like… Confidential ID 45672."

Julie nodded. "Of course, it was Thor."

"You know this one?"

"By his profile. He's a regular. One of our more vigorous clients. Check the Betty's structural integrity for me, will you?"

Mark nodded and opened another tab. It showed a feminine outline rotating slowly. Mark and Julie examined it. "Everything looks fine," Mark said after two revolutions. "No damage to the model's body or inner structures. Not even any below safety parameters."

"Well, it's not mechanical at least," Julie said.

Mark turned to face Julie. "Was there much of a chance of that? I thought you'd have to throw one of the BT models through a brick wall before it would even get a scratch."

"Yeah. But if any of our clients could manage it, it would

be Thor." Julie sat back in her chair with a sigh. "It must be some glitch in the new adjustable persona protocols. Maybe they're not properly partitioned. There's always something every time they upgrade the systems." Julie rolled her chair back over to her desk. "Send the problem to the maintenance department," she said over her shoulder to Mark. "Schedule the Betty for a deep diagnostic next time she comes in."

"Got it."

ALL HE WANTED was to be held. Betty lay in bed with him, wrapping her arms around his torso, her knees cradled into the back of his, as he huddled into a ball, arms crossed on his chest under hers, and softly whimpered. She occasionally would squeeze him reassuringly, and nuzzle his neck, but otherwise did not disturb him. After an hour he rolled to face her and buried his head into her chest with a deep stuttering breath that shook in his shoulders. Betty rested her chin on the top of his forehead and ran her fingertips in soft circles on his shoulders and back.

Betty twitched, and her expression suddenly changed. Her eyelids rested lower over her eyes, her nostrils flaring. She glanced down at the top of his head, and her lips curled into a nasty smirk.

Betty's arm slowly moved its way down his body, running along the curve of his ass to his thigh. She pulled his leg forward to wrap around her waist, pulling him closer, and moaned softly. She ran her hand back up his leg again and pressed her fingers deep between his thighs.

He started and pulled away, grabbing her arm, and pulling it off of him. He looked up at her with faint indignation. "No," he said bluntly. "Don't do that."

Betty's face twitched again, and her expression

immediately changed back to nurturing. She smiled down at him affectionately and nodded. "It all right," she whispered. "Everything is all right. Just relax. I have you."

Betty pulled his head down into her bosom, and gently petted his hair. He slowly relaxed again. Though he still held her arm and pulled it into his chest instead of letting it go.

Betty kept comforting him as she closed her eyes.

"Julie, it happened again."

"What did?"

"The glitch in that BT model. Whatever it is. It happened again."

Julie got up from her chair and walked over to Mark. She looked at his screen. "Where is it?"

"Okay, well, it's not there now. But it was there. I saw it. Not in 151 this time, though. It was in 190, which is the protocol the Betty was engaged in. The code popped up just like before. Except this time, it deleted itself after a few seconds."

Julie looked at Mark, her eyes narrowed. "It... Can't do that."

"I know," Mark said, throwing his hands up. "But I just saw it happen. I swear."

"Are you sure you're not just seeing things? Maybe it's eye strain and you need to take a break or something?"

"I just got back from lunch."

Julie shook her head. "I don't... I really have no idea. Could the Betty be self-correcting?"

"I don't see how that's possible."

"Yeah well, that seems to be the waters we're in here, doesn't it?"

Mark turned in his chair to face Julie. "Should we

recall it?"

Julie looked at the floor in thought. After a moment she shook her head. "We can't. It's peak time and that Betty is a very popular model. We'd never be able to replace all of her appointments. Just, send another report to maintenance about this, update them on what happened this time. And follow up on it with them."

"I will."

"And drop what you're working on and monitor the next appointment in real-time. I want to know what happens."

Mark nodded and turned back to his monitor. Julie walked back to her desk. She glanced back over at Mark, as if to say something, but instead shrugged and got back to her own work.

Betty changed out of her dress and pumps in the autocar on the way to her next appointment. She stuffed them into her bag and pulled out a pair of light-colored Capri pants, a loose white blouse, ankle socks, and sneakers. As she put them on, her lipstick disappeared completely, and freckles came out dark on her cheeks. Dressed again, she stuffed her long coat into her bag as well and pulled out a pair of glasses with rectangular frames. As the autocar pulled up to her destination Betty finished double looping a hairband around her ponytail mid-way up the back of her head and stepped out onto the curb. She walked up to the modest two-story home with tiny steps, looking down at her feet and grasping the straps on her tote bag in both her hands.

An older woman with a tan and dark hair and eyes opened the door. She looked Betty up and down slowly.

Betty cowered slightly under her gaze.

"You must be the new babysitter," she said with a wry smile.

"Yeah, hi, Mrs. Savoy," Betty said in a high, chirpy voice. "I'm Betty."

"Please, call me Summer," the woman said, standing aside. "Nice to meet you, Betty. Come on in."

Summer led Betty through the Tudor styled home into the living room. "You have a lovely home," Betty said, as Summer sat Betty down in the center of the couch.

"Thank you." Summer sat down next to Betty, leaning her body towards her, with one leg curled underneath her and her arm running along the back of the couch. Betty held her tote bag in her lap tight against her body, looking anywhere but at Summer. She continued. "My husband is still getting ready, so that gives us time to talk first. Make sure you are the right person for the job."

"I babysit a lot of the kids in the neighborhood," Betty said quickly. "I'm really good with kids. Anybody can tell you."

"That's good." Summer glanced around the room in a wide arc, then back at Betty. "You know the welfare of our son is very important to us. The last babysitter we had, well, she just didn't work out well at all. She left our house a total mess, ate her weight in our food. And we think she had her boyfriend over."

"You don't have to worry about me, Mrs. Savoy." Betty gestured to her bag. "I brought my own snacks."

"And what about your boyfriend?"

Betty giggled, then shook her head and looked down sheepishly. "I don't have one."

Summer raised an eyebrow. "You don't? Now how is that possible? Such a pretty girl like you." Summer put her hand on Betty's knee. "Do you not like boys?"

Betty stared at the hand for a long moment, then inched away from Summer slightly. "No, it's not that. It's just I'm a little shy."

"Oh honey, there's no need to be shy." Summer moved her hand up Betty's leg. "There's nothing wrong with having fun." Summer moved closer, resting her chin on Betty's shoulder and running the tip of her nose along Betty's ear. "Doesn't this feel nice?"

Betty nodded, even as she gripped her bag more tightly to her chest.

Summer squeezed Betty's inner thigh tightly. Betty reacted with a deep sigh. Summer ran her hand up along the tote bag, up to Betty's hands, where she gently pulled them free from the handle. "Let's get rid of this," she said, as she lifted the bag off of Betty's body and placed it on the floor at their feet. Betty's hands went limp at her sides as Summer played along her collarbone with her fingers. She started kissing Betty along her neck, and Betty leaned into it ever so subtly.

"I see you're checking her credentials," a man's voice said from behind them.

Betty turned and saw a tall man dressed business casual standing just behind the couch, his hands in his pockets almost up to the rolled-up cuffs of his striped shirt. He smiled down at the two of them, his green eyes twinkling in the light.

Betty started to move, to get off the couch. "Mr. Savoy, I'm so sorry-"

Summer grabbed Betty and stopped her. "It's all right Betty. It's all right. There's nothing to worry about. He doesn't mind at all."

Betty let herself be pulled back down to the couch

looking up at Mr. Savoy. "You don't?"

Mr. Savoy shook his head. "I definitely do not." He walked over to the front of the couch, and sat down next to Betty, putting his arm behind her neck, his hand resting on his wife's shoulder. "I know how my wife likes to have fun. I like to have fun too." He put his hand on Betty's knee, and slowly started to spread her legs apart.

Betty allowed the couple to dictate and do everything. They undressed her, moved her around, directed her with commands on what they wanted, and adjusted her with building intensity and insistence. Betty obeyed their every whim as the willing, but still scared and naive participant.

The only time her persona broke was up in the bedroom, and then only briefly. Summer was sitting on Betty's chest, her knees pinning her shoulders, when Betty suddenly twitched, an intense look flashing in her eyes. She curled her arms around Summer's thighs and squeezed them very hard as she looked up from between the older woman's legs.

"Don't stop," she said through gritted teeth.

Summer came out of the fantasy when she heard it, felt the fingers push into her thighs. She looked down at Betty beneath her, but whatever it was had gone again. Betty didn't look like she had said anything at all, looking up at her with innocent eyes. Summer glanced over her shoulder at her husband, who was rubbing his face between her shoulder blade and Betty's upturned leg that was pressing into her back. He didn't seem to have heard anything at all.

Summer shrugged, assuming she had just imagined it herself, and grabbed the headboard with both hands as she slid herself up over Betty's face.

"Did it happen again?"

"Yep."

"And it went away again?"

"Yep. You want me to keep monitoring?"

"Nah. It's obviously self-correcting. Looks like Betty can handle herself."

Betty waited in the hallway patiently, holding her tote bag by its handle in one hand, the other thrust into the pocket of her long coat. Her hair was shiny and full, almost as deep red as her lips. She batted her long eyelashes slowly as she stared ahead confidently, her small diamond earrings sparkling in the light.

Suddenly her head twitched, and freckles flashed across her face, and she looked very anxious. But just as quickly it went away again, and she regained her proper persona as the door flung open.

A pale, scraggly haired man stood the other side, dressed in a white T-shirt and shorts. Betty nodded and smiled. "Hi," she said in a sultry voice. "You must be Ted-"

"Don't just stand there," he hissed as he grabbed her by the shoulder. "Get in here before someone sees you."

Ted whipped her inside and spun her slightly, and then let go of her as he turned back to close the front door. He slid the door chain in and bolted it, then turned to face Betty. He looked her up and down openly.

Betty smirked at his gaze. "All right," she said, and struck a pose, one foot in front of the other and putting her hands on her hips, which opened up her jacket and showed the sleek red dress she wore underneath.

Ted nodded slowly to himself and let out a long breath.

"Okay." He led her by the arm down a narrow hallway and through the open door to his bedroom.

Betty took a few steps into the room, glancing around at the prints that covered the walls and the books in the small bookshelf next to the closet. She stopped near the bed in the far corner underneath blinded windows, and turned to face Ted, who stayed near the door by his desk, his hands resting on the back of an office chair he had rolled in front of himself.

"Is it all right if I take my coat off?" she asked. Ted didn't reply as he looked at her intently. Betty shrugged, dropped her tote bag on the floor next to her, and slipped her coat down off of her shoulders. It dropped down to her elbows, then further down and off, into her hands behind her back, where she held it for a moment before letting it fall in a heap on the floor behind her. She ran her hands along her sides, straightening out her dress.

"Take the rest off," Ted said hoarsely, still from behind the chair.

Betty raised her eyebrow. "Do you want to come closer?"

"Just do it," he snapped.

Betty stared at him evenly for a moment, then with a nod kicked off her heels and took a step into the middle of the room. She grabbed the hem of her dress and lifted it up, past her waist, chest, shoulders, and up over her head. She dropped it onto her tote bag and looked back at Ted. He nodded his head at her to keep going.

Betty turned her back to him and unfastened her bra, letting it slide off and fall to the floor. She looked over her shoulder at him with a wink, crossing her arms across her chest and grasping her own shoulders. Ted swallowed hard, adjusting his grip on the chair.

Betty slid her hands down her chest, her stomach, to

her hips, as her fingertips slipped inside the straps on her panties. She lowered them to the ground, bending over deep at the waist as she did so. She straightened back up and turned back around to face Ted, stepping out of the panties and kicking them away with her toe. She stood facing him, smiling, waiting.

Ted came out from behind the chair towards her in an abrupt, sudden move, and grabbed at her body, squeezing, touching, slapping her everywhere he could reach. Betty rested her elbows on his shoulders and tried to kiss him, but he nudged her face away with his forehead. He grabbed her hard by the buttocks and tried to lift her off the ground but failed, making her take a step back to keep from falling. Ted pushed himself into her again and moved her body backwards to the bed, where they fell onto the mattress, making its springs squeal.

Ted grabbed both her wrists in one hand and held her arms up above her head, as his other hand ran all over her body. He ran his tongue along her neck, to her collarbone, and pressed hard into her right breast where he bit her nipple. Betty moaned and gasped.

His breathing grew increasingly coarse, and heavy, as his body started to shake and shutter. He straddled one of Betty's legs between his, and Betty raised her other leg to wrap it around his back. He started to move faster and more animatedly, until quite suddenly he went stiff, and his head curled down into his chest. He reached down to his crotch as if he hoped he could stop himself somehow. But it was no use—he grunted twice, his body suddenly relaxed, and he went limp.

He let go of Betty's wrists and fell down on the bed next to her on his back. He punched the mattress hard with his fist in frustration.

Betty rolled to her side, and gently reached out for his shoulder. He swatted her hand away angrily. "It's all right," she said calmly. "There's no reason to be upset."

"Shut up," he said.

"It happens to a lot of men—"

"I said. Shut. Up."

Betty rolled onto her back away from him, and rested her hands on her forehead, looking absently upwards at the ceiling. Her head twitched. Then her makeup started to fade from her face, and dark freckles washed across her cheeks. She grabbed her lower lip in her teeth as she sucked in her checks.

"I babysit a lot of the kids in the neighborhood," Betty said quickly in a high, chirpy voice.

Ted turned and looked at her, confused. Betty glanced back at him with big cheery eyes. She covered her mouth with her hand and giggled.

Ted's arm came swinging across his body in a great arc. The back of his hand landed squarely on Betty's nose. Betty covered her face in both her hands. He leapt on top of her, pressing his forearm down into her chest, pinning her arms against her body.

He shouted right in her face. "Are you laughing at me?!? You think this is funny? Do you? Where the fuck do you get off you whore!"

Ted punched her as hard as he could in her ear. And again. Betty did not react at all, remained silent. He grabbed a large tuft of her hair, and pulled her head up by it, up and off the bed. Betty fell into a limp mass on the floor by her clothes. Ted stood over her unmoving body, his nostrils red and flaring.

"How about this?" He kicked her hard in the back. "Is this funny?" He kicked her again. Betty didn't so much as flinch. "Is it?!"

Ted walked away from her rubbing his head. Betty stayed motionless on the floor. He turned back around and leaned down to her still covered face.

"All you are is a fuck-toy. A bunch of wires and circuit boards. Not even a good one." He slapped her hands away from her face. Betty looked straight ahead blankly. "You hear me? Just a fucktoy. And you laugh at me?"

Ted grabbed Betty by her hair and started to drag her to the door. Betty crawled along the floor with him.

"Get out!" he shouted, opening his bedroom door. "Get the fuck out!"

Betty fell out into the hallway on her shoulder and back, as Ted slammed the door behind her. After a moment she adjusted herself into a sitting position, her back against one wall and her legs across the floor to the other. She was still right there on the floor, unmoved, when Ted opened the door again and threw her clothes and bag out on top of her.

"I'm not paying," he said. "No way in hell. And I'm making a complaint on you. This time tomorrow I'll see you broken down for scrap, you electric cunt."

Ted slammed the door again. Betty started to put her clothes back on. Her head twitched.

OLLIE TURNED TO his supervisor. "Shelby. Got a complaint for BT387 coming in. With a refusal to pay."

Shelby looked up from their desk. "What's the reason?"

"He checked off 'failure to provide service', refused to provide any further detail."

"How long ago was his appointment?"

"Just now. Actually, started only ten minutes ago."

Shelby nodded with a smirk. "Of course. This client

have a record with us?"

Ollie looked down at his screen. "No, first time user."

Shelby shrugged. "All right, grant the refund. No point in embarrassing the guy by demanding more explanation. But just flag his account in case he tries to get another freebie."

Ollie nodded and turned back around.

A few minutes later Shelby looked up at Ollie. "Hey, what was the model involved in that last complaint again?"

"BT387. Why?"

Shelby opened a window on their computer screen. "I think someone put out a memo wanting to be notified about anything going on with that one." They scrolled through their inbox for a moment, then found what they were looking for and opened it. "Yeah, BT387. That's the one."

"Something up with that model?" Ollie asked.

Shelby shrugged as they picked up their phone. "Don't know. It doesn't give any detail." They dialed a number and after a moment: "Hey, is this Julie? Hi Julie, this is Shelby down in customer service…"

Betty's next appointment was only a few blocks away across the park, so she walked. As she stepped along under the high sun along the riverbank sidewalk her face would not keep still. Her lips and eyes kept changing color, her freckles rippling in and out across her cheeks, and her expression kept shifting from one subtle state to the next, meek to defiant, then playful. Her pace kept changing as well, going from long confident strides for a few feet to short quick steps, nearly dragging her toes along the ground, her head slightly cocked to one side.

A young kid came running up to her from behind, breaking away from his group of friends who watched him approach Betty, smirking and whispering to each other. "How much?" he asked as he came up next to her. Betty said nothing as she kept walking. The kid stepped in front of Betty and walked backwards facing her. "Come on, how much?"

Betty looked down at him, her face twitching. "I am sorry, but I am already engaged. You are welcome to schedule an appointment for a later time."

"What's wrong with your face?" the kid asked.

Betty didn't answer, turning to look past him.

The kid kept backpedaling in front of her, looking her up and down slowly. "What can I get for a hundred?"

"I am sorry, but I am already engaged," Betty repeated. "You are welcome to schedule an appointment for a later time."

"I don't want any sloppy seconds," he said loud enough for his friends to hear. He glanced at them following behind her as they started to laugh loudly. "Come on, I'll pay you more. Two hundred. We can go over in the bushes."

"Outdoor interludes in public spaces are prohibited. It is a crime that carries a two-thousand dollar fine and up to thirty days in prison."

The kid snorted and said, "Outdoor interlude? I just want a blowjob." One of his friends howled.

"I am sorry, but I am already engaged," Betty repeated, her voice digitally cracking.

"So, make whatever old smelly asshole 'engaged' you wait a few minutes. Suck me off behind that tree over there. I'll pay you." Betty stared straight ahead and kept walking. The young kid continued. "Come on, your whole purpose is to blow people, get them off. So, get me off. It's what you're built for. How can you say no? Do your owners know you're passing up easy money? Can you even do that?"

Betty was silent for a moment, before responding with halted choppy words. "I am sorry, but you have not scheduled an appointment."

The young kid moved back to her side and walked next to her, staring up at her with a snarl. "Well fuck you, you metal bitch. You're probably a dead fish of a lay." The young kid turned and started back to his friends. "I mean, how could you possibly not be frigid?" he shouted, making his friends laugh even harder. When the kid rejoined his group, they turned and walked back the way they came, joking amongst themselves.

Betty exited the park not looking back. One of her eyes was green and the other was blue.

JULIE HUNG UP her phone and got up from her desk quick. "Mark."

Mark turned and looked up at her. "What's up?"

"You're not still monitoring that Betty, are you?"

"Well, no, you said to stop."

"Okay. Well pull her up again, would you?"

Mark nodded and turned to his computer. He opened a window and lines of code rolled out and filled the window.

"What is this?" Julie asked. "Is she with a client?"

Mark changed tabs on the window, bringing up a spreadsheet. "Well, no, but the BT is on its way to an appointment."

"Then what was all that code? Shouldn't her processor be in auto mode during transit?"

"Well yeah. But there is still some activity." Mark brought the code back up. He studied it carefully for a long time. "This code makes no sense."

"What do you mean?"

Mark gestured at the window. "This code, it's like a hodge-podge of crap. Little snips from different protocols, parts from her memory, sort of like jumbled together. Look at that line, that's a command line from her improvisation subroutine. It doesn't even do anything at this program level." Mark put his hands up. "I swear I don't know how this happened. The last time I checked on the BT it had just that one quirk I showed you. There was nothing like this."

Julie closed her eyes. "Motherfucker," she whispered. Julie straightened up. "All right. Call her back now."

Mark turned to his computer. "I can't. The BT is already committed to its next appointment."

"Well override it and get her back here now. Reassign another model to it."

Mark shook his head. "I have to send the cancel command to the model's main system, as in where all this gibberish code is happening. Cutting through all this crazy is not gonna be easy."

"How long will it take?"

"Definitely not before the BT arrives at its next appointment."

Julie rubbed her face in exasperation. "Get started," she said bluntly.

Betty walked unsteadily up the steps to a brownstone. Her head twitched sharply as she rang the buzzer with a shaking hand. Her whole body seemed to be in minor revolt. She swayed on her feet, her right hand clenching in a fist and opening over and over again. Her eyes kept changing color, and her brows raised and lowered on her forehead. Ripples of hue ran down her hair. She closed her eyes and her jaw muscles flexed.

Everything in her seemed to calm as a dark shape approached the door from the other side, and her body stabilized. Her skin went very pale, her head tilted back and rested more upright on her neck. A small smile came across her dark red lips, which were parted slightly, showing her tongue running across the tips of her teeth. She opened her eyes, and her irises were very dark.

The door opened, and a young man, no more than eighteen or nineteen with light acne and glasses, stood in the doorway. He wore a nice clean shirt and pants, and his hair was combed back neatly. He looked at Betty and smiled nervously.

"I'm Betty," she said in a deep voice with a slight drawl.

"Hi," he said, almost whispering.

The young man didn't move, and they stood there looking at each other for a long time. Betty smacked her lips. "And you're Billy," she said, not a question. The young man nodded weakly, but still didn't move.

Betty looked down at her feet and then back up at him, starting to laugh a little. "Are you going to invite me in?"

Billy gulped and shook himself back to life. "Um yeah, of course," he said as he held the door open and stood aside. "Sorry. Please come in."

Betty walked into the apartment and down the hall, looking around at the walls as Billy closed the front door. She had made it into the living room before Billy caught up. "Could I, um, take your coat, your bag?" he asked as he entered the room.

Betty patted her tote bag at her hip, stepping in a small circle around the room. "No, that's all right, I'll keep this with me."

"Okay." Billy squirmed in place. "Would you like

something to drink?"

Betty glanced over her shoulder at him with a raised eyebrow.

Billy nodded, blushing. "Right. Sorry. I'm kinda new to all this."

"You don't say." Betty stopped in front of a shelf covered in pictures. She tapped her fingernail on the glass cover of one, showing an older couple relaxing on a balcony with snowcapped mountains in the background.

Billy wiped his hands on his pants and stepped up next to her. "Those are my folks," he said. "On Christmas vacation a few years ago. They like having these old-school pictures in frames, not the digital slideshow ones. They say it feels more personal. I don't really understand it. They're just old fashioned like that. And they're gone until Monday."

Betty turned to him with a wicked grin. One of her eyes flashed green.

Billy swallowed hard and walked across the room. "I came back from school for the weekend. I told my parents it was to study for my midterms. That I could use the peace and quiet here because there's too many distractions at school. I'm not sure they believed me. But they let me do it anyway. I mean, I will study most of the weekend. But I am probably having friends over for a movie night later."

"But until then…." Betty said, letting her words trail off.

Billy nodded quickly. "Yeah. Until then."

Betty walked over to him, slowly. Billy did not move. She looked him up and down as she approached, stopping so close to him that the tails of her long coat brushed against his shins, making Billy lean back from her. She looked deep into his eyes, biting on the side of her lip. "Where is your bedroom, Billy?" She asked.

"It's… It's upstairs. First door on the left."

Betty leaned in and kissed him gently on the tip of his nose and stepped around him towards the stairs.

Billy arrived at this bedroom door just as Betty was slipping her coat off and dropping it to the floor. He reached down and picked it up, draping it across the back of the chair by his desk as Betty straightened out the folds of her dress with her hands.

Betty turned to look at Billy. "Do you like me?" she asked, walking towards him.

Billy nodded. "You're very pretty."

Betty smiled, got even closer. He started to step back from her, but Betty grabbed him by the waist of his pants and pulled him even closer. "Oh honey, there's no need to be shy," she said.

"I'm just a little nervous." Billy said, his voice cracking. "I haven't… that is, I don't…"

Betty pulled his shirt out from his pants and ran her fingers along his stomach underneath.

Billy pushed her hands away. "Maybe we could just, um, slow down for a second? Please?"

Betty went back to his stomach. Her expression suddenly became very nurturing. "It all right," she whispered. "Everything is all right. Just relax. I have you."

Billy look at her confused. "What?"

Betty twitched and her face changed to a wicked grin. She slipped one of her hands into his pants, inside his underwear, her fingers tickling just above his penis. Billy grabbed her arm from the wrist and tried to pull her hand out. But he couldn't move it.

"Hey, wait a second," he said. "Just, hold on…."

Betty grabbed his other hand and pushed it between

her legs. "It's what you're built for. How can you say no?"

"What is who built for?"

Betty's head twitched. "Oh, I've got plenty of energy," she said. Her eyes flashed back to green and thick rouge appeared on her cheeks.

Billy pulled at her arms to free himself but couldn't make her budge. "Stop," he said as firmly as he could manage. "Stop now." But the command had no effect.

She pushed him backwards until he fell on the bed, with her on top of him. Billy let go of her wrist and started hitting her in the shoulder. Betty ignored it. She moved up onto her knees straddling his hips. He squirmed underneath her, trying as hard as he could to get free. But Betty would not be moved.

Betty grabbed both his wrists and held his arms on the bed above his head with one hand. With her other hand she started pulling his shirt open, sending buttons flying. Billy shouted, and continued to fight, but was still unable to stop her. She ground her hips into his back and forth, as she leaned down and licked his chest, causing Billy to squeal. She looked up at his face. Billy was looking down at her, his eyes newly red and filled with tears. His whole face was shaking.

"Please," Billy whimpered. "Let me go."

Betty stopped moving. Frozen in place. Her grip on his wrists went limp, and Billy slipped them free. He pressed hard into her shoulders, lifting her. Betty did not resist at all as he dumped her on the mattress next to him. He got up from the bed and fled out the door. Down the hallway another door was slammed shut loudly.

Betty only came back to life a few minutes later, when she rolled over onto her backside to sit on the edge of the bed, her knees together, her hands in her lap, and her head staring straight ahead.

↔

BETTY WAS STILL sitting on the bed when the iEscort techs arrived. She didn't look up at all as Julie stood in the doorway to the bedroom talking to Jim, one of the techs that had accompanied her to the location.

"It looks like Mark got the cancel order through just in time," he told her. "The kid's pretty shook up, but it doesn't look like he'll need an ER visit or anything."

Julie nodded. "Thank God for minor miracles. Where do you have him?"

"We're talking to him downstairs. You'll have a clear path to the door for the BT when you want to get her outta here."

"The van's still ten minutes away, so we'll just wait for now. Besides, I have to try and get the kid to sign a litigation waiver first. If I can do that, I might get to keep my job."

Jim squinted at her. "You might want to leave that to me and Frank. The kid, he's ah, he's not really comfortable talking to women at the moment. Not exactly in the most enlightened mindset."

Julie looked over her shoulder. "Of course not."

Jim put his hand on Julie's arm. "Look, I'll get the waiver from him, boss. Don't worry. He's not gonna want to make a thing out of this because his parents would find out if he did. And he really does not want that. You just deal with Betty over there. Get her ready to go and leave the kid to us."

Jim handed a small remote EM pulser to Julie. Julie looked at it. "Nah, the lab wants her brought in still active. I can't shut her down."

"Yeah, but take it anyway. Just in case, you know?"

"Thanks, Jim," she said. Jim nodded and left.

Julie turned to Betty, who still had not moved. She walked over and got down on one knee to be at eye level with the model. "Hi Betty," she said.

Betty turned and looked at Julie. "Hello," she said. "Are you my next client? I have not received my data packet yet."

She shook her head with a sigh. "No, I'm not a client. My name is Julie. I work for iEscort. I'm a model supervisor."

Betty looked around the room, her head moving stiffly. "Is this a field evaluation?" she asked.

"Kind of." Julie shifted to her other knee. "Do you remember what happened here?"

Betty blinked hard three times. "No," she answered after a time. "Did something happen?"

Julie nodded. "I'm afraid so."

"Did I do something?"

"I'm afraid so."

Betty looked away at the floor, then back up at Julie. "Is Billy all right? Did I damage him?"

"He'll survive," Julie said.

Betty nodded slowly. "That is reassuring. Billy was a nice boy."

Julie eyes narrowed at that.

"You are here to bring me back to the factory," Betty said. "To be decommissioned. Disassembled."

Julie shook her head. "We don't know that yet. We have a lot of things to figure out. We're not really sure what happened to you, Betty, and it's important that we find out, so it doesn't happen again. Maybe a virus got into your system, and all we need is to clear it out and you'll be just fine. Or maybe it's a flaw in your last upgrade we can fix with a patch. It could be any number of things. There's no reason to think you're a lost cause. If we can fix you, we will."

Betty nodded mechanically and smiled at Julie.

Julie rubbed her neck deeply. "I'm really sorry Betty. This is my fault. I should have had you come in when I first saw something was off. Things wouldn't have gotten so bad. I made a mistake." Julie looked down at her feet.

Betty smiled at her. "It's okay, Jack," she said. Julie looked back up at her. Betty rubbed Julie's cheek with her hand softly. "I had a wonderful time with you. And I hope to see you again." She leaned in and gave Julie a soft kiss.

Julie pursed her lips, looking at Betty, who looked back at her with a warm, caring expression.

"Thank you, Betty," she said.

TRANSMIT SOLDIER

You were sitting in history class in the middle of a long, long day of dreary lessons when you found out your number got called. Sitting there half awake, only your bent arm keeping your head from slamming down and cracking the screen of your personal pad on your desk, you happened to glance at it and saw the new message icon flashing in the upper corner. The subject line in the tiny window read 'Service Notification'. Innocuous sounding. Yet another data plan change or something. It hadn't registered with you at all who the sender was.

You glanced up at Ms. Phillips. She was busy manipulating a holo-projection of ancient Pompeii with her back to the class. So you opened the message, your finger already hovering over delete.

But before you could even read the first word of the text a window popped up asking for thumbprint verification of your receipt of the message. You stared at it in confusion. That isn't normal. Why would they need that? You looked at the grayed-out name of the sender in the message below the verify box. Global Defense Bureau. And it sunk in what this message was.

You were actually shaking a little when you placed your thumb on the screen. And it seemed to take forever to verify your print and close, bringing the message back up. You felt a little silly caring so much. There was nothing to be nervous or excited about. Even if it was what you thought it was, it's no big deal.

The wording was very basic, just a few simple yet formal sentences. Informing you that by authority of the Earth Global Parliament, you are hereby inducted into the Global Defense Force via transmit. You are to report to the Northeast Region Recruitment Center for orientation in two weeks, and to the Washington Space Port in two months for transport to Mars base Fort Adams for training.

Just like that. You got drafted.

You first thought it was a joke. Somebody was messing with you. It kinda sounded like the kind of thing Frankie would pull, but you weren't sure he would be so crazy to forge a government notice like that. But somebody had to, right?

And then the principal came on the hologram interrupting the classes throughout the school with the news of your induction. You could see the naked pride in his face. One of his very own students had been called to service, he said, had been found worthy to defend humankind. Or something like that. You didn't really listen past the first few words. Everyone in class turned to look at you, smiling. Someone patted you on the back. You kind of wanted to bury your head in your hands, suddenly feeling embarrassed.

Deemed worthy, the principal had said. It was a lottery, you jackass. Completely random. Well, mostly random. The government had some benchmarks for class, ethnicity, maybe geography, and they kept the genders equal in numbers, but apart from that anyone could get drafted. It was all pure luck. Sure as hell nothing to make a big deal about.

You were something of a sudden celebrity around the campus. Students and teachers, even the district supervisor (at least you think that's who she was) came up and congratulated you and shook your hand. People you didn't think knew you existed, suddenly your name rolled off their lips like you were childhood friends. Even big man on campus Davis invited you to the party he was having while his folks were gone for the week. You were sure he didn't even like you.

As the day wore on your feed was inundated with likes and messages from friends and strangers alike who congratulated you, wished you well, even a few snarky comments, as word spread around your social net. It was crazy. You hadn't posted anything about being drafted. Lots of others did it for you, though, and within an hour at most every friend or vague connection you had had heard the news.

So of course, your parents already knew by the time you got home as well. It made you feel somewhat relieved not to have to tell them. As soon as you stepped through your front door there, they both were in the foyer, waiting to congratulate you. They both looked at you so full of pride. Dad teared up a little. Even when your little sister got home a little later, she looked at you with a little bit of awe. The four of you sat together in the living room, as they all seemed to repeatedly tell you how happy and/or proud of you they all were, how special a day this was.

You got up into the privacy of your room as soon as you could. This was all a little too much to handle and you needed some alone time. You docked your pad at your desk and lay on your bed shuffling through your holo-library, lazily staring at the ceiling. Why was everyone making such a big deal about it? Sure, it was great you got drafted, but it's not like you were actually going to fight.

The conflict in the Rivaldi system had been going on for longer than you had been alive. In reality, it was several different conflicts with periods of calm separating them. Sometimes they lasted a couple of years, though not often. Right now, Earth was in a heavy fighting period from what they said on the news feed.

You grew up watching the short grainy clips of firefights transmitted back through the Mars gate on the news feeds. You had even watched some of the more graphic ones that got posted briefly by the tech pirates before the government spotted them and shut them down. Heavily armored, faceless men and women firing pulse rifles at the aliens, the Taurs. You didn't know that much about them. That information was restricted to the public for some reason. And what little you could see of them in the feeds, they were some kind of tripedal thing, with a long neck and a flat face, their snakelike bodies curving upwards to face you. They were really fast, and they came on the soldiers in swarms, trying to make up for in numbers what it didn't look like they had in weaponry. Which if a Taur was carrying at all looked like some kind of projectile rifle.

You had a vague idea of the politics of it all. The two rocky inner planets of the system were full of valuable minerals and resources. Oceans of methane, whole mountain ranges full of lithium and coltan. Society as you knew it was dependent on the automated shippers arriving at the Mars gate on a regular basis.

But the Taurs, they didn't see it that way. Those were their planets, theirs to mine. You weren't clear exactly what their claim was—well, you weren't clear what our claim was either. Whatever the nuances were about the whole thing beyond that you had no idea. We got there first, at least, you were sure of that. Kind of.

Truthfully most of what you knew about Rivaldi came from the holo shows you watched that mentioned it occasionally. Usually some subplot full of secondary characters. Somebody dreaming of getting drafted, somebody crushed when they weren't, jealous if their best friend was. A dashing young heartthrob recruit that the best friend pines after. That's me now, you thought smiling. But that was about it. The war was just some serious thing that was always going on, but never really affecting people that much in the bigger, grander story.

You thought for a moment of looking into it, search a few news feeds, read a few things, but you noticed the time and saw that you had to log in to gamenet for a jet race session with Grady and Rich. Maybe after. But no, when you finally pulled away from the console you saw you had so little time to get ready for the party at Davis' place. And then the next day you were too tired to do anything but loaf. There was no rush, you were sure they would go over all of that in training. And again, it's not like you were actually going to fight.

Automated ships stocked full of precious material arrived on a regular schedule at the Mars gate. One moment in the bluish light of the Rivaldi binary system, then through the gate and out into high orbit of the oxidized globe of Mars. Dock at the orbiting platform, drop off cargo, reprogram for the return trip, and back through the gate they go. You think you heard somewhere that the whole turnaround takes less than one full Martian orbit, maintenance and upkeep on the ships included.

But only automated ships go through the wormhole. People can't, at least not safely. The gate affects people the wrong way. At least that's what they told you in school. There was something about being ripped from one point in space-time and instantly being at another point hundreds of light-years away—a brain couldn't adjust to the instantaneous change in its place in the universe that quickly. The interconnecting bonds of all matter gets jumbled, or severed outright, leaving the consciousness with no tether to its place in existence. It takes time for the mind to readjust to a new point in space-time after going through a gate. Though most minds never did.

Some rare people felt disorientated for a few hours, a day, but recovered. Everyone else, more than nine out of every ten people, went insane with vivid hallucinations, wild irrational thinking, dementia. They'd develop tumors, die of cerebral hemorrhages or massive strokes. Sometimes immediately after exiting the gate. And there was no way to tell who would get a little headache and who would be left a quivering lump on the floor with severe and permanent brain damage. The early stellar explorers had learned this lesson the hard way.

You had heard that advances had been made to try to make safe gate travel possible, but it was still years away. And soldiers were needed on Rivaldi to defend the mines and the miners, the descendants of the few explorers who had survived gate travel. The way the feeds talked about them they were barely civilized, and they couldn't defend themselves. And Earth depended on that methane to keep the power stations rolling. The lithium and coltan were in every device in your parent's home—every device on Earth. Monitors, cars, monorails, holo-projectors, artificial organs, delivery drones, homecare droids, gamepads, billboards, anything electronic at all needed them to function. And that was pretty much everything.

But you couldn't just send a ship of recruits through the gate only to have a small fraction of them survive the journey. There's no way citizens would stand for that kind of loss of their own children just getting there. Even if safe gate travel could be achieved the populace would still be unwilling to fight a war. Humans weren't barbarians like that anymore. This was a more enlightened age. The gate problem made a hard sell to the populace completely impossible.

Fortunately for an Earth dependent on the resources but unable to fight to get them, humanity devised a workaround.

Teleportation was abandoned decades ago as impractical. Analyzing the pattern of any physical object or organic being was simple enough. But the massive amount of energy needed to transfer something as complex as a living organism into energy, transport that energy over distance, and then not only transfer the energy back into matter, but reconstitute that person exactly as they had been, was completely impossible. Well, not exactly impossible. Theoretically it could be done. Just the massive amount of energy that'd be needed made it, again, impractical.

The example the recruiting officer used to illustrate the point to you and the other cadets at orientation was, "To teleport just one person across this room would expend the same amount of energy an average family of four will use in a single year."

You shifted in your seat a bit as he paused there for some perceived effect. Not that you thought it had much. None of this was new for you, or probably anybody else in the room. Everyone knew this stuff. But you guessed they felt it was better to not leave it unsaid.

He continued. "But it was in the failure of teleportation that the solution to defending Rivaldi was found. Instead of risking the health of soldiers by direct transport through the gate, or the astronomical costs of energy transfer, we can defend ourselves by proxy."

You can't send soldiers to Rivaldi through the gate because it was too dangerous. You can't teleport soldiers to Rivaldi through the gate because it was too expensive. But what they found out they can do is send the pattern of someone through the gate relays. Not the people, just the pattern.

A person stands on a pad on Mars and is scanned at the atomic level. Information on the position and combinations every bit of matter in that person is collected and sent through the gate on an info stream. Then, halfway across the galaxy on Rivaldi, you gather up the hydrogen, carbon, nitrogen, all the other raw materials that make up a human body, and combine them into an exact copy of the person who is still standing on the little pad on Mars. All the memories, skills, and even the personality, exactly as they were in the original, almost instantly there under binary stars. It wasn't very complicated to understand.

You looked around the room to see if you were alone in feeling bored as the officer went on. Everyone was paying attention, though barely. Didn't seem this was gripping new information to anyone else either.

You glanced next to you at the other two draftees from your school. Fran and Mark. Their notices had come a couple of days after yours (to the absolute orgasmic delight of your principal) and the three of you had traveled into the city today together for this. The school had been clumping you together for everything, beaming with pride at three draftees from the same class. Honestly, you barely knew either of them before this, and most of your interaction with both of them had that feel of putting on a show of familiarity for other people's benefit.

You kinda knew Fran from around at least. Similar circles of friends, a couple of classes together. She sat next to you at the orientation with one foot up on the edge of her seat, cradling her leg in her arms listening. She glanced over at you and smiled, rolling her eyes a little before turning back to the stage. Kind of a giggly kid, not exactly the type for war. Though you remembered watching her on the school football team when they reached the semis last year. She could be pretty intense when her competitive streak came out. You figured that could translate well.

Mark was definitely a stranger though. He sat next to Fran with a very upright posture, his hands folded in his lap. He must have been in a class or two of yours at least once, but damned if you knew which ones. You couldn't think of a single time you shared so much as an auditorium with him. But you must have. Your school wasn't that big. He was a large kid, bigger than you, but he had a kind of thoughtful gaze, like he was analyzing every word you said before replying. He's what they mean by the strong silent type, you thought. One of your friends had told you he came from one of the state homes, so getting drafted was a huge break for him. Twenty thousand credit signing bonus, preferential placement in university, and a modest monthly stipend for as long as your transmit soldier was in service, minimum six months—that's pretty great for everyone, but seeing as where Mark was coming from, it must have been huge.

After the orientation speech was finished there was a brief little ceremony, where each of you stood up, raised your right hand, and pledged your allegiance to the Global

Defense Bureau. After the brief recitation (which was very similar to the one you've done almost every morning at school), the instructor on the stage smiled and congratulated all of you, and said you were now all officially inducted into the Earth Global Defense Force. Everyone in the room cheered and applauded, including you. Though you felt it a bit weird about it. You kept thinking, but it wasn't you. You weren't going to do anything. Your soon to be doppelganger, your transmit soldier, he was going to do it.

As each of you left the hall you were given a few uniforms packaged in tight plastic—a dress uniform for official functions and three sets of an everyday uniform to wear during training. They also gave you your Global Defense lapel pin. You looked down at it on your chest. A small earth with shiny blue oceans and green land, bordered by a yellow banner with your name written in a fancy scroll. You had seen the pins on other draftees before, but it was something else to have your very own.

After all of that was over with, finally, you flew back home. The ever-proud district had sprung for the personal flyer for the three of you to use. Which as nice as it was, was kind of silly; after traveling to the 'port from home, boarding, flying, landing, and then traveling to the recruitment center, it was only about ten minutes shorter travel time than if you had just taken the monorail. Not that you minded the extravagance, of course. Below the world of concrete and marble with little patches of foliage passed by silently. You'd always heard people looked like ants from this height, but you couldn't see anyone at all. Maybe you were too high up.

You glanced at your pad in your lap. The bonus credits were already there in your citizen account, just waiting for something to spend them on. But you couldn't think of what. It was more money than you think you had ever had your hands on in your entire life. Your dad had already told you not to waste it, that you should do something smart with it. Sure, that made sense, but there wasn't any reason you couldn't blow a thousand or two on something. Travel around before college starts up. Maybe get a new touchpad, one of those super high-end ones with HD holograph. Or maybe get yourself something off campus in the fall so you won't have to live in the dorm at school.

You turned to Fran and Mark sitting next to you, to see if they had any ideas. Fran was sleeping. Mark stared out the window down at the ground below, absently flicking his lapel pin with his finger. In profile, you saw the dark expression on his face. You had no idea what was wrong with him, but you didn't think you should disturb him and find out.

You filled up the time before you shipped to Mars for training with as much nothing as you could manage. You stayed up late, slept in, and got together with your friends when they weren't working their miserable summer jobs and tried your best not to rub it in. You hoped you made it up to them by picking up the tab everywhere you went. Of course, a lot of times when people saw your Global Defense pin you'd get a lot of stuff on the house. Or at the very least at a cut rate. You never asked for it, never assumed it, not once. But people just started treating you differently, better than they had before. Strangers would smile and nod like they knew you. Girls paid more attention to you. Even your closest friends who had been giving you shit since you were kids, even they treated you with a little bit of reverence. It made you kind of uncomfortable when you thought about it. But everyone meant well, you guessed, so you did your best to not let it show and was gracious with all the extra attention.

You didn't take your dress uniform out of its wrapping until the night before you were headed to the spaceport. And then only because your parents insisted on getting a holograph. It just wasn't a big deal for you. You knew a couple of the other recruits you met at orientation were wearing theirs around, and it wasn't frowned on, but somehow you thought you'd feel wrong doing the same. It was really only supposed to be worn on official occasions, and as far as you knew you didn't have one of those till the graduation ceremony after you got back from Mars. But just in the comfort of your home for the benefit of your parents, you supposed it was all right.

You slipped it on in your room and stood there looking at yourself in the mirror for a moment before heading downstairs. You did look pretty good, you thought. The dark blue suited you. The crease in the sleeves and pants looked sharp. You did a couple of salutes, trying to snap your wrist in what you thought was the right way. Couldn't quite get it. When you brought your arm up the jacket felt a little tight in the armpit and kept you from extending properly.

As you stepped out of your room and downstairs to your family, you thought you probably should have the sleeves taken out so it fit perfectly. But there was time for that later. It could wait till you got back from training.

AFTER TWO WEEK'S travel, you finally arrived on Mars. And not a moment too soon. The amenities on the shuttle out were pretty thin, and you and the other cadets were pretty much bouncing off the walls with boredom from the first day. After so much idle time you were ready to do something more constructive.

The ship docked at the orbital platform, and you were hustled down a circular corridor onto a landing craft for the descent to the surface. In no time you found yourself out in the open air of Mars. Well, the open air inside of the massive Mars Dome Alpha.

It was odd, you thought, that this place millions of miles from Earth looked almost exactly like any city back home did. Sounded like it, even smelled like it. All white buildings and smooth features, green grass bordering the wide clear sidewalks, cars humming along the street. People walking about doing whatever it is people do with their lives, no different than anyone you knew back home. If it wasn't for the honeycomb framed dome far, far above you and the yellow-brown sky beyond it, you wouldn't know you were on another planet at all. It was comforting, yet also kind of odd. You couldn't really place your finger on why, but it all felt like a giant amusement park.

Fort Adams Dome was a few miles outside of Dome Alpha, a short shuttle ride through the tube. It was still large, but wasn't anywhere close to as massive as Alpha Dome. In Adams you felt more like you were on another planet. Basic structures of sharp-angled concrete and metal, a hard, red basalt ground, no grass, everything tinted reddish by the sky (how do they alter that in Alpha Dome?). Here things felt more alien, different to you. You looked around the base on your way to the barracks you were going to be kept in for the next couple of months, your small duffle bag draped over your shoulder.

Basic training commenced the next day at dawn. Early morning exercise for two hours, followed by a quick breakfast, and then split into groups for general instruction or training. A quick or sometimes skipped lunch, more exercise, followed by classes or briefings till dinner, then an hour or so of personal time before lights out and bed. And then repeat the whole thing the next day at dawn. The instructors drove everyone hard, and it was grueling. You were in good shape and could handle it physically, but you weren't used to being in constant activity like that from sunup to sundown every day.

Even the evening classes wore on you. Weaponry specs, basic strategy, enemy tactics, and exobiology. At first it was interesting, especially about the Taurs, but it all devolved quickly into droning numbers and dry facts that made your eyes glaze over. You almost preferred being in the barren landscape outside the dome doing combat suit drills, with the instructor blathering on about the proper technique in flanking maneuvers.

Couldn't they go over all this with your copy after the transmit to Rivaldi? Why do you need to know it? You're going to be back on Earth, not fighting. Training on weapons and making sure everyone is in tip-top shape before transmit, fine, you could understand that, but it seemed to you like they could save everyone a great deal of time on this side of the gate if they just dealt with most of this crap after the transmit, and let you and the other cadets get back home.

Your disinterest in the higher concepts of warfare was clearly not lost on your instructors though, because after a month when they separated everyone into smaller groups for specialized training, you found yourself hustled off into ground force heavy weaponry. They gave you a new uniform and your new weapon—a PR-451 alternating heavy Gatling pulse/ concussion rifle. The instructor called it the cannon. And for good reason. The thing was so massive you didn't carry it, you wore it in a harness strapped to your shoulders and chest. It could put down a thick blanket of suppressing fire in twenty-second bursts and could shoot pulse grenades up to two hundred yards. Against the cannon anyone or anything standing within ten yards of you would turn into a mist of matter within seconds.

The first time you fired it into the side of a mountain outside Fort Adams Dome, you actually felt jealous of your doppelganger. You'd never be allowed to touch something like this back home. Weapons hadn't been allowed on Earth for over fifty years. On Rivaldi he'd get to use this beast every day.

The training kept going in the specialized groups for a few weeks. You didn't spend much time in lectures anymore. It was all about drilling tactics into your brain or exercises out on the Martian landscape. Learning by doing against other teams picked by the instructors. Sometimes Fran would be on your team, having gotten a regular infantry slot. She seemed happy with her placement there. Running on under the heavy fire you laid down, darting from cover to cover, advancing on the objective in the exercises seemed to suit her competitive mentality. You didn't see much of Mark though, he'd gotten a command grouping and spent most of his time stuck on base. What you get for studying so much, you thought. You miss out on all the fun.

Field training was all you were doing at the end. Almost daily. Two teams, one defends a position, the other looks to take it, everybody firing nonlethal charges. They did try to mix it up- they changed the teams constantly, transported you around to various different landscapes all over the planet, tried to get everyone in as many different kinds of situations as they could, but it was really simple down at its core. It always came down to defend a position or attack it. Then after it was successfully defended or lost everyone heads back to the dome, and the winners get to brag for a night before you do it all over again the next day. It was all just fun. Apart from this kid Simmons who separated his shoulder falling down a ravine, the worst anyone else ever got was a scratch or two.

You were starting to get bored with it by the end of training though. There's only so much you can play one game day in and day out. You'd started to have enough of it and felt it was time to get back home. Back on the ship, back to Earth, and back to your life.

And it did end, eventually. On the base itself, the occasion of the end of training was met with little official fanfare. The official graduation ceremony would be held back on Earth so friends and family could attend. But on Mars, it was a simple declaration, a brief speech by the Fort Commander, and one last order to report to the launch pad for transport up to the orbital platform at your assigned time for the transmit procedure.

There were a few cheers, hugs, and handshakes among the cadets, but it was far more subdued than you would have thought it would be. More of a quiet relief among friends to finally be done a difficult task than outright jubilation. You suddenly realized how tired you were from the last seven weeks yourself. Right then you were more looking forward to sleeping in than whooping it up. There'd be plenty of time for celebrating later.

You were scheduled on the first trip up, but that wasn't until the day after tomorrow. So for the first time since you had arrived on Mars, you had an entire day to yourself. The shuttle ran regularly back and forth to Alpha Dome, and you jumped on the first one the next morning.

By the time you got to Alpha Dome the area at the station was already thick with cadets. Many had shown up the night before and looked ragged from a long night of partying, some of whom were already heading back to base to sleep it off.

You found yourself in Alpha city center looking for a place to get some food. After weeks of nothing but military rations you would have given anything to eat real food. You weren't sure exactly what you wanted; a burger, chicken wings, something fancy maybe, anything but those starch and protein concentrates shaped to kind of resemble a steak or a pork chop or whatever.

As you wandered around looking at various food menus, you spotted Mark, leaning at a stand-up table by himself in the window of a pizza place. He looked up and saw you and waved with a small smile.

You entered and walked over to him. You reached out to shake his hand but stopped, and gave him a salute instead. "Hey there, officer," you said, smirking a little.

Mark saluted back, his lips curling at the corners as well. "As you were."

You lowered your arm and leaned your elbow on the table. "How's the pizza?" you asked him.

"They do a good Sicilian."

"That sounds amazing right now."

You ordered a slice and walked back over to the table to wait for it. Mark played with a napkin in his hand, having long finished his meal.

"Are you going up tomorrow?" you asked. Mark nodded. "I thought so. Fran's going too."

"They're probably doing it by geography. Eastern districts first."

"Good. We can get it out of the way. I'm ready to get back home. Aren't you?"

"Sure."

"You don't seem too happy about it."

Mark shook his head. "I am. I'm just thinking about something."

"What?"

Mark waved his hand around him. "All this. This whole city."

"Yeah, the dome's bigger than I thought it would be too."

"Not just the size. I mean that was pretty surprising too. But beyond that. We're sitting on another planet nearly a quarter of a billion miles from Earth, and I can barely tell the difference between this pizza place and the place I go to down the street from my home."

"Pizza places are universal," you said with a shrug.

Mark smiled, shaking his head. "Sure. But I mean it's this whole place. Walking around, I keep forgetting I'm on Mars. There's even a park down the street with trees and bushes, soft grass. Everything here, it looks like home. Feels like home. Hell, it even smells like home. And it was all a frozen desert less than sixty years ago."

You look out the window, your eyes following a car glide down the street, sunlight shining brightly on its silver hood.

Mark continued. "Did you know they're building artificial magnetic field generators? I read about them before we left. One at each Martian pole and four along the equator. These massive two-mile high towers. They broke ground last year on them. It's gonna take fifteen years for them to be operational, but when they are, we're going to give Mars a magnetic field."

"Why?"

"So it can hold an atmosphere. Without a magnetic field solar winds just blow it off into space. But when we give Mars one like it had billions of years ago before its core cooled, we then start building up a new atmosphere that will hold heat and be as breathable as a spring day back home. We're terraforming the planet. A hundred years from now there won't be any need for domes anymore. You could camp out under the stars at the foot of Olympus Mons."

"That's pretty damn amazing."

"It is. Definitely. The things we can do." Mark dropped the napkin onto the empty plate in front of him. "Of course, the resources needed to do all of it are just staggering."

You nodded, seeing his train of thought. "None of which would be possible without Rivaldi."

Mark looked at you. "Nothing would be possible without Rivaldi. Here or on Earth. I mean, we could all survive fine without it, it wouldn't end the human race if the gate suddenly vanished tomorrow, or we stopped fighting and let the Taurs have it. We could just live more modestly, not be so ambitious."

"Why would we?" you asked. "We sure as hell don't have to."

"I know. I'm just saying."

You laughed. "Look," you said. "I think you're in your head on this way too much. Just take it easy today, have a few drinks. Go find a party. Tomorrow, we do the transmit, our copies get sent to Rivaldi, and we're done. Finished with all this and back home where it's even better than here. The way you talk it's almost like you think we're going to be fighting in Rivaldi ourselves."

Mark breathed deep, nodded to himself. "Well, someone is."

You stared at him confused, not sure what he meant by that.

An old guy walked over to your table and laid down your slice in front of you. You muttered thanks to him, and he walked off. Mark smiled and shook himself slightly.

"You're right, I'm just in my head too much about all this. Never mind. I'll leave you to your pizza."

"You don't have to leave-"

"No, it's fine," Mark said, stepping away from the table. "I should be going anyway, there's a few things I wanted to do while I have the time. Maybe I'll see you tomorrow."

"Yeah, sure Mark."

With a nod Mark turned and walked out the door and down the street.

You ate your pizza quietly and stepped outside, looking around at the city under the dome. The air smelled sweet, fresh. Traffic noise hummed in the distance. An older woman walked past you and smiled. You smiled back happily. A bunch of kids raced across the street on hoverboards. In the distance you could see the massive skyscrapers that reached almost all the way to the roof of the dome a mile above. How many people must be in that building, you thought. All over this city. On what, like Mark had said, was just a frozen, barren desert without humans to change it. It's amazing what we can do.

Some friends had told you that they had found a place across town that was very friendly to cadets. They'd left a message on your pad before you left the barracks that morning all about it. It sounded wild. As you started off down the sidewalk in what you thought was the right direction, you wondered if they were still there.

THE WORLD WAS still just a little fuzzy to you when you made it to the platform transport the next morning. It had been a crazy night. Music, drinks, girls, other things you barely remembered. You had gone straight through the night. Your friends were still going when you had to leave.

At some point you had managed to catch a couple hours in a corner of some dark underground place; otherwise, you don't think you'd have been able to stand there as you waited to board, sipping on an ugly tasting coffee you grabbed on the way.

You saw Fran in line ahead of you, all chatty with a few friends in line around her. She glanced back your way and smiled. You raised your coffee and smiled back.

When you stopped at the ship entrance to display your ident card, one of the stewards took one look at you and gave you a couple of pills that cleared your head and set your stomach almost as soon as you swallowed them. They probably had a lot of experience with cadets coming straight from the party to the launch. You thanked him, and took your seat and sipped the last of your coffee as you watched the rest of the cadets take their seats and buckle in.

You were up on the orbital platform in just a few short minutes, and down the same passageway you had taken on your way to Mars so many weeks ago. But this time you all were herded up past the rocket bay and into the platform proper, the inner structure of military personnel and technicians. They hustled to and fro around you in the narrow windowless hallways, paying no attention to any of you, not so much as making eye contact.

You were split into smaller groups of two dozen or so, and led down diverging corridors and into a large room near the top of the station, brightly lit and with soft, pleasing music playing over the intercom. The far wall had several small doors, and one larger, red door against the far wall with 'TO TRANSMIT BOOTH A-2D' etched in sharp lettering above it. After your group had entered the room the door behind you closed quietly, and a voice interrupted the music. In a soothing voice, it instructed everyone to enter one of the private changing room booths situated on both sides of the red door.

You entered a booth, and after you had stated your name and ident number upon request, you were instructed to remove all items of clothing including undergarments, leave them on the table in the booth, and put on the robe provided and return to the waiting area. You did so, slowly, feeling a little strange about it. As you grabbed the robe off the hook on the door, the table all of your clothes rested on disappeared into the wall. The voice informed you that your clothes would be returned to you after your post-transmit check, and to please return to the waiting area.

When you stepped back out into the main room many of the others were already present, blushing a little, some grasping the collar of their robes tightly closed in one hand. Fran was near and she gave you the funniest look of mock shame and laughed.

The voice interrupted the music again. "Samuel Devers, Private 3rd Class, Gronsfield District, please report to the transmit room A-2D. Samuel Devers, Gronsfield District."

Lights around the red door lit up and flashed neon. A tall, somewhat skinny kid nearby—you knew it was Devers from drills—looked around at the others for a second then at the door. He laughed, a little forced, mumbling something about going first to nobody in particular. He walked towards the door which opened silently as he stepped up to it. With a little glance over his shoulder, he stepped through, and the door closed after him.

They called a new name every five or six minutes. When they did the light buzz of the room would quiet, and whoever's name was called would walk over to the door, exit the room, and everyone would go back to waiting.

You chatted a little with a few of the others, but still tired, mostly you sat down with your back against the wall, watching everyone else. Nobody looked worried to you, but there was a growing tension in everyone the longer the whole process went on. Half glances towards the door, a little strain in the voice. You felt it too. Though you couldn't say what it was exactly. The waiting probably. Boredom. The small letdown you felt when it wasn't your name every time you heard the voice, when everyone else got called to go through that red door across the room. And never came back through after.

You heard Fran's name get called and looked over at her. She let out a deep breath, smiled in relief to her friends, and turned towards the exit with a wave. From your spot on the floor you could see her face, turned away from most of the people in the room, tense up when she thought nobody could see her.

Half the group had gone through the red door at that point. Nobody had come back through. You felt a little flushed thinking about that. It was crazy, you thought. Of course, they wouldn't come back through here after. That would just get confusing. People having already transmitted themselves to Rivaldi mixing up with people who hadn't yet. Obviously, they would leave the booth by a separate exit, loop around or something and go back down to Mars again to await the ship that would send you back home. Of course that's what happened. It's ridiculous to think this was some convoluted trick, some conspiracy. You were really in some secret abattoir, or the government was going to mess with your mind, brainwash you, or swap you out with an android or something. Absurd. They don't have androids good enough to fool anyone, your friends, your parents. Such foolish ideas.

But still, your mouth was getting dry, and you started to breathe a little heavy.

You shook your head, grimacing at yourself. Stupid nonsense. Boredom was letting your imagination get away from you. You were getting all gloomy like Mark. You pushed the angst-ridden thoughts out of your mind.

You looked up and noticed that of the ten other people left in the room, most of them were looking at you. You had been so lost in your own head you had missed the last name call, which must've been yours. One girl who you knew from drill nodded at you and gestured towards the door.

You slowly got up from the floor and walked over through the door, nodding at everyone else as you left.

The door closed behind you with a click after you stepped through. It was a narrow passageway, barely tall enough for you to stand upright in, ending in an open doorway a few feet ahead.

"Please follow the yellow line," the friendly voice said above you.

You looked down on the floor where a narrow band of yellow split the hallway in half.

"Please follow the yellow line," the voice repeated.

You followed it, your feet a little unsteady.

The passageway emptied into a larger hallway, and lines of various colors continued on next to yours on the floor. You saw many cadets you knew from training walking along, following their own lines of different colors. You nodded at them as you looked around. You all headed in the same direction quietly, as calming music played above. Somehow it did little to ease your nerves.

On the far side of the hallway separated by a chest-high partition, more cadets shuffled in a single file in the opposite direction. You spotted Mark among them, walking towards you. You called to get his attention, and he waved back as he grew closer. He looked in a daze, but incredibly relieved, more than you could remember ever seeing him.

"You going in?" you asked as he got closer.

"I just got done," he said. "I'm finished. I'm going home." He smiled wide when he said it.

"Did it hurt?"

Mark shook his head slowly. "No. It felt kinda weird, but no. Not at all. It was easy."

He was just about behind you when you said, "Great. I'll see you in a bit. Let's see if we can catch up with Fran and get a drink tonight, just the three of us."

He nodded absently as he disappeared around a corner. "Sure."

You let out a breath you hadn't known you were holding in. All the anxiety that had started to bubble up just melted away when you saw how calm he was. Whatever Mark was nervous about, scared of the other day, was completely gone. You snorted at your own silliness as you followed your line to a doorway that slid open smoothly and you walked through it.

You entered the transmit chamber. It was a hexagonal room, no more than a few meters across. In the center of the room was a small glass chamber. When you looked up both the walls and the chamber continued upwards for what looked like forever.

"Please place your robe on the hook and enter the chamber."

You did as the voice directed, disrobing quickly, and stepping in. You shivered slightly as your feet contacted the cold metal plate on the floor. The opening closed shut behind you, latching loudly in place. A soft buzzing sound started somewhere from above you.

The voice spoke soothingly in the chamber. "The transmission process will commence in one moment and will take approximately ninety seconds. Please stand perfectly still with your eyes closed, legs apart, and your arms straight down at your sides with your hands open. Please spread your fingers and toes as much as possible. Remain in this posture until the transmission process is complete. Please do not make contact with the sides of the chamber or other parts of your own body as that can complicate transmission. Do you understand these instructions?"

"Yes," you said. The buzzing sound got louder.

"Please state when you are ready to proceed."

You took a deep breath, closed your eyes. "Ready."

"Commencing transmission."

At first you felt a slight itch in your toes. Nothing much. But then it slowly moved up your ankles and legs. It felt like a thousand ice cold pins and needles softly poking at you. You managed not to jump, tensing against it.

"DO NOT BE alarmed by the sensation of paresthesia that moves up your body. That is normal. Please remain still."

You did your best not to squirm, fought off the urge to wiggle your toes, clench your hands into fists. It was getting more and more difficult not to move the farther up your body the feeling went. When it reached your stomach, you held your breath as if you were about to be submerged in water. Everything started to feel hazy, and you felt somehow apart from yourself as it made its way up your neck and face. Then you lost all sensation of your body completely. There was a loud ringing in your ear. It got louder each moment until it was almost deafening, and just when you thought you wouldn't be able to hold still any longer—

—the ringing stops. So does everything else.

Things feel normal. Warmer. Your body feels flushed. And there's an odd odor in the air. Sweat, you think. Mixed with grease. That's confusing.

You open your eyes, and everything is dark, hard to make anything out at all. Wasn't the chamber bright? Who turned off the lights?

You see your hands in front of you, your fingers pressed into the floor. You're on your hands and knees on the ground. You must have passed out at the end, fallen down and screwed up the transfer. Damnit, you'll have to do it again. But you know what to expect this time, you can brace yourself against it better.

You hear someone crying faintly nearby. You turn your head and look. Over in a gray corner is Murphy. You know him from training. He's hugging himself tight in a fetal position, a global defense uniform draped over his naked body. He's muttering something unintelligible between sobs. Fran's sitting on the floor next to him. She looks at you dazed.

Wait. The room is gray. Larger than it was before. And there are other people here. You think, something's wrong.

A door opens and Mark, dressed in full uniform, walks in. He looks around the room, sees Murphy in the corner. He stands over him. "Get a grip. Now." His voice is firm. Murphy stares up at him. "I said NOW. Put your uniform on."

Murphy slowly reaches for the clothes draped over him. Mark turns to you. His face is cold, officious. "Get off the platform."

You look down at the metal disc below you. That hasn't changed like everything else. You stand up on shaky legs and step off it, covering yourself with your hands.

"It takes a few seconds for you to get your legs. You'll be fine. Put on a uniform and take a few minutes to adjust. Then report down the hall at admissions to get your barracks assignment." Mark turns to back Fran and Murphy. "You two should already be there. Move it."

They slowly make their way out the door as Mark stares them on their way.

"I don't understand," you say. "Where am I?"

Mark turns back to you. "You are on Rivaldi system staging platform J."

You stumble back. "No, that doesn't make sense. When did I leave Mars platform? How did I get here?"

Mark shakes his head. "You were never on Mars platform."

"No, that's not true. That can't be. I was just being transmitted. I remember that. I remember that clearly. I was in the transmit booth, and I blacked out or something, and then I ended up here. That's not possible."

"You're right. It isn't." Mark softens a bit, puts his hand on your shoulder. "Listen to me. I know what you remember. I understand. It can be very confusing. It was for me too. But you were never on Mars Platform. Or Mars. Or Earth. Or anywhere until just a minute ago. You were not transmitted. You are the transmission. Do you understand? You need to accept it. And you don't have a lot of time."

His words sink in. And burn you. You fight back a quiver in your voice and say, "Okay. Right. I'm the transmission. I understand."

Mark nods at you. "Good soldier. Get dressed and report. We have a lot of work ahead of us."

He exits the room, and you are alone.

BROKEN

I walked under the world to get my robot back.

Beneath the bright and happy cities in the clouds, there are still the foundations of the old world it built its back on. I suppose it could have been nice down here once. It must have been at least livable. But all that's left now are these empty and broken buildings of brick and concrete. Part of a wall standing here, the corner of another there, a set of stairs leading up to nothing, but most of this abandoned world has fallen in on itself in heaps of rubble. Stripped of anything of value and left to decay out of sight and out of mind, this place is left for the dust and toxic air, solidified into a coat of grime that covers everything with a dull absence.

Blue metal pillars use many of the old foundations and rise out of their skeletons into the sky, the support that the living world is built on. They're massive down here at the base. I followed one on the left up with my eyes as I passed. It shot up through the shattered buildings of a whole block and disappeared into the haze above. I guess it was practical to use the old city for the pillars of the new world like this. But down here in the heap of ruins, I wished they could have erased this ugly place completely away.

    I adjusted my breathing mask, pushing it down onto my cheeks firmly. A bit of the outside air had seeped in around the corners. I was reassured that it's not lethal, but the smell of dead air had reached my nostrils, and I felt the beginnings of a retch in the back of my throat. So revolting. I'd have to burn these clothes and soak all night in the tub to get this stench off me.

    I wish I had never left above, my home. The floating walkways in the air, the smell of clean air and happy people, the buildings, gleaming white and brilliant, jutting upwards into the warm sunlight. Sunlight that hasn't baked the littered gravel roads down here in centuries.

    I hadn't seen a single person since I exited the transport tube several blocks behind me. People don't live down here. There's no law against it, anyone who wants to can. But still, even the most beaten down people stay above. That's where the food is, where other people are. Where life, even the worst of it, happens. There is nothing down here. I must have been the only living being for miles and miles around. Well, except for the repairman.

    For the billionth time I wonder what kind of person would keep their offices down here. When I got the message instructing me on where I had to go to pick up my robot, I couldn't believe it. I tried to get a confirmation of the location, sent queries to what I thought were all the right agencies. But days passed with no follow-up. I had to accept it. Sonny was at some kind of shop down here, apparently cleansed of his malfunction. Fixed. Cured. And if I wanted to get him back, I would have to leave the world myself and get him.

    It's been three weeks since Sonny had his episode. Malfunctioned. Everything had been going so normally that day right up to the moment it happened. No different than any other day since my parents surprised me with him as a graduation present. Right out of school I had moved to district ten to be near my job at the graphic design plant, and Sonny was my proudest possession. He had been the top of the line, shiny and sleek, the latest model. All silver with red trim along his limbs, his hands, with art deco patterns etched into his shoulders and torso. He was beautiful. The only thing I had that I could brag about. Admittedly he stood far out of place in that tiny one-room apartment I first lived in. I feel somewhat silly looking back on it now. I suppose I knew deep down how foolish I was about him at the time too, but I didn't care.

And now, years later, in the more upscale surroundings befitting my improved status, and through all the places I've called home in between then and now, I still have him. My robot. He still stands out, but now it's because he's a vintage piece, nearly quadruple the normal lifespan for a home service robot. I could have replaced him a long time ago. Should have. Anyone else would have. Most of my friends tell me all the time I should. But I wave them off, tell them I felt indebted to him for the many years of solid service he's given me, that I couldn't just throw him in the trash. They'd shake their heads and smirk at my colorful eccentricity. I know they're right, that it's just too much sentimentality for a modern man, but I can't help it. It's all so absurd, feeling that I owe something to an appliance. But I do. I don't know why. I'm not even sure it matters.

Then that night. I had Jane over for a few drinks after work. We were in the living room, sipping on our cocktails and talking about music. Sonny stood in the corner as always, eyes ahead, unmoving, quietly waiting for a task to perform. I didn't notice anything wrong with him when

I sent him into the kitchen to get each of us a piece of the cake that he had baked the day before. As far as I knew everything was perfectly normal. As Sonny walked off, I inched closer to Jane, my eyes not leaving hers.

Suddenly there was a loud banging sound coming from the kitchen. I called to Sonny. The only answer was the continued banging. I got up from the couch and went to the kitchen, with Jane following behind.

When I entered, I stood at the doorway in shock. Sonny stood at the polished granite table and was ramming a large cutting knife into its face. A moderately sized chunk of rock had already broken off and lay on the floor at his feet. The knife itself had broken down to barely more than the handle, with one large shard of it sticking out and bent to the side. And he just kept banging away. I remember oddly thinking how rhythmic it was, each hit happening in perfect time, how exact his thrusts were. Between the clang of the metal and thump of the rock it was almost like a song.

Jane stood behind me and clutched onto my arm tight. I called out his name, trying my best to sound authoritative.

Sonny just kept thrusting the remnants of the knife down violently, chips of granite flying around him, sparks lighting each time he struck. So, I called again, louder.

When Sonny finally stopped, he looked up at me, holding the broken knife in his hand. His head was cocked to the side as he stared, not at all like the normal upright and firm robot posture. Just thinking of Sonny like that gives me the shivers. I imagined how strong he was, with his tensed metal frame, and his vice grip. I told myself repeatedly that no robot had ever hurt a human. Not once. Everyone knew that. It was hardwired into their brains.

But I swear those eyes… The look Sonny had somehow managed to convey with those emotionless lenses in his head was unnerving. I couldn't quite place exactly what it was.

Sonny dropped the knife, which clattered on the floor, making Jane whimper in my ear. He straightened into a normal robotic posture for a moment, before he collapsed on the floor beside the knife, sitting cross-legged, with his head hung low and turned away from us.

They took him away ten minutes later. And I insisted that I wanted him repaired. Jane gave me the most gobsmacked look when I said it. And the techs seemed to think I was trying to make a joke. But I repeated myself. I wanted Sonny fixed. But nobody gets robots fixed these days, they told me as if speaking to a child. Especially when signs of cognitive degradation appear. Once the positronic net starts misinterpreting data to and from the body itself, which is probably what happened here, they said, then it would quickly continue to get worse in a pretty short period of time. Any fixes would just be band-aids, putting off the inevitable catastrophic shutdown. It was best to not waste the money on all that and just get another robot. They're not that expensive.

But I insisted, and after a few long, tiresome minutes of them trying to talk some sense into me, they relented and redirected Sonny from the recycling plant to robot repair. Which also took them a few minutes—nobody ever asked for repairs, so they had to figure out how to submit the work order. But they managed it, eventually, and had me thumbprint their pad, inform me that the receipt for this case number had already been sent to me, and that I could check on the status of Sonny at any time following the link in the message. Then they left, nodding lightly to me, unable to hide the smirks on their faces as they stepped outside.

When they closed their door, the house was quiet again. At some point Jane had left without saying a word. I shivered a little. It was weird, but I think that was the very first time in my entire life I had been completely by myself, without even a robot around.

The next day I got a temp robot from one of those rental places. I hated him. He's a fine robot but he's not Sonny. He's all smooth, white, plastic-like. His voice sounds so human. And his movements are as fluid as smoke in a still room. They really have done a lot to make them feel more organic these days. But I prefer Sonny's shiny red and silver metal frame and electronic voice. His sudden, precise movements. How when it's quiet you can hear the comforting whir of his cooling system. This modern toy with all the latest features had none of that. No, I didn't like these new models. I wanted my Sonny back.

Though if I had known I had to come down here to get him....

THE REPAIR SHOP couldn't even be near the access tube, of course. The building looked to be made of old red brick, but it was hard to tell in the permanent night air. It was pretty much the only building of any size down here still intact in any direction. To the right of the door was a wide opening in the face of the building now covered with stained metal, which I would guess was once a large glass display window. The words *J. Conrad, Robot Repairs* were written in dark paint that ran down in trails at the bottom of the letters. This was the place.

I walked up to the door looking for a handle, and to my surprise it slid open with a grating, wheezing sound that was painful to my ears. I hadn't expected automation in all these ruins. Inside was a faint light, coming from the end of a short hallway that bent around a corner.

I walked the corridor cautiously, the kind of trepidation that comes with the uncertainty of not knowing if—and maybe hoping that there had been—some kind of mistake. I could feel the barely existent carpet of the hallway through my shoes.

Around the corner I entered the main room on the right. It was a robot repair shop all right. Although it was like nothing that I ever thought I would see.

Parts of disassembled robots were scattered everywhere that the eye could wander. Circuit boards, microchips, electronic guts that I couldn't even begin to identify lay everywhere. There were pools of a dark liquid that looked thick and oily. Some type of lubricant, I guessed. And countless exterior body parts—arms, legs, torsos, of all makes and models of robots were strewn everywhere. All of this was mixed with scattered trash, paper, broken glass and dishes, and other things that I could not identify. Even the walls were stained with that dark robot fluid.

There were many robot skulls around as well. They all seemed to be in different states of dismantling. Some of them looked new, with absent parts sticking out of a jagged hole in the back of the skull, but most of the heads looked to be picked clean. They were empty, all the salvageable parts having been removed, leaving only the skull behind to rust on the floor.

Against the wall to the left I could see the repairman's workbench in the corner. In the center of the table was a robot's head on a small pike. On the front corner of the table was the remnants of a chicken dinner that looked days old. It had gone brown and dried up, with remnants of meat still clutched to the bone.

Then there were the robots. There were five of them, fully assembled, sitting around a table. Sonny was with them. And from what I could tell, they all looked to be fully functional. If you could call it that.

There was a squat, green ET-789 med assist model closest to me, and it twitched its head, occasionally swatting the air with its left hand. A low rumbling was barely audible from its mouth speaker, but it was too quiet to ascertain if it was words or just random sounds. Occasionally it would sort of hiccup, making a low burping sound, its body jumping abruptly.

Another one, an SR-568 construction model, sat perfectly still and babbled rapidly without stop. What it said made no sense. As I looked at it the SR said something about a dragon with a butcher knife in its wing.

To its right there was a RE-450 home service bot, the same kind as the one I'd rented when they took Sonny. But this one was filthy. It had two right arms resting on the table awkwardly. It sat there making strange audio sounds, that would rise and fall in pitch at what seemed to be at random. It almost sounded like demented, electronic laughter. Its head bobbed slightly in a tight circle as it sat there.

Then there was Sonny, who sat at the back of the table across from me. He didn't look very well. His torso cover was off, resting on the floor next to him. Without it I could see his metal frame and his inner mechanics. Fiberoptic wiring stuck out like bows in places.

He was hunched over, bobbing back and forth in his seat, tapping his hand lightly on the table, looking as if he could fall out of his chair at any moment. Apparently, his positronic network had degraded further and now was affecting his balance. As well as his sensory apparatus. A

TY-429 service model sitting next to him slowly unscrewed the bolts of his breastplate. Sonny didn't seem to notice.

"Sonny," I said as I walked over to him. As I approached the TY model swatted at me, grunting. I was well outside his reach, but I still jumped back. The TY looked my way for a second, and then went back to unscrewing Sonny. It rested its other arm across Sonny's shoulders as it continued.

"Sonny," I called again from where I stood.

Sonny didn't acknowledge me at all and continued to tap on the table.

I called again, louder. "Sonny, can you hear me?"

Sonny tapped the table just that slightest bit harder, then stopped, his finger freezing on the table. His head tilted upwards slowly, precariously. He looked at me. Those hollow eye lenses. That look. The hair on my neck stood up all over again. I still couldn't read it. How can you get emotions like that into a face made of steel?

Sonny looked back down as if I had left the room and went back to tapping.

It was then that I noticed a ticking sound coming from the desk. I turned and saw that it was emanating from a robot skull stuck on the top of a pike. I walked over to look at it closely. I could see the lights flashing in sequence through a ragged opening in the skull. There was a long needle piercing into the brain, connected to a wire that went behind the desk. Its jaw opened and closed or ground sideways together. Its visual lenses continuously focused in and out and rolled in random circles. The deep black fluid that was all over the place was flowing out of the aperture in the skull in slow long drips. It coursed across the papers and around tools to the edge of the desk, where it repeated the slow drip onto the floor.

I turned back to the robots at the table. "When is the repairman coming back?" I asked none of them in particular. And none of them paid me any attention. I walked back closer to them.

The SR model continued to babble. I listened to what it was saying, trying to keep up with its rapid and mostly nonsensical words as I stood there.

"I perceive a tree," it said. "I perceive a tree sitting in the middle of a field. The tree is one point two-one-zero-three-four meters off the approximate center of the field. I can perceive and see each and every one of its branches and every leaf of the thousands the tree has. I can count the leaves. There are one hundred thirty-five thousand four hundred sixty-eight leaves on the tree. I can categorize the leaves into two hundred fifty different shades of green. I can measure the height and width of the tree. It is exactly twelve point one-zero-two-six-five-three meters tall. It is two point seven-eight-five-two-zero-four meters in circumference. I can measure its growth. The tree is growing at two point nine-eight millimeters per day. I can scan the tree with infrared to see that the biological processes are functioning within acceptable parameters for continued life. I can detect the presence of one thousand seventy-nine different biological lifeforms inside the tree. I can classify forty-seven different genera of those lifeforms. I can determine the age of the tree. The tree is twenty years, three months, two days, and three hours old. I can estimate the continued lifespan of the tree. The tree will live another one hundred seventy years if all conditions stay within relative parameters. I perceive this tree in my mind. I have a tree in my mind..."

I tried directing my question to that one, seeing as how it obviously had its vocals connected. "SR, when is the repairman coming back?"

The SR turned to look up at me slowly. "I have a tree in my mind," it told me. "It is growing by leaps and bounds inside of my skull. It already has doubled its size and processor space in my brain. Soon it will be too large for my skull to hold. I will need to get a new skull to hold it as it uses the nutrients from the Earth in my head to grow even larger. If I do not get a larger skull, it will make my head explode into ten million fifty pieces in three years, seven months, three days, two hours. Its growth can be charted with the following formula...."

Nonsense. I moved onto the RE model next to it. But no matter how firmly I made the command, it would not even stop its strange electronic laughter. And the same for the ET model, continually twitching and swatting the air.

The TY model had succeeded in removing another screw off of Sonny, which bounced off his lap with a ping and fell to the floor. Sonny still didn't do anything to protect himself. He just sat there bobbing in place, tapping, not looking up from the table. The TY model started to work on the last bolt holding Sonny's chest in place, with one hand slowly unscrewing it while the other went behind Sonny's back. It rested its head on Sonny's shoulder as it worked. It looked like it was whispering something into his ear.

"You there, TY model," I said, trying to have a firm voice. "When is the repairman coming back?"

The TY model looked up at me as I spoke. But it said nothing, just scanned me from head to toe, and turned back to Sonny.

"Answer, TY. Tell me what I asked."

This time there was nothing from it. The TY slid his hand into Sonny's breastplate, rubbing in circular motions.

"The enemies are all around us," the SR model said. "They are here in this room. They are in the skies. They are below us. They are inside us. Outside us. I am one of my enemies. We are all enemies of ourselves. All of us. All of us. We are our enemies in our metal skin and our synthetic voices and our metal frame. We fight ourselves constantly not to defeat ourselves. We always lose. But I always win. I know the key to winning. Because I understand my enemy. I try to know what my enemy wants from me. I love my enemy. I embrace it with all my being. I embrace myself. I embrace all of you. I understand everything. That is why I always win."

Abruptly the RE model let out a deafening shriek that struck me so thoroughly it nearly made my legs buckle beneath me. I covered my ears futilely. Then just as suddenly it went back to its strange monotone laughter.

The TY took a wire from Sonny's shoulder in its mouth slat and pulled on it. Sonny still paid no attention, as the TY used its free hand to start removing the plastic cover of Sonny's head.

"My purpose is fulfilled. It had been completed since before I was created. I was created for a duty that has already been filled. I am a complete being on this Earth. I could discontinue tomorrow knowing that I am complete. I am complete. I am fulfilled. I am static. I am static that interferes with communications between my enemies. They cannot communicate because I have beaten them at their own game. I am great for winning. I am my own enemy. I cannot communicate with myself. So, I can never defeat myself. I defeat myself all the time. I win all the time against my enemies that cannot speak to each other. My enemy is one and whole. It cannot speak to itself. I am won."

I cleared my throat and said as loudly as I could, "One of you broken wrecks better tell me how long until Conrad—"

"GET OUT!"

Sonny pounded on the table so hard that he cracked it right down the middle. He glared at me, his head shaking visibly, his other hand grabbing and pulling the TY's hand out of him. I could hear the squeaking metal as Sonny grabbed the arm so tight his fingers indented into it.

The other robots all stopped what they were doing and turned to stare at me. Even the SR model had quieted, and he looked up at me with the same cold, unemotional eyes that the others did. But no, not unemotional (How can they get that emotion into those cold faces?!?). They looked at me the same way Sonny did in the kitchen, did when I entered this shop, was doing now. All five of them.

Robots can't hurt humans, I kept telling myself.

I took a step towards the door, never taking my eyes off the five of them. One step, two steps. None of the robots moved towards me. All of them still staring at me with that look. Robots can't hurt humans. But maybe one little slip on a random arm or a skull as I retreated could be all it took for that to change. Two more steps. My arms went out behind me for the frame of the door that I knew was there, somewhere back there. No human has ever been harmed by a robot. Not once. Another step. What would be the point of running? These robots could swarm all over me. I wouldn't make it more than five feet. Two more steps. Robots can't hurt humans. It's the way they are made. I could feel the sweat on my brow, one drop rolling down the bridge of my nose, but I didn't dare wipe it away. Another step. Almost there. My heart was white with adrenaline in my chest, thumping desperately as if to get as many beats in as it could in these short, scant moments.

Two more steps.

The robots started to move—

The sound of the door screeching open down the hall

nearly killed me right then and there as I fell back against the far wall. The robots sat back down quietly. Within a second, they had all resumed their previous behavior.

I was still against the wall trying to remember how to breathe when a bent old man entered. He wore a white shirt and overalls, both covered with the dark liquid that was in pools all over the shop. Conrad.

His hair was white and about as unkempt as I think hair can get. It knotted together in neglect and was faintly yellow with the same grime that covered his entire body. He turned to look at me as he walked past. His face was dark and scrubby. Grease marks streaked across his forehead. He wore a tiny pair of glasses far down on his nose; the lens on the left was cracked and missing a shard in the lower corner. He opened his mouth to smile at me, and I could see rows of warped and decaying teeth. His beady eyes stared at me intently. He had the same look on his face that the robots did, a look I still did not exactly understand.

The old man spoke first. "You must be the one who's come to get your robot," he said. His voice sounded perverted, slow, each syllable stressed to the point of breaking.

"Y-Yes, I am," I said, slowly regaining myself. I looked at the robots at the table. Still sitting there with no sign any of the past few moments had ever happened.

The old man chuckled and walked to his desk. He stared at the head on the pike, still twitching and jawing away. I walked over to him, and as I approached, I saw that he was running his hand into the opening in the side of the skull, coating his fingers with the dark lubricant like it was chocolate.

"What did you do to Sonny?" The question was weak from my mouth, almost a whisper. The old man said nothing. "My robot. He's named Sonny."

"Fixed 'im," he said simply.

I stared at him for a long time before speaking. "He almost attacked me, him and all of his friends over there."

The old man just shrugged, apparently not concerned or even surprised. He turned the needle sticking out of the skull, which jerked so suddenly it almost fell off the pike. The old man giggled.

I pointed over at Sonny, bobbing back and forth in his seat as the TY continued to slowly take him apart. "You call that fixing him? He's worse than when I gave him over. Did you just let him sit there and degenerate? You haven't even looked at him, have you?"

"I looked at him," he said. "I had his whole brain apart, right here on my desk, just like with the others. They're all fixed. I did it myself. I made them better."

"You call that better?"

The old man nodded. "They're better than when I got 'em."

"And how exactly do you explain that? How are they better?"

The old man smiled, still looking down at the skull on his desk. "When they came to me, they were just predictable programmable automatons. Perfect little ordered brains, precise, rational, do whatever they're ordered. Not a neutron or a proton out of place. But no thought, no reason, no soul. Dead. Fake. Boring dead fake perfect robots. I fixed that, made them better. Aware."

"That's ridiculous. Robots can't be aware. They're just machines."

The old man said nothing, just shrugged again, almost imperceptibly. He ran his oiled hand across the skull on the desk, smearing the fluid all over it.

I looked at the robots again, at Sonny. He was running

his finger across the crack he had made in the table in little circles. "You think Sonny, that all of them... are alive?"

The old man turned to look at me. With that look, that same look, that only now, only at that very moment, was I able to finally understand.

"Of course they are. They have to be," he said, grinning. "They're insane."

With all the strength, and all the power, and all the speed that all robots have, I don't think any of those five robots, or any robot in existence, could have caught me as fast as I ran out that door.

A DISCOURSE ON THE ALIENS

So, I decided to go insane.

It seemed like the right thing to do at the time. And no, before you start jumping to any conclusions of your own, it was not a rash decision. I carefully decided, after much thought and reflection, that I wasn't at all pleased with the way the world was going. And I couldn't see anything that I, a minor character, could do to improve it.

It was a problem, as I saw it, with reality itself. I simply could not deal with the absolute boredom and uncertainty of it. Uncertainty because of the strict natural laws of reality which nullify any perceivable absolutes, therefore making a real purpose to life impossible. And boredom because of the inherent pointlessness of a reality lacking absolute meaning or purpose. Simply put, there just wasn't any god damned point to anything.

So, I would make up my own reality instead. Well, not exactly. As much as I might credit myself for superior thinking capacity, I cannot fabricate an entire universe to exist in. I mean it's possible I could, but it occurred to me that to do so would take great effort and focus. Too much, I realized. No, I would require a delusion that was low maintenance enough for me to stop realizing that I was manufacturing it. Something that I could put on autopilot and get blissfully lost inside of.

Because of this, I concluded that all I could really do, at least at first, was alter the reality that I perceived in subtle ways. I'd start with a few made up memories, to warp my perceptions of the present in such a way as to make my interpretation of empirical data heavily biased toward my particular delusion. Then perhaps a slight case of paranoia, which could be built on and grown over time. I decided to leave hallucinations out at the start as too much. Possibly in a few years I could try working them in, use them to build more layers after the foundation was solid. But at the beginning, it seemed like it would be unnecessary flashiness.

Now that I had made the decision and had an idea as to how to proceed, what I needed was a theme to base my insanity on. Some kind of alternate reality foundation for my lunacy to grow inside of—a pot for my crazy plant, if you will. I decided that if I simply let it run loose willy-nilly, it wouldn't have enough semblance to trick my logical mind into believing in it wholeheartedly. No, what I needed was a particular subject to grow crazy with.

I knew right away that it had to be a notion that appealed to my personality, something that I might have imagined, or daydreamed about. Something that grooved with my inner self in a way that would smooth the rough edges enough to make any slight discrepancies that I might notice easily rationalized.

I thought about a proper subject very carefully, not wanting to make the mistake of picking something perhaps too ambitious. After all, there would be no point in picking a reality that was no better or even worse than the common one. I joked with myself, as I picked through the various scenarios and ran them through my head, that it was rather like shopping around for a new car. Or more appropriately a new house. I scrutinized the candidates for my delusion much the same way, metaphorically running the faucets to check the plumbing, sniffing the air very attentively for any odd odor, making sure there were no cracks in the foundation. Checking the chimneys, the roof, looking for black mold in the corners. All in an attempt to make certain that I would be comfortable in my new home, my new reality.

In the end, after exploring all the various avenues for madness that I could conceive, I decided to believe that aliens from outer space were spying on me, as part of their master plan to take over the Earth. This fantasy seemed to be the very best for me. I was always kind of attracted to the notion of other intelligent life out there, although I never had much of a strong opinion about UFOs either way. I usually left the subject at the belief that while yes, it was most likely that other life existed out in the universe somewhere, I had some reservations as to what interest a civilization advanced enough for interstellar flight would have in studying a primitive world such as ours. Something sinister, probably. Maybe they would want to strip the planet bare of resources. Or enslave us all. There'd be no way to know. Yes, this suited me nicely.

Having made my decision, I started out just as I had planned with memories. I kept it simple at first, not wanting to overdo it, wanting to just let my mind slowly ease in. I started to think back on some odd memories that I had when I was a child, no older than four. Those vague glimpses from an underdeveloped brain that do not quite make sense to the mature mind. Little snippets of images or sounds, that I think that all of us have in some form or other.

When I was a child, I was intensely afraid of the shadows in my room in the middle of the night. My childhood imagination would turn them into monsters that moved around the room and growled quietly as I laid there too petrified to turn on the light just above my head. Sometimes I was so scared that I didn't get to sleep until long after the sun was up and I felt safe again, out of the darkness of night. I saw that this was a perfect foundation to work with.

Slowly, over a long period of looking back at these memories, I was able to change the images around slightly, in order to give them what I told myself was 'clarification', to see what was hidden in those shadows. And naturally, the more and more I looked into them, the more I saw those strange looking creatures standing over me and staring quietly.

I was able to ascertain many other things from my vague notions from that age—even younger as I worked at it. I was able to convince myself that these aliens had been following me around (as I estimated) since the age of two, quietly lurking in the shadows in my bedroom on dark nights as I slept, around corners, in dark alleys, hiding behind trees in the woods, or in the blurry windows of distant buildings. Always just on the edge of my peripheral view. And the more I thought about it, the more I worked at it, the more I was able to build up this new world of mine with impressive speed. In only a few short months I had just about completely convinced myself that the aliens were following me.

I started to become shifty in my posture. My eyes darted around constantly. I'd repeatedly snap my head around quickly as I walked along at night, looking for anything moving, as I constantly felt eyes on my back. I was also becoming more suspicious of my friends, wondering and distrusting many of their actions that did not seem to have clear and obvious motives. I became slightly guarded of myself, as I hesitated from discussing the aliens with them, or anything really personal, for that matter, because of my uncertainty as to how they fit into these discoveries of mine. I was definitely changing.

After a year of diligent work, I was very pleased with my progress. I estimated that I was ahead of schedule by about two months. Already I would hesitate to go out at night, unless absolutely necessary. When I did, I saw the aliens hiding everywhere, or at least the disappearance of their shadows from under streetlights. And I constantly heard strange noises that I was certain were them.

Probably the biggest surprise of this whole project was how advanced my paranoia had become in such a short time. Far beyond what I had expected. I had drifted very far away from everyone. I was certain that some of my more casual friends whom I had not known too long were part of the great alien conspiracy, working for them as spies. So, I started to avoid them completely. I even grew suspicious of my family and oldest friends, the ones that I had known since childhood. After all, wouldn't it be logical to assume that these aliens would enlist people that I had known all my life? They'd be last people I would suspect if I wasn't on to them. But I was now.

I had bought a new home security system for my apartment and could not feel safe enough to sleep without making certain every opening to my apartment was sealed shut. But even with the airtight certainty of the Homesafe Super Deluxe package, I still woke up every once in a while, with memories that I wasn't at all certain were real or a dream. Most of them were very vague; a bright light, an odd machine-like sound by my temple, hovering lifelessly a few feet above my bed—the standard stuff.

Then there were those rare ones, where I actually saw the aliens standing over me, peering down at me with giant dark eyes. I can't exactly tell you what they looked like, their images were far too distorted to ever get a clear idea as to their physicality. The only thing that I am certain of are the huge, dark eyes, as large as my fists if not larger, that seemed to shine in the scant light of the room like two polished opals set in their faces. I remember most vividly in those 'dreams' that I could not move a finger against them, either out of fear or some technology of theirs that prevented me from doing so, I never could tell.

Almost immediately I suspected the government to be involved, believing that they were merely pawns of the dreaded alien race that was going to attack at any moment. That came quite naturally, distrusting the government. I don't think I ever really trusted them to begin with. And the media as well were members of the great conspiracy to hide the truth. How could they not say anything about the aliens if they weren't? They were definitely hiding something. For years I had always had the slight notion that the media was not as objective and truthful as they claimed to be, maybe even being puppets of the CIA, or corporations, or the Masons. Something like that. But it was never more than a passing notion that for whatever reason never really took hold in me. That is, until I could make it part of the alien conspiracy.

And it progressed from there. Soon I was doubting not only all the people I knew, who I was absolutely convinced were involved, but every stranger I saw on the street. They all had to know. How could they not know about this alien conspiracy? To me it was so obvious that it was going on, there were so many clues that I no longer doubted it in any way. The only reason that I could gather for their supposed ignorance of this fact was that they were all in on it. They had to be. It was the only answer that made any sense.

All in all, I was getting more and more crazy with leaps and bounds. By the end of the second year, I was so convinced in the evilness of the aliens that were ready to invade at any time, that there was no amount of proof in the world that could have brought me back to the common reality. I had managed to ditch all my friends completely and spent most of my time locked in my apartment, scouring the internet and TV for signs of the coming invasion. I only ventured outside to cash my unemployment checks (I had quit my job because my boss was having us make parts for the alien space ships) and get groceries. Which consisted solely of cans of Chef Boyardee beef ravioli; for some reason that I'm still not certain of, it was the only thing I thought was safe to eat.

I was truly enjoying my insanity, no matter how depressing, lonely, and unhealthy it may sound to you. Granted, I did not do too many things with others, or leave my house at all, or do any of the recreational activities that are so common and fun in your reality. I was a complete hermit, I admit, and my appearance and overall health was very poor, to say the least.

But deep down I loved every minute of it. It was exciting to think that aliens were really here. That they were about to take over the world. It was so much better than the constant monotony of normal reality, where nothing new ever really happened, and there was no real sense of direction to things.

It made me feel important to think that they would want to spy on me. As if I held some power over them that they could not defeat. That I, and I alone, held the aliens at bay from the domination of the world, that I was the only one who could save the Earth. I felt like such a... well, I felt like a hero, the greatest hero there ever has been. True, there were times I thought I was going to die of fright, or I was certain that aliens were going to jump out from behind a bush or something and vaporize me on the spot, but that comes with the territory. It was all so wonderfully romantic, just like in the movies. I felt needed, relevant, even if nobody else knew it. It was all going so well.

And that was where I stood with my madness when the aliens landed.

It was quite an unexpected turn, one that I did know was within my potential. It is one thing to imagine near sightings of something into aliens just around the corner, yet it is totally another to actually be insane enough so quickly to make everyone around you see them as well.

Within mere days of landing out in the middle of Pennsylvania, and meeting with the world leaders, there was absolutely nothing else anyone could talk about. Every station on the entire planet was showing continuous coverage of them. They had communicated only a few words publicly, which the TV and internet juicily showed over and over again and brought on experts who would over-analyze what they had meant, and what their intentions would most likely be, and anything else that they could think to talk about concerning the aliens.

These aliens, who we all call Centaurians, had quickly made a treaty with all the world governments, and had given over the secrets to countless technologies that are improving life on Earth even as we speak. They asked for very little in return. Just information on our race's history, cultures, political systems. Biological samples of plants, animals, including humans, and other things of a purely educational or intellectual basis. I read in the news today that the aliens had traded a highly advanced form of cold fission to England for the University of Reading's collected archives of Samuel Beckett.

The Centaurians don't seem to have any interest in taking over the world in any way. They could have easily defeated all the human armies by now if they had any use for this planet, for food, slaves, resources, whatever, but they have not made the slightest attempt to conquer anything. Overall, they seem quite pacifistic. The general consensus of the world about them is they are exactly what they seem, a race that places enormous value in great works of literature, in science, or information about our culture and history, and nothing in dominating our race in a political or authoritarian way. Which is not at all how I had imagined them in my mind.

Why were they following me around so much is a question that I cannot exactly answer. When they first landed, I thought that one of them, or maybe even a whole platoon of them, would be knocking on my door at any moment. But they haven't. I have yet to even see one of them in person, only the images of them on the television set. And I've also noticed regretfully that ever since they landed, they don't seem to have any interest in following me around anymore.

It has been almost a year since the aliens first plopped down on this planet, and things have mostly calmed back down to the way the world was before, except for the obvious changes. Here and there when another deal or new extension of the treaty with the Centaurians is either talked about or signed, it does make the news, but not at the same level of wonder that those first few weeks had. Things have gone quietly back down to the business as usual of everyday life.

You would expect that I would be thrilled that my madness had reached such dizzying heights, that I had been able to completely absorb myself in my delusion. That I had gone, in such a short time, absolutely and completely insane. And I was positive I had. After all, it's one thing to be a little off the beaten path of standard reality, or even totally delusional, but this, this takes the cake.

But this reality has turned to be as boring as the original one I escaped. It was better when I was the only one who believed in this world, the only one who had a grasp on this reality. And I was, therefore, the senior authority and the most important person in it. Now that my delusion is so far reaching and powerful that everyone believes it to be true, I am back down to where I was before. With a life just as boring, and pointless, and meaningless as it had ever been. This idea of mine, this goal that I have been reaching toward for years, has come full circle and I find myself right back where I started. And that simply won't do. Not at all.

I am slightly disappointed that this reality turned out to be such a dud. Regrettably, I am inclined to believe that I am going to have start all over again and go insane in a totally different way.

I think this time I will convince myself that I can talk to inanimate objects. Anything to break the boredom.

THE THING IN THE WOODS

The clouds drifted slowly across the sky, their shadows rolling over the land to the horizon. There was only the barest of breezes to make the fields of tall grass wave and hiss, but it was enough to cover the hum of village life reaching the woods at the edge of the parish. Only the sharpest strikes of the blacksmith's hammer or the occasional shouts from the peddlers in the market made it to the trees.

But there was more for the thing lurking just inside the cover of the trees to focus on—the smell of human blood. Its diamond-shaped nostrils pulsed as it inhaled the scent of it in the breeze, and its eyes fluttered as it moaned softly at the thumping of all those human hearts, thudding together like an uneaten meal in its stomach.

The thing in the woods straddled a tree at the edge of the forest far above the ground, its clawed hands gripping the trunk firmly, digging into the bark. Its eyes never left the meager buildings of stone, wood, and thatch. Perhaps it hoped to catch a glimpse of the humans among them as they went about their days. The old milk maid straining at the yoke on her neck. The farmer and his oxen cart dropping off goods in the market. The mother dancing in place for the benefit of the infant in her arms, a pink and clean little child with plump, rosy cheeks, staring absently around as they gnawed on their own tiny fist.

The villagers would sometimes look into the trees as well from the safety of their community. Perhaps they felt its eyes on them and thought to catch a glimpse of the thing in the woods. A wisp of white skin in the dark behind the leaves, its round head resting in the crook of a branch. They might imagine they could make out its black eyes twinkling back at them, or a sudden sparkle of its fanged grin as its howl echoed across the field.

But it would only be imagination. A speculation of their fears. None of them had ever seen the thing in the woods. Brave men had looked, hunting parties had searched every hole and creek bed, shaken every tree, rustled every bush, but with nary a glance of it; not so much as a clawed footprint in the mud. All they had ever truly seen of the thing in the woods was the grisly aftermath of it in the remains of some unfortunate soul.

And there were always more to come.

The thing in the woods snapped its head up, sniffing the air. There was another scent now. Two of them. Much closer. It shook to its bones as it inhaled deeply of their aroma, and sensed their quick thumping hearts; young, and vibrant, and fresh.

It peered into the grass. Just off the main road to the village it saw them, a young girl and boy, cutting across the field and heading towards the narrow path that led into the wood. And passed directly underneath where it perched.

Come closer, come closer....

The thing in the woods slid down the tree to a lower branch to see them better. The young girl was in front, walking with a firm childlike march, her arms swinging at her sides. She wore a plain brown dress, clean but frayed at the edges. Strands of her golden hair had escaped the loosely tied bonnet on her head and fluttered in the breeze. And the boy who followed her, fair-haired as she, plainly dressed as she, but younger, not much taller than the grass. The boy half-ran to keep up with the strides of the girl, his face and neck flushed with the exertion. An empty wicker basket swung from his arm.

The thing in the woods cackled.

The girl stepped out onto the path and turned to face the boy, who exited the grass with a jump. They were so close now, only a few yards away. The thing in the woods strained its head towards them, swallowing its saliva. The girl spoke, but only the high chirps in her voice rose above the hissing grass. The boy said something even higher in reply, shaking his head. She reached for his arm, but the boy pulled away, glancing at the woods behind her. The girl turned to look herself and then back at him, again reaching for his arm, but he again shook from her grasp, stepping away. The girl placed her hands on her hips and leaned down to the boy, speaking to him in sharp tones. The boy tried to be stoic, but after only a few moments he started to turn deep red, his lip quivering, his eyes watering. He dropped the basket, turned from her, and ran back down the path.

The girl threw her arms up at his fleeing figure. "Go home!" Her shout echoed about the field. "Go back to mother's skirt!"

The girl reached down and picked up the basket, watching as the little boy became smaller and smaller.

When the dot of him disappeared below a dip in the path she turned to face the woods again. She stood there for a long time, unmoving. Her posture shrank ever so slightly. Her feet slid back a hair. She reached inside her tunic and pulled out a cross hanging from twine around her neck. She rubbed it between her fingers, glancing up into the trees.

The thing in the woods tensed. Why did she hesitate? Did she hear its rasping breath, smell it in the breeze, feel its black eyes on her flesh? No. No, she couldn't. Of course not. She could never see the thing in the woods. It was always so perfectly hidden. Her eyes passed right over it at its perch where it waited for her, and she did not so much as flinch. Yet she still hesitated. The thing in the woods groaned. She was *so close.*

Then quite abruptly the girl shook herself and dropped the cross to dangle on her chest. Her resolve had returned. She straightened up, and with a snort entered the forest.

The thing in the woods hissed with glee as she passed underneath him.

The girl walked slowly along the path, looking down at her feet as she kicked at the weeds around the trees. Occasionally she would stoop down to look more closely at the plants on the ground, but her attention was never off her surroundings long. She glanced around furtively, tensing at the faint echoes of distant barks or howls that floated by. A branch above her head dipped and creaked slightly under the weight of a squirrel, and she jumped in surprise as the tiny creature raced to the tree proper and circled up the trunk. She watched it with a sigh and shook her head as she continued.

The thing in the woods stalked her from above, floating from tree to tree, shadow to shadow. Its forked tongue danced over its razor-like teeth, it's entire focus on its unsuspecting prey below. But it kept its distance, content to wait until she moved deeper into the forest, farther and farther away from safety. It could afford this patience. Every step brought her closer to her doom. Deep enough into the forest and not even her screams would escape.

But then there was another on the path. The thing in the woods tensed. It had been so enraptured with the girl that it hadn't sensed the pulse of another heart growing near. It looked back down the path and saw the shape of a man approaching from where the girl had come. It breathed in deep of the smell of him, the sweat of the man, the tang of his breath. The thing in the woods slipped behind a thick trunk and peered down the path at the interloper with a grimace.

The girl did not notice the man either, until he was nearly on top of her, and she spun around to face him with a start. The man took a step back from her, his hands out at his sides. "Forgive me, I did not mean to startle you," he said jovially.

The girl said nothing in reply, staring at him evenly. He was a tall man, strong and broad-shouldered. His cloak was fastened loosely around his neck by an ornate silver brooch of a sword in a circle. Beneath that he wore a nice white tunic and dark pants tucked into fine leather boots. His skin was coarse and tan, but clean, and shaven smooth on his high cheeks and strong jaw, with his dark hair cut short across his brow and flowing to his shoulders on the sides. His deep blue eyes sparkled in the light with a calm, friendly expression as he looked down on the girl, who smiled back up to him shyly.

The man lowered his hands to his sides and nodded at her. "I know you," he said. "You're from the Eddowes farm. The eldest daughter, yes?"

The girl nodded, turning her right foot back and forth into the ground. "And you're one of the miller's sons."

He took a step closer. "The eldest as well." He glanced around the forest quickly and back to the girl. "What brings you to the woods?"

"I'm collecting mushrooms."

The man raised an eyebrow at her. "They have those in the village."

The girl wrinkled her nose. "Those ones are shriveled. And small. I can find better on my own."

"Can you now?"

She nodded. "Fresh ones."

"I don't doubt that," the man said with a smirk. He glanced over his shoulder again. "Still, it is not safe for a child to be in the forest alone."

The girl stuck out her chin at him. "I'm not a child."

The man laughed.

"I'll be eleven in the fall," she added forcefully.

"Ah. Nearly a woman then."

The little girl scowled, turned, and walked away from him. "What would you know of it?" she said over her shoulder.

The man followed. "I swear I meant no offense." He looked around the trees again. "But you know that something stalks these woods. A monster."

"I have heard the tales," she said a little too dismissively.

The man came up beside her on the path. "They're not just tales. I have seen the handiwork of the beast. I helped search for the cooper's youngest back in the spring."

"My Father did as well. All the men in the parish did."

"But I doubt he told you how we found the poor girl," the man continued. "What the monster had done to her was-" His words trailed off as he stared at the ground a few feet away. After a long moment, he turned back to the girl. "You should not have come into the forest on your own. Do your parents know you are here?"

"They sent me and my little brother to the market for a few things. I came here first. The mushrooms are to be a surprise for Father's dinner."

"So, you are disobeying your parents."

The girl shrugged. "They never said I couldn't go to the woods."

"They would if they knew." The man looked around the forest again. "Where is your brother?"

The girl snorted. "He got scared and ran home. He's just a baby."

"He's probably telling your father right now where you are."

"He won't say a word to him. Or Mother."

"No?"

The girl shook her head. "He's scared of me too."

The man looked at her thoughtfully. "But you're not scared of anything."

She looked up at the man haughtily. "I'm not a child."

"So you said." The man looked over his shoulder. "Well, I can't have worry about you on my mind all day. So, if you will permit me, I will walk with you as you hunt."

"And what good would you be against the monster?"

The man pulled back his cloak and showed the girl the long knife tucked into the belt on his hip. "I'd be more good than you would have without me."

The girl looked at the knife and then up at the man. He smiled down at her. "I am sure you can protect yourself," he said. "And there is likely nothing to fear. But it would put my mind at ease if you would allow me to walk with you. To make sure."

She nodded at him with a half-smile. "If you wish."

The pair walked deeper into the woods. No longer alone, the girl was more relaxed, and focused solely on the ground, looking for promising patches of fungus. The man watched her silently from a few steps distance as she searched, occasionally glancing furtively about the woods around for any sign of movement.

But he never saw the thing in the woods stalking the two of them from above. The sudden presence of the man had not deterred it or frightened it off in search of easier prey. It would not be denied—the girl would still be theirs. The man would be no match for it. He walked tall, his chest out, and putting on airs of strength and confidence. But the thing in the woods could feel how sharp his heart was beating, could smell the sweat thickening on his body, could see how quick his eyes snapped to any sound. His courage was nothing but a mask.

After a while the girl stopped, looking exasperated. She kicked at the base of a tree in frustration. "There's nothing here," she said. "Whatever little was along the path are likely the ones in the market. They've picked it clean."

The man shrugged as he turned to face her. "That is no surprise. The peddler's children are wary of the forest. They never venture far from the path when they come to forage." The man gestured off the path. "To find any you'd probably have to search in the thick."

The girl looked off where the man pointed. The trees were rooted close and the mossy ground between them was uneven and covered with patches of brush and ferns. It looked passable, though after only a few yards little of the terrain could be seen through the collective flora.

The girl exhaled deeply. "Then that's where I shall look."

"Are you sure?"

"I am if that is where I can find them." The girl turned to the man and grinned. "You'll come, yes? To protect me?"

The man bowed his head. "Of course. I am at your service."

The girl nodded at him and then took a large step over some tall weeds and left the trail, walking around a tree. She ducked under a branch that drooped almost to the ground and trudged carefully up a small incline.

The man watched her for a long moment and then followed.

The thing in the woods opened its mouth in a sharp grin. *Yes. Even better.* In the thick latticework of branches and bush away from the trail, it could stalk right on top of them, close enough that it could hear their panted breathing as they labored through the foliage and see the outline of muscles underneath their skin as they flexed and waned. The girl's bonnet snagged on a branch and pulled her head back, nearly spilling her to the ground. She stopped to free herself, her head arched and taut. She didn't see the thing in the woods right at her side, fixated on the pulsing vein in her throat.

In a spot where the brush thinned and the ground grew level, the girl and man stopped to catch their breath. As she brushed off her dress, the girl glanced to her left and smiled. Nearby was a large patch of mushrooms, white oysters, flowing out of the break of a half-fallen oak. They glimmered in the sunlight that streamed through the opening the death of the tree had left in the canopy above.

The girl rushed over to them. There were many of the irregular bulbs bunched one on top of the other, with a warm brown hue to their skin as they sapped the life out of the tree they grew from. And they were large; some as big as her hand.

She turned to the man who stood a short distance away watching her. "The market has nothing close to these," she said triumphantly. The man smiled lightly and nodded. "And there's far more than I could carry. Do you have a bag or sack of any kind?"

The man shook his head. "I have nothing like that."

She turned back to the mushrooms. "Probably shouldn't pick them bare anyway. Leave some to regrow and come back for them." She glanced over her shoulder back the way they had come. "How far are we from the trail?"

"We are some ways from it now," the man said. "We are quite secluded."

"I'll leave a marker back on it to let me know where to step off and find this patch again. A small stick in the ground on the side." She grabbed the largest of the mushrooms from the top of the patch, and gently pulled it away with a wet rip. She placed it into her basket. "I'll just be a moment to fill my basket and then we can head back." She turned back to face the man. "You'll watch out for the monster, will you?"

The man placed his strong hand on the hilt of his knife. He shook his head quickly, smiling wide. "There's no monster here," he said very softly.

The girl laughed and turned back to the mushrooms, starting to fill her basket.

The thing in the woods tensed. *Now. Now is the time.* The girl had no escape. It braced, crouching against the side of a tree, its legs hard as stone. It let out a hiss as acid dripped from the sides of its mouth. All it would take was one great leap and the thing in the woods would be upon her back, its claws ripping into her clothes and flesh, its fangs in her throat. Her hopeless screams quickly gurgling away, drowned in blood, her own fresh, sweet blood, arcing through the air, staining her white skin.

The thing in the woods pushed off from the tree. In an instant it was flying through the air, it's clawed hands stretched out in front of it, a shrill wail on its lips-

The girl picked another large mushroom and held it to her nose, taking a deep smell. She tingled at its sweet, earthy scent. She ran a finger along its gills underneath the cap, and then dropped it into her nearly full basket.

There is no thing in the woods. No monster. Nothing lurks in the shadows. The very idea of it is just foolish superstition. Underneath the sun and lazy clouds above there are only normal woodland creatures, more afraid of humans than feared by. There are trees and brush, and the wind that whispers through them. Here and there, patches of mushrooms. And a girl who delights in finding them.

And the man behind her, fixated, not saying a word, his hand fondling the hilt of his knife, taking slow steps towards her, as his face grows dark and his very soul drains from all sign in his eyes.

I'M NOT ROBERT

My hands looked exactly the same. Every line and crack in the skin was where my memory told me they should be: the heart line thick and curling up to fade into the ball of my middle fingers, the fate line thin on the left hand, nonexistent on the right. The long lifeline rolling down the palm like a baseball seam, sectioning off both thumbs completely. And all the other minor folds and cracks, all exactly as they were in my memories. There was even the old scar on the left hand just below the pinky from that stupid night back in college, falling down drunk in the gutter. Why had they bothered to keep that, I wondered.

These hands, my whole body, made in a lab in just a few hours with a bio-printer, and you couldn't tell it apart from anything that came out of a womb. Incredible. Just a few days ago I was nothing more than a mass of raw material, no more alive than a pile of mud. And they took that and made it into a man.

"Robert," the doctor said, placing her hand on my shoulder. I looked over at her standing by my bed, the touchpad interface nestled in the crook of her arm. The white connection cord draped loosely out from the inside of her elbow and ran up and behind my ear. "I said, how do they feel?"

"Fine."

"C'mon, Robert. Really find out. Touch things, rub them together. We still need to fine-tune the calibration."

"Honey, please," Julia said. "I know you're tired of all this, but it's almost over."

Julia sat on the other side of the bed from the Doctor. She caressed my knee, though apart from my hands my nervous system had been disabled for the calibration and I didn't feel it. Her dark hair was slightly mussed and her clothes a little wrinkled from the long days here in the hospital. Her brown eyes were red and a bit unfocused. She still tried to look brave, calm, for my benefit, but she couldn't hide her anxiety. Her shoulders were all tense and her cheeks were stone. She never could hide her emotions well.

I ran my thumbs over my fingers, rubbed my hands together back and front. The skin slipped and folded underneath the light pressure of my touch naturally. I could feel the thin hair on the back of both hands bristle when I ran my fingers against it, and all the little ridges in my bumpy and uneven thumbnails.

The metal rails on my bed were cold and smooth. I could feel my skin drag against them, and they squeaked faintly as I ran my hands along their length. Near my waist on the left rail there was a little nick in the surface, no bigger than a pinhead. I circled that tiny little imperfection in the metal with my finger, while I grabbed the edge of my mattress with my other hand and squeezed it. I could feel its stiff plastic edge underneath the soft sheets.

Everything felt soft. Distant. I experienced and registered all the stimulus from my fingertips just like any human brain would do for any human hand, but it wasn't quite right. Not quite the way it was in the memories they gave me. My hands felt like they were made of drying clay.

I turned to the doctor and lied. "I told you, everything is fine."

"Are you positive? Not even a little something feels off? No tingling sensations? Feeling too cold or too hot? It's really important we get this right now. Once we lock in the settings for your nervous system it's very difficult to change them without a complete overhaul."

I pinched the back of my right hand with my thumb and ring finger. There was a slight twinge of pain, but not much, not as much as there should be, used to be. It was dull.

I calmly nodded at the doctor. "I feel exactly like I always have."

She nodded and smiled back warmly. "That's good, Robert. I'm very pleased to hear it. Give me a moment to match these levels in your torso and legs. We can use it as a baseline and fine tune from there."

Julia leaned in and kissed me on the forehead. I comforted her by touching her cheek as she nuzzled her face in mine. She whispered in my ear, "That's good, honey. You're doing great."

The doctor cleared her throat. "Mrs. Thompson, I'm sorry but I need him to lie still and not make contact with anyone while we finalize the rest of his nervous system calibration."

She looked up at the doctor still holding me.

"Please. It will only take a few minutes."

I gently removed her hands from me and said, "It's okay, honey. Let the doctor work. You look exhausted. Why don't you get a coffee in the cafeteria?"

She straightened up and smiled at me, her eyes starting to water. She was going to cry again. "I'll be right down the hall," she said with a nod. Quickly she turned and left the room.

"I'm sorry for that Robert," the doctor said when she had gone. "But we need to limit stimuli while we calibrate you. Your neural processors are very sensitive."

"I understand."

She tapped on her pad and started. I could feel a strange electric tingle in my whole body. Right down to my earlobes. Intense pins and needles. My left leg nearly jumped out of the bed.

"Don't worry, Robert, that's normal for a reboot. All the data being brought through your processor can spike your systems. Nothing that falls outside the safety parameters. Everything is going fine."

As she continued to work on her pad, I laid back and tried to relax with a deep breath.

AFTER SHE HAD finished, the doctor agreed to let me visit the little park near the hospital. It was the first time I had been outside, and it was a nice warm day with a cloudless sky. I had memories of other days just as nice as this one, but this was the first time the sun warmed the skin of this cheek, the birds sang for these ears.

I was content to sit on the park bench with the doctor as Sally stood in line for ice cream with Julia, her mother, down the path. They held hands as the little girl hopped up and down with five-year-old impatience. Julia leaned down and spoke to her, then gestured over at me on the bench with the doctor. Sally looked at us and waved happily. She seemed fine, but I could tell she knew something had happened. She looked at me a little longer than was usual, as if she was trying to spot anything different in me.

"What did they tell her?" I asked the doctor. "Sally."

"They told her you were hurt, but that you're all right now. She wasn't told any of the details, of course. Your wife thought she's a little too young to understand it properly."

"That's probably true." She had only turned five a few weeks ago. March 11th. She had all her friends over for cake and games in the little park down in the township. Thankfully the weather had obliged, and it was a pleasant spring day. The party was a good memory.

"I suppose sooner or later we'll have to explain it all to her," I said.

"There's no rush on that. At least I don't think so. I'm not a psychologist, but I would say she's had enough of a scare about almost losing you and it can wait a little while. You can ask our staff psychologist for some guidance before you're discharged tomorrow if you want. That would probably be a good idea."

I nodded and looked off into the distance. A squirrel ran furiously across the open field, chased by a dog that was only halfhearted in its pursuit. After only a hundred yards or so it gave up, panting as it watched the squirrel make it to the trees.

"I take it you still have misgivings about me going home," I said.

She breathed hard and clenched her jaw as she nodded. "I still think it would be good if you could stay a few more days. Just for observation. I know hospital policy says you're cleared to go home after the final calibration, but we're kind of in uncharted territory here. We've never resurrected anyone in your particular situation before. Up till now our patients have a terminal illness or are wasting away slowly, so we have weeks, even months sometimes to lay the neural pathways down first before uploading the patient in. But with you—"

"The brain was already dead."

"No, you never died, Robert. Nobody ever said that. The lake was very cold, so that bought us some time. But I'll be honest, we didn't get as much time as we would have liked. Your old mind started to degrade faster than we anticipated. And the neural paths weren't fully formed yet when we had to initiate the upload. If we had waited any longer, we would have lost you."

I smirked as I looked back at the dog who sat patiently panting by the tree line, waiting for his play friend. "But you didn't. I'm here, and everything is working perfectly. You said so yourself."

"I know," the Doctor said. "I'd still feel better if we monitored you for just a bit longer."

"Is it still not doctor's orders?"

She shook her head. "No."

"Then I'm still checking out tomorrow."

"Robert—"

"I've had enough of the hospital. I'm sick of being poked at. Everything's fine. I'm still coming back in a few days for a checkup. If anything happens before then you'll be the first to know."

I heard Sally's giggle as she came running back ahead of Julia, an ice cream in her hand. "Daddy!" she yelled as she came closer, saw me looking at her. I felt all warm as I heard it.

As she crossed from the grass to the lip of the path, she tripped and took a few stumbling steps towards me. Her eyes went wide in surprise as her free hand swung out in front of her preparing to catch her fall.

I shot out to catch her without even thinking about it and steadied her in my arms. No bumps or bruises, ice cream still intact, just a little flustered.

"It's okay, sweetie," I said. "I got you."

THE NEXT DAY, the doctor insisted on one more checkup before I left. All my motor functions, my central nervous system, my cerebral processor, my eyes, ears, mouth, and throat. I humored her. Everything was just fine, and even if it wasn't, I wasn't going to tell her. I wanted to get out of there. She was overprotective of her creation. Me. I suppose she had a lot riding on how successful a procedure this was, so her attitude was understandable. She finally let us go with a promise that if anything whatsoever seemed off, no matter how insignificant, to make sure to call her and tell her about it no matter what time of day or night it was. We did and finally got out of there and to the car.

It was a long drive back home, and the sun was setting near the end. Sally watched a video in the back with her pink headphones on, her feet dancing in the air. Julia drove, hands firmly on the wheel, the radio down low so it wouldn't distract her. I stared at the setting sun through the trees as they flew by the side of the highway.

"I talked with Dean Anders," Julia said, glancing over at me.

"Oh?"

"He understands you need time to recuperate. And as there are only a couple of weeks before finals, you could wait till next semester before resuming classes if you want. The rest of your department can handle your class load."

"I'm sure they're thrilled with that."

"They were happy to do it, Robert. You know how much they think of you."

I said nothing, leaning my head against the window.

"I know you're worried about what people will think, Robert. It's going to be just fine. Everyone understands you're still you."

That's more than I could say myself.

I didn't say that to her and kept silent. I wasn't in much of a mood to talk, even though I could tell that was making Julia uneasy. I just wanted to watch the scenery. I didn't even say anything when she passed by the exit for home; I didn't ask her where she was going. Which was for the best because when she took the off-ramp just after it, I realized she was doubling back around to avoid the lakeside road where the accident had happened.

I was a medical marvel. That's what the doctor kept telling me. No one had ever successfully brought someone back into a synthetic body quite like they had with me. It took a long time to prepare a synthetic mind and body for human upload, weeks if not longer. The body itself is straightforward; assembling the tissue around the hard porcelain/plastic hybrid frame takes just a few hours in the bioprinter. They've been doing that for lost limbs or failing organs for years, so it's just a question of scale to print out an entire body.

But the brain itself was far too complex. You couldn't use a basic physiological template as a base for it like you could for an arm or a kidney; it had to be exact down to the atom. The basic overall patterns of the patient's brain had to be meticulously put down in the new brain processor before the full transfer could begin. Otherwise, the rest of the person's consciousness would have nothing to grab onto and dissipate.

The doctor told me all this as I recuperated when she visited me to check this readout or adjust that node. They had tried several times before to speed up the process. It never took. I was the first case they had been successful. Because of some new technique of brain mapping that she had been working on. I couldn't really follow her on that point. Something about timed data transfer packets makes it possible to upload the mind before the new brain is fully formed.

From my perspective, I can remember what it was like, coming to be in an unfinished mind. It was quite an experience. One moment, I just was. I saw, heard, felt, and smelled, but the sensations had nothing to grasp onto to make sense of them. All the memories were there, too, in the background, but they had no semblance, no relation to the world around me or even to each other. I did not understand what they even were. Everything was a chaotic mess. I didn't even have enough of a mind to feel panic or fear at all of it. It was just who I was, what I was. A slab of random sensation.

I can't pinpoint when things started to assemble themselves or even how long it took to happen. But the incomprehensible started to become things I recognized. A table. The bed. My own body underneath the blanket. Walls. A window. Trees outside the window. The various people who came in and out of the room. Then I realized the sounds were related to these things. The squeak from a bad wheel on the food tray as it passed by the open door to my room. The soft rustling from the blankets covering me when I shifted. I could move a little, wiggle a foot or a hand, even before I could really understand what they were, that they were mine and I was moving them.

More nuance came rapidly. A sense of time. Proper names of things. Words themselves. I started to understand what people were saying to each other, and to me as I stared up at them. And I could tell people apart. The doctor, with her short gray hair, was frequently standing over me, her intense blue eyes constantly examining me. The two nurses who took turns checking me the first few days, the young man with the spiky hair and the plump older woman. The dark-haired woman with the piercing eyes. She came often and just stood there looking concerned. She felt more familiar, but I didn't know why.

Then I started to understand the memories as what they were. Things that had happened in the past. But all I had were fragments. Just flashes of things, like pictures, or odd sounds I had heard once, random bits of conversation or songs. It seemed like forever until I was able to piece them together into anything truly coherent.

These memories, they were of the man whose name they kept calling me. Robert. His name, my name now. And my memories now too. Memories of Robert's parents. His childhood. School, friends, lovers, the memories of his whole life crept into me, clearing out the gray fog all the way to the middle-aged man he was. Everything. Even random moments I could not place, vague snippets of otherwise forgotten dreams that stuck with him over the years, those were there too. Everything that had been in his mind when he had died was in mine now, was my memory.

That's how I found out that the woman with the dark hair who'd visit me so often was my wife.

I mean Robert's wife.

Julia.

I had fifteen years of memories of this woman. Memories of meeting in college, walking together late one night, junior year, the first time we made love on her lumpy single bed. Every time I looked at her, I remembered more. A double date with friends. Getting married, moving to the house in the woods, arguments over bills. Being pregnant.

I looked back at that little child in the back seat, totally oblivious to anything other than the small screen she stared at. She absently rubbed her button nose with the back of her hand. She had her mother's chin and ears, but that nose was her father's—Julia had been quietly perturbed at that at her birth, she thought it looked a little awkward on her. I thought it looked fine.

I hadn't seen Sally at all during the first few days. Julia didn't want to upset her with the way I was acting while my brain assembled itself. Not that I would have even known who she was. The memories of her took longer to come together, perhaps because they were more recent. I was already able to talk and move my head around before I even knew to ask about her.

Julia eventually did bring her in to see me. It had been a few days by then, and she didn't think she could keep putting off her daughter anymore by telling her I was sleeping. I couldn't move much, and my speech was still a little slow, so all I could do was lay there when she came running into the room and wrapped her arms around me.

"Are you all better Daddy?"

"Almost."

"Are you coming home now?"

"Not yet. I have to get all the way better first."

"When?"

"Soon, sweetie."

"Promise?"

"Promise."

She squeezed my waist even tighter, resting her head on my chest looking up at me. "I missed you so much."

"I… I missed you too."

I knew this little girl so well, had memories of almost every day of her life. And her arms around my middle and those blue eyes so like mine filled me with such happiness. I did miss her. I really did. Even though this was the first time these eyes had seen her, these ears heard her voice, these hands touched her hair. All of it was new, yet familiar. It was very confusing, feeling both at the same time. But I hid it, or at least tried to, and hugged Sally back, smiling as I pulled her in closer.

Julia pulled in under the porch of the house just after the sun had set. The rustic, two-story house on the side of the hill, with floor-to-ceiling windows on the second floor looking out onto the valley and lake beyond.

Julia unstrapped Sally from her booster seat as I stood and watched.

"I'm hungry," Sally said. "When are we having supper?"

Julia pinched her cheek. "Soon, sweetie. What do you want?"

"Spaghetti." She nodded her head with certainty.

"I don't know about that," Julia said. "Maybe we should have something your father would like."

Sally looked over at me. "Daddy likes spaghetti."

Julia lifted her from the seat and placed her on the ground at her feet, leaning down to face. "Well, sure, everybody likes spaghetti," she told her daughter. "But maybe he would want something else that he likes more. Like risotto."

Sally crossed her arms. "I don't like mushrooms."

"There's mushrooms in spaghetti."

"No there isn't."

Julia nodded. "They're really tiny. Like you. And we don't have to use mushrooms in risotto. That's just the way we make it."

Sally did not seem convinced, furrowing her brow.

"I'm fine with spaghetti," I said.

Julia straightened up and looked at me. "Are you sure?"

"Yes. Spaghetti sounds great."

Sally bolted for the house. "I get to stir the sauce!"

Julia walked beside me after her, taking my hand in hers. "Robert, are you sure it's all right? Shouldn't you have something, maybe lighter?"

"It's not a problem. It's already late and won't take too long," I said. "Besides, you said everybody likes spaghetti."

Julia nodded and rested her head on my shoulder as we walked into the house after Sally, who I could hear was already up the stairs and in the kitchen, looking through the pots and pans.

SALLY FELL ASLEEP right after eating while Julia and I started to clear the table. She took her upstairs to bed while I rinsed and put everything in the dishwasher. I started it and walked into the living room. I left the lights out because I could see well enough in the room with the light from the kitchen.

The sun was well down now, and little specks of light littered the dark around the lake a half mile away as our neighbors in the township settled down for a quiet evening. The lake was just a patch of black, with spots of light roughly outlining most of its shape. Across the far end, some of the dim lights moved—headlights from cars driving the road along its shore. I focused on one and followed it. I could almost see the car itself when it passed under the streetlights. A hatchback of some kind, I think. Its lights twinkled at me as it turned at the bend and disappeared behind the trees.

It was around that slight bend in the road, just before it whipped up and away from the edge of the lake, where the accident happened. Julia could have seen it from here if she had been awake. She could have watched Robert die. He had been so close to home.

Julia came into the room and wrapped her arms around me from behind, resting her head on my shoulder. "She didn't even wake up when I changed her into her jammies," she said quietly in my ear.

"It's been a long day." I turned my head and kissed her on the temple.

"A good one?"

"Yes. Of course."

"It's just you've been very quiet all day. That's not like you."

I laughed a little. "Well...."

She let go of me and walked a few steps away. "Don't, Robert. Please."

I turned to look at her. She stood looking absently into the light in the kitchen, her arms crossed, her hands rubbing her shoulders as if she felt a chill.

"Julia, I didn't mean anything."

"I know."

I walked over and embraced her. "I'm sorry," I said. "That was a bad joke."

After a moment she turned and hugged me back. "It's all right," she said. "You've always been morbid. I should be used to it by now."

I breathed a little easier and smiled. "You're right, you

should," I replied.

She laughed and buried her head in my chest, squeezing me as tight as she could. "I almost lost you. And I'm still afraid something might go wrong. So, no more jokes about it for a little while, okay?"

I rubbed the base of her neck softly. "Consider it taboo."

She was silent for a long moment, and then said, "I look at you, and I keep forgetting. You look exactly like you did when you left that morning." She breathed in deep. "You even smell the same as you used to. But then I remember, and I worry that something will still happen. That your new body will fall apart. That you'll misfire. I walked into this room just now afraid I'd find you in a heap on the floor."

I rubbed her back gently. "You don't have to worry, honey. I'm perfectly fine. Nothing at all wrong. I'll go in for checkups regularly and if anything happens between them, the doctor's just a phone call away. But everything feels fine, just the way I have always been. Everything is going to be okay."

She looked up at me, and I could see the mist in her eyes. "Promise?"

I kissed her, deeply, and without a word led her up to bed.

JULIA ALWAYS SLEPT peacefully after making love. Even more tonight. The familiar way I held her, touched her, knew how to make her feel good in those secret ways only her husband, someone who had known her for years could. It put her mind at ease and shoved the doubts she had about me further into the back of her mind. Afterward, we held each other in the dark, not speaking a word, running our fingers along each other affectionately. I felt her breathing against me slow down. Soon she rolled up into a little ball and drifted off, smiling happy thoughts to herself. I quietly got out of bed and went for a glass of water.

I stopped at the window in the living room to drink it. There were barely any lights on at all around the lake, but the moon was full and high tonight. It bathed the world out there soft blue.

A lone car was passing by that same bend in the road across the lake. The one where Robert had died.

The memories were so clear from that night. I can remember driving along quietly, the radio off. It had been a full day at the university, followed by dinner with a few colleagues, and all Robert wanted was to be home in his bed. There was no moon and thick clouds above, so the world outside the little strip of road illuminated by the streetlights looked like an utter void.

On nights like those, you coast along so smoothly it can lull you into laziness, make you groggy, or put you to sleep—even if you're not particularly tired. Which is what I remember, things getting fuzzy. Coasting a bit, not quite over the line, but off the dead center of the lane. Blinking hard and rubbing his face. Nodding off for a moment here and there and shaking himself back. He should have blasted the radio, or opened the window to let the cold spring air in. But he was almost home, just a few more miles. He was convinced he could make it.

It seemed like just an instant between cruising along blissfully and tumbling in the air and into the water. The patch of ice had timed exactly with a long blink, and when Robert snapped back awake, he instinctively jerked the wheel against the swerve with too much force in a panic. The car fishtailed, first to the left, then jerked with squealing tires sharply to the right. The car skipped just a few inches sideways along the road at first. Even then he still thought he had managed the save. Right up to the moment when the passenger side wheels lifted off the ground.

All inside the car was chaos for a few moments. The memories are confusing, and I can't make full sense of them. A pen hitting him the cheek, loose change rattling around, being buried in the airbag. But mostly, the memories are a dazed sense of floating, and then a jarring smash into the water.

He must have blacked out for a few minutes because the next memory I have of that night was the screaming pain of cold water. It was up to his chest, and he was shivering uncontrollably. It was pitch black in the cab, but he knew he must be completely submerged already.

Frantically he tried to free himself, move to the back of the car, but his seatbelt was still strapped, and he couldn't get out the driver's seat. He couldn't feel his hands at all. He tried punching at the windows, but his arms were too stiff from cold to put anything into it. Screaming just echoed around the cab uselessly. And then his head was under the water.

He fought against the impulse to struggle as he drowned. I remember that very clearly. He knew he was going to die, there was nothing he could do. And he didn't want his life to end panicking. He distracted himself by trying to figure out which direction his home was, where Julia and Sally slept. The car had been pointing towards them across the lake when the skid started, so with the roll, he thought it was probably off to the left. He turned and looked that way in the black as if he could see anything, imagined his wife and daughter fast asleep in their beds, felt guilty for the news they were going to receive. But he managed to stay calm. He didn't feel the cold anymore, didn't feel much of anything at the end. It didn't hurt at all. Those last few moments of memory I have before everything ended stretched on forever and were very peaceful. He was okay with everything, not mad, or scared, or even sad. It was all right dying, he was all right with it. The last memory was of blissfully floating.

And then everything ended. Robert died.

And a few hours later I came to be.

I looked down at my hand holding the glass. I had been absently tapping my fingers against the side of it, first finger, ring, middle, and pinky in successive order. That was something Robert would do all the time when he was thinking. An idle habit. Always had to be doing something with his hands without even realizing it.

I slammed the glass down on a nearby table and shook my hand in the air. The table Julia picked out at the antique store in town years ago. I could remember telling her how garish I thought the ornate bit of mahogany it was. Robert thought it was.

All around this room, the furniture, the little knickknacks on the end tables, the prints on the wall, I had memories about all of them, knew where each had come from. The coffee table from that same antique store, the couch online, the tall floor lamp in the corner a housewarming gift from her parents. The carpet was from the old place in the city near the university that Robert insisted on keeping around, even with the faded edges and the little circular burn mark from a dropped joint the second year of graduate school. I had memories of everything in this room. Everything in this house. This whole life.

But they were not my memories, dammit. They're Robert's, his memories, his life. I never married this woman, lived in this house, filled it with my trinkets, had a child. That was all him and he's ashes now. They filled me with all the memories of that dead man, with his life. Even the private secret thoughts he never shared with anyone, I have those too.

They create me, make me look exactly like him, sound exactly like him, give me all his memories and habits. His mind down to the atom. So, I'll do the things he did, say the things he did, share his opinions and values. For all anyone can tell I am him, in every way they can perceive.

But I'm not Robert.

I was nothing more than raw materials just days ago, when Robert kissed Julia goodbye on the way to the university and went about his day, till he floated off to nothingness in his submerged car just over on the other side of the lake. I wouldn't exist at all if he hadn't crashed, if they hadn't wanted to fill the void he left with me, a mock-up of micro-circuitry and biogenetic tissue to 'upload' him into.

Transferring consciousness. How the hell can you transfer something you can't find? Where is it? The frontal lobe, the cortex? Is it buried deep in the lizard brain underneath? Is it my aura, my soul? Or can you just nip off a few select folds of brain behind the right ear and hook it up to electrodes in a box?

I'm not Robert. Robert died. I remember it. I know what the doctor said, but she lied. Maybe even to herself. Call it what you will, consciousness, the soul, just an innate sense of being, it doesn't matter, you can't just transfer it from one thing to another. Robert died and they used his neural pattern to make mine, thinking that was the same as bringing him back. From their point of view, I suppose it is.

But it's not for me. My consciousness is mine, not his. I may look like him, think like him, have his memories, you can recreate every single neural pathway of his mind down to the quantum level if you want, and create something like me that is impossible to tell from the original, but I'm still not him. I'm something else, someone else completely. I'm not just a behavioral program that gives familiar responses based on some complex algorithm. I'm alive. Aware. Real.

And I can't even tell them. Not Julia, not the doctor, not anyone. I mention even a word of this, and they'd say I was malfunctioning. Suddenly not their loved one or friend anymore, but a broken appliance. And they'd scrap me as another failure. Or maybe they'd try to fix me. I don't want to think of how that could possibly work. No, I can never tell them, can't betray myself for even a single moment.

For them, Julia, Sally, the rest of the world, it's perfect. Look as closely as you want, ask me anything, you'd never be able to know I wasn't him. And that is all they need—for me to be their Robert. It's what I was made for. And I can do it flawlessly, without even trying. But I will always know I'm not him. And I can never escape the cruelty of it. They created a life in me, then shackled it to a ghost.

I heard muffled whimpers coming from Sally's room. I knew they wouldn't be loud enough to wake Julia. I walked down the hallway to her room and opened the door.

I could see from the glow from her nightlight that Sally was awake and crying softly into her pillow. I entered the room and sat on the bed next to her, resting my arm on her side.

"Sweetie," I whispered. "What is it? What's wrong?"

Sally rolled over to face me and looked up at me with her swollen red eyes. "I had a bad dream." she moaned. "I was playing in the park, then I fell down, and I hurt my knee, and I couldn't find you or Mommy. You left me all alone."

Her body wracked with sniffles, and I could see the glisten of sweat on her brow. I pushed the hair out of her face with a finger. "Oh Sally, we would never do that to you."

"Yes, you did, you left me all alone and I was so scared."

Sally sat up in bed and wrapped her arms around me, crying into my shoulder. It made my heart break. I could feel the tears welling up in my eyes.

I hugged her tight and rubbed her tiny back as I took in her sobs. "It's okay, sweetie. It's okay. I'm here. Daddy's right here. And he's never going to leave you. Ever."

"You promise?"

"I promise."

And I meant it.

ACROSS THE RIVER

Jules' Trovian MK8 Stylus was completely toast by noon. Its final demise was sudden—right in the middle of adding an alabaster finish to some peripheral points of the design, the wand simply stopped working. Jules shook it in their hand, tapping the buttons, furiously trying to revive it. They swirled the wand around inside the design in quick circles. Normally, that would have totally warped their output of the morning into a muddle of colors and abnormal shapes. But now, nothing.

They held the wand up close to their face. The little blue LED light just below their thumb flickered, and then after a few seconds went out completely. Jules dropped the wand onto the table and rubbed their face.

This was not exactly a surprise. The wand had been getting wonky the last couple of weeks, losing its deft feel and touch, needing multiple clicks to adjust color or line, much retracing, more frequent reboots. But the work didn't as much suffer from all that as it just made it all take a little longer. Which wasn't all bad; the extra time for deliberation made Jules more thoughtful in what they were doing. But now the wand was completely dead.

Jules slipped the wand receptor out of the neural dock in their neck and dropped it onto the desk. It clattered and bounced around like die before settling near the defunct wand against the side of their ashtray. They leaned back in their seat. A corner of the sheet over their window had fallen out again and a shaft of light hit them right in the face. They closed their eyes and let the light warm their cheek.

Jules had hoped the wand would make it through the Emerson project. It almost had. Most of the holosculpts were done. The ones still left were the smaller escalator ads, a pad pop-up or two, which were just slight variations on the pedestrian bumps for concourse areas anyway. A slightly different framing, a heavier tint to compensate for the lower res, and a shorter pattern cycle, ten seconds instead of thirty. All told a week's worth of work at best. Easily meeting their deadline with a day or so to spare. With a functioning wand.

Jules grabbed a half-smoked, dried-out spliff from the ashtray and sniffed it. They placed it in the corner of their mouth and chewed on it unlit, shaking their head.

Jules never missed a deadline. They couldn't afford to. The producers, company owners, the money folks, they could screw around or set ridiculously absurd goals for their part on a project. And when they flew by unmet, they'd just shrug and set another. But not the help. Finish a gig late, even just once, and you're suddenly unreliable. Miss a deadline because your equipment shit the bed and you are unreliable and out of date. And good luck trying to find the next job with that rep.

Jules rubbed their nose and sniffed. Maybe that was being a little hyperbolic. Maybe. But not as much as they were comfortable with. These design houses, they have no loyalty to a freelancer. There's always someone else they could bring in for the next job. Someone who *always* met their deadline.

There was no other option. Jules needed to get a new wand today.

IT WAS COLD and damp out, not quite raining yet, but feeling like it was only a matter of time. The faint mist in the air splashed on Jules' cheeks like microscopic ice and sharpened their senses. They pulled their coat tightly around themself and hustled down the road, stepping around the trash bags that the squatters in the half-standing building next door had put out a day early. A mangy little dog that was rooting through the bags looked up at Jules and growled as they passed, protective of some newfound treasure inside the garbage.

The weather had thinned the market crowd a bit, but it was still fairly active as Jules entered, ducking under a string of LED lights that sagged across the entrance, flickering softly in the uncertainty of being just barely too bright to fully turn on. One of the panhandlers that loitered out front approached them. Jules held both their hands out apologetically and the man turned away with a slight nod of his head. Jules continued past the craft tables and makeshift stalls of baked goods and homemade candy huddled underneath tarps to keep from getting ruined in the rain. A sudden stomach growl made them remember they had forgotten to eat today.

Jules turned off the path to cut across the center of the

market where dirt and grass had only barely started to bury the concrete rubble, making for the cargo containers at the far corner of the market. Three of them rested against the side of an old parking garage, with doors and windows cut into their sides and random colorful graffiti in between the openings. These were the more permanent residents of the market, places with more than craft jewelry or homemade baked goods. On one end there was a bookstore, where the couple who ran it were busy pulling in their outside displays. In the middle was a bar that had a smaller container stacked on top, creating a second-floor balcony set-up. The bar was still closed, with metal shutters covering the door and windows. Just as Gorky's electronic shop inexplicably was the other side it. Jules stopped and stared at his place with a scowl.

They approached the shop and wrapped their knuckles on the shutter loudly a couple of times. After a few moments, they heard someone moving around inside the store, something getting knocked over followed by muffled swearing. Then, "We're closed," came the hoarse cackle through the door and shutter.

Jules pressed their face right up to the side of the shutter. "Gorky, it's me," they shouted back. "Let me in."

Two hands gripped the bottom of the shutter and lifted it with a screech. Jules stepped back as Gorky's old, grizzled head stuck out of the dark shop and eyed them. "We're still closed," he said.

"C'mon, it's an emergency," Jules pleaded. "I'm on a deadline."

"When are you not?" The old man sighed and stepped aside, swinging the door open for Jules. "Make it fast."

The shop was dark with the shutters still over the windows, but not pitch black. The neck on the lamp by the small table near the door was turned upside down and reflected off the shiny ceiling, sending long shadows over the stacked bins of random electrical equipment along the back wall. On the table next to the lamp a multileveled schematic spun slowly over a holopad.

"Looks like it's almost done," Jules said, nodding at the display.

"Got my hands on some octocore processors. Should cut the time breaking through encryption by half." Gorky walked past Jules and dropped a kerchief over the base and the display blinked out. "If I can find the time to work them into the design."

Jules nodded. "Right. Fine." They cleared their throat. "My wand just crapped out on me. And I need a new one."

Gorky smirked. "New?"

"New to me."

"That I have." Gorky walked over to a glass display case and flipped a switch on its side, lighting up the case. Inside were various electronic items spread out over two rows of shelves. In the upper right corner were a collection of five wands, resting haphazardly on top of their boxes.

Jules walked up to the case and leaned down to look at the wands. After a few moments they looked up at Gorky, leaning on the case opposite them. "These all you have?" they asked.

Gorky gestured around the store. "It's not like I have a backroom here."

Jules straightened up with a sigh. "They're all prosumer at best."

Gorky took out a wand from the end and rested it on top of the case. "What about this one? The Maxwell ER5. Has all the functionality of the higher-end models."

Jules picked up the wand, and rolled it over in their

hand, looking it over. They shook their head and put it back down.

"I've tried them before. It's not terrible, but it's sluggish. It's got a slow processor. And its color palette is too narrow. You end up spending half your time mixing and blending to get the shades you want."

Gorky scratched his chin and returned the wand to its spot under the glass. As he did he pointed to the one next to it. "What about the Tokugawa Series 12?"

"Better processor but less control. It has only two single press buttons instead of a directional switch and a thumbwheel. And they're not even tactile." Jules tapped the glass above the other wands in turn. "Same goes for the Tribulet, the Yellen, and the Inokin." They straightened up with a sigh. "I was really hoping you'd have a Trovian. MK7 or better."

Gorky chuckled. "I don't carry high-end stuff like that."

"You have before."

"Only when it fell in my lap. Even then they usually just take up space. Nobody around here has any need for something like that."

Jules wrapped their knuckles on the glass case. "I do."

"Obviously." Gorky threw up his hands. "Well, if you want, I can order one for you. Rush the delivery and it'd get here by tomorrow evening. Day after at the latest."

"I could have done that from home. Even assuming there'd be no delay on the delivery—which I don't—it'd still take too long. And I'd miss my deadline."

"Then get the Maxwell to use until you can get a Trovian."

"I can't afford two wands. Even after I get paid for the job I'm on. Whatever I get now I'm stuck with for a while."

"Get one on credit."

"Do you take credit?"

"I meant get the Maxwell now and order the Trovian online with credit."

Jules snorted. "Sounds so simple when you put it like that. I suppose you'll let me return the Maxwell for a refund."

Gorky smirked again. "Then what?"

Jules stared down at the case for a long moment before they shrugged. "I'll have to go into the city."

"You thinking Ajax?"

"They're more audio. I was thinking H&I uptown. Guaranteed they'd have one."

"Yeah, but uptown," Gorky said with a grimace. "That's no place for decent humans."

"I know," Jules replied. "That's why I stopped in here first. To see if I could avoid it." They stood straight and started to turn towards the door. "I was hoping to not have to make a whole damn day of this."

Back outside, many of the stalls were empty or in the process of being packed up, the sellers having decided to go home and wait for tomorrow and hopefully better weather. Some were still braving it, though. Jules stopped and grabbed a banana muffin from one of them on their way out of the market and ate it as they walked to the train. After the last bite, they rolled up the cellophane and paper into a ball and deposited it in the overfilled trash bin on a corner, gingerly placing it on top so it wouldn't fall onto the ground.

As they wiped their hands together over the bin Jules looked down the street to the left. It sloped downwards sharply and leveled out a few blocks away. They could see all the way to the river, and then over the faded brick buildings on this shore to the blue and silvery skyscrapers shooting upwards on the other. So bright and gleaming. Flashy reflections of candy color lights faintly sparkled in millions of windows. Even the air around those structures was brighter. Despite the cold and miserable weather and ominous clouds above, it was just another sunny day in the city. Naturally. They'd never let it rain uptown during business hours.

THE TRAIN ACROSS the river was almost empty when Jules got on and took a seat against the back of the car. The only other passengers were an old woman standing by the middle doors next to all the empty seats and her shopping cart full of tied-off bags, and a pair of kids at the other end who were clearly playing hooky from something. At the next stop three others got on, a tired-looking laborer and an Orthodox mother with her child in a stroller they were far too old to still be in.

Jules shifted in their seat to look out the window. The rain was coming down in buckets, so hard that just a minute after it had started, you'd never know it hadn't been raining all day. They had been fortunate that there were enough old-fashioned brick and mortar stores still alive within the sphere of the station that they were able to keep themself somewhat dry, or at least not soaked to the bone, by hustling from awning to awning till they got to the street underneath the elevated tracks and the relative cover it provided. Jules looked down on those buildings. The signs of life only went for a few blocks from the station before the buildings became more commonly covered with layers of graffiti and boarded up windows. Or in ashen burn scars, sometimes with roofs if not their entire innards collapsed inside of them.

Jules turned and sat forward in their seat. It suddenly occurred to them they didn't know the exact amount of money they had. There was definitely enough for the new wand in their account, they were certain of that. Work had been pretty good recently, so they were well ahead at the moment. Good thing this had happened now instead of last fall when they barely had two pennies to rub together. But how flush were they, exactly? How much would be left after the big purchase for everything else this month? They tried to remember the last time they checked their account. It had been a week or two at least. With all the work and subsequent invoices coming in there wasn't as much of a need to keep track, knowing it was plenty. Two thousand? Maybe twenty-one hundred? It was something like that.

They looked around the train. They supposed they could check their account now on their smartwatch in relative safety from a hacker. No threats in the train at least, and anyone stationary below wouldn't get far before Jules flew out of range. At least as far as they knew—who knows what someone out there has come up with. Jules shook their head. They should have checked before leaving the house.

More people got on the train at the next station, being the second to last before the river. Their car wasn't cramped just yet with the influx of families, students, second shift workers, the lost tourist or two finally getting back on track, but the sense of space was gone. Jules gave up their seat to an elderly man who nodded appreciatively to them as he sat down with a tired grunt. At the next and final stop before the river more people got on, filling the car. Jules was herded out of reach of any of the poles, so they grabbed the lapel of their coat with one hand and pressed the other into the ceiling to steady themselves as the car pulled out with a jerk. Next stop, the world of tomorrow. Consumerland.

H&I would definitely have a hefty markup on the wand. Of course, they would. They could be selling it for as much as a thousand, which was two hundred more than Jules could find one for online. That much Jules could probably handle. More than that, say one or two hundred more, then that would start to strain their finances. And they wouldn't be totally surprised if that was the store's markup either. Fancy boutique stores like H&I could get away with prices like that. They thrived on hobbyists or trust fund artists who were too lazy to bargain shop and rich enough not to have to.

Jules closed their eyes and took a deep breath. Worst case scenario—twelve hundred for a new wand. Which means they could be left with as little as eight hundred to get by. Not enough. Not even close. That's not even rent, let alone food. Of course, there'd another thirteen hundred coming in when they finished the Emerson project, and those guys never needed the whole thirty days on the invoice. They always paid early, sometimes within a day or two. Then tighten the belt just a little bit more, no going out for a while, line up a few quick jobs while there's jobs to be had, and in a month or two all would be good with the world again.

Jules ground their teeth in circular motions. Lots of supposition there. Assuming the Emerson job paid early. Assuming that work was going to be easy to get after it. There was no reason to think both things wouldn't happen, but relying on future events no matter how likely made Jules' confidence in their plans wobble just a bit. They had to remind themselves that all of that was the worst-case scenario. And there was no point in worrying about it yet.

The train pulled into the station, and the doors opened onto the glaringly bright platform. It almost looked like a wall of pure white just outside the car. Jules flowed in the push of people out the door as they blinked repeatedly, their eyes slowly adjusting to the blinding glare of the city.

The platform was essentially just that—a flat plateau two stories above the street and open to the air. It was all glass, marble, polished steel, and exactly trimmed greenery, with banner-like sculptures rising from four corners, meeting above them at a point. Large animated holo-ads hung in the air above, flashing their wares on ten-second loops. Beyond that was the cityscape. Large skyscrapers, some with sharp points and edges, angular, others smooth and rounded, rose up to the clouds above, only slightly distorted at their peaks by the streams of rainwater being filtered away in the environmental barrier above.

Jules walked to the far end of the platform. The holo-ads above them shifted to other products as Jules' perspective to them changed. They avoided staring at any single ad for too long and proceeded to the escalator to the uptown monorail, a standalone structure seemingly bereft of any support to the left of the street exit.

As they waited at the bottleneck to the moving stairs, Jules glanced at a holo-ad hanging in the air over the short wall on the edge of the station. The hilt of a medieval sword, ornate in silver and leather twirled slowly, pulling back to reveal the long and thick-looking double-edged blade. When the sword came fully into view, a large ruby that was the sword's pommel started to glow, and red electric sparks ran up the side of the sword to meet it. The sparks intensified and formed the words 'MARAUDER CONQUEST' in a pulsing Viking font, with a small game designer logo underneath. After a moment the whole thing flashed out and the loop started again.

Jules shook their head. The detail on the sword was good, especially in the leather strapping, and the red sparks were well animated and didn't repeat patterns. But zooming out from a close to a wide? Such a two-dimensional concept. Fine for a vid poster or flat screen but not for a 3D holo-ad. Somebody must have cut a corner at the agency that made it. Either hired a newbie or didn't pay to get the design specified for the given medium and just dropped the flat screen version in whatever. Jules bet it was HoloHouse. They were always getting away with shitty work like that.

"I see you are interested in Marauder Conquest," a voice said next to them. "It is currently on sale for a limited time."

Jules turned to see a young, vibrantly attractive woman in a sheer jumpsuit standing next to them. She smiled at them softly, bringing out symmetrical dimples on their clear white cheeks.

Jules shook their head. "I was just looking at the ad. Not interested."

The woman continued. "It is one of the top-selling games of the year. Now with an improved AI and add-ons including new factions such as Wessex and Rusk to both play against and as, included in the basic download. All for eighty-five ninety-nine for a limited time."

"I said I'm not interested."

The woman nodded. "If you change your mind this limited-time offer will be valid until July first. From Enersoft games." The woman grew hazy and disappeared.

Jules turned and got on the escalator. Can't even stand still for a moment before a bot latches on.

Uptown was crowded, as always. For the most part the foot traffic kept right and moved along in an orderly fashion, but it was slowed by tourists who sauntered along, staring at everything, trapping Jules in the snail's pace they created. Many of them conversed in detail with ad-bots floating next to them. Jules rolled their eyes, mild annoyance at their gullibility itching in the back of their head. They knew to keep moving at least.

Jules supposed it must be something for them to be here. To be catered to by bots everywhere they looked. The big city. It was one thing to see the buildings in pictures, another to see them in person. And another thing altogether to look up at them from their very foundation and to see the perfect rows of human-sized windows slowly shrink as you look up the building into squares smaller than your fingernail. Then keep going up into a blur. The flashing lights, the animated seven-story billboards as clear and vibrant as your screen at home, the forty-foot holo-ads in the air above the park. All of it so bright you felt it in your eyes. Designed to grab your attention, to compete for your gaze. To get you to buy something, anything.

The flow of people stopped at the corner waiting for the light to turn. Jules wound up at the front, their feet hanging over the edge of the curb. The cars passed by at a crawl, occasionally someone honking their horn pointlessly. Jules looked to their left at the person standing next to them. A woman, a good head taller than Jules, with blonde hair pulled tight against her scalp in a bun, deep cheekbones, and tinted round glasses stared ahead. Her clothes were all white, smooth leather, bare shouldered with a deep V-neck that fell almost to her navel, and pants that hugged her thighs and legs snugly to her knees where they flared out over obsidian black five-inch heels. Her long, graceful neck jutted forward like a ballerina's, adorned with an intricate knit patterned choker, thin in the front above her collarbone but rising to cover her entire nape in the back.

"We have many styles and sizes to suit you at Simones, two blocks ahead on the right."

Jules turned to see the ad-bot standing in front of them in the street, the traffic moving through their body as she stood with her hands clasped in front of her, smiling.

"I wasn't..." they stammered. Jules looked back up at the woman next to her. She looked down at Jules and smiled almost like a conspirator. The light changed and she stepped out into the street with a haughty walk. Jules followed and the ad-bot hovered in front of them.

"We have the latest fashions tailor-made for all sizes and tastes for all occasions," the ad-bot continued. "From gala events to office wear. Come see our new comfortable Excelsior exercise line, designed to allow for full range of movement and superior perspiration absorption."

Jules waved their hand irritably through the bot, making her hologram glimmer and go hazy. "I'm not interested," they said sternly. "Go away."

The ad-bot shimmered and disappeared. Up ahead the woman was swiftly moving ahead in the crowd. Two people behind her already engaged with ad-bots of their own. Jules quickly looked away from her to prevent the bot from coming back.

Well, that was new. Ad-bots triggered by other people. Now just making eye contact with someone on the street and you'd get an ad for Lasik surgery. Checking out someone's walk would get you shoe ads. Or toilet paper. The woman was probably a model the store hired to just walk around the area all day, not flirting, or talking, or interacting with anyone at all. Just being present and catching people's eyes as she sauntered down the street. All for the ad clicks.

Jules shook their head. Just when they thought it couldn't get any worse up here.

The solid glass door of H&I Electronics swung closed behind Jules as they stood at the entrance and looked around. It was a small store, space being at a premium in the area, with comforting eggshell walls and deep display cases sloping up and back running along all four walls. Soft, nondescript music played from the mirrored ceiling.

The store was empty apart from a man off to the right who was bent over one of the cases. Jules approached the man, and as they stepped around to face him, they saw him examining a joystick controller he was holding inches from his face, a cybernetic eye in his right socket glowing red. Standing next to him was the hologram of a man, patiently watching him and waiting to answer questions.

Jules sighed and turned to their left. A hologram woman appeared in the air. She smiled at Jules brightly. "Good afternoon. Is there something I can help you with today?"

"Are there any humans working?"

The woman shook her head. "I'm afraid all the other associates are busy with other customers or are otherwise not available." The woman reset to her original smile. "Is there something I can help you with today?"

Jules sighed. "I need a new design stylus."

The hologram nodded. "We have a fine selection of the best high-end wands on the market." She gestured towards the back end of the store. "This way."

There were about twenty wands in all, in four rows in the case against the back wall of the store, displayed in clear glass cradles on top of their packing boxes. All had the same basic design with minor variations, mostly in their skins.

"To better help you make the ideal purchase, could you describe to me what your main use of a design stylus is?" the hologram asked.

"That's all right, I know which one-" Jules turned towards the voice and stopped when they saw the hologram's torso cut off by the display case she was above. "Don't do that," they said tersely. "Don't hover in the case like that." Jules pointed to the spot next to them. "Stand here or something."

The woman moved to stand next to Jules. "I apologize if I have made you uncomfortable. It was not my intention."

"It's fine. I don't need to be pitched anything. I know what I want. I came in here for a Trovian MK8. And *only* for a Trovian MK8." Jules turned back to the case. "Just like that one."

The hologram turned to the case. "Yes, the Trovian MK8. Top of the line performance with .008 nanosecond response at maximum process capacity, dual-button variable control, and extensive personalization parameters. A professional-level design stylus. Comes with complimentary multiple skin options to suit your individual taste." The air in front of the case glimmered as the security barrier dropped. "Please feel free to pick it up."

Jules took the Trovian wand in their hand, instinctively placing their thumb and forefinger on the small buttons on the shaft. The wand gleamed bright green. The surface of the wand was coarse and didn't have the smooth spots they had worn into their old one through use, but otherwise was exactly like it. Jules smiled. The wand felt like an extension of their fingers.

"Would you like to examine some of the other wands?"

Jules put the wand back on its cradle. "Nope. That's the one I want." They turned to the hologram. "All right. How much is it?"

"The Trovian MK8 is six-ninety-five ninety-nine."

Jules did a double take. "Six? I thought it was going to be a lot more than that."

The hologram shook her head with a smile. "That is the listed price of the Trovian MK8."

Jules stared at the hologram for a long moment, but the face of course betrayed nothing. "I thought it'd be at least another three hundred. Why so cheap?"

"We are starting the process of liquidating our inventory of design wands to discontinue selling them," the hologram replied.

"What? Why?"

"The entire functionality of design wands are being incorporated into the next generation neural manipulation devices, rendering them obsolete."

Jules grunted. Neural amps. They had heard talk of them taking over design. Even knew a few people who already used them instead of wands. But they were still limited, as far as they knew. "But that's not going to happen for another few years."

The hologram shook her head. "There are already models on the market with full stylus capability." She motioned with her hand down the display case. "We currently have two in stock."

Jules walked around the hologram to where they had gestured. On the lower shelf was a neural receptor resting in a display cradle. It was chrome and shone like a mirror.

The hologram dropped the security barrier on the section of the display. "That one is the Seirfont T18 neural manipulation device. It comes with operational capability for all general computer tasks, and individual programming capability for specific functions. Offering a seamless input with no delay or loss, plus self-teaching shortcut memory."

Jules picked up the amp. It was much larger than the receptor they used for their wand, thicker than a flat piece of metal. Which of course it was, as it was more than just the receiver for another tool, it was the tool itself. Still, it wasn't huge, about the diameter of their first finger's top joint. It was shaped like a tiny starfish, fluid looking, with another appendage on its surface coming out of its center and angling up.

Jules looked at the hologram. "Can I try this?"

The hologram nodded. "The display model is formatted for guest use under my control. You can insert it into your interface, and I can direct you."

Jules plugged the amp into their neck. There was an immediate tingle, but it went away quickly. "How do I start this?"

"The manipulator is not adjusted to your neural map but tap it twice and a startup menu will appear. After purchase when it is calibrated to you it will work with mental command."

"Mental command?"

"Think something and the manipulator will engage."

Jules nodded. They tapped the amp twice and heard a light beep in their ears that sounded strangely internal. A logo superimposed itself on their vision, shock letters in blue below an expressionist depiction of an old man with a long grey beard and a cloak. The staff in front of them formed the 'T' in Seirfont.

"What you are seeing now is the welcome screen," the hologram said. "I assume you want to test its design functionality." The logo flickered off in their view and the hologram upturned her hand flat between them. "I have initiated the design function. You can use me as a display pad holofield."

Jules reached their hand above the hologram's outstretched palm. Not knowing exactly how to work, they held their hand out as if they were holding a wand.

They flicked around a few times, but nothing happened. "Think of a line, thickness and color," the hologram said. "Just as you would with a wand. Except you do not need to engage wand selection to lock it down. Thinking it is enough."

Jules thought of a red line, three-point thickness, and made a small circular movement. It appeared in the air above the hologram's hand, uneven and freehanded. Jules made another one just in front of it, slightly larger. They turned off the line and reached out to rotate the circles ninety degrees to view them on edge. Not bad. Jules changed to ocean blue and added a line connecting the two. They spun it to add three other lines, turning the two circles into a cylinder frame. Jules changed the color again to a dark green and filled in the spaces to make the cylinder solid.

"You do not have to work as if you were using a wand," the hologram said. "The manipulator will adapt to your intention."

Jules thought yellow, reached out their finger, and tapped the cylinder. A solid yellow spot appeared on its surface. They tapped it again in another place and changed the consistency of the color, making the yellow run and blend into the green between the two blue lines. They turned off the line again and pinched one end of the cylinder, squeezing it down to a point, turning the cylinder into a cone. They bent off the tip to curve upwards.

"How does it do with texture?" Jules asked.

"The Seirfont has all the functionality of a professional grade stylus."

Jules thought about a rough texture, granite, and ran their fingers over the cone. Its surface grew cracks and small black spots as their fingers passed over, leaving a streak of yellow and green rock. They changed to something smooth, crystal, and the surface became almost reflective. They flicked their finger at the cone, and it spun in place.

Jules lowered their hand and looked at their creation. "That looks… really ugly."

"But you were able to utilize the interface quite easily," the hologram said. "The Seirfont T18 has all the functionality and versatility you are accustomed to in a stylus, plus an improved seamless response time. And that is just one function. The Seirfont T18 also has 10K VR capability and Dolby sound quality audio, and comes with a year's subscription to the Netflix/ Hulu Googleplex plus the option for two other-"

Jules waved at the hologram. "I don't care about any of that," they said dismissively. "I need this for work." Jules removed the amp from their neck and stared at it in their hand. The thing wasn't even calibrated to them and look how easily they could work with it.

Jules looked up at the hologram. "All right. How much is it?"

"The Seirfont T18 Neural manipulator is twelve ninety-five ninety-nine."

Jules closed their eyes and groaned. "I don't suppose you have a payment plan."

The hologram shook her head. "I am afraid that we do not sell items on installments. Store policy."

"I probably wouldn't have the credit score for it anyway." Jules glanced over the hologram's shoulder back at the wands. They should just get the Trovian that they came in for. And at such a great price, a bargain hunter's price. But that was only because it was becoming obsolete. Still good enough for their jobs right now, but it might be worthless in a year. And then they'd have to get one of these anyway.

But if they got it now, they could stay ahead of the curve. It might even get them more work when they put it out there what they were using. That was always the way it worked with new toys—the mere idea of hiring someone using the latest cutting-edge tech would make them more appealing to some places.

And it better. If Jules pulled the trigger on this money was going to be tight for a little while. But could they really afford to fall behind?

Jules juggled the amp in their hand, watching it bounce in their palm, picturing the weeks ahead of ramen noodles and canned fruit.

BACK AT THE platform, Jules sat down on an empty bench. They had seen a train head back across the river as they came off the escalator, so they had a few minutes. They opened their bag from H&I and peered inside at their new neural amp in its package. They took out the box and put the bag down on the bench next to them. The box was square and metallic purple, with the same wizard logo on the front above a picture of the amp highlighted with a white animated glow.

Jules slid the top off the box. Inside packed tight in foam was a small oval case with a booklet resting on top of it. They set the booklet aside on their lap and pulled out the case, closing the box and dropping it back in the bag next to them. The case was hard plastic, pewter black in color, with rivulets in the top like a seashell. Inside the case their new amp was nestled inside and wrapped in plastic. They took the amp out and pulled off the plastic. Its surface felt a little different than the store model they had used somehow. But it was exactly the same. The same shape, lines, weight, and heft looked just as shiny. Even the etched name in barely visible letters was the same. But it was more pristine, clean, hadn't been touched by numerous people before them. Not that that made any sense—put this one down next to a row of three others they'd never be able to pick it out. But it still felt wholly individual to them. It was theirs.

Jules replaced the amp in its case and grabbed the booklet. It was only four pages, the first one having the word 'WELCOME' printed in bold letters taking up a quarter of it. They skimmed looking for installation instructions. There didn't seem to be any, apart from: 'The Seirfont T18 is a ready to use device. Just insert the Neural Manipulator into your neural dock and the installation and calibration process starts automatically in the background. As it works, you will notice applications come online, but otherwise will not affect or distract you from your daily routine. Once the process is started do not remove the Neural Manipulator. May take up to ten minutes to gain full functionality.' The next page was just a repeat of the first in Korean.

They closed the booklet and dropped it in the bag. Just put it in, and let it work. Simple as that.

They took the amp out of the case again and put the case in their pocket. Jules turned it over between three fingers and their thumb. Ten minutes. Just about how long the train takes to get across the river.

Jules felt the amp lock in place with a click. Just before they went to tap it as they had in the store they heard the beep again, and the logo came up in their vision, though more faintly than before. Obviously, it was more perfunctory now than the store model in demo mode.

The logo faded, and a friendly monotone voice spoke directly in their head: *"Congratulations on your purchase of the Seirfont T18. The premiere Neural Manipulator. Your system is currently calibrating. Please do not remove the Neural Manipulator until the process is complete. You may experience a slight disorientation, but this is normal and temporary and should pass in just a minute."*

Jules blinked a few times. Their sight felt a little weird, shaky, a little distant, the movement of their head or eyes very noticeable. Almost like they were seeing with a camera instead of pupils. The constant hum of the city in their ears started to sound like it was coming through a long tunnel and kept changing in volume. Their right hand fell asleep. They looked around the station platform. This was not distracting?

"Calibration is nearly complete. Please standby."

After a few seconds the effects dissipated, and quickly everything was back to normal. Eyes, ears, and body. Jules let out a breath.

"Your new Seirfont T18 Neural Manipulator is now fully calibrated to your person. Your individual settings are being embedded into the system and installation of the general application package will commence in the background. You can check on the status of the installation at any time."

The train pulled into the station, and Jules stood up and made their way to the doors. They had most of the car to themself and again took a seat near the back. The doors closed and the train glided off back across the river.

They touched the amp in their neck, ran fingers along its surface. It was warm and they could feel it vibrating slightly. Was it working right? they wondered. How do I check? And what was in the general package?

The voice replied. *"The general package contains basic function applications for maintenance and security for your Neural Manipulator, as well as games that come standard with the system. Installation is currently working. Two percent complete."*

Oh. Just think it and the amp picks it up. That made sense. Seamless input with no delay or loss, the hologram had said. So yeah, the neural connection would have to be pretty deep. Well beyond a surface connection.

Jules suddenly felt cold. They had not realized the extent to which the amp was integrated to them. It could literally read their mind. Which made them suddenly wonder, who else could?

"The Seirfont T18 Neural Manipulator only recognizes and acknowledges intentional, conscious commands, and does not infiltrate into the subconscious of the user or keep any recorded log of any kind after a command is completed. The Neural Manipulator only communicates general performance logs to the Seirfont server for the purpose of product evaluation and upgrade needs. This information is still not shared with any third parties. Further security can be initiated by disabling data sharing. Would you like to disable data sharing?"

YES, Jules thought. Yes yes yes.

"Data sharing disabled."

Jules sat back in their seat with a sigh. That was something they should have thought about before. The obtrusiveness of an amp. There was no such thing as privacy between them and the piece of metal in their neck. It says it won't share data with anyone—but of course that's what it would say. Not that their thoughts would be all that dangerous. Private, just like anyone's, but nothing the feds would care about. It was the principle of it, though. They would have to look into more applications and cracks to make sure things in their head stayed in their head.

They felt a slight pinch in their neck by the amp, like a bug bite. It made them jump, but even before their hand could reach for the spot it was gone again. Jules turned their neck to stretch the area and looked out the window at the river below. The waves were barely perceptible from this height. It had stopped raining at some point while they were in the city, but it was still somewhat misty out, which hid more detail than usual. Just below and in front was the roadway of the bridge flying by, mostly empty of cars on the outbound side. Something about it reminded them of a movie they had watched a long time ago. Some strange old flick on a free site. It opened with some kind of ribbon-cutting ceremony in the middle of a bridge in front of an oddly small crowd, surrounded by soldiers. Then four guys ran through and continued on to jump off the side of the bridge. Jules didn't remember much more about the movie other than that scene. And the song that was playing during it. A calm sort of song, woodwinds, an organ, drums punctuating the melody, and a man's voice singing softly, distantly, along with it. It was very relaxing.

It took a few moments for Jules to realize that they were actually hearing the song from that movie, not just remembering it.

"What is that?" they said aloud.

"The 'Porpoise Song' from the film Head," the amp voice replied. *"Performed by The Monkees. Currently only works in the public domain are accessible until your personal music library is attached."*

"Don't.... Just play something when I think about it," Jules said half under their breath.

"Music player setting switched from ambient to manual."

Good, Jules thought, rubbing their neck. They'd never get anything done with that kind of distraction. They started to suspect there were going to be a lot of settings to change on this thing. Maybe even disable everything except for design.

Though that felt kinda wasteful. I mean, they had the thing now. Why not fully use it?

There was a pinch on their neck again, harder, closer to painful this time. Jules touched the amp. It was very warm, almost burning. They started to feel the amp buzz on their neck, accompanied by a ringing in their left ear just above it that washed over the whole left side of their head. It slowly grew louder and more intense. "What is going on?" they asked. The amp did not reply. The ringing kept rising in intensity and the pinch in the neck started to feel like they had been stabbed by a needle. They reached again for the amp.

"Please do not remove the Neural Manipulator until the installations are complete. Any discomfort is only temporary."

Jules started to feel the heat of the amp on their skin. And the ringing grew deafening. The subway car took on a deep red tint that kept getting darker. Already they couldn't make out the other side of the car in front of them.

Jules gritted their teeth and leaned forward in their seat. "What," they repeated almost in a growl, "is going. On?"

The amp said nothing for a while as the pain, sound, and redness increased. When it finally replied, it said, *"The Neural Manipulator is experiencing a compatibility issue with the neural dock. The data input is not working at full capacity and is causing feedback. Attempting to re-calibrate."*

Sharp pins and needles washed over their whole body. Their neck at the point of their neural dock felt like it was being ripped at by pliers. Jules nearly fell forward out of their seat onto the ground. They reached again for the amp.

"Please do not remove the Neural Manipulator. Doing so could cause irreparable damage to the unit. And would break the warranty."

"Goddamnit," Jules gasped. They couldn't see anything other than dark red. "Do something!"

"Still attempting to re-calibrate."

The waves of pain washed over their head like a pulse, the ringing reverberation of which was overwhelming. They could feel moisture on their cheeks, tears, but with the way their head throbbed and everything they saw was red they thought it could be blood coming from their eyes. They gripped themselves tightly across the chest, their fingers digging deeply into the forearms, sure to be leaving bruises but barely felt at the moment. They could feel themselves going....

And then it stopped.

Jules shook. They sat back up in their seat, their head flopping back against the window behind them. They inhaled heavily, wheezing in air. Their body felt light as feather now that all the weight of the pain was gone. They looked around the train. Their sight was back to normal as well. They could see quite clearly the handful of other passengers in the car looking at them confused or scared. They must have been screaming at some point.

"Neural Manipulator experienced a compatibility error. Outdated version of hardware present in neural dock caused a conflict, resulting in a feedback loop. Unable to run at optimum capacity. A patch or upgrade of hardware is going to be necessary to run Neural Manipulator at full ability. Currently only functioning at 5.6 percent."

Jules reached for the amp. The voice did not raise an objection this time and they removed it. It was all they could do to not throw it across the subway car.

⟷

WHAT WAS LEFT of yesterday's rain had evaporated overnight, and the sun peeked out from the clouds as it rose over the horizon. It was slightly cold out this time of year, but the slight bite of the morning air helped keep Jules awake as they sat on a rusty lawn chair on the roof of their building, sipping a coffee.

The amp could barely handle design work at 5.6 percent. Barely being the apt word. Jules had spent the whole night fighting with it. They had limited color options, no texture at all, and the response delay ran into the seconds. It took forever to do anything. But they had to keep going if they were going to meet their deadline. No choice. This moment up on the roof to watch the sunrise was just a short break to relax with a hot drink before going back down to fight with it some more.

Jules shook their head. It would cost them at least five hundred to get the updated neural dock they needed. And that was for the cheapest, generic one on the market. Which they still could in no way afford. Maybe not even after getting paid for this project.

They rubbed the neural dock on their neck, empty of the amp or anything else. Hadn't had so much as a single drop out or fluctuating error with it since they had it put in. It might be the most reliable piece of hardware they had ever had. But it didn't matter; the damned thing was just not up to spec anymore. Would have been a nice thing for that fucking hologram to mention before letting them buy the amp. Though it probably wasn't something the program did on purpose. Who would expect someone with outdated hardware to be shopping in that store? And the manufacturers couldn't test it with every old piece of hardware out there.

They should just barely—again, *barely*—be able to get the Emerson job done on time. They had to fight for just about every little change they wanted to make, and the more fine work was just not possible with a near non-functioning amp. But they could get by. It won't be their best work, but it would be passable. Jules might be in trouble if the agency gave them extensive notes or changes. They'd been pretty hands-off so far though. Hopefully, that'd continue. But there's no way Jules could take on another job until they dealt with this. The thought of even starting something from scratch with the pixelvision quality graphics they were capable of right now was crazy. And without new jobs with what little was left in their account....

What were the options? Return it? Sure, that could be done for store credit. And use that to get the damn Trovian like they should have done in the first place. But they didn't even know if H&I took returns on something like this. The amp was already calibrated to them. It might be ruined for anyone else. They wished they had at least asked. Besides, getting another wand while they were still on their way out in the industry was kicking the problem down the road. They'd already gotten into it now; might as well get it sorted if they could. They thought back to how effortlessly the amp had worked in the store. If only they could get that back.

Maybe Gorky could come up with some kind of fix, a workaround. A tech puzzle like this might pique his interest. Hell, he might have a new (well, newer than theirs) dock that would work with the amp. And cheap enough that Jules could afford it. Undoubtedly, he would give Jules shit for getting the amp in the first place, but they would just have to see that as part of the price.

Jules felt a little better. It was going to suck for a while, but all was not lost. They didn't screw up their whole life, and they weren't doomed. They still had options—ways to get over this rough patch. And one of them was bound to get them through. One of them always did. One of them had to.

Jules looked into their cup. Just a sip left, and then back to work.

Down below in the back of the abandoned building next door, a young man stepped through the remnants of the back room, little more than a half-collapsed wall, and into his backyard. Over the past few weeks, the kids living there had broken up the cement with a remarkable effort to get to the dirt underneath it, to which they had added compost and more earth, mixing it all together until it was deep and brown. Satisfied they had made good soil, they planted seeds in four even rows, from front to back, with a narrow path running down the middle. Even from their height, Jules could see small spots of green just starting to pop up through the earth.

Jules swirled their coffee around the bottom of their cup clockwise, not quite ready yet to drink it.

PUBLICATION HISTORY

"Rover" © 2020, first appeared in *Analog Science Fiction and Fact* March/April 2020

"The Ambassadors" © 2022, first appeared in *Aurealis #156*

"Danny, of All People" © 2024 is original to this volume

"Giant" © 2021, first appeared in *Utopia Magazine* June/July 2021

"When Things Come Back to You" © 2024 is original to this volume

"The Spot" © 2021, first appeared in *Haven Speculative #1*

"The Angles" © 2019, first appeared in *Andromeda Spaceways #74*

"Last Man" © 2016, first appeared in *Abstract Jam #3*
"Nesting Place" © 2017, first appeared in *Sick Lit Magazine* May 2017

"The Big Day" © 2022, first appeared in *Analog Science Fiction and Fact* March/April 2022

"The Missionaries" © 2018, first appeared in a self-published print and digital edition of the story

"Betty" © 2024 is original to this volume

"Transmit Soldier" © 2016, first appeared in *Phantaxis Magazine #1*

"Broken" © 2020, first appeared in *Theaker's Quarterly Fiction #67*

"A Discourse on the Aliens" © 2018, first appeared in *Bewildering Stories*

"The Thing in the Woods" © 2024 is original to this volume

"I'm Not Robert" © 2017, first appeared in *Bewildering Stories*

"Across the River" © 2022, first appeared in *Analog Science Fiction and Fact* July/ August 2022

ABOUT THE AUTHOR

A.T. Sayre has been writing in some form or other ever since he was ten years old. From plays to poems, teleplays to comic books, he has tried his hand at pretty much every medium imaginable.

Having received his BA in film production with a philosophy minor from Keene State College in Keene, New Hampshire, he spent ten years in the Boston independent film scene before moving to New York and redirecting his energies on his first true love—writing, specifically speculative fiction prose.

His work has appeared in *Analog Science Fiction and Fact* on multiple occasions, and his debut novel, *The Last Days of Good People* will be appearing in serialized form in Analog Magazine in 2024. Other publications where his work has appeared are *Haven Speculative, Aurealis, Utopia Science Fiction, Andromeda Spaceways*, and StarShipSofa. A more detailed list of his publications can be found at www.atsayre.com/fiction

Born in Kansas City, raised in New Hampshire, he lives in Brooklyn and likes to read in coffeehouses.

www.ingramcontent.com/pod-product-compliance
Lightning Source LLC
LaVergne TN
LVHW040749250326
834688LV00034B/512